Willie and Maud

Willie and Maud

A LOVE STORY

Barry Shortall

The Collins Press

Published in 2002 by
The Collins Press
West Link Park,
Doughcloyne,
Wilton,
Cork

Copyright © Barry Shortall

Barry Shortall has asserted his right to be identified as author of this work.

The material in this publication is protected by copyright law. Except as may be
permitted by law, no part of the material may be reproduced (including by storage
in a retrieval system) or transmitted in any form or by any means; adapted; rented
or lent without the written permission of the copyright owners. Applications for
permissions should be addressed to the publisher.

British Library Cataloguing in Publication data.

Printed in the Ireland by Betaprint

Typesetting by The Collins Press

ISBN: 1-903464-23-4

For Nancy and Jim
For Kevin Barry
And for Zita, Claire, Carys and James

While still I may, I write for you
The love I lived, the dream I knew.

To Ireland in Coming Times

Acknowledgements

It is difficult to single out for special acknowledgement any one of the many biographies and books concerning W.B. Yeats. Each contributed to the research which was crucial to making this story of Willie and Maud as true to their lives as possible.

The biographies relating to Maud Gonne were also essential reading, as was Maud's autobiography, *Servant of the Queen*, and the autobiographies of Yeats himself. The books relating to the life and times of Lady Augusta Gregory were also invaluable reading. I must also pay tribute to the many theses and works relating to the formation of the Abbey Theatre, the Easter Rising and the early years of revolutionary Ireland. The work of Anna MacBride-White and Norman Jeffares, *The Gonne-Yeats Letters*, was particularly inspiring, both as a study of their relationship and the historical perspectives which accompanied it. I am pleased to acknowledge the use of extracts from these letters and from the poems of Willie Yeats.

Finally, I must also acknowledge the thousands of websites dedicated to W.B. Yeats which yielded so much information and allowed me to hear Willie Yeats' mellow, musical brogue reciting some of his own poems. These, of course, need a very special acknowledgement for their everlasting beauty and source of contemplation and pleasure.

BARRY SHORTALL, JUNE 2002

1

'SHE'S HERE, father. She's here.' The excitement in the girl's voice was contagious, her sister and two brothers crowding into the small bay window of the neat, red-brick house in Blenheim Terrace, a quiet, tree-lined street in west London.

The parents showed little excitement as the hansom cab pulled up outside, the father unmoved, hands folded behind his back, unwittingly blocking the heat from the blazing coal fire on a damp January day in 1889. Near him, Susan, his wife, sat quietly and uncomplainingly in her usual chair near the fireplace, now a mere onlooker to the family's life since her last stroke.

'She's so beautiful. And so tall, isn't she Willie?' There was awe in Lolly's voice as she stared from the window. 'Just like when she was presented at court. See.' Her sister, Lily, held a newspaper cutting with grainy pictures of their visitor standing next to the Prince of Wales when, as a debutante, she was presented at court. 'It says she was the belle of the season and caught the eye of Prince Edward who danced with her. And that she is one of the great beauties of Anglo-Irish society.' The girls' excitement was quieted by a gesture from their father as the family waited for their visitor to follow the short path to the front door.

'Let her in girl. Don't just stand there gaping.' Lolly left the room at her father's bidding, returning almost immediately and ushering their visitor before her.

There was a long moment of silence, even the elder Yeats taken aback at the sheer presence of the woman, though her looks and reputation had preceded her. She was statuesque, perhaps six feet in height, a full figure with a tiny waist, and a peacock green, French-styled dress falling in shimmering waves to her ankles, a loose shawl over it, and a wide-brimmed, feathered hat crowning tresses of magnificent red-gold hair which curled to her shoulders.

She seemed to glide over the floor to greet her host, her hand outstretched.

'My dear Mr Yeats. I'm Maud Gonne. It's good of you to see me. I believe Ellen O'Leary mentioned my name?' Her voice was rich and melodious.

'She did that. As did my good friend John, her brother. She tells me you would like to discuss literature with us. And Ireland.'

She inclined her head, accepting that the introduction was a ruse, formally requiring her visit to be to the head of the household, though his eldest son was the real reason for her presence there.

John Yeats introduced her to the others in the room, his daughters, Elizabeth and Susan, their brother Jack, and his eldest son, Willie, last of all. 'You must know of Willie's work; we think he is going to be a great poet.'

She stared hard at the tall, thin, raven-haired young man with the small goatee beard and moustache, wide-spaced, lively eyes staring admiringly at her. She took his hand. 'I think you are that already, Mr Yeats.'

As tall as himself and almost hypnotically beautiful, he felt her magnetism immediately. His response stuck in his throat. 'I'm very glad to meet you, Miss Gonne ...' His voice trailed off lamely. He spoke quickly, hesitantly, strangely shy and uneasy as those hauntingly dark, golden-brown eyes stared into his.

She turned away, glancing at the cutting from the *Illustrated London News* which Lily still held in her hand. Maud took it from her and laughed, speaking to the two girls as if they were the only people in the room. 'It was a beautiful dress. It was covered in beads which made it look like a fountain and the train was of white satin. It was over three yards long ...'

'Did you like the Prince of Wales, Miss Gonne?'

John Yeats frowned at his daughter's question.

Maud laughed throatily. 'I did. And he asked me to dance and talked to me more than any of the other debutantes. I was told he admired me and wanted to invite me to supper but my father disapproved of his reputation.' She gave a wry smile. 'Father took me away to Bayreuth to see Wagner before I could receive the invitation. That was the end of that.'

Again she laughed before turning her attention back to John Yeats. 'Just what else has Ellen told you about me, Mr Yeats?'

'Very complimentary things, Miss Gonne, although she warned me your politics may not be ours.'

She acknowledged his reply with a slight inclination of her head, a quiet smile on her face as she moved across the room, leaning over Susan Yeats and taking her hand, speaking briefly to her before moving to the chair John Yeats had pushed forward. He ushered all the children except his eldest son from the room.

Maud Gonne spoke first. 'I've seen some of your paintings, Mr Yeats. I think they are very good, particularly the one of Mr O'Leary.' She turned to Willie. 'And your poetry, Mr Yeats. I admire that very much. I have your new book, *The Wanderings of Oisin and other poems*. It is so good.'

Willie Yeats mumbled a reply, still staring at her. Beauty such as hers he had never expected to see in his home; tall, her movements like a goddess. Already he was captivated.

She took a lacquered cigarette case from a pocket of her dress, his father refusing the offered cigarette, but Willie accepting and leaping forward to light hers with a taper from the fire. When it was alight she continued, staring intently at him. 'I so much wanted to meet you. You know that John O'Leary tells me you are destined to be recognised as one of Ireland's greatest poets?' She raised a hand at his obvious embarrassment, drawing on her cigarette and exhaling slowly. 'You should not be embarrassed, Mr Yeats. O'Leary is a man of fine intuition.'

Willie Yeats was slow to reply. 'He gave me the encouragement to publish, particularly about Ireland and its legends. He taught me about the Irish poets ...' He stopped, blushing shyly as his father spoke for him.

'We do have hope for the boy. O'Leary, not long back from exile, said at one of the meetings of the Contemporary Club ...' He waved a hand as he explained. 'It's a gentleman's meeting place in Grafton Street, in Dublin. He said Willie was the only person in the room who would ever be reckoned a genius.' He nodded his head in emphasis, his back still to the fire, stroking his grey-flecked beard as he continued. 'O'Leary and I are old friends. Since before ...'

She cut him short, almost brusquely. 'I know his history, Mr Yeats. His official publication, the *Irish People* for the Irish Republican Brotherhood, was too inflammatory for the English. They arrested him on the pretext of organising a revolution.' She looked from one to the other, nodding her head to emphasise her words. 'But I can assure you that there were many in England who thought that twenty years prison and exile was a terrible sentence for a man with beliefs.'

John Yeats nodded. 'Aye. He is a great man.'

She smiled almost arrogantly. 'You may be surprised to know that I also met him in the Contemporary Club. I believe I was the first English gentlewoman to be admitted. I had sympathy with the Nationalist cause and my work with the starving peasants in the west helped strengthen those beliefs. And, as John O'Leary was the leader of nationalist Ireland, I asked him to show me how to work for Ireland and he saw no problem with a woman helping him with his work.' She laughed. 'He really took quite a shine to me. He said I was the most beautiful woman in the world, and of such dramatic beauty it would be of great use to the cause.' She smiled, a smile which sent a sudden pang of longing through Willie Yeats. 'But then he spoiled the compliment by saying that even if I was not an intellectual, I was surely an activist.'

John Yeats frowned. 'John O'Leary may be a special friend of mine, Miss Gonne, but I find his are extreme views.'

She shrugged. 'If you mean his belief that the Supreme Council of the Irish Republican Brotherhood is the legitimate government of Ireland, then yes, they may seem extreme. But I accept his beliefs.' She paused, suddenly reflective, inhaling slowly on her cigarette before continuing. 'At one time I shared my father's belief in Home Rule but then, because of O'Leary, I joined the Irish Republican Brotherhood.' She leaned forward in her chair, her head inclined toward the older man. 'You don't believe in complete separation from England then, Mr Yeats?'

'What good would that serve us, Miss Gonne? We are mutually dependent, surely? I have no religious beliefs and it seems to me that too much of the nationalist cause is based on religion, and Roman Catholicism in Ireland is strong to the point of foolishness. And anyway, John O'Leary cannot be a true republican if he believes a constitutional monarchy is the best and safest form of government ...'

Maud remained silent, an inquiring lift of her eyebrow her only response, as Willie Yeats ventured an opinion for the first time, impatiently pushing back a long quiff of hair from his forehead. It was a soft, humorous voice with a strong brogue. 'John O'Leary argues that a political revolution cannot succeed unless backed by a cultural revolution. And he condemns individual acts of terror.' He paused, embarrassed by his forwardness.

John Yeats supported his son. 'There is another way, a way without violence and bloodshed.'

Maud gripped the side of her chair, her face shining with a fierce animation. 'But first the power must be gained, Mr Yeats. And then a purer nation will follow.' She pushed herself to her feet, walking to the window and staring into the fine drizzle and the great beech tree which dominated the garden. Beneath the window, on a tall plant stand, was a wide-necked bowl of cherry blossom. Willie Yeats gazed from it to her. The winter daylight was on her face, her complexion luminous, matching the blossom. He wanted to speak, to show his conviction but was too overwhelmed by her beauty and the strength of her personality.

John Yeats stroked his beard thoughtfully, mild sarcasm in his voice. 'So you and your supporters preach war Miss Gonne. Surely ...'

She cut him short. 'War is the only way. The exciting pure way. Ireland must be freed by physical force if necessary. Freedom from England will only be gained at the barrel of a gun.'

There was a fervour about her voice which made the two men uneasy. A strained silence ensued, John Yeats shaking his head, at a loss for words, as Willie exhaled a lung full of smoke, in awe of this fierce and beautiful woman who had aroused strange, new feelings in him. He stared at her, fascinated, and then glanced at both their reflections in the ornate mirror over the fireplace. He straightened up, pleased he was equal to her height or more, even more pleased to know, as the conversation continued, that she was a year younger than himself.

John Yeats was visibly shaken by the aggressive politics advocated by so young a woman, vexed at her praise for war for its own sake, and the almost impertinent forthrightness of this guest in his home. He was searching for a response, his anger obvious, when his son attempted to defuse the situation.

'Women should have an opinion, father. Politics is not just for men.' He was reckless in their guest's defence.

The elder Yeats shook his head again, looking from one to the other. Political argument with his son was not new. He stuffed tobacco into the bowl of a stained clay pipe, ignoring William's words as he smiled rather patronisingly at his visitor. 'So you would be a ruthless revolutionary, then?'

'As ruthless as the daughter of a British Army Colonel can be.' She smiled at his obvious surprise. 'I was born in Aldershot, Mr Yeats. My father was in the army there. I acted as hostess for him when my mother died and my father was posted to Dublin. He was part of the garrison to keep the peace against the Fenians. But he was a sympathiser, he kept his men in the barracks when the Land League marched through Dublin.' She smiled sadly. 'He was a good man, proud of his Irish descent. He felt the injustice of the Land War so much that he resigned his commission and joined the Home Rule party.' There was a slight moistness in her eyes as she continued. 'He taught me so much that I believe in. Two things in particular: never be afraid of anything, even death, and that will is a force that can achieve anything.'

John Yeats took the pipe from his mouth and stared at her, suddenly disarmed by her sincerity. 'In that case I think you are more Irish than many born there, Miss Gonne.'

She inclined her head, a smile of acknowledgement on her lips, before swiftly and easily changing the subject. 'Perhaps Ellen told you I have been in Donegal, working for those evicted by the landlords.'

John Yeats' expression changed and again there was a strained silence. Willie glanced at his father before the older man spoke, a touch of irritation in his voice. 'I was a landlord once, Miss Gonne. I know the difficulties they face. I was forced to let my tenants buy their holdings. The Land War meant that our Kildare land, in our family for generations, was taken from us.' He was suddenly angry, shaking a finger at her. 'You cannot understand. You are an outsider to what is happening there.' He was fighting to restrain himself.

She took out another cigarette, standing to casually discard the stub of the previous one into the blazing coals, and again Willie lit the fresh one for her, refusing one for himself. She inhaled deeply before staring challengingly at John Yeats. 'I try to understand, Mr Yeats, but I do care greatly for the peasant people.'

Maud sat down again, glancing around the room. The carpet before the fire was threadbare, the furniture old and worn. It was not as she expected. She knew John Yeats had been a successful lawyer in Dublin and had given up his career to move to London, to make a living as an artist, so far without much success. And his son's poetry could not yet be selling sufficiently to keep the family in a decent standard of living.

Almost an hour after arriving she left the house, leaving John Yeats angry and bemused by his son's support for Maud Gonne's ideals. He shook her hand testily as she left, unable to hide his irritation.

Maud refused to acknowledge his annoyance, thanking him for his hospitality before turning to Willie. 'Mr Yeats. Perhaps you would be so kind as to dine with my sister and cousin and I this evening. At my rooms in Ebury Street?'

Willie blushed, his shyness returning as he mumbled an acceptance, his two sisters rushing back into the room and crowding around him as the hansom cab pulled away.

Lolly's nose was turned up in dislike. 'I don't think I like her, Willie. She thinks she's royalty.'

Lily was more impressed. 'But she'd be a good one for you, Willie.'

A BROWN velvet smoking jacket, the better of the two jackets he possessed, a loose bow tie like a scarf at his neck, large pocket handkerchief overflowing from his top pocket, pince-nez tucked neatly below it. Over this an old Inverness cape which his father had tired of and which he thought gave him a bohemian appearance; Willie Yeats dressed with unusual care that evening

At Ebury Street in Belgravia a young maid opened the door to him and led him up a flight of stairs to Maud Gonne's rooms, his shyness returning with the sheer magnetism of her presence as she came to meet him. She was dressed more formally than on their previous meeting, in a dark blue ruched jacket with a high collar, a long string of pearls and a wide belt pinched in at her waist.

She smiled and gestured around the room. 'Please, don't let my small friends alarm you, my dear Mr Yeats. They all know their place.'

Yeats tried hard to hide his astonishment as he stared at her small menagerie of pets. There were caged birds on the sideboard; a small monkey and a black Persian cat perched on the back of an overstuffed sofa and a huge, tawny Great Dane in place on the hearth rug.

Maud gestured to the monkey. 'My spiritual friend, Mr Yeats. And my chaperone. Isn't he the perfect thing? And this is Daghda.' At the mention of its name the dog lifted its huge head to gaze unblinkingly at Yeats as Maud introduced the other two occupants of the room. 'This is my sister, Kathleen, and my cousin May who was with me in Donegal.'

Yeats nodded shyly, shaking hands with the two women before taking his place at the table, the meal already prepared. The two other women stared appraisingly at their new acquaintance as they ate, occasionally firing questions at him, Maud curiously aloof, a slight smile on he face.

Kathleen was the first to compliment him on his work. 'I loved your poem, "The Salley Gardens", Mr Yeats. The words are so nice. So comforting.' She repeated a few lines slowly and with a voice as mellow as her sister's.

She bids me take life easy, as the grass grows on the weirs;
But I was young and foolish, and now am full of tears.

She looked at him. 'Where did you get the idea for such a lovely thing? Where does your inspiration come from?'

His answer was immediate. 'I remembered an old woman singing in Sligo. It kept returning to my mind when I was homesick. The words followed.' He shrugged modestly.

Now the questions were continuous, Kathleen and May both intent on impressing him with their knowledge of his work. It was May's turn. 'And your other poem, everyone's favourite, "Innisfree"? Where did you get the idea for that?'

Patient and polite, Yeats was hardly able to hide the nostalgia. 'My sisters and I miss the west of Ireland so much.' He smiled ruefully. 'I suppose it's the old race instinct thing, the need to hold a sod of earth from a field of home.' He paused, his thoughts distant. 'We were walking past a shop on Fleet Street and heard the tinkling of water and saw a fountain in a shop window which had a ball balanced on its jet. I suddenly began to remember the sound of lake water at Innisfree. It's a little island which just seems to float in the waters of Loch Gill.' He shrugged. 'That gave me the idea for the poem.'

May quoted from it.

And I shall find some peace there, for peace comes dropping

11

slow
Dropping from the veils of morning ...

She leaned across the table, her hand on his arm. 'I think they are the most beautiful words ever put together in the English language. You write like no other poet has ever done, Mr Yeats. Will you recite for us?'

He smiled and nodded. 'I call this "The Song of the Wandering Aengus".' His voice was soft and musical.

Though I am old with wandering
Through hollow lands and hilly lands,
I will find out where she has gone
And kiss her lips and take her hands:
And walk among long dappled grass,
And pluck till time and times are done
The silver apples of the moon,
The golden apples of the sun.

There was silence for a few moments after he had finished, smiling modestly as Kathleen was the first to speak.

'You speak that so beautifully, Mr Yeats.' Her questions continued. 'Do you know many other poets? Are they among your friends?'

His modesty was now replaced by a sudden need to impress. 'I did meet Lady Wilde. I was interested in her book on the ancient myths of Ireland, and then I met her son, Oscar. He was marvellous company! He must be the greatest raconteur of our time.'

Maud interrupted, the first comment she had made since her sister and cousin had begun to bombard Yeats with their questions. She had been leaning forward, elbows on the table, resting her chin in her hands, her great wide eyes swallowing him as his mind dissolved every time he glanced at her. 'I've met Oscar Wilde.' She laughed. 'He called me an utterly charming European sophisticate.'

Yeats nodded politely. 'I am sure he is right, Miss Gonne.'

She smiled at his flattery. 'You like him?'

'Very much. I had Christmas dinner with Oscar and his wife and children in his home in Chelsea. It was all very elegant and Oscar was very helpful to me. He told me that writing tittle-tattle letters and reviews for newspapers is not a fit occupation for a gentleman.'

'And Bernard Shaw? Have you met him?'

'Yes. He also ...'

'Is he really eccentric, Mr Yeats? That great yellow beard. And knee breeches. Well, really ... He looks like a gamekeeper to me.' May's question was serious.

Yeats shrugged. 'Perhaps. He is a socialist after all.'

'He gives political talks in the parks!' May sounded shocked.

Kathleen broke in. 'And Mr Wilde is not too enamoured with Mr Shaw, it is said.'

Yeats laughed. 'I believe so. Oscar said Bernard Shaw has no enemies but is intensely disliked by his friends.'

They all broke into spontaneous laughter before the questions continued.

'And who else?'

He shrugged. 'Well, a group of us have a regular meeting at the Old Cheshire Cheese, in Wine Office Court, off Fleet Street. It's where the old writers used to meet, Dickens and Goldsmith and Oliver Johnson. Nowadays Bernard Shaw and William Morris come, and Arthur Symons, Lionel

Johnson and John Masefield. Oscar comes sometimes. We take a room on the second floor. We call it the Rhymers Club.' He chuckled. 'We read our verses and drink a little beer or wine. It is very pleasant.'

Willie Yeats was unusually modest. The meetings were now an important part of artistic life in London; the Cheshire Cheese was situated in the centre of the newspaper publishing district where most of the Rhymers worked as journalists or critics. Inside, up a winding, dark stair, they met around long, stained tables, drinking from tankards, some smoking clay pipes like the poets and writers of years before.

By now, every answer to every question was weighted in his mind as to how it would influence Maud. The evening passed quickly until, as he left, she invited him to dine there again the following evening, and invitations followed for every evening of the coming week.

Intoxication with her moved seamlessly into infatuation, as evenings passed in a haze of conversation during which he poured out his dreams and ambitions. Without the company of her sister and cousin on some occasions, the easy comforts were the same. She would sit on the huge low sofa which dominated the room, the Persian cat on her lap, a pile of coloured cushions behind her, large, hauntingly-beautiful eyes turned to him. He would sit facing her, standing only to light her constant chain of cigarettes as they discussed the theatre of the day, her questions often unnervingly direct. 'What is your greatest ambition, Mr Yeats?'

He leaned forward intently. 'I have a dream of creating an Irish National Theatre.' He paused. 'Perhaps based upon the nationalist movement.' Again he wanted to impress.

'Yes. Yes. That would be so right, Mr Yeats.' She leaned forward, even more intense. 'You want a theatre and I want freedom for Ireland. But how? There is so much oppression to be overcome first. So much more to turn our energies to.' She ignored his questioning look as she continued. 'The evictions, Mr Yeats, whole families are being wiped out, dying at the roadside even as we speak.' There was passion in her voice as she continued. 'In Donegal I saw homeless families, near death from cold and starvation, sheltering in ditches, loved ones dead and stiff beside them. May and I did what we could for them; we took them to food and shelter. But we were helpless to prevent the evictions. Families who had lived in the same cabins all their lives were thrown out, and the walls tumbled down with battering rams and crowbars in front of them.'

She clenched her fists as she continued. 'I fought for them in the magistrates courts, children charged with stealing turf for the fire, women for taking milk to keep their children alive and men threatened with eviction for not paying the rent.' She stopped, shaking her head slowly. 'I paid their fines and gave them all the help I could. The women kissed my hands, the men thought I was a queen or a saint.' She gave a rueful smile. 'But I'm neither, Mr Yeats.'

Yeats shifted uncomfortably. The terrible truth of life and death were not what he had come to discuss. Poetry and theatre and the beauty of Maud Gonne had brought him there that evening.

There was a slightly mocking, challenging smile on her lips when she changed the subject to a more personal theme. 'But tell me about yourself, Mr Yeats. Where do you come from?'

Yeats was taken aback by her forwardness, his long,

sensitive fingers pushing back the lock of dark hair which was continually falling over his eyes. 'Sandymount, near Dublin originally. After that we lived in Howth before moving to London.'

Maud clapped her hands together, cigarette ash dropping to the folds of her dress. 'Then we have more in common. I too lived in Howth. And loved it.' She inhaled deeply, sitting back against the cushions, her eyes locked into his as she spoke. 'Do you have religion?'

He hesitated before replying, searching for the right answer. 'John Yeats, my great-grandfather, was rector at Drumcliffe, in Sligo.' He laughed. 'I remember being frightened of God, and by my sins. But, like my father, I hated church.'

'And school?'

The questions seemed never-ending and he sat, captivated, willing to please, answering her obediently, as if in a witness box. 'I went to school at Erasmus Smith High School in Harcourt Street. When I left school father wanted me to go to Trinity but I decided to go to the Metropolitan School of Art.' He puffed at his cigarette and smiled. 'It was less expensive and less demanding.'

He stopped abruptly, embarrassed he had said so much, annoyed that she could have prompted so much from him. He struggled for something to carry the conversation, her beauty completely captivating. He suddenly realised she was speaking.

'I think that you and your father must disagree over many things, Mr Yeats.' It was almost a statement.

He nodded. 'Money is short, as you must know. The income on my father's Irish properties fell as the tenants' rents were unreliable. He had 500 acres at one time.' Yeats shrugged. 'And since he came to London as an artist he cannot make a living and, I'm afraid, he is too generous for his own good.' He smiled, showing even, good teeth. 'Or the family's good. But we are able to borrow against the future. My poetry pays some bills and Lolly is an art teacher. She and I support the house.' He sighed. 'But father gets depressed at his failure to sell his paintings and then we row over the lack of money.' He laughed quietly. 'Yet you are from a wealthy background, Miss Gonne. You would find our situation difficult to understand.'

'I have an inheritance: a trust, some family possessions, some land and a small income. I should never want, Mr Yeats but, more importantly, it gives me the opportunity to do the things I believe in.' She was staring intently at him, her dark eyes fixed on his, the intensity of her gaze increasing his nervousness. He felt strangely uncomfortable as she leaned forward. 'Do you believe in magic, Mr Yeats?'

Surprised at the question he hesitated, again wanting to give the answer which would please her most. Finally he nodded. 'Yes. I think so ...'

'I am not sure that I do, although I am superstitious. And I do believe I am psychic. What about the supernatural. Do you believe in such things?'

He laughed, embarrassed. 'I once went to a seance. It rather frightened me.'

'And the tarot cards. Do you use them?'

He nodded, almost guiltily. 'Sometimes. For fortune telling.'

Maud's mind was never still. 'You write plays as well, Mr Yeats?'

His modesty was assumed. 'I try to. You know Florence Farr of course?' Without waiting for an answer he continued.

'She's a good friend of mine and a wonderful actress. I try to write plays which are worthy of her.' He laughed. 'A very emancipated woman and very hard working.'

'And?'

He looked bemused.

She prompted, with a rise of her eyebrows. 'She has other friends ...'

He laughed. 'Bernard Shaw, you mean?' She nodded her acknowledgement. 'Yes. They are lovers, I believe. She is a lady of generous talents.' He blushed at his forthrightness.

She leaned towards him. 'Could I be worthy of a play, Willie? Will you write one for me? One which will tell an Irish story. I was an actress, you know. I still could be.'

He felt a sudden, almost child-like elation as she used his name for the first time. 'I will. Of course I will.' He sought for inspiration. 'A play in which a beautiful lady is admired by a young poet.'

She smiled. 'Now you are flirting with me, Mr Yeats. That will never do.'

Oblivious of the amusement of the few passers-by on the streets of Chiswick, he walked home later that evening in a haze of cigarette smoke, muttering to himself, the stirrings of a play flickering in his mind. It would be based on one of his Irish fairy stories, about a philanthropist, a woman who sells her soul to the devil to ransom the souls of those suffering during the famine.

That night, Maud filled his dreams. Next day, in his first-floor study, in Blenheim Terrace, he stared thoughtfully out the window at the bare tracery of the Virginia creeper clinging to the small balcony, the fireplace and floor littered with paper from his first attempts at the play.

2

THEY MET at every opportunity, the intervals bridged by a continuous exchange of letters as his terrible pangs of first love intensified. By December his play, *The Countess Cathleen*, was nearly ready. It was a story of the Sidhe. In it, Maud Gonne would ransom her soul to the devil.

While he was working in London Maud was making her first public speech. It was to an English audience. She had been invited to canvass and to appear, in June 1890, at a meeting for the Irish Parliamentary Party in the by-election for the strong conservative seat at Barrow-in-Furness. There was an audience of over 1,500 when, without warning, the chairman introduced 'Miss Gonne, a young Irish lady'.

Slowly she got to her feet, unsure of what to say, intimidated by the large audience. Then, as the evictions came to mind, the story flowed easily. Of the dead at the roadsides; the old couple driven from the home they had lived in for 50 years, walking slowly away together across the fields; of the woman with the day-old baby left homeless; of young children trying to light a fire in the rain; of the desolation of the workhouses and the families torn apart.

The audience, at first curious, were stunned. There was

an almost shocked silence until, as emotion took hold, Maud could no longer control her tears, sinking back to her seat and weeping freely.

There was silence when she sat down, apart from the muted sobs of the audience, before they rose to their feet. The applause was prolonged, almost rapturous, and, as she left the stage, people crowded around wanting to shake her hand, expressing their sorrow at the atrocities their countrymen were committing.

Maud Gonne, the public speaker, was launched.

After that, each day for the next week, she spoke at up to five meetings, her confidence growing and, as news of her appearances reached the newspapers, she became sought after socially in London, old pictures of her in court dress resurrected by the newspapers.

The following July, in Dublin, Yeats called to see her in her rooms at the Nassau Hotel in South Frederick Street. Although it had been almost a year, during that time her image had seldom been from his mind.

He waited in the lobby, standing to greet her, his manicured beard and moustache now gone, suddenly apprehensive as he walked towards her, anticipation giving way to sudden shock. Her magnificent beauty had faded. She was thin, her face wan and pale, her high cheekbones exaggerated. And, with the change in her appearance, her youthful vitality had disappeared. There was an air of sadness about her which, for the first time since they had met, made her seem vulnerable. He stared at her, overwhelmed with emotion: more in love with her than ever, wanting to help her, comfort her, as she greeted him.

'I am so glad to see you, Willie.'

His concern could not be hidden. 'You don't look well,

Maud ...'

'I suppose I've been doing too much. That's all.' She shook her head, the great mass of curls falling over her shoulders, her voice full of weariness when she spoke, the old assertiveness gone. 'But I'm all right now.'

He followed her to her rooms overlooking the lawns of Trinity College and, after her maid had served tea, it was as if their conversations of the previous year had never ceased. Perhaps a deeper closeness existed between them.

'I was in Donegal, working for the rights of the tenants, but I had to leave for France. My work had helped stop the evictions; court orders were now needed to get the people out, and the landlords blamed me. One landlord had friends at Dublin Castle and there was a warrant out for my arrest for helping the Plan of Campaign.' She shrugged. 'But I have friends also and eventually it was withdrawn. When I was in France I gave lectures; it was the first time the people had heard the truth about Ireland's troubles. I told them about the famine of 50 years ago when whole families, who had nothing more to eat, would barricade themselves into their cottages so that no one could look upon the agony of their death.' She shook her head. 'People found it all so hard to believe.' She hesitated, glancing at him sideways, not meeting his eyes. 'When I was in Donegal I dreamed of you. We were brother and sister in the past and I had been sold into slavery in the Arabian desert.'

He stared at her, sudden elation coursing through him. 'And I tried to reach you in my dreams.' He leaned toward her. 'Perhaps I'm in your thoughts as well as your dreams, Maud.' He leaned forward, suddenly very nervous, speaking without conviction. 'Scotia.' He used the pet name he had given her but now, in his fumbling shyness, he suddenly became formal, his hand shaking with nerves, the cup and saucer he was holding rattling. He placed them on a side table before leaning forward again and taking her hand. It was the first time he had physically touched her and a sudden pulse of desire shot through him at the sensation of her smooth flesh. He swallowed hard before continuing, stuttering with nervousness before blurting out his need. 'Maud, Miss Gonne, ever since we met, almost two years ago now ...' He stopped, his courage almost deserting him, breathing deeply before continuing. 'Ever since then I have been in love with you. Deeply and terribly in love with you, but I have never been able to tell you.' He held her hand in both his. 'Please, dear Maud. Will you marry me?' He paused, staring at her face before continuing lamely. 'I want you to be my wife.'

There was a long silence as she stared at him before overcoming her confusion and drawing her hand away. 'Oh no. No, my dear, dear Willie. Not marriage. Marriage would spoil what we have between us. I feel it is so special, so spiritual, we must not spoil it. We have so much more than any marriage could offer.'

He stared at her, deflated and embarrassed. He had misjudged the moment.

She stared at him with concern, this time taking his hand in hers, feeling guilt at her refusal and pangs of regret at his dismay. 'There are reasons I can never marry. But I will always be your friend. Believe me, Willie, the world would not thank you for marrying me.'

EVERY DAY the following week was spent together, his love deepening as daily she recovered her old spirits.

Almost a week later, in her rooms in the Nassau Hotel, Willie started to read aloud his first love poem for her. 'I call it "The White Birds".'

And the flame of the blue star of twilight, hung low on the rim
      of the sky,
Has awaked in our hearts, my beloved, a sadness that may not
      die.
Soon far from the rose and the lily and fret of the flames would
      we be,
Were we only white birds, my beloved, buoyed out on the
      foam of the sea.

When he had finished her smile was reward enough. 'It is beautiful,Willie. I can't thank you enough.'

He put the pages on the table, encouraged by her words. 'Tomorrow I'm going to the west. Why don't you come with me? It is beautiful, so different. You can tell me what you think of the play I have been writing for you.'

She hesitated and he gave her no chance to reply. 'We could work together. There is an old uninhabited castle, Castle Rock, at Lough Key, in Roscommon. It would be a place for us to work on Celtic stories. Our castle of heroes, somewhere we could write and meditate and help one another.' She made no reply and he tried to persuade her. 'All the hidden forces of nature could give us strength for the freeing of Ireland.' His enthusiasm ran away with him. 'And the best of Ireland's men and women could go there for inspiration and teaching.'

She smiled gently at him, raising his hopes. 'I'll think about it, Willie. In time, maybe.'

But it was not to happen. Next morning he struggled to

confused wakefulness as the loud knocking on the door of his hotel room interrupted his sleep. It was Maud. Her face was drawn, her eyes wide. He was instantly awake.

'What is it, what's wrong Maud?'

'I have to go to Paris. Immediately. A child I adopted is dangerously ill. I must go to him.'

'Then I will go with you.'

'No. But thank you, Willie. You have your work here. But I will write to you; as soon as I arrive.'

He nodded quickly. 'Of course. You must go. Our trip can wait. Perhaps when you come back?'

She gave a sad smile. 'Perhaps, Willie. Perhaps.'

He stood at the door until her hansom cab had disappeared from sight, wondering if she would write; if he would ever see her again.

His love was now his obsession, often precluding all coherent thought but driving him to a frenzy of work, on poems dedicated to her. Melancholy, sad and beautiful poems to be completed in time for her return to Dublin.

Their exchange of letters had never faltered, her last, in October 1891, asking him to meet her from the boat at Kingstown. This was the same boat which was carrying the body of Charles Stewart Parnell, the leader of the Irish Parliamentary Party, who had recently died in London.

Willie took Maud straight to her hotel for breakfast, staring at her across the table in her room. 'I am sorry the child died, Maud. So very sorry. You must have been close to him.'

The letter had been short and simple and he had read it and re-read it. It was full of sorrow and sadness but there was a depth of feeling and closeness that had not been there before.

She was still thin and terribly tired but needed to talk. Then it all came out. It was the first time he had seen her lose her self control, great racking sobs heaving through her until she regained her composure, pushing herself up in the chair.

'It was meningitis. It was so sad.' She smiled through her tears. 'I had a lovely tomb built for him.'

'He must have meant a lot.'

'I loved him as if he were my own, Willie.'

'You're too caring, Maud. It's taken too much out of you.'

'I'm well now, thank you, Willie dear. I was coughing badly when I reached Paris but I spent some time in the south of France to recover in the sun. I was looking for French support for our cause.'

'Our cause, Maud?' He stared at her, not understanding at first and then shaking his head despairingly. 'All Ireland has a cause but with you it is a battle. And you cannot win it by yourself.' He stopped abruptly before he said more than he would have wished, taking her hand and leading her to the large sofa in the drawing room. Beside him was a gentler woman than the one who had left Dublin four months earlier. He pushed his pince-nez back on his nose, preparing to take the opportunity, his voice now more assertive.

'Maud. Surely now you will marry me. Let me look after you. You know I will support you in all you try to do. Let us get married and share the best things in our lives. The theatre. Poetry. Everything.'

She shook her head sadly and slowly. 'I cannot marry, Willie. I can never marry.'

He went to speak but she stopped him with a finger to his lips. 'Don't question me, Willie. If you love me just accept my wishes.'

There was a firmness in her voice which stopped further discussion. He pursed his lips in disappointment, although a refusal was little more than he had expected. When she was away he had confided his feelings to John O'Leary but his old friend's response had not been encouraging. Maud Gonne was not for marrying. She was unreachable. Men courted her for her beauty and qualities but were deterred by her aloofness. She was a woman seeking something, her vanity needing recognition.

O'Leary's remedy had been succinct. And rejected out of hand. 'There are other women, for relief.'

But Willie Yeats had to succeed with her. Nothing less would do.

There was still one more approach. He brushed his hair back nervously, taking both her hands in his. He faltered as he spoke. 'If you don't want to marry, Maud, then would you consider ...' He stopped, taking a deep breath as he plucked up courage. 'Would you consider being my mistress?' He tried to smile but found it impossible. 'I am so troubled by thoughts of you and the need for you. It affects my work.' His despair suddenly spilled out. 'My friends claim to have mistresses and yet I have never even kissed a woman on the lips. I want to spend special times with you. I want to be able to kiss you ...' His voice trailed off in embarrassment before he plucked up the courage to continue. She stared at him in silence as he continued. 'I am poor, very poor, Maud, you know that, but ...'

She leaned towards him, taking his hand. 'Money doesn't matter, dear Willie. I am very flattered.' She turned away, staring from the window as she spoke, as if unwilling to face him. 'But that sort of relationship, sexual, would spoil so much that is beautiful between us.'

A terrible sadness filled Willie, his words hardly audible as he spoke. 'Then what do we have? A marriage of minds? Nothing more?'

She stared at him, nodding her head slightly. 'Perhaps the fruits of such a marriage could be a free nation, Willie.'

He sighed inwardly as again her politics intruded on their most intimate moments. But now was not the time to force the issue; that time would surely come. He forced a smile. 'Let me read from the play I have written for you. I call it *The Countess Cathleen.*' He took a sheaf of papers from his pocket and, making her sit back on the sofa, began to read.

When he had finished she reached out and took his hand. 'I will be proud to play her part. Thank you for writing it for me.'

He had another surprise. From his pocket he took a small, vellum bound book, the title, *The Flame of the Spirit,* in gold lettering on the cover. He placed it in her hand. 'It has some poems written for you. Just for you. Perhaps some time you will read them and understand something of my feelings.'

3

IT WAS in the spring of 1893, almost four years after their first meeting, that they had their first argument. They were in her new apartments over Morrow's Bookshop near the National Library in Nassau Street, Dublin. Much to his disapproval it had become the meeting place for nationalists, mostly young, idealistic, working class Catholics.

The meetings did little for Maud's standing with the British authorities. Her reputation as a leading nationalist was now such that two Special branch members, the G men, kept her under surveillance. The G men were the detective division of the political crimes unit of the RIC, an undercover organisation based at Dublin Castle.

Yeats was more than unhappy about the direction in which the meetings, and those who attended them, were taking her. 'They are dangerous friends, Maud. They take your ideals to dangerous limits.'

She defended them angrily. 'People like Arthur Griffith, you mean, Willie. Good people, Catholic or not.' Griffith, a reserved, rather austere young compositor and journalist was a particular friend of Maud's.

'They preach violence. You shouldn't mix with them or be influenced by them.'

She stared coldly at him. 'You should know me better by now. I would never willingly discourage a constitutionalist or a realist or a writer or even a dynamiter. All that matters to me is how they can help the Irish separatist movement.' She waved her arm at him disdainfully. 'Anyway, you're just a snob, Willie Yeats. And snobs have no place in my life.'

He shook his head angrily. 'Don't you think you would be better spending your time on literary matters? Your presence, your fame, Maud, would attract people. We could form a National Literary Society. You could lecture, bring books to the people, organise libraries. There is so much you could do, we could do together.'

She shook her head forcibly in disagreement. 'It's not the only way. Feeding the people is more important than giving them stories.'

His dismay showed. 'Then you will only pander to the interests of the Catholic clergy and their vested interests. They don't want the people educated.' For the first time in their relationship he showed anger, standing over her, shaking his finger at her as his frustration poured out. 'You have too much lust for the extreme ways, Maud. The wrong ways.' His face was flushed with his annoyance.

Maud hid her surprise at his outburst. There was a sudden strength about him she had not seen before, a rudeness even. She waited until his tirade was over, a sudden, icy silence settling over them before she ordered him from her rooms.

That night Maud lay awake, trying to cope with the change in Willie's manner towards her, surprising herself with a sudden fear that she would lose his love and, even more, his spiritual friendship. She went to sleep determined, the following day, to make friends with him again.

But it was not to be. During the night she developed a heavy fever, her maid sending for the doctor who refused to let Yeats see her when he heard that she was ill. Later that day he left for Sligo, depressed at her rejection of his feelings. And of his advice. And possibly, himself.

FEELING GREAT despair at losing Maud, it was June 1894 when Willie Yeats was invited to a formal literary dinner at the Hotel d'Italia in Old Compton Street, in London's Soho. There was good food and easy conversation, with a beautiful and intriguing woman sitting near him. With dark hair in a bun, large soulful eyes and full, sensuous lips, she caught his eye, nodding slightly to him after the meal, before moving away.

Later, as Florence Farr and he took the underground railway back to Bedford Park, he asked about the woman. Florence smiled, amused at the intrigue. 'She asked your name, Willie. I think she likes you.'

A few months later he saw her again. It was at a dinner at the home of Lionel Johnson, a fellow poet and old friend, and a member of the Rhymers Club. Yeats discovered that the woman was Johnson's cousin, Olivia Shakespeare.

Again conversation was easy. 'Florence has told me much about you, Mr Yeats. And I do so enjoy your poetry.' She leaned forward, smiling engagingly. 'Perhaps you would be kind enough to comment on my amateurish efforts.'

He smiled disarmingly. 'I am sure they are far from amateurish, Mrs Shakespeare. And I would be only too delighted to read them.'

She nodded her head gratefully. 'I just hope they are

worth your time.'

He stared at her. She was the first woman he had felt any real attraction to since his first meeting with Maud. Exquisitely dressed, she contrasted markedly with himself: a thin young poet, strikingly handsome, with lean features and crow-black hair, but lacking in many social graces, his clothes old and worn. He was surprised and flattered by her attention and yet, despite this apparent lack of anything in common, except for a love of poetry, their meetings over the following year led to an exchange of letters. Comments on their mutual interest in poetry and the theatre gradually became more intimate as he told her of his sadness over his relationship with Maud.

It was not until the spring of the following year that they met again at a dinner in London. After their letters and exchange of confidences they were able to talk freely, at ease with one another.

'You met some other friends of mine, I believe.'

He stared at her, puzzled until she prompted him.

'At Lissadell, in Sligo.'

He smiled as he remembered. 'Eva and Constance Gore-Booth.' He smiled wryly. 'I like them both very much. I was close friends with Eva and even thought of proposing to her, but I'm afraid her father would not have let her marry someone as poor as me.' He shrugged. 'That, I'm afraid, was that.' He paused ruefully. 'Like you, she also thinks I waste my time over Maud Gonne.' He saw her raised eyebrows, lifting a hand apologetically. 'I'm sorry. She's something of an unhappy obsession with me.'

She reached across and took his hand. 'I am unhappy also, Willie. My husband is fourteen years older than me. He is, I'm afraid, rather dull.' She stopped, not looking at him as she continued. 'He stopped being a husband to me soon after we were married.'

Yeats blushed, the revelation too intimate, unsure whether or not there was a signal there. Availability? Something which Maud denied him? Embarrassment turned to an excitement which he had only felt before with Maud. In a sudden rush of confidence he took the initiative.

'Perhaps you will have dinner with me one evening, Olivia?'

'No, Willie. You will dine with me.' She laughed and placed a hand on his arm. 'Please don't be offended, but I do know how poor you young poets must be. And my husband is a wealthy man.'

A frisson of sexual excitement surged through him. She was married and had agreed to dine with him. Confidence gained, it was the opportunity to take the relationship further.

Their first evening together was charged with sexual tension, she waiting his advances, he naïvely incapable of approaching her. After several hours of small talk he finally blurted out his needs. 'Olivia. Will you come and live with me?' Clumsily he leaned towards her and kissed her on the cheek. She looked at him, surprised by the gentleness of the kiss, unaware that, at 30 years of age he had never kissed a woman in any other way.

She shook her head gently, stroking his cheek with her hand. 'I can't do that, Willie. I'm sorry. I've far too much to lose.'

He tried to hide his disappointment. 'Then perhaps we can see each other more often. Perhaps tomorrow we could go out for the day to Kew Gardens?'

'I'd love that. And then in the evening we can again

dine together.'

His preparations for the following evening were painstaking: a silk tie, saved for the best occasions, his best suit and fresh polish on his good shoes.

On the train to Kew they sat at the rear of the carriage, Yeats excited, unsure of how to manage the occasion. 'I wasn't sure if you would come. Because of your husband.'

'I wanted to come, Willie. You must have known that.' He took her hand, leaning towards her and again kissed her gently on the cheek. It was another chaste kiss which changed quickly as she turned to him, her arm around his neck, pulling him to her, natural instincts guiding him as it became a long, passionate and erotic kiss. Something so greedy and sensual he had never before experienced.

He pulled away, frightened that his arousal would be obvious, suddenly aware of how public a place they were in, only to lean towards her again, kissing her greedily, his hand on her side aware of the fullness of her body beneath the light dress.

As they walked through the gardens at Kew his passion faded, suddenly shy and embarrassed. But slowly, easily, his reserve evaporated as the day passed in increasing sexual tension, their conversation building an expectancy.

'I wasn't sure you would return my feelings.'

'I wasn't sure myself, Willie. I have never thought of another man but my husband.'

'And now?'

'There will be no going back. Unless you have doubts?'

His answer was to pull her to him again, this time his hand smoothing the contours of her body before they pulled apart.

Willie Yeats thought he was in love again. He spoke

quickly, before his nerve went, asking her again. 'Leave him now. Come and live with me.'

She smiled ruefully, gasping as his hand caressed her. 'I can't. You know I can't. We can spend time together but we will have to be careful. The risk of divorce is too great.' She stopped, hesitating before continuing. 'I have already asked for a separation but he became upset and ill. I don't want to lose everything, Willie. My home, my daughter. And, if we were discovered, you would be sued for all you have.'

Yeats smiled ruefully. 'I have very little to lose then.'

She smiled and gave an almost imperceptible shrug, unable to meet his gaze. 'I think it would be kinder to deceive him.'

But Willie Yeats' ardour had to wait. For over a year he was filled with desperate longing. They met clandestinely, in art galleries and railway carriages, their mutual friend, Florence Farr, recently divorced herself, acting as the go-between.

Their feelings for one another grew stronger until, in the early spring of 1896, at Olivia's prompting, Yeats decided he needed a home of his own, a place which would provide privacy for their relationship. And Olivia helped him find it.

The apartment was in Woburn Buildings, a tenement in a quiet passageway off Euston Road in Bloomsbury. It seemed secretive and exciting, the gas lamps outside casting romantic shadows from the trees lining the street.

It took several days to get some basic furniture and, in between fits of embarrassed giggles, a large and second-hand double bed.

On the day the furniture was delivered, Yeats waited in a passion of anticipation for Olivia to arrive early that evening. Her mind was made up. She had no reservations about the affair, smiling at his shyness as she took him by the hand and led him to the bedroom, her fingers to her lips, motioning him to be quiet so as not to arouse the attention of the other tenant on that floor. She walked ahead of him into the room, he remaining in the doorway, sudden confusion overwhelming him as his need suddenly subsided. She stared at him, a gentle smile on her lips.

'Don't be frightened of me, Willie.'

He closed the door behind him. 'I'm frightened of myself, Olivia. I have a confession to make.'

She stared at him, sudden concern crossing her features.

He took a while to reply, suddenly blurting out his confession. 'I'm thirty years of age.' He hesitated. 'And I've never been with a woman before.'

She stared open mouthed and then laughed aloud, covering her face with her hand as she saw his embarrassment. 'I'm sorry, Willie. But that's beautiful. I'm the first. Oh I do like that.' She was suddenly serious. 'And you will be the first man except for my husband.' She turned his face to her, kissing him long and sensually before pulling away, her hands moving to the buttons at the front of her dress. He moved away from her, standing at the window staring out, too shy to look, reluctant to spoil his images of the beauty of a woman's body, her body. There was silence except for a nightingale singing from its perch in one of the plane trees outside. The rustling of her clothing seemed magnified. And then there was silence.

Except for her voice.

'Willie ...?'

Hesitantly, eyes lowered, he turned towards her until, in the dim candlelight, he could see her naked feet by the side of the bed, surrounded by layers of discarded clothing. A goddess emerging. His gaze moved upward slowly, as if to prolong the pleasure of expectation. Long, slim thighs, a dark mystery between and then the fullness of her stomach. He had been holding his breath, as if in a trance, as the mysteries of a woman's body were at last revealed to him, and now he suddenly exhaled, gasping, as he stared at the alabaster heaviness of her breasts.

Large, larger than her outer clothing had made him believe possible; larger, heavier than the small, bulbous breasts which he had gazed at wistfully and lustfully in galleries and museums.

But this was no statue. His gaze met hers and there was a quizzical expression, a gentle smile on her face as she held out one slender, graceful arm.

'Come to me, Willie. A gentleman never keeps a lady waiting.'

Another vision flashed into his mind, a head thrown back, a full body silhouetted against a thin dress. Was Maud's naked body ever this beautiful? Were her breasts so white and rounded? Was her skin as smooth and unblemished. He closed his eyes, trying to force thoughts, wishful comparisons from his mind, and they slowly evaporated as he moved towards her, trance-like, aware suddenly of his own clothing but with no thought or confidence to even attempt to remove it.

He stood before her, perhaps a pace from her as she reached for his hands, lifting them to her breasts. He held them, his palms upward, gingerly lifting, marvelling at their soft weight, their firmness and softness, their smoothness as her hands went around his neck, her mouth to his.

Then the trance was broken, thoughts of Maud now

completely dissolved from his mind and he responded, returning her kiss greedily, his hands moving now, massaging, fingers pinching, hard, arousing. He groaned with the sensuality of it, suddenly in need as she helped him pull his clothes from him, excited at the sensation of naked bodies pressed together.

He held her as she lay back on the bed, leaning over her, his head going to the soft pleasure of her skin, to her breasts, tasting, savouring for the first time the sweetness of a woman's body. He made her wince, his mouth greedy at a nipple, unaccustomed to such sensuality, before moving to lie on his side, one arm around her, his other hand smoothing the long sweep of her thighs, exploring.

She sighed with pleasure and lay back, eyes half closed, fingers ruffling his hair. She was so good. It was all so good, the touching, the sensations. The closeness. At last his need to be satisfied. By Maud.

It was Maud. It had to be Maud. He could never be unfaithful to the most beautiful woman in the world. He moved over her and opened his eyes.

It wasn't Maud and the moment passed. Suddenly there was nothing. No response. The wonder of her femininity not enough. He closed his eyes in despair, hardly able to meet hers, half closed with passion. He looked at her blankly, cursing himself. Disbelieving.

'I'm sorry. Olivia.' His disappointment and embarrassment was obvious.

She smiled, breathing deeply and holding her hand to his cheek. 'It's all right, Willie. It doesn't matter, really. It takes time and we have all the time we need.' She smiled teasingly. 'It will be all the more worthwhile.'

Yet despite all her assurances, her caresses, her gentle

hands, there was nothing. Finally he sat up, shyly pulling on his clothes, hating himself and for a few moments hating Maud for causing this refusal by his body, this failure of his masculinity.

Olivia was already dressing and he sat looking at her as she fought with buttons and laces and hooks. There was an almost embarrassed silence between them before she left the flat.

But the need was too much, lust soon to overcome guilt, and several nights later he achieved a release he had never dreamed of: the preamble a sensuality he had never thought possible. Gradually even the images of Maud, the comparisons, all disappeared as for the next few weeks he left the apartment only to buy food and drink. They were days of happiness together, Olivia revelling in his newly released vigour, the frustration which she had freed and now devoured until, regretfully, it was time for him to leave London for an arranged visit to the west of Ireland.

4

IT WAS a castle from his Celtic dreams, a turreted, ancient splendour, dominated by a great square tower, older than the castle itself and set in grounds which went on forever.

It was soon after the idyllic, exhausting days with Olivia, in the July of 1896, that Willie Yeats went with Arthur Symons, one of his Rhymers Club friends, to meet an arts patron who was interested in his ideas for an Irish National Literary Society. Edward Martyn was a wealthy Catholic landlord; Tullyra Castle in Galway was his home.

Inside, the great Gothic mansion it was as Yeats imagined a home of the Anglo-Irish landlords would be. Walls decorated with paintings by the great artists, suits of armour, sculpture and exquisite old furniture in the rooms. It was both a Camelot and a Windsor; a home fit for the kings of Ireland.

But nearby there was a smaller house which took his heart even more, a house built by the British in a country of romance that reminded him of the beautiful home of the Gore-Booths at Lissadell. It was approached down a long, flower-bordered drive, dappled with sunshine and shade, and lined with tall beech, ash and hazel trees, manicured laurel bushes giving way to the sudden gloom of a great arch of ilex and lime trees. Surrounded on two sides by thick dark woods, the house was set beside a broad lake and well-kept lawns.

Built of buff-coloured stone and under a slate roof, Coole House was the home of Lady Isabella Augusta Perse Gregory who, visiting Tullyra in her two-wheeled jaunting car, had invited her neighbour and his friends for lunch.

Recently widowed, dark-skinned and attractive rather than beautiful, the 44 year-old Augusta Gregory was still dressed in mourning black as she greeted them, her fifteen-year-old son, Robert, on holiday from Harrow school, beside her. Willie Yeats was in admiration as she led her guests into the hall, through a room lined with books, statues and more paintings. It was a house of wealth, luxury and taste.

Some of her views on politics, aired during the conversation over lunch, seemed provocative. Lady Gregory was fiercely against Home Rule for Ireland. 'Talk of it only fuels some of the more extreme nationalists. It is not for the good of Ireland, I am afraid, and the position of people like myself, Irish landlords, will be terribly threatened, Mr Yeats.'

Seeing a frown cross Yeats' face she leaned toward him. 'Don't misunderstand me. I do believe in Irish nationalism and in bridging the gap between the educated classes and country people.'

The next afternoon Lady Gregory invited her guests to join her in a visit to the home of a French neighbour, the strongly Catholic Count de Basterot, who lived in nearby Kinvarra, his home, Duras, reflecting the beauty of Lady Gregory's home.

After tea they left the house and strolled across the lawns, Symons and Martyn following behind, Yeats pushing the Count's wheelchair. Yeats told Lady Gregory of his literary ambitions and how, since forming the Irish Literary Society in London in 1889, which most of the Irish journalists in London had joined, his latest ambition was to create an Irish National Theatre.

Lady Gregory nodded approvingly. 'You have certainly made a grand start, Mr Yeats. Your poetry, your articles, your speeches. The ground work has surely been laid.' She stopped in her stride and turned to him, her hand on his arm. 'Could I be of help?'

Yeats was taken aback at her enthusiasm. 'Of course. Any help at all would be very welcome, Lady Gregory.'

A penetrating cold rain from the sea began to fall and they returned to the house, to sit in the drawing room where, despite the time of the year, a fire had been laid. They were relaxed, all but Lady Gregory smoking pungent cigarettes, Yeats monopolising the conversation; his comments on her work, a collection of Irish folklore, some of which she read for her guests, was both complimentary and sincere.

It had become a meeting of like minds, the other guests mere onlookers and occasional contributors to the conversation.

Almost an hour later Augusta Gregory stood up and walked to the window. 'It would be good to have our own permanent national theatre, Mr Yeats. Somewhere we could put on our own plays. And those of others like us.'

Yeats shook his head ruefully. 'It's always been my dream, Lady Gregory, but it will, I am afraid, remain a dream. There is no money in Ireland to support it. I have tried but I couldn't even get the few pounds needed to start.' He shrugged. 'I've given up on the idea.'

Later, when they returned to Lady Gregory's home, the

conversation was continued. Lady Gregory looked at Yeats pensively. 'You know, since my husband died, I have been searching for something to give me a fuller life. This could be it.' She sat down, addressing all three of her guests. 'When he died the house became my obsession. Although I have a home in London this is the land where my heart is. I want to save this house, these lands and woods, for my son. But I could still work with you. I need more to my life, Mr Yeats.' She nodded her head vigorously as the idea took hold. 'Surely together we could raise the money to start a theatre for Irish plays?' She clapped her hands together. 'I will help collect money. We could all collect money, talk to friends.' She glanced at each of her guests in turn, nodding her head positively. 'We could do it.'

The three men glanced at each other. Even as they talked things became possible, shared enthusiasm overcoming Yeats' initial doubts. He waved his hands animatedly. 'It will be our chance to get rid of the Irishman of English comedy.'

Lady Gregory wasted no time, quickly typing out their suggestions for the theatre, suggestions which, over the rest of the afternoon, were converted into a three-year experiment to put on Irish plays in Dublin.

Drinking tea as the windows were lashed by the rain from the Atlantic, Edward Martyn was the first to promise money, Lady Gregory pledging Count de Basterot's support. It would be enough to guarantee the first season. At the end of the afternoon there was pleasure on all their faces as they sat back, excited by the new venture: the Irish National Theatre was born.

As her guests left, Lady Gregory invited Yeats to spend the remainder of that summer writing at Coole. It was an invitation not to be refused, as the peaceful, quiet surroundings of Coole Park were the ideal place for a young poet to work.

It was an invitation which would change his life and that of the theatre in Ireland. And it was enough for Arthur Symons to turn to him, as their carriage drew away from the house, convinced that there was an ulterior motive behind the invitation. 'She's out to get you, Willie.'

Yeats laughed uproariously. 'She's thirteen years older than me, Arthur. And I have other affections just now.'

His visit to Coole was the start of a new relationship as Lady Gregory now entered his life. But another, closer relationship was to cause pain and despair. His friendship with Olivia was by now well established, their affair less than a year old, their lovemaking continuing at almost every opportunity, their time spent together in the bedroom of his flat at Woburn Buildings both exhausting and fulfilling. Happiness seemed complete until Maud's letter came early in the January of 1897.

She had been in America on a fund-raising tour for the Land League and for the amnesty campaign for Irish political prisoners, another of her favourite causes. Now back in London, her letter was an invitation to join her for dinner in her rooms.

The moment he saw her he was again lost. Tall and graceful, a vision, though he could see the journey had tired her. Again the immense pangs of love as she sat opposite him. Over the meal, he asked her about America.

All her old vitality had returned as she she launched into a recital of the visit.

'It was wonderful, Willie. It was sponsored by Clan na Gael and when I arrived I had rooms at the Savoy Hotel. John

O'Leary gave me letters of introduction and I went all over: Boston, Chicago, Denver, Cleveland, New York. And they liked me.' There was a fierce, positive pride in her voice. 'I spoke to 2,000 people in the Opera House in New York where the Irish-American women of Brooklyn gave me an embossed resolution of their gratitude. They thanked me as Ireland's Joan of Arc.' She went to a table at the side of the room and showed him the illustrated manuscript.

'Every meeting was crowded with Irish people who wanted to hear the latest news and to be told how they could help Ireland. There were lectures and receptions and banquets. There was a charge for every one I attended and by the time it was over I had collected £1,000.'

She continued to describe the tour, excited at its success, recounting tales of the people she had met, what she had worn, until, tired, she smiled her wonderful smile. 'But now I am boring you, Willie.'

Then it was as if they had never been apart, conversation easy, turning, inevitably to her latest political schemes as, for the next week, they were constant companions.

But for Willie Yeats, sadness would be inevitable.

HER EXISTENCE could never be forgotten and avoiding her had been difficult.

But some time she would have to be faced. It was late one morning when Olivia called to see him: distraught, accusing and tearful. 'Why Willie? Why have you been avoiding me? We were so happy together. You don't even write to me any more.'

He stared at her, the blush of guilt on his face, unsure of how much she knew about his meetings with Maud. She answered for him. 'There is someone else, isn't there? Maud

Gonne is back. Is she back in your life too?'

He went to hold her as she burst into tears but she pushed him away. He held his arms out in a gesture of innocence, sudden, terrible despair and fear flooding through him that he might lose the love and the physical affection of this beautiful woman. 'There is nothing of what we have in my relationship with her, Olivia. We are friends, brother and sister almost.'

But she had made her decision. 'It was so beautiful with you, Willie. I don't want to lose your friendship but I can't compete with what is in your heart.' She turned to leave the room, pausing at the door. 'Goodbye.' She shook her head at him. 'Please, dearest Willie. Don't let her drag you into her crazy life.'

He stood and watched until her footsteps vanished down the stairs.

Olivia's warning was no surprise to him. At the back of his mind were dark forebodings of coming tragedy as Maud's political intrigues increased. The first outlet for the fervour she had created in him came in the spring of 1897. His involvement in politics had become more pronounced, his speeches increasingly revolutionary, when he accepted Maud's invitation to become Chairman of a committee to design and raise funds for a memorial to celebrate the centenary of Wolfe Tone and the Fenian revolution of 1798. The executive committee consisted of members of the IRB and its President was John O'Leary. It was a committee which many recognised as the nucleus of a fledgling Irish Parliament.

The first meeting was at Maud's rooms in Nassau Street, and among those present was Arthur Griffith, for all his revolutionary ideals a man of mild appearance, with gentle eyes behind small round glasses, above a neatly-trimmed moustache.

Griffith had a request. He had promised James Connolly, Chairman of the Irish Socialist Republic party, that he would ask Maud to speak at a public protest against the celebrations for the sixtieth anniversary of Queen Victoria's accession. Griffith was persuasive. 'He will be disappointed if you don't speak. At least talk to him, Maud? He believes in you, what you can do for him.'

She shrugged. 'I'll meet him, Arthur. But I'm making no promises.'

Yeats travelled in a cab with Maud and Griffith to Connolly's tenement flat in Gardiner Street. It was a Dublin he had heard of but never before experienced, the poverty unimaginable. A family, often six or more, shared one room; outside there was one water tap, with two lavatories in the yard shared between up to twenty rooms.

Barefoot children were playing on the stairway which led to the small room in which Connolly, his wife and four children had to live. The stale stench of dampness and decay pervaded, the ceiling stained and sagging, patches of damp on the wallpaper, a hole in a window covered by a piece of cardboard. The furniture was minimal.

But the room was as clean and decent as Lily, Connolly's wife, could keep it and the welcome they gave their visitors was overwhelming. Maud Gonne was a woman who represented freedom; Willie Yeats a man whose poetry had brought pleasure to many a sad, drab life. Lily, despite a racking, bronchial cough which brought tears to her eyes, was charming and polite, but the pain of that despairing poverty could be seen in her eyes as she offered them strong, pungent tea from chipped mugs, and milk from a cracked enamel jug.

'Where are you from, Mr Connolly? Not here, I think.' Maud stared at the short stocky man who stood respectfully beside his wife, a full flowing moustache making him appear older than he was.

'From Scotland, Miss Gonne. I served in the army here ...' He paused before continuing, almost defensively. 'Now I work for socialism and social justice.' He paused again, unsure of her response as he continued. 'I believe the only way to help the people is by direct action.'

Maud tilted her head admiringly. 'We have much in common then, Mr Connolly.' She took a sip from her mug as Connolly nodded his acknowledgement, his arm around his wife's shoulder, smiling broadly as Maud continued. 'And I will speak at your meeting, Mr Connolly.' Connolly's smile slowly dissolved. 'But at a private meeting only. Not in the open air. Anything I might say at a Socialist rally might damage my wider cause.'

A T THE protest meeting Maud Gonne stood on a chair, towering over everybody. It was the first time that Yeats had experienced her power over crowds, her beauty alone having an immediate effect, her eloquence masterful. He stared in admiration as she spoke, her mellow, musical voice at that moment vibrant with emotion.

'Today is Jubilee Day and a public holiday, and all the public places are closed. But is it right that this morning at the cemetery at St Michan's Church in Dublin, because the gates were chained and locked, I was unable to get in to honour past Irish heroes, to lay a wreath on the grave of Robert Emmet and the graves of the United Irishmen executed for their part in the 1798 revolution?'

The crowd shouted their support as she continued in a slow, measured, theatrical voice. 'Must the graves of our dead go undecorated because Victoria has her jubilee?' The intensity of her voice and gestures incited the crowd further, the meeting continuing with speaker after speaker taking up her rhetoric against the Jubilee.

The scenario for the day's events was well established, so much so that, after the protest meeting and throughout the day there was tension in the city, the emotions aroused repeated that evening at a meeting of the 1798 Committee at the City Hall, attended by delegates from all over the country.

Inside the hall the noise of the demonstrations outside could be clearly heard, Maud gesturing to the window. 'Come on, Willie. Those people speak for us. We must join them.' She turned to the Chairman, John O'Leary, asking him to suspend the meeting so that they could give their support to those outside.

Yeats stood up, moving to her side, speaking quietly. 'You can't, Maud. Your presence will only incite the crowd further and you could be in danger yourself.'

Arthur Griffith joined him, adding his support, pleading with Maud, their protestations ignored as she marched from the building, striding imperiously down the steps to be greeted by cheers from the crowd. Yeats grabbed her arm as they stepped into streets decked with flags; Union Flags held by the Unionists and black flags, which she had herself made and which bore the names of those hanged for treason in 1798, draped from windows or waved by some in the crowd, each of the flags with white lettering giving the numbers who had died in the famine during Victoria's reign, the number of houses destroyed, and men gaoled.

There was an atmosphere of festivity as Yeats allowed

himself to be pulled into the crowd. 'Come on, Willie. Come on.' Watching was not enough for Maud and sudden irresponsibility overcame Yeats, masking his inhibitions until, abruptly, the festivity turned to violence as the excited crowd threw anything which came to hand at buildings which showed the Union flag. Yeats tried in vain to stop them, his voice soon hoarse and almost non-existent. He glanced at Maud, his hand still tightly grasping hers. Her head was thrown back, laughing, her face flushed with excitement as windows nearby continued to be smashed. 'Come on, Willie. This way.' He allowed her to pull him through the crowd, as a band organised by Connolly marched with the demonstrators as he led it towards Sackville Street. In the centre of the parade a hand cart, pulled by some of the demonstrators, carried a black coffin, with the words 'The British Empire' painted on it, the band playing the Death March. It had been another of Maud's ideas to add to the protest.

'The coffin, Willie. Into the river with it. To hell with the British Empire.' Her eyes were blazing with fervour as, with Connolly and others, Yeats helped her haul the coffin to the parapet of the bridge, the cheers of the crowd resounding around them as it was launched into the river.

Then, sudden screams and cries of alarm, almost masked by the clatter of hooves as police reinforcements arrived, forcing their way towards them through the crowd. Yeats grabbed Maud as they were pushed backwards in the crush, the music from the band coming to a discordant halt, bandsmen on the ground as police baton-charged the marchers.

Yeats dragged her with him, merging with the throng, looking back in time to see Connolly fall to the ground before being pulled to his feet and marched away, flanked by two of the police, as the crowd continued towards the National Club in Rutland Square.

Her presence was like a wand, the crowd parting miraculously for her until they reached the club. Yeats groaned in apprehension. Again she had managed to incite the crowd. She had given Connolly lantern slides which showed the police in attendance at eviction scenes and, after pictures of Queen Victoria, these slides were flashed up on a giant screen, arousing the crowd still further. Their mood suddenly became hostile, and cobble stones and pieces of paving were pulled up and used to bombard the watching police.

Yeats pulled Maud inside the club, attempting to calm her as the riot continued outside. The police again charged the crowd, Maud struggling against Willie as he held her back. 'Come on. We must go outside. We must show our loyalty.' He ignored her, pinning her to the wall inside the doorway.

'Why go out, Maud? What do you want to do? What can you do?'

She struggled against him 'For Christ's sake, Willie. How do I know until I get out?'

He restrained a sudden urge to laugh. 'No, Maud. Not yet. Let it calm down a bit.' He held her back by the shoulders, nodding to one of the porters to close the doors.

It was early the following morning, Maud cold and distant towards him, when they visited Connolly at the Bridewell, Yeats waiting quietly in the background as Maud, impatient with the gaolers, calmly issued her orders. By the time they left she had arranged for all those in custody to be fed and had agreed to pay their fines or get bail and lawyers for those who needed them.

Her fury was directed at Yeats as she argued her justification for Connolly's behaviour. 'He saved Dublin from the humiliation of an English Jubilee. The only one who had the courage to do it.'

Yeats spoke quietly, pointedly. 'An old lady was knocked down by the crowd and killed. Two hundred people were taken to hospital. Was it really worth that?'

She turned on him, still angry, ignoring his question. 'You should not have stopped me, Willie.'

He sighed wearily. 'If I hadn't stopped you, Maud, you would be inside with all the others. Would that have helped your cause?'

She glared at him. 'You had no right. You and everyone who remained in the club and did not go to the rescue of the people being attacked and batoned by the police ought to feel ashamed of yourselves.'

He started to protest but she cut him short, glaring at him, her face fiercely beautiful. 'By keeping me in the club you made me do the only cowardly thing of my life. I was born to be in the middle of a crowd.' She waved her hand disparagingly at him. 'It's no good, Willie. We can never work together where there is likely to be physical danger. I don't need your protection and you must no longer involve yourself in this side of politics. That is for me. You have higher things to do.'

A pained expression lined his face as he stared at her, hiding the hurt and resentment which boiled inside him. Her arrogance was indescribable; her fervour only to be admired.

She still had not finished. 'And if we can't work together, Willie, what is the point of our friendship continuing?'

5

∞

In the summer of 1897 the serenity of Coole Park was a convalescence. He had been writing and publishing continuously. The depths his emotional creativity needed, his ambitions for the Literary Society, together with his political ideals, ideals confused by the need to accept some of Maud's revolutionary politics, had drained him. His work for the 1798 convention, closely followed by the Jubilee riots, had also taken their toll, as had Maud herself: his increasing obsession with her, her rejection of his proposals and the frustration his poverty still caused him. And a new, emotional relationship was taking its toll.

Florence Farr had been a friend since teenage years, a dramatically beautiful brunette, a gifted actress and free-thinking, liberated woman who shared her charms with a number of men friends, her liaisons eventually leading to her divorce. She had been the willing conspirator and go-between for Yeats and Olivia, amused at the affair and pleased for the involvement of her two close friends. Perhaps it was inevitable that she would become more than a go-between.

It was Florence who Yeats had turned to in an outpouring of sorrow at Olivia's rejection, her's the comforting words which quickly turned to more; the warm comforts of her bed and full body. It was an affair he fell into so easily that it felt it had been ongoing since he met her years earlier, his feelings such that he was sad when he had to leave her to return to Ireland and the different comforts of Coole Park.

On his arrival there was concern on Lady Gregory's face as she stared, without immediate comment, at her pale, thin guest. Later that first evening, after dinner, as heavy clouds moved across a vaporous moon, she walked with him through the walled garden beside the house, an evening mist falling as she took his arm and voiced her concern. 'You aren't well, Willie. Your beautiful voice has almost gone, your nerves are terrible and you are smoking far too many cigarettes.'

Yeats knew she was right. Physically and mentally he was near breaking point. He had eye strain, which meant he found it difficult to read for too long, and the face that stared at him from his mirror every morning was white and haggard. He gave a half smile, stopping and removing his glasses to stare after a nocturnal animal, a badger which nonchalantly crossed their path in the moonlight, glancing back at them disdainfully before disappearing in the impenetrable woods. 'I'm just tired. I've been so busy.'

'But most of all you have been troubled by your love for Maud Gonne? She has been giving you a rare old time, Willie.'

He glanced at her, smiling ruefully and absentmindedly running his fingers through his thick, black hair. 'You know?'

'Everyone knows. You are a couple. Why don't you marry the woman. Calm her down?'

He shook his head wearily. 'It's not for want of asking,

believe me. All I seem to do is write to her, think of her and sometimes see her. But I just don't understand her. One minute she talks politics; the next she talks about brood mares and the very next moment poetry and the theatre. I never know whether I'm coming or going with her.' He paused, embarrassed at his openness. 'And of course, I've fallen out with Olivia.' He fell into a confused silence, unable to express the terrible sense of loss he felt. 'We are still friends but she couldn't put up with my feelings for Maud.'

'Poor Willie.' Lady Gregory felt strong, almost maternal instincts towards him. 'We'll have to get you better. Tomorrow, if your voice has improved, you can relax and read some of your beautiful poetry to me. At least Maud Gonne has played her part in that.'

The following day was passed as she had promised, and he readily gave himself up to her care and affection. And to the special quality of Coole – peace. Quiet, restful, ordered peacefulness. Even the house itself was comforting. The library, with its shelves of leather and vellum-covered first editions to browse through, and the cellar full of great wines, majestic clarets laid down by Lady Gregory's husband to be enjoyed over dinner.

And outside there was the lake sheltered by woods, a ruined castle thrusting above the trees on the far bank, blue-green hills in the distance and with its own resident swans, wild geese and ducks. Willows hung low over the water, small streams fed it, and around it was an abundance of wildlife, woodcock, squirrels, badgers and foxes.

Gradually the calm serenity of these surroundings forced his worries to the furthest recesses of his mind. Walks eased his frustration, walks intensified by fantasy and solitary sexual release, surrounded by visions of her. Sometimes, in a trick of light, he saw her waiting in the shadow of the trees as a misty harvest moonlight filtered through, time passing slowly, darkly in the wood until a pale dawn eased above the trees to the east and the stars went out.

At Coole, for the first time since leaving his family home, there were regular meals. Irish meals. Filling, satisfying meals. Lamb, peas, bacon and blood-rich black pudding, sausages and fresh eggs, bread and imported fruit, rich desserts and the best red wine. A meal fit for the Celtic kings and English lords who should have lived in such a place.

Days eased into weeks, which merged into months, as Willie Yeats spent the remainder of the summer in an organised schedule of work and relaxation. The young, romantic poet from the small family house in Bedford Park, the tenant of a cheap flat in Bloomsbury, had become part of the life of a great Anglo-Irish mansion.

And it was Lady Gregory, quietly and almost unnoticed, who facilitated his work, putting him in the master bedroom, approached by a corridor lined with Augustus John etchings, and giving him her husband's old study where he would spend several hours each morning and afternoon.

Even his relaxation was catered for as, one morning, Lady Gregory gave him her husband's fishing rods. He took them gratefully; it was the one pastime he enjoyed.

And there was work to do together, collecting material for his poetry, spending time in the peasant cottages of the surrounding countryside, where he listened eagerly to the folk tales of the hero, Cuchulain, or, visiting the poor house in Kiltartan, sitting quietly fascinated by the stories of the sad wretches interred there, despite their initial suspicions of him.

It was soon after he returned to London and the different comforts offered by Florence Farr that Lady Gregory first visited his home. He was waiting on the pavement outside Woburn Buildings when her carriage drew up. He ushered her inside. 'Welcome to my humble home, Lady Gregory.' He followed her, pointing out the other occupants of the building: on the ground floor a shoe maker; a labourer and his family on the first floor, his rooms above them and in the attic, an old man who painted watercolours.

He opened the door to the barely-furnished rooms he had chosen with Olivia. Lady Gregory glanced around; a shabby Persian carpet covered bare floor boards and a dilapidated wicker chair stood in one corner next to an old bookcase. Above the fireplace was his favourite picture, a painting by his brother Jack of Memory Harbour in Sligo. On other walls there were Blake engravings, a Beardsley painting and a framed portrait of himself painted by his father.

But his visitor could also see the moths in the curtains, books on the shelves covered with dust, the mattress uncovered and the dusty floor littered with paper.

Willie followed her as she went through the rooms, inspecting them almost item by item, taking an inventory of what was needed to make it moderately comfortable. The rooms which were suitable for his trysts with Olivia were not good enough for Lady Gregory's young protégé.

The following morning a large and comfortable leather arm chair was delivered, later that day a delivery of fruit and wine and, in the evening, Yeats helped Lady Gregory take measurements for a set of blue curtains which would match the colours in the carpet.

Later, when she had left, he found four crisp five-pound notes tucked behind the clock on the mantleshelf. He stared at them, shaking his head slowly, sudden tears of affection and gratitude welling in his eyes.

The following evening she took him to dinner. During the meal she handed him a small parcel. 'Just a small gift, Willie.' He put on his glasses, momentarily lost for words as he stared at the handsome inlaid fountain pen. Emotion threatened to overcome him as he reached across the table and took her hand. 'It's something I will use forever. Nobody has ever shown me such kindness.' He shook his head. 'I don't think I should really let you do all these kind things for me.' He reached into an inside pocket as he fought to control his feelings. 'I have this for you.' It was a photograph of Lady Gregory and himself, taken on his last visit to Coole Park. Across it he had written a brief dedication to her.

Though loud years come the loud years go,
A friend is the best thing here below;
Shall we a better marvel find
When the loud years have fallen behind.

She took it and placed her hand over his as he continued. There was even more she had done. 'And I have to thank you for seeing my father and commissioning him to paint my portrait.'

'And my own, among others, Willie. I think he has a very special talent as a portrait painter.' She paused, sipping her tea. 'But I don't think he approves of my interest in you. He thinks I'm too bossy.' She became serious again, her face showing her concern, her voice faintly sarcastic. 'Where is she now, Willie? Fighting the good fight?'

He shrugged wearily, leaning back in his chair. 'She's back with the starving people in the west.' He sighed. 'In Kerry, and now she incites them to kill their landlords and seize food.' He looked grim. 'She has published a leaflet with Connolly. They call it "Rights to life and rights to profit" and quote St Thomas Aquinas.'

Lady Gregory raised a curious eyebrow as Yeats continued. 'She says ... *in case of extreme need of food, all goods become common property. No human can stand between starving people and their right to food, including their right to take it.'*

Lady Gregory stared at him, shaking her head slightly. *'Perhaps the famine has been exaggerated. But there are other ways than murder. Those who are better educated should not encourage others to murder and steal. They must be taught to die with courage rather than live a thief. Those of us who have money must share it with the starving.'* Again Lady Gregory shook her head disapprovingly. 'Her ideas can only lead to worse things.'

'It's the effect this work has on her that worries me. I try to talk her out of it but she is hell bent on it.'

'My poor Willie.' She shook her head sadly, his concern so desperate.

'She won't let me help her. She says I must consider first what is best for my genius which belongs to Ireland. And that nothing must injure that.' He smiled across the table. 'Although I can't say I'm sorry.'

'She is right, Willie. The only wrong that matters is not doing your best work.' She leaned across then table and took his hand. 'If you really need her, Willie. If you feel she must be part of your life then you must persevere. Make her marry you.'

He shook his head sadly. 'She has a will of her own and I can't fight it. Just now she's in Paris getting support for one cause or another.'

'Then go to her, Willie. Now. I will pay for your ticket.'

He shook his head as he refused. 'Thank you, Augusta dear. You are very kind. But no. I'm too tired of chasing after her.'

Lady Gregory was persuasive. 'Give her this one last chance Willie. For her sake as much as for yours.'

He stared at her for long moments before finally nodding his head in acceptance. She smiled and waved a finger at him. 'Just don't leave her side until she agrees to marry you.'

PARIS WAS a new world. A wider, more fulfilling world. It was a world of change, with artists like Lautrec and Monet fighting for recognition; of famous literary figures and poets. It was the capital of the artistic world.

And in Paris he adopted the look which marked him out as one of that literary élite, an elegance he had copied from Oscar Wilde. A soft black hat, a silk shirt with a loose bow tie, an overflowing handkerchief in his high-buttoned velvet jacket, his pince-nez hanging from the top pocket, and a long black cloak. A cigarette was always casually between his fingers. The only thing missing was the flower in his buttonhole which his meagre finances could not afford.

The Hotel Corneille, in the Rue Corneille, near to the Sorbonne and the Luxembourg Gardens, had been recommended to him by John O'Leary who told him that many famous Irishmen had stayed there.

It was during this visit, on New Year's day of 1898, in a small café in the Rue Saint Jacques, that Yeats met a 25 year-old aspiring poet, penniless like himself, who was renting a small attic room in the hotel. John Millington Synge was a quiet, introspective Irishman with a mop of unruly hair, a moustache and a wispy beard. He was dining alone, paying for his meal by playing sad old Irish airs on his violin. A student of French literature at the Sorbonne, his ambition was to be a literary critic.

It was several days after arriving in Paris that Yeats took his new friend to meet Maud, his excuse for the visit being to discuss the formation of a Young Ireland Society. Her apartment contrasted strongly with the Hotel Corneille. Beautifully furnished, it was on the Avenue d'Eylau, in the sixteenth arondissement, with views over the Seine and of the Eiffel Tower from her balconied windows

Although she greeted them both warmly and they talked until the small hours as Yeats outlined his ideas for the Society, she only seemed intent on telling him about her work for the Irish political prisoners. Synge remained coldly aloof, making no effort to hide his disapproval of her Fenian politics.

Willie Yeats' real reason for visiting Paris was not touched upon; the time not right, Maud's mood too distant, her mind so wrapped up in her other causes that a proposal at that time would have been dismissed out of hand. Except for the meeting with Synge, the visit to Paris would have been pointless.

On his return to Ireland, later in the summer, after Synge had taken his advice and visited the Arran islands to study Irish folklore at its peasant source, Yeats took him to meet Lady Gregory.

It was a meeting of like minds, Lady Gregory pleased to have an Irish-speaking writer to share her enthusiasm and help with her work. With Synge's help she would now be able to give her stories of the Irish peasant the realistic speech patterns it needed.

It was a time of exciting collaboration between the three, together collecting pages of Irish myths and legends which led to the publication of a collection of folk tales, *The Celtic Twilight*, which Yeats, now becoming increasingly business minded, knew would appeal to Irish emigrants throughout the world.

6

IN THE August of 1898 the Wolfe Tone centenary was celebrated. There was a banquet at Frascati's restaurant in
Soho, and the following day Yeats chaired a meeting at
which Maud Gonne was the main speaker, again provocative in her denouncement of the British Empire from the
heart of its capital.

Yeats stared at her. There was something frighteningly
impersonal about her, her face not just that of flesh and
blood but sometimes as cold as that of a statue. And
although modest about her own startling beauty, she was
well aware of its affect on others, and was able to use it to
advantage when she had an audience.

A day later they left for Dublin where John O'Leary was
to lay the corner stone of the monument to Wolfe Tone. It was
Monday, 15 August, and the occasion was attended by John
Redmond, the leader of the Irish Parliamentary Party at
Westminster, and eleven other MPs. Yeats and Maud Gonne
were greeted rapturously by the crowd as they travelled to
the Lord Mayor's banquet in a cart draped with the tricolour.

Willie Yeats was asked to speak, his nationalist sympathies as inflammatory and cliché-ridden as anything Maud
could have said. 'England thought Ireland was about to

submit but we have answered her. It is the people who have made today, the inextinguishable fire of patriotism rises like smoke from the breasts of the peasantry ...' He faltered, frowning, as there were shouts from the crowd, 'It's Maud Gonne who made it.'

Her patriotism for her adopted country was revealed further when she refused to share a table with the Lord Mayor due to his pro-British leanings, the upper-class, Protestant woman now taking a special place in the hearts of the people. She and Yeats were new heroes of Ireland, recognised as a couple and as a couple, almost legendary, their closeness like a marriage, with rumours constantly circulating about their relationship. Yeats was still full of inner despair that it was little more than a deep, almost mystical friendship.

The day after the Lord Mayor's banquet they visited the National Gallery together, other visitors more interested in them than the Whistler exhibition showing at the time. Their appearance was striking: of the same height, he was wearing a dark cloak, she in a shimmering green dress. Yeats was uneasily aware of the stir they were causing as they studied the pictures. Later, walking through Grafton Street, people turned and stared at them, total strangers nodding warmly to them, her arm in his, her head high, an almost regal air about her, Yeats beside her holding the leash of the aging Daghda, still her constant companion.

IN AND out of focus, a dream or a vision, neither complete, she leaned over him, her red dress enveloping him. And then she kissed him and the vision dissolved, fresh images taking its place; castles, derelict cottages, coffins floating in a black river.

Slowly he came to consciousness, confused and then fully awake, leaping from his bed, dressing quickly and running to her hotel.

She met him at the door to her room, taking his hands, questioning, before he could speak. He stared at her, dumbfounded, as she spoke. 'Did you have a strange dream last night, Willie?' Maud gave him no chance to reply, repeating the question, a strange urgency now in her voice. 'Did you dream of me last night?' Her grip on his arm was so intense it made him wince.

He looked at her, unsure. 'I always dream of you Maud. Always. But last night it was different.'

'What did you dream?'

'You came to me in the night. You wore a red dress, you leaned over me and kissed me.'

She leaned towards him, flushed and excited. 'I had the same dream, Willie. But it was a white dress. I saw a great spirit who put my hand in yours and said we were married. And I kissed you and I believed we were married. It was a mystical experience, it truly was.' He stared at her, too stunned to speak, as she continued. ' It was so mystical and beautiful. What I always believe of us.'

He grabbed the chance, taking her hands in his. 'Then why don't we make it a real marriage, Maud? At last.'

She leaned towards him, suddenly affectionate, and kissed him on the mouth. Yeats stared at her as she moved back, elation and excitement mixed with confusion.

The kiss had been ten years in coming. He pulled her back to him as her eyes opened in surprise, and she pushed him brusquely away, suddenly aware of what she had allowed, her defences weakening.

Her sudden change of mood, her rejection, hurt him.

Without a word he turned and left the room.

It was cold for early December in Dublin and a roaring fire was blazing in Maud's drawing room when Yeats arrived the following morning. She had sent for him and was contrite and depressed, staring out at the leafless trees through the window before turning to speak to him.

'I'm so sorry for yesterday, Willie. For leading you on in that way. Can you forgive me?'

'Of course, Maud.' He smiled. 'I'm sure I will remember it always but there is nothing to forgive.' He stood beside her, a doleful expression on his face. 'I did think you had come to me at last.'

She stared at him, intense sadness in her eyes, and something more. She was suddenly tearful but if aware of it he made no comment. Her hands were clasped in front of her, still contrite, as he took a sheaf of creased and folded papers from the pocket of his long jacket.

'This summer, in Coole, I finished another collection of poems. I'd like you to read them. It's yet to be published.'

She took the slim sheaf of papers from his hand, reading the title page aloud. '*The Wind in the Reeds*?' She looked at him and smiled through her tears. 'It has a nice sound to it.'

'I want to read one to you. It will always be one for you alone, Maud. I call it, "He Wishes for the Clothes of Heaven".' He leafed through the pages until he found the poem, standing before the fire, his mellow, musical voice resounding through the room as he read it slowly, every word emphasised.

Had I the heavens' embroidered cloths,
Enwrought with gold and silver light,
The blue and the dim and the dark cloths

Of night and light and the half light,
I would spread the cloths under your feet

He stopped, staring at her questioningly. Her mouth
trembled, her eyes moist with tears, her hand raised to him,
as if in supplication. 'Don't do this to me, Willie. Not just
now. It's so beautiful. Please don't.' Her voice choked. 'I
don't deserve something so beautiful.'

He ignored her plea, no need now for notes as he continued, leaning forward, one hand, fist clenched, across his
chest, the other angled expressively towards her.

But I, being poor, have only my dreams;
I have spread my dreams under your feet;
Tread softly because you tread on my dreams.

When he had finished there was a long silence, her tears
now flowing freely; then a muted sob before she lifted her
face to him. She was agonisingly beautiful in her sorrow.

'It's so perfect, Willie. The most beautiful yet. And written by a genius. You are such a wonderful man.'

Now he seized the moment. 'Then for God's sake marry
me, Maud. If you think so much of me marry me now.'

She wiped the tears from her cheeks, her eyes terribly
sad. 'I can never be your wife, Willie.'

'But why? Do you love someone else? Is it my poverty?'

'No.' She almost shouted, searching for the right words,
unwilling to hurt him. 'But there is someone else.' She
buried her head in her hands in desperation.

He turned pale, stunned, unable to speak, a sudden,
pain ripping through his insides. 'Who? Why?' A terrible
despair swept over him.

7

SHE WAS no longer the Maud Gonne he had known: confident, sure of herself and of her convictions. Suddenly vulnerable, she looked slight and tired, aware of the hurt she was about to cause him; fearing things between them might never be the same. But there could be no hiding anything now.

He waited, still stunned, for his world to be torn apart.

She took a deep breath, crossing the room and perching herself on the edge of the sofa, gazing for long moments into the fire before standing again and pacing the room. He gave her no help, waiting, as she lit a cigarette before returning to her seat.

Her tears were gone and she glanced quickly to where he was standing by the window before starting to speak. It was a confession and a penance, a melancholy dullness about her voice.

'Years ago, late one evening, sitting by the fire as I am now, when I was only nineteen and after my father died, I felt terribly alone and wondered about my future life. I wanted so much to be my own mistress.'

She glanced at him for some acknowledgement but there was none. Her gaze returned again to the fire as she continued. 'I was looking through his books and among them I found one on magic. It gave me awful and evil thoughts. And ideals. It made me pray to the devil, asking for help, for control of my life in return for my soul.' She stopped, breathing heavily. 'And as I prayed the clock struck twelve and I suddenly felt terribly afraid. I knew then my prayer had been answered; that I had given my soul in exchange for the freedom to live as I please.' She shrugged. 'I don't really know what I was looking for but soon after that I met a man in France called Lucien Millevoye. He was, is, a lawyer and journalist.' She stopped and turned to face Yeats, almost defiantly. 'I made a pact with him also.'

Yeats' voice was bitter. 'Was he the devil?'

She frowned, an almost childish expression of resignation on her face. 'No Willie. It was a pact that we would fight together against England. It was at Royat, in the Auvergne. I was with my aunt and my sister and we were taking the waters. My aunt introduced us.' She paused, a reflective look in her eyes. 'He was handsome, he paid me compliments and he said I was the most beautiful woman he had ever seen.' She sighed, shaking her head.

'I remember it was raining and when I went to watch the lightning storm he followed me to the verandah and tried to kiss me.' She glanced at Yeats, adding quickly. 'But I wouldn't let him. Then we talked about Ireland. I told him England was our enemy and he told me that his whole ambition was to win back Alsace for France, and that England was the natural enemy of France also as it defeated Bonaparte who would have liberated Ireland.'

She stared down at her hands clasped in her lap, shaking her head sadly. Yeats waited. When she resumed her voice was almost apologetic. 'He said that together we could achieve anything we wanted, that I did not understand the power I had and that my ambition should be to free Ireland.' She gave a small half laugh. 'But I already knew I had that power when I sold my soul. Then we swore allegiance to each other, a pact to the death, and he said he would help me free Ireland from England if I helped him regain Alsace-Lorraine from Prussia.'

Again she tried to laugh. 'I became a spy for him. I carried secret documents to Czarist Russia, to St Petersburg, with them sewn into my dress. Millevoye said it was my first work for our alliance against the British Empire. He even gave me a small revolver to carry with me.' She paused, her eyes still cast down. She breathed deeply, hardly daring to look at Yeats who had slumped into a chair opposite her, her words hardly discernible as her voice lowered. 'Soon after that we became lovers and I took an apartment in Paris to be near him.' She stopped, her face turned away from Yeats when she continued, her voice now barely audible. 'Then I became pregnant.' There was guilt in her voice as she continued. 'He was, is, married, you see.'

Yeats face was ashen, his eyes closed, a long sigh escaping from him as, at last, she turned to face him, her eyes pleading with him to understand. She raised her hand against the sudden protest on his lips, recoiling at the hurt in his eyes. 'He said he would get a divorce and marry me.' Again she paused, searching for a way to tell him. There was no easy way. 'We had a son, Georges.' There were tears in her eyes. 'I thought I loved him, Willie, I really did, but then I realised I did not. Even though it lasted for ten years.' Then, almost defensively. 'It all started before we met.'

Her voice was muted as she continued. 'It was not what

I expected. Not what I had dreamed of as a young girl. I hated the physical side with him.' Her voice was now pleading. 'Believe me, Willie, I did. It was so painful, so distasteful that I would reject him more often than not.' She shrugged. 'Since then I have believed that sexual love is only justified by children.'

A sudden stabbing pain in his temples made Yeats close his eyes before shakily lighting a cigarette, his need for her dissolving into despair. He only half heard her as she continued. 'He didn't really love me. He even wanted me to become the mistress of someone else just to further his political aims.' She stopped and stared at him, the pain of his hurt shooting though her. She needed him to look at her, to show he understood. Her words were penitent and pleading. 'Forgive me, Willie. Please. Try to understand.'

She waited for a response but there was none. He climbed to his feet again, unable to settle into the chair, tears of despair stinging his eyes as he stared out of the window. Her voice was hushed as she continued. 'I told you that my adopted child had died in France, and a child did die but he was not adopted. Georges Sylvere was my child. He was only nineteen months old. We had a special tomb built for him in the graveyard at Samois.'

Still he listened in silence. It was as if she was purging her soul as she recited every intimate detail of the affair, every breath of the child. Sudden wrenching compassion made him want to reach out and comfort her. But a huge void between them held him back, making it impossible to even face her.

Her voice was both penitent and reflective. She was somewhere else. 'It was the largest tomb in the small graveyard and I went there with Lucien and we put flowers in the tomb. Then ...' She stopped before breaking into hysterical laughter. 'It was bizarre, a heresy. A crime against Christianity, something the devil made me do.' Tears poured down her cheeks. 'I forced him to make love to me there, on the floor beside the tomb. I wanted him to recreate Georges inside me.' Deep sobs wracked her body and this time she took several moments to compose herself. Yeats made no effort to help. 'It was brief. There was not a word of love spoken. I just needed another child to replace the son I had lost.' She stared hard at Yeats. 'Do you believe in reincarnation, Willie? I wanted my child reborn.'

He sighed deeply and at last turned to her, his hands at his sides, the cigarette drooping from his fingers, ash falling unnoticed onto the polished boards. Even now, despite his hurt, he had to help her; to reassure her, his words barely discernible. 'People do say children are reborn into the same family.'

She lifted frightened eyes to him, the only person who could ever see her innermost emotions. 'I told you of the grey lady. I saw her again soon after that but this time she was evil. She said she was the murderess of children.' She fought back more tears. 'Then we had a daughter, Isoeult.' She glanced quickly at Yeats. 'She's four years old now.' She answered his unspoken question. 'When I was pregnant I hid it from you under a shawl.'

'When I thought you were ill and I couldn't see you?'

She nodded, adding lamely. 'I haven't been intimate with him since.'

'You still see him?' He had turned back to the window, unable to look at her.

She shrugged. 'Only occasionally. We had a useful political allegiance but, since Isoeult was born I have lived way from him. Please believe me, Willie. It is finished.'

And she had finished, her confession over. She remained seated on the sofa, unable to meet his eyes, her own fixed on her hands still clasped tightly in her lap.

Yeats sank back again into the chair, facing her, his eyes fixed on her, unblinking. It was all still unreal. A nightmare. His voice was full of hurt. And bitterness.

'You? But why?' It was all he could say. The woman he loved, the woman he breathed and dreamed of and wrote for had betrayed him. There was dreadful bitterness in his voice. 'I needed you. I lived for you and to be with you. Hoping ... But the woman I thought of as my mystical virgin is the mother of two illegitimate children. Two! And all that time, while you had them, I loved you.' Contempt replaced the bitterness in his voice. 'But that Maud I loved was just an illusion she allowed me to love.' Now his voice became full of anger, his hurt boiling over. 'You lived a lie to me, Maud.' He paused, fighting to control his emotions, his hands shaking as he lit yet another cigarette from the remains of the previous one, neither of them speaking, both of them now staring into the flames of the fire.

When eventually she spoke her voice was subdued. 'You should not have given me such a place in your life. It was wrong.'

His words were measured, his voice resolute as he turned to face her. 'I was so deeply in love with you but now I just feel sorrow for you. I'm finished with you, Maud, I can't go on after this. There must be someone else to help me forget you.'

Bᴜᴛ ꜱʜᴇ was impossible to forget. It was the early summer of 1899 and *The Wind in the Reeds* had just been published, a book of sad and despairing poems to Maud, poems of need and hurt.

But then other things that summer helped push her to the back of his mind.

It was the launch of the Irish Literary Theatre. Florence Farr was appointed Director and lead player, taking the part which Maud had asked him to write for her.

The two main Dublin theatres, the Gaiety and the Royal, were booked and *The Countess Cathleen*, in which the Countess sells her soul for gold to save her starving peasants, was premiered at the Ancient Concert Rooms in Pearse Street.

The publicity had been immense, adverse publicity which only served to increase the interest in the play. The church had condemned it without seeing it and ordered that no Catholic should see it. The press had varying views; one journalist in particular, Frank Hugh O'Donnell, an old enemy of Maud, and therefore of Yeats, had distributed pamphlets throughout the city, damning the play as heretical and calling it an insult to Catholic people and an attack on Irish womanhood. Yet despite his public outrage at such criticism, Yeats was secretly pleased, since such publicity could only make himself, and the Literary theatre, better known.

The first night was a great social occasion, men in dinner jackets, women in the audience dressed in traditional Irish cloaks with Tara brooches, Florence Farr playing the role of the Countess to perfection.

Arthur Griffith had given his support, bringing others with him to cheer anything the church might disapprove of, with noisy protests breaking out after an embarrassed silence when, in the first scene, an evil peasant tramples on a Catholic shrine. The protests were countered by cheers from Griffith's friends, the disturbances continuing until the police were called.

It was a play which helped change the direction of Irish theatre, a play to make people think. Yeats' young friend, James Joyce, in the audience that night, was one of those deeply impressed.

There were, however, other important objectors. Edward Martyn, one of the first sponsors of the Literary Society and a devout Catholic, considered the play to be a heresy and threatened to withdraw his backing, a compromise only reached when Yeats offered to change some of the more offensive lines. Martyn no longer complained when his own play, *The Heather Field*, sharing the bill with *The Countess Cathleen*, met with enthusiastic applause.

A FTER THE efforts and difficulties of their first production, the wooded softness and peace of Coole Park was again a refuge from the hurt, the sadness and despair which Maud had brought to him.

At Coole Lady Gregory became more than a friend and hostess. She became a focus for peace and understanding, and the stability he needed to continue his work. He no longer used the study which had been Lord Gregory's retreat; instead he worked in a small, quiet drawing room at the back of the house where Lady Gregory ensured that a table was laid, every morning, with an array of pens, ink and paper, a fresh blotting pad and, every two hours when he was working, a glass of warm milk and biscuits brought to him by one of the maids.

Lady Gregory was the mother he had lacked, organising his day to get the best from his work. After breakfast he read for an hour, after which he walked in the woods, before spending several hours writing until lunch. Many afternoons were spent in a small boat, fishing for pike and perch in the cold, deep waters of the lake, at times in the company of John Synge, another keen angler, if he was also visiting Coole. Then, in the early evening, there was more writing and reading until dinner, the day finishing with an evening walk through the still woods with Lady Gregory as twilight approached, returning to the house as the sun set over the Burren and the dark Connemara hills in the far distance.

Life was good again, but, despite Augusta Gregory's efforts, thoughts of Maud Gonne could never be taken from his mind.

'I AM Lady Augusta Gregory.' It was a few weeks later, when both were staying at the same Dublin hotel, that Lady Gregory first met Maud. The introduction was as imperious as her manner, deepening feelings for her protégé having made her decide to call on Maud Gonne.

Maud's greeting was as formal. 'Good morning, Lady Gregory. I do, of course, know of you.' She invited her visitor into the drawing room, concealing her surprise. The woman before her was not the elegant beauty she had expected; instead she was a plump, matronly, slightly greying lady, more like Queen Victoria than the person Willie had described.

And to Lady Gregory, Maud Gonne was more startlingly beautiful than in any picture. She was now at her loveliest, her great mop of tawny hair loose about her shoulders. Her strong face and frank eyes were transformed by her smile. Dressed simply, the only ornament she wore was a

Tara brooch at her waist.

Taken aback by the sheer presence of the woman standing before her, Augusta Gregory soon recovered her composure, wasting no time. 'I'll come straight to the point, Miss Gonne. I've been working closely with Willie Yeats. Helping him; typing his poems and plays.'

There was no smile from Maud, just a cold, disconcerting stare. Lady Gregory was not put off. 'But he needs help. Your help. I, and others who care for him, are terribly worried about him. Whatever you have done or said to him, it has affected his health. He is wrecked with self-doubt and torment. I fear he is obsessed with his feelings for you.'

Maud still showed no emotion. 'I am sorry, Lady Gregory. I do care for Willie, you must know that.'

'He is so unhappy because of you. He wants to marry you.' She stopped, staring contemplatively at Maud. 'I may not approve of all you stand for, Miss Gonne, although God knows most of the people in this country do, but I believed that he should persist in his proposals until you agree to marry him. Now I think he is ready to give up.' She paused, shaking her head in a show of disbelief. 'He wants to help you; save you from yourself, to shape you into his image of what is good for you.'

Maud raised her eyebrows, an expression of indifference crossing her face. 'I do not wish to be shaped into anyone's image, Lady Gregory. You have to understand that. My salvation is here in Ireland, working for the poor, for the evicted peasants, and organising those groups which will help give Ireland its own political future.'

'But that should not stop you marrying the poor man?' Lady Gregory added, with a trace of sarcasm. 'I suppose you would be good together.' She continued with a passionate plea, taking Maud's hand, the younger woman pulling it away.

'Can't you see what he has to offer? He is one of the most brilliant and charming men I have ever known. Good humoured and gentle and marvellous company ...'

Maud smiled. 'Might I ask why you are so interested in him, Lady Gregory? Perhaps you should marry him yourself.'

Augusta Gregory looked taken aback but ignored the comment. 'Can't you see I am only doing for him what I would do for my own son. And I do feel for him as if he were my own son.'

Maud shook her head sadly. The matter was none of Lady Gregory's business, her reply as blunt as it was brief. 'There can be no question of my marrying Willie Yeats, Lady Gregory.' She stood up, peering down at her visitor from her great height. 'I have more important things to think about than marriage. And so has he. I am sorry that you have had such a wasted journey.'

Lady Gregory inclined her head in acknowledgement, her expression hardening as she left the room. 'I think you are only playing with him, perhaps from selfishness, perhaps from vanity.' She shook her head sadly, immense dislike for Maud in her voice as she spoke quietly, almost to herself, as she walked quickly away down the hall. 'I don't wish you any harm, but God is unjust if you die a quiet death while you continue to make him suffer like this.'

8

IT WAS the beginning of revolution. Maud's nationalistic ideals were increasing, so much so that, in the October of 1899, Yeats had deep forebodings when she helped form the Irish Transvaal Committee, she herself chairing the first meeting at the offices of the Celtic Literary Society in Lower Abbey Street.

The Committee, which even before that first meeting had been banned by the authorities, had been formed to oppose recruitment for the British Army fighting in the Transvaal, and to raise money for anti-war protests against British involvement in South Africa. One month before the meeting, the Boers had gone to war with the British Empire over the ownership of the gold fields which the British had developed. To some in Ireland, Britain's exploitation of the Boers reflected the situation between Britain and Ireland

On the way to the meeting, when Maud shared a horse-drawn cab with Arthur Griffith and James Connolly, mounted police tried to stop them, dragging the driver from his seat. Quickly Connolly took the reins, moving the horses on and scattering the police until they were forced to a halt, Griffith sent sprawling when the police tried to snatch the Transvaal flag he was carrying. It was enough to incite even the mild-mannered journalist to action as he grabbed a sword from one of the policemen, waving it and the flag above his head before throwing them into the huge crowd surrounding them and now stopping the police as they tried to follow.

When the meeting eventually started, Maud's voice was quiet and determined.

'Gold is man's greed and British settlers are pouring into the gold fields. It is only right that the Boers should resent British attempts to steal from their lands.'

Arthur Griffith had been working in the Transvaal and had only recently returned to become editor of the *United Irishman*, a newspaper which continually attacked the British presence in Ireland, its banner headlines arguing for 'An Irish state governed by Irish men for the Irish'. Griffith now pledged the newspaper's support for the anti-recruitment campaign, the most recent issue of the paper being full of praise for a new hero for Ireland, praise which he now continued at the meeting. 'I move that congratulations and a flag be sent to Major John MacBride, Deputy Commander of the Irish Brigade in the Transvaal in which 1,000 men had enlisted by September.' Griffith paused for effect. 'I know John MacBride well. I was working in the mines with him in South Africa. When I came home he stayed to fight for the rights of an oppressed people.'

John MacBride was a member of the Supreme Council of the IRB, a nationalist Catholic and follower of John O'Leary. He had first gone to South Africa in 1896, his friendship with Griffith starting through their membership of the Celtic Literary Society. A year later he had persuaded his old friend to join him, Griffith working as a machine supervisor and assayist in a gold-mining company.

One week after the meeting in Lower Abbey Street, Maud invited Yeats and Griffith to dine in her rooms. By now, Yeats himself had become an active sympathiser, writing a letter to *The Times*: 'Victoria was the head of an Empire robbing the South African Republic of its liberty as it had robbed Ireland of hers. People choose to ignore this at their peril. Today, but for her fleet and soldiers, would any representative of English rule sleep easy under an Irish roof? The spectacle of John Bull amassing 70,000 or 100,000 men to fight 20,000, and slapping his chest while calling on heaven to witness his heroism is not exhilarating.'

Maud had devised a crazy and ruthless scheme, arguing that if one of the troop transports to South Africa could be blown up, it would deter men from enlisting. A French contact, the Transvaal representatives in Europe, had agreed to give £2,000 to fund the scheme and to supply bombs disguised as lumps of coal, her friends in the IRB arranging to get the bombs on the ship.

Yeats was in despair when he heard her plan, reminding her that there were many patriotic Irishmen serving in the British Army who would be on those ships. Without any qualms she waved his objections aside.

But to Yeats' relief the money had gone missing, the plan was abandoned and Frank O'Donnell, who had objected so strongly to the staging of *The Countess Cathleen*, was suspected of redirecting the money to the Irish Parliamentary Party at Westminster.

Griffith looked grimly from one to the other. 'It's bad ...' He paused. 'The IRB have decided O'Donnell must be killed. To set an example.'

There was shocked silence, despite all the revolutionary rhetoric, even Maud blanched at the thought of cold-blooded murder, her voice near breaking when she spoke. 'Maybe he deserves to be shot but I would never ask a man to do a thing I was not ready to do myself.'

Yeats was the first to regain his composure. He turned to Griffith. 'We can't let that happen. Maud and I will talk to them. There must be no murder.' He paused, shaken by such lawlessness. 'It's wrong, Arthur. Violence like that is not what we want.' He shook his head, looking from one to the other. 'There is only one thing for me to do. I cannot support that kind of justice. I am resigning from the IRB.'

There was a moment's silence before Maud spoke. 'As am I.' She was adamant. 'Only Arthur, the IRB and I knew of the money. It is not fair to let young, enthusiastic men risk their lives for Ireland in an organisation where things like this can happen.'

Later that evening, when Griffith had left, Maud and Yeats were both quiet, shocked at the easy way in which political dispute could escalate to murder. Yeats was more worried at Maud's growing involvement, his appeal to her to change falling on deaf ears.

'You're much too involved Maud. Not only is it danger- ous but you could be arrested or worse. Now is the time to let me protect you. And help you.' He paused, preparing himself for another rebuff, an almost resigned look on his face. 'Marry me now, Maud. Before it is too late for both of us. Before you get dragged further into this awful fight.' He looked at her sadly. 'Neither of us are getting any younger.'

Irritation at yet another proposal, yet more pressure from her friend, showed in her expression. 'I won't marry you. For God's sake Willie, why do you persist?' Her voice softened as she saw the hurt on his face. 'I can't explain again, Willie.'

He sighed wearily. 'If you don't I will sacrifice myself for you. I won't marry another, even if you will only be as a sister to me.'

She shrugged, staring at him with something close to remorse. 'I don't want you to go and love any other woman, I really don't, but all that matters for me is my work. I'm happy. The life I have chosen seems the only one for me.' She took his hand in both of hers, her voice gentle and almost sad. 'I think I understand your feelings for me and I love you for them. And I am happy that you have so many beautiful things in your life. Your poems, the peace and rest you have in the country with Lady Gregory.' She laughed aloud, her smile softening his sadness. 'I know you think I am in my own sort of whirlwind but believe me, in the middle it's dead calm.' She looked at him affectionately. 'Believe me, Willie. I do have my own peace and I know marriage would bring peace to neither of us.'

THERE WAS a sad start to 1900. In London, on the last day of January, with her husband and eldest son at her bedside, Susan Yeats died. Although she had suffered the effects of several mild strokes for a long time and was confined to a chair, there had been no sign that a sudden end was near. She was buried three days later and to the family it was as if a close friend had gone; they had lived with the detachment the illness had brought and now little changed in the lives of the rest of the family.

Maud was in America at the time, canvassing for support for the Boers and for the *United Irishman*, but had sent Yeats her condolences, wishing she could have been there to support him.

In America crowds had attended Maud's every appearance. At her first speech, to a huge, mainly Irish-American audience in New York, the flags of the South African republic and Ireland decorated the platform side by side with the stars and stripes, every word greeted by cheers as she described the heroism of those fighting against the British. She knew there was little support for the way the Boers had treated the native South Africans and made no attempt to support their behaviour. 'It matters not to the Irish people whether the republics are right or wrong. The fact that they are fighting England makes us their friend. England's methods of warfare have not changed since she turned loose the red savages armed with scalping knife and tomahawk to make savage war on the American colonists.'

Her final words could hardly be heard, the crowd now on their feet, cheering every word. 'To Ireland I say that freedom is never won without the sacrifice of blood. The end of the British Empire is at hand. Your motherland calls you. She has been the land of sorrow long enough.'

It was fierce, patriotic melodrama, with stronger vitriol already delivered. While Maud was in America, Queen Victoria had visited Dublin, ostensibly to celebrate 100 years of the Act of Union, but the nationalists saw it as a recruiting visit, enlistment now at a virtual halt. Before leaving Ireland Maud had written an article for the *United Irishman* which she called 'The Famine Queen'. Even when not in Dublin, she still managed to fuel revolt as her outrage poured through. 'Taking the Shamrock in her withered hand, the Queen dares to ask Ireland for soldiers ... to fight for the exterminators of their race. Queen, return to your own land, you will find no more Irishmen ready to wear the red shame of your livery. In the past they have done so from ignorance and because it is hard to die of hunger when one is young and the sun shines; but they shall do so no longer.'

They were words which aroused strong passions among the Irish Americans but were without the same support in Ireland. Although the early Boer victories had caused some excitement among the nationalists, the majority of the public resented this support, people proud of their men, their relatives; husbands and sons serving with distinction in the Irish Regiments; the Inneskillings, the Connaught Rangers, the Dublin Fusiliers, regiments which had all suffered losses in the war. This support for their menfolk meant that the efforts of Maud and the nationalists were virtually ignored by the general public, with the Queen's visit a massive propaganda success. The warmth of her reception was even greater than expected, with the majority of Irish people still loyal to the throne. Special events had been organised, one of them a Queen's breakfast attended by 15,000 children in the Phoenix Park, special trains bringing the children into the city from all over the country.

A student band played the National Anthem as the Queen's procession appeared, a small lady in an open carriage, wearing the shamrock on her bonnet and jacket. It was a moving occasion with a strange warmth for the Queen Empress from both unionists and even many nationalists, despite her known opposition to Home Rule which, to her, was a danger to the unity of the Empire.

With Maud in America, Willie Yeats was still showing his loyalty to her cause, writing protests about the Queen's visit to the papers. 'What can these Royal processions mean to those who walk in the procession of heroic and enduring hearts that have followed Cathleen ní Houlihan through the ages ... Anyone who would cheer for Queen Victoria would cheer for the Empire and dishonour Ireland.'

It was a thoughtless involvement, rational behaviour suffocated by his obsession with Maud, leading to the loss of many friends Willie had made in society circles in Dublin.

When Maud returned from America she would not let the success of the Queen's visit remain unchallenged. Within days, at a meeting in the rooms of the Celtic Literary Society, a group of women under her leadership arranged a late demonstration against Victoria's visit. It would be their own patriotic children's treat. 30,000 children who had not attended the breakfast party carried bouquets of green leaves to symbolise their nationalism, and were led in procession through the streets of Dublin, to Clonturk Park, where nationalist supporters had brought refreshments, sweets, biscuits, ginger beer, cakes, fruit and sandwiches; enough to feed the hunger of that vast crowd.

Despite the lack of formality, Maud addressed the crowd with an inflammatory speech, telling the children she hoped Ireland would be free by the time they grew up. There was a spine-chilling moment for Yeats as she made the thousands of children swear in unison an undying hatred of England until freedom for Ireland had been won.

Yeats spoke to himself as he gazed despairingly at her. 'Why, Maud? Why instil such hatred?' He turned to Arthur Griffith who was standing beside him. 'How many of those children will carry a bomb or a rifle when they are a little older?'

9

〇〇

I<small>T WAS</small> late in the summer of 1900 when Maud found another role for the women who organised the patriotic children's treat. With them she formed a new association, Inghinidhe na hÉireann, the 'Daughters of Erin'.

They had one main objective: to work for the complete independence of Ireland. Their first activity was to organise free classes in Irish history and language, dancing and music, while still carrying on their campaign against recruitment for the Boer war.

It was the first society with open revolutionary ideals and Maud, elected as the first president, had designed a uniform with a sash of green and blue and a replica of the Tara brooch as a badge, her adopted name that of Maeve, the warrior queen of the west.

Revolution was brought a step nearer at a meeting of the leaders of the Irish Transvaal Committee on 30 September 1900, with delegates from various literary, political and athletic societies attending. Again Maud was in the chair. As the twentieth century began, it was a meeting destined to change the course of Irish history.

Willie Yeats and Arthur Griffith were with Maud on the platform. By now the journalist was more than a friend to

Maud, addressing her publicly as 'my Queen', admiring her not only as an astonishingly attractive woman but also for her revolutionary ideals which, if alien to his more moderate nature, were doing more for nationalist Ireland than any other person in the country. She had been working closely with Griffith, writing articles for his paper, his feelings for her concealed from all but Maud herself, who quietly but firmly disillusioned him when suggestions of more than a political alliance were tentatively suggested. His feelings for her were more openly revealed when Griffith reacted strongly against an article in the socialist paper, *Figaro*, which had launched a campaign to try to stop the anti-recruitment movement. It had defamed Maud as the daughter of a dead British army officer, with a pension from the English and accused her of being an English spy.

Griffith had attacked and beaten Ramsay Collis, the editor of the paper, before being arrested and sentenced to a month in gaol. Yeats, at first laughing at what took place, used his influence to have Griffith released on bail, and the incident closed when Maud sued Collis for libel, Collis retracting his accusation and apologising.

Now, ten days after Griffith was released, the relationship of the three friends was firmly established, a friendship cemented during the Jubilee riots and throughout the anti-recruitment campaign; friends who shared a mutual feeling for the literary as well as the political renaissance in Ireland.

The meeting was open to all present, philosophical at first but, since the threat to O'Donnell's life and Yeats' refusal to support violence by the extremists in the IRB, many present were concerned that the activities of the IRB were getting out of hand. Most agreed there was now a need to control the number of organisations working for

Irish independence, yet at the same time they wanted to use the growing nationalist spirit as a route to independence.

Even Maud, who had seemed unusually subdued after her resignation from the IRB, was seeking something less violent. She, more than the others, saw that something new was needed, an umbrella organisation which would bring all these nationalist societies together into an open separatist movement – societies such as the Celtic Literary Society which had branches throughout the country, the Daughters of Erin, the Young Ireland Societies and Literary Clubs, Athletic Clubs and Hurling Clubs, the 1798 Clubs which had become defunct once the centenary was over. And, of course, the Transvaal Committee itself.

Eventually a format was agreed, Griffith suggesting a name which all those present agreed with. 'The Federation of the Gaels, Cumann na nGaedheal. And its voice will be the *United Irishman*.'

Maud clapped her hands enthusiastically. 'It's a strong name, Arthur. At last we have a revolutionary movement from which freedom will grow.' She made notes as Yeats, Griffith and others helped draft a policy of self-reliance for Ireland which called for the withdrawal of Irish members of Parliament from Westminster and the establishment of an Irish Council responsible only to the Irish nation.

It was an exciting occasion for all those present, Maud's eyes gleaming as the idea took hold. 'It will be the party for all disaffected nationalists and poets and the IRB and the Gaelic League. It will preserve Irish nationalism, help our industries and protect our people.'

Even the moderate Griffith was caught up in the fervour of the moment. 'And first of all it will work to stop recruitment for the British Army. People have to see that enlistment is treason to Ireland.'

Maud nodded. 'We should stop local authorities giving jobs to those who have served in the British Forces.' She clenched her fist. 'Remember the ruined homes, the emigrant ships. The English have so much to answer for. But they won't get our young men now.'

By now all those present were caught up in the excitement. Something new for Ireland. Freedom? Or just rebellion? Or perhaps protest and then revolt for its own sake.

Maud was scribbling furiously as she drew up a list of objectives, the others throwing ideas at her, entrenched in the aims of the Daughters of Erin.

'Support industry ...'

Yeats was not to be outdone. 'Teach Irish history, language, music and art. Give prizes for poems and plays on nationalist subjects.'

'And fight against anything which continues the anglicisation of Ireland.'

'And find a national anthem to go with it. "A Nation Once Again", or "God Save Ireland" or "Let Erin Remember". We must choose ...'

The suggestions were continuous, gradually whittled down until, when Maud had finished writing, she proposed John O'Leary as President, Griffith proposing herself and John MacBride as Vice Presidents, refusing a position for himself at that time. He had much to do running the *United Irishman* which would be the voice of the new movement.

They had made the first tentative steps towards the rebirth of a nation.

I T WAS Bastille Day and the leaders of the Dublin Transvaal Committee were guests of honour of the Paris Municipal

Council, the evening one of tradition and pomp, and dressing for the opera. It was Wagner, Maud's favourite composer, and she was escorted to the performance by Arthur Griffith, dining later at a small restaurant nearby where their evening was marred by an unexpected confrontation. It was Lucien Millevoye, who had also been at the opera.

She stopped at his table, Millevoye rising to greet her, calmly introducing her to the young woman seated opposite him. He was unusually subdued. Maud stared at him, formally polite. 'A wonderful performance, don't you agree, Lucien?'

Millevoye looked at her and shrugged. 'De Valkrie is always great opera.'

Cold, unwelcome realisation hit Maud. She had known about his most recent affair for some time and although it hardly mattered to her, it had been over a year since she had seen him. It stung that the relationship, built upon their shared political ideals, and which had also brought her a daughter in whom he showed no interest, was now at an end.

She glanced down haughtily at Millevoye's companion, a strange bitterness inside her, needing to know. 'Is she something to you, Lucien? Has she your interest in politics?'

'She's a singer, better than the one we have just heard, and she has the same beliefs as me over Alsace.' He glanced quickly at Griffith who stood quietly by. 'But less demanding than your beliefs.' He stared hard at her. 'Your absurd Irish revolutions. You have no real cause; no real hope.' He waved his hands at her in dismissal.

Griffith stepped forward, fury on his face, Maud grabbing his arm and pulling him back. It was the end. And although there was hurt, with it was relief that the relationship was truly over.

The reception party at the Gare de Lyon was lost in billowing gusts of steam, the noise of the welcoming band drowned out by that of the engine as it slowly came to a shuddering halt against the buffers. Waiting on the platform, standing behind the red carpet, was the President of the Republic, there to greet another head of state, President Kruger of South Africa, on a state visit to Paris.

Some distance from the official party was another, smaller group of three, shivering in the December cold as they waited to greet one of the returning heroes of Irish nationalism, the 35-year-old John MacBride.

The old Fenian and Francophile, John O'Leary was there at the invitation of Arthur Griffith; Maud Gonne there to meet a man who already, in her mind, had become one of the heroes of Ireland, a man whose name had become a nationalist rallying cry and who even Willie Yeats suggested should be a Parliamentary candidate at the next by-election.

Maud tried to conceal her curiosity as she stared intently at the wiry, red-haired man, almost a head shorter than she, his face dark from the African sun, striding along the platform towards them. Griffith greeted him warmly before introducing him to Maud.

'Major John MacBride, allow me to introduce my very good friend and believer in Irish freedom, Maud Gonne.'

MacBride took her hand, bowing slightly, his heels formally together. 'I am honoured to meet you, Miss Gonne and to thank you, as did all of us who were out there, for your work for our lonely brigade.'

'And I, in turn, am very pleased to meet you at last, Major MacBride. I have heard so much of you. I feel I know you already.' She felt a sudden frisson of excitement, both from interest in the man himself and for what he stood for, an interest which deepened as she sat next to him at the official government reception in the Hotel Seine that evening, when the 70-year-old John O'Leary, speaking fluent French, presented the Boer president with an illuminated address.

After the reception, Maud invited MacBride back to her apartment, where Griffith was also staying, their conversation continuing late into the night as MacBride told them of events at the front. Maud was an eager and questioning listener.

MacBride struck a match, leaning towards her to light her cigarette. She inhaled deeply before continuing. 'Did you join the Boers first, Major MacBride, before you joined the Irish Brigade?'

'I did. But the Brigade formed itself. We had Irish, Irish Americans, even French. Anyone who would fight against the British. Colonel Black, an American, was our leader but when he was injured I took over.' He grimaced. 'We found it terribly sad that so many of the British troops were Irish.' His expression changed as he smiled charmingly at her. 'And please call me John.'

She smiled her acknowledgement. 'And those troops now see you as a traitor?'

'Possibly. But to hell with them. And the English. They treat the South Africans as they do us.' He leaned towards her. 'I have to thank you, for the flag the Daughters of Erin sent to us. It became a sacred thing. At night, before going to bed, in the light of the campfire, some of the lads would go up and kiss it for luck.'

Maud hid her emotion. The Daughters of Erin had designed and made the flag – green, gold fringed, with a harp in its centre inscribed, 'Our land – our people – our language'. Hiding her feelings she continued her questioning.

'You were wounded, I believe?'

'I was. At Colenso, when I was blown from my horse. But others suffered more.'

Her questioning persisted, Griffith a quiet listener as MacBride told them of the hardships and casualties suffered by the brigade. 'We were in action early in the winter. We fought about twenty battles, Spion Kop among them. And then we were caught up in the siege at Ladysmith for three months, the British unable to relieve it.' He smiled disarmingly. 'Your flag waved over our camp. Then, when the British threw 3,000 more men into the war, although they weren't as good as the Boers, it turned into a guerrilla war.' He shrugged and shook his head despondently. 'Our Brigade was no longer of value. We couldn't speak the language and had no knowledge of the country so they stood us down.'

The conversation turned inevitably to politics, Griffith telling MacBride how the IRB had failed them. MacBride, who had been a member since a boy, showed his disappointment as Griffith outlined another way MacBride could help their cause. He paced the floor. 'A lecture tour to America, John. The IRB's links with Clan na Gael over there will help. You will be welcomed everywhere.'

MacBride nodded his approval. Clan na Gael was an Irish extremist organisation, the IRB's counterpart in America. 'It's a good idea, Arthur. I can't go back to England or Ireland and I have friends in America. Most of the Brigade chose to go there when we stood down. They will drum up support. But I'm not a writer or a speaker.' He smiled challengingly at Maud. 'I would need you to come and write my lectures for me, Miss Gonne.'

Griffith was unhappy with the suggestion. 'Is that

necessary? Maud has much to do in Ireland.' He could see Maud was enthralled by MacBride's story, hiding a fleeting jealousy at her obvious attraction to his old friend.

AMERICA WELCOMED John MacBride but the tour was not the success they had hoped for. His appearances were warmly applauded, the publicity generated by Clan na Gael preceding him. He was modest as he related his experiences in the war, finishing each talk with an emotional appeal, written by Maud, asking for help for the Boers and for moral and financial assistance for revolution in Ireland. But MacBride was not a charismatic speaker, unable to generate great enthusiasm, the talks receiving an indifferent reception, with audiences falling off as newspapers stopped reporting on the visit.

MacBride was aware of his failings, aware also that not all Irish-Americans supported terrorism or the prospect of a violent war in Ireland. Most of them, the rational majority, happy in their new and successful lives, believed that freedom could be won by peaceful and political means. His letter asking Maud to join him was not unexpected and, encouraged by both Griffith and Yeats, Maud left for America.

Now the presence of the famous and beautiful revolutionary brought the crowds, as she built on the fame she had achieved on her previous visits. She was received enthusiastically everywhere, her clothes, chosen for the tour, striking; on one occasion a startling red dress with a silver belt and broad picture hat; on another a blue velvet dress with a Tara brooch. To many who listened in awe she was a Celtic goddess visiting her migratory people.

A goddess who spoke passionately about England, about famine, the Boer War and Cumann na nGaedheal.

Her rhetoric to the Irish Americans was strong.

'Why should we not succeed in our fight for independence as you Americans did, as the Boers will surely do.' She stood with arms raised dramatically as she appealed to their patriotism. 'Freedom is never won without the sacrifice of blood and your motherland calls for your help.'

Her words were intoxicating, the audience brought to its feet, their emotions stirred with the intensity of the feelings she had aroused. She knew instinctively how important a hero was to those whose forefathers had left a poor, impoverished country. 'For what he has done, the Irish race owes a deep debt of gratitude to Major John MacBride. Of all Ireland's children, he has served her best by fighting for right and justice. He saved Ireland's name from dishonour when there was great need.'

And there were more inflammatory words, some without substance, some inaccurate but enough to exploit the emotions of the emigrant Irish, those of second and third and fourth generations to whom Ireland was a green and fertile country exploited by England's rule.

The tour continued, MacBride's need for her changing from admiration to awe to infatuation, as much for her rhetoric and enthusiasm as for her beauty and presence.

At the beginning of the third week together he proposed. Flattered but non-committal, her reply was the same reply she had given, on so many occasions before, to Willie Yeats. 'Marriage is far from my thoughts, my dear John.' But adding quickly. 'At least while this war is on. And there is always an Irish war on!'

But she was flattered. And despite her refusal she realised that perhaps marriage to a hero could only further her cause.

10

IN THE summer of 1901 Yeats was again working at Coole, periods of deep concentration interspersed with intensely private times. He was often alone, casting for the fish or painting excellent pastels of the hills and lakes at Coole, though never matching the work of his father and brother.

One morning, after several weeks in those idyllic surroundings, Augusta Gregory was already seated when he came down to breakfast. He took his usual chair and she could see his excitement as he leaned towards her across the table. 'I had a dream last night, Augusta. Or perhaps a vision. Maud would call it a vision.' He stared at her intently. 'It was of a cottage where there was contentment and firelight and talk of marriage, and into that cottage came a woman in a long cloak.'

He paused, shaking his head, a puzzled expression on his face. 'I think that woman was meant to be Ireland herself.' He pushed his long hair impatiently back from over his eyes. 'That dream was a message. Perhaps for the play I am meant to write.' He grasped her hand. 'But I will need your help, Augusta. It will need peasant dialogue.'

She squeezed his hand in return, his enthusiasm capturing her. 'It sounds very dramatic, Willie. And very emotional. Of course, I would love to help.'

Together they drafted the outline of the play, an allegor-
ical story, set in Kildare at the time of the French landings in
1798. They chose the name of a family who were tenants of
Lady Gregory.

Bridget and Peter Gillane were a relatively prosperous
peasant family, looking forward to the wedding of Michael,
their son, the following day.

Lady Gregory was sitting at the table, writing quickly as
he continued the story. 'Then the poor old woman, Cathleen
ní Houlihan, enters. They offer her hospitality. Immediately,
the atmosphere must change. Now there must be a sense of
doom, of mystery.' Yeats face furrowed in concentration as
he paced round the room. 'She is grieving for the loss of her
four beautiful green fields.'

'For Ireland?'

He nodded. 'Then she must become pitiful and sinister
as she tells the family of her loss and how so many died for
love of her. She refuses the mother's offer of money and
insists that those wanting to help must give themselves to
the cause, give themselves for love to get the strangers out
of her house.'

'The English out of Ireland. And freedom? Good, Willie.
It's very good.'

He continued. 'She is very persuasive and Michael is
torn between self-sacrifice for Ireland and his love for his
fiancée, Delia.'

He paused, waiting for Lady Gregory's approval.

'The old lady then leaves to meet her friends. There is
cheering and Michael, his decision made, follows her, leaving
his young bride and future happiness, to join the French.'

He stopped, staring from the window for inspiration.

'There must be a final, dramatic moment.' He nodded to himself as in his mind's eye he saw the small cottage in Kildare. 'The bent old woman suddenly becomes a beautiful young girl, standing straight like a queen.'

Lady Gregory leaned on the table, her eyes excited. 'Ireland again?'

They reached out and grasped each other by the hand. They knew that together they would create something immortal.

L ATE THAT summer, Maud Gonne's journey back from America after a gruelling tour was itself exhausting and, although reluctant to meet Yeats until she had rested, he had insisted on visiting her. He joined her and other family members in London for her cousin May's marriage to an English civil servant, her sister Kathleen already married to an English army officer whom Maud disliked intensely.

There was a vestige of sadness and concern as Yeats greeted the sisters. Kathleen, although recovering from a recent illness, was elegant, dressed in high Edwardian fashion. Maud sat next to her, on the sofa in the drawing room, looking tired and dishevelled, still in the dark clothes and black veil she always wore when travelling.

He complimented Kathleen on her dress. 'You look like a beautiful, tall lily, Kathleen, with your lovely golden hair and white evening dress. You look younger than ever. And very beautiful.'

She nodded her head in acknowledgement, pleased at the compliment from someone who, in the past, had often ignored her completely in his infatuation with her sister. 'Thank you Willie, but it's damned hard work being beautiful.'

The following day the streets of the capital were crowded,

hansom cabs jostling for space with pedestrians, the horse trams forcing their indisputable route down the centre of the road, passengers hanging over the top rails, staring at the ebb and flow of summer in the capital.

Yeats was bubbling over with excitement about the new play, telling Maud about it on the way to Westminster Abbey, climbing from the tram in Parliament Square, their arrival creating a stir, their appearance, even in London, well known. She stood tall and straight, strikingly attractive despite her tiredness, wearing a tight, head-hugging cream hat with a wide brim, a pale blue suit with a long jacket and skirt, and short grey boots; he was equally tall, exceptionally handsome, thin and elegant. Both behaved nonchalantly, as if unaware of the interest they caused.

The Abbey was hushed and quiet, cooler than the warm afternoon they had left outside. Maud rested her hand on Yeats' arm as they strolled slowly over the flagged floor to stand in front of the great grey stone, Lia Fail, the Irish Stone of Destiny, on which the kings used to be crowned, and which was embedded under the British throne.

'It should be back in Ireland, Willie. We could do it. Take it from the throne for Ireland. Perhaps for your castle of heroes?' She looked at him questioningly, teasing, as he shook his head in mock horror, unsure whether or not there was another wild scheme brewing. She laughed as she saw his expression. 'Well, maybe not. Perhaps it's a bit too heavy for us. But it will be our destiny to remove Ireland from the throne.' She grasped his arm firmly. 'We can do that.'

He let out a long, exasperated sigh as she continued to talk rebellion, stopping in the shadowy quiet of Poets Corner. Yeats stared at the tombs and plaques before turning to her, his voice quavering with irritation and emotion. 'Don't you think you spend too much time and effort seeking a destiny, Maud. For yourself or Ireland, I never know which?'

He grasped at her arm, turning her to him. 'I look at you and I just despair. You don't take care of yourself, your lovely face is worn and tired.' There was a catch in his voice as he continued. 'Even your sister Kathleen, ill as she was when I saw her last night, looked healthier than you.'

He smiled gently at her, softening the criticism, his voice now almost a whisper. 'But you will always be beautiful, Maud. More beautiful than anyone I have known.'

He lifted her chin gently, gazing deep into her eyes. 'Oh my sweet Maud. Why don't you accept a comfortable life. Marry me, for God's sake, marry me and I promise you will find peace. We could have a wonderful life among the poets and artists and writers who would understand you. All my friends would be yours. And our children would be shown the way to beautiful things.' He took both her hands in his. 'And there would be other, less demanding ways you could work for Ireland.' His voice broke in a final appeal as he gestured around him. 'Then perhaps we too could be remembered among the poets here.'

Emotion had thickened his words, the mellowness of his voice enhanced by the intensity of his feelings. It was a heart-rending appeal and Maud made no effort to remove her hands from his as her heart went out to him. At this moment she thought he had never looked so handsome and yet, at that moment, so vulnerable.

But her answer was as always, her face intensely sad as she shook her head despairingly. 'Dear, dear Willie, aren't you tired of asking me that question? I keep telling you to thank the gods that I won't marry you. I have told you that you wouldn't be happy with me. You know I wouldn't want to hurt you, Willie, but poets should not marry. You have too much to give the whole world which would be grateful to me for not marrying you.'

He stared glumly at her. 'But I will never be happy without you, Maud.'

'Of course you will. Because you will make such beautiful poems out of what you say is your unhappiness. Anyway, Willie, marriage would be dull and our friendship means so much to me. It has helped me when I needed help, more than you or anyone will ever know.'

He shook his head. There was no way he could understand the continual refusal of what he offered her. 'But can you ever be really happy, Maud?'

She shrugged. 'Sometimes happy, sometimes unhappy. I don't think about it, Willie. But I'm happy with the work I am doing. It is my life. And I do pity those who have dull, uneventful lives.'

She leaned towards him, her hand on his cheek as she artfully changed the subject. 'But there is something we will do together Willie. We will put on your play, *Cathleen ní Houlihan*. And I will play Cathleen.' She grasped his arm. 'I have to play her. I saw her once, Willie. From the window of a train at twilight. A tall, beautiful woman, hair blowing in the wind as she crossed a bog, leaping from one white stone to another. I heard a voice telling me that I was one of those white stepping stones stones on which her feet had rested on the way to freedom. I was meant to be Cathleen ní Houlihan. I will be her!'

WILLIE HAD been busy with other things that summer. A month after Maud's return from America he had helped his two sisters start their own business, Cuala

Industries, in a small house near their new home in Dundrum, south of Dublin. Among other things it would publish hand-printed first editions of his books.

Soon after, another of his plays for the Irish Literary Society, *Diarmuid and Grainne*, had its first performance in Dublin, Maud with him on the opening night.

It was a great social occasion and they had prepared well. A promising English composer, Edward Elgar, had been retained to provide music for the play. It was a year in which he had produced the first two of his 'Pomp and Circumstance' marches and his music for the play was perfect for the occasion. It was melancholy and sad with a great horn dirge at the end marking the death of Diarmuid.

The play was a great success, the audience giving the cast and author a standing ovation, a recognition which continued outside the theatre as Yeats and Maud climbed into their cab to go to the first-night supper party. Some of the more excitable members of the audience undid the horse from its straps, dragging the cab to the restaurant. They turned to each other, laughing, holding hands, never before as close, as they smiled into each other's eyes, his love for her now deeper than ever, her lips evading his as he leaned towards her, she laughingly pushing him away.

The occasion was another step in their recognition as two of the greatest figures in the Irish cause: she Ireland's greatest daughter; he Ireland's greatest poet.

A great patriotic fervour was growing in the city, fuelled by the exploits of John MacBride, the publicity given by Arthur Griffith and the less publicised work of John Connolly. Yeats, however, felt a sense of foreboding, a sometimes suffocating sense of doom; that things yet to come, would lead only to tragedy.

11

○Ⓒ

ON 2 APRIL 1902, the small hall of St Theresa's Total Abstinence Association Theatre in Clarendon Street, behind Grafton Street, was rented for the opening night. The theatre was crowded well before the curtain rose. Gleaming white shirt fronts mingled with the rough serge clothing of the Dublin worker, those at the back craning over bonnetted and capped heads in an effort to see. Outside the theatre many were turned away.

Maud prepared the stage for the occasion. Over it she had hung the banner of the Daughters of Erin, who had agreed to produce the play and, at Maud's insistence, supply the female players. It was a golden sunburst on a blue background, which she herself had designed. In the small orchestra pit was the String Band of the York Street Work Men's Club which Lady Gregory had hired specially.

Cathleen ní Houlihan was in one act and, to extend the evening's performance, a play in three acts, *Deirdre*, a tragic love story, was performed first. It was received with generous, almost tumultuous applause by an audience eager for the main play of the evening, which had been rehearsed in private. The plot had remained a secret to all except the actors and authors, even Maud's costume for Cathleen still a secret to all in the cast.

She had prepared well. She had worked on the part in Paris before returning to Dublin, walking in the Wicklow mountains to perfect her lines. She was ready for her greatest performance yet.

Yeats stood at the side of the hall, dressed elegantly for the occasion, as the band played, on Maud's instructions, an overture from Wagner's *Siegfried*, her favourite opera.

As the play opened, Bridget Gillane was standing at the table, unwrapping a parcel which contained her son Michael's wedding clothes, stopping suddenly as her husband Peter and youngest son Patrick moved to the window. Off-stage was the sound of cheering, Patrick turning from the window to tell his mother that an old woman was coming towards the cottage.

A ripple of reverent applause moved through the audience and slowly died away as a bent old crone shuffled in ghostly robes along the centre aisle. The audience was now mute, the atmosphere in the small theatre almost electric as, purposely, the old woman made her way towards the stage.

On her head Maud wore an unkempt grey wig, a long plait hanging to her breast, her feet bare, her clothing a torn grey flannel dress, one of her own dresses cut short, a dress similar to those worn by peasant women. Those in the audience away from the centre aisle stood to see her as she approached the stage and threw back the dark blue hooded cloak which flowed behind her, her face dramatically intense and pale.

God save all here.

The old crone gave the traditional welcome before

accepting Bridget's invitation to sit by the fire, Bridget asking her why she was wandering the roads.

There are too many strangers in my house ... my land was taken from me ... my four beautiful green fields.

As she grieved for the loss of her green fields, the audience remained in tense silence as the woman began to sing. Maud Gonne's voice was melodic and haunting, and yet still the voice of an old woman as she sang for the golden-haired Donough who was hanged in Galway.

I will go cry with the woman
For yellow-haired Donough is dead,
With a hempen rope for a neck-cloth
And a white cloth on his head ...

Michael Gillane stared at her, bewitched by her singing.

What was it brought him to his death?

He died for love of me: many a young man has died for love of me, she answered.

The Gillane family gathered around her, sympathetic and curious, offering her a cup of milk and a shilling to help her on her way.

That is not what I want ... If anyone would give me help he must give me himself, he must give me all.

Michael asked her what hopes she had. She turned to

him, her arms wide as she replied:

The hope of getting my beautiful fields back again; the hope of putting the strangers out of my house.

Innocently Michael offered to help her, to go with her, his mother reprimanding him, reminding him that his fiancée was coming to the house. She turned to the old woman and asked her name.

Some call me the poor old woman, and there are some who call me Cathleen, the daughter of Houlihan.

It was a magical play, with an almost dreamlike quality, and Maud Gonne dominated it. The audience were swallowed up by her performance, hardly breathing, sucked into that desolate cottage. She was Cathleen, all that was magnificent in Ireland; she lived the part.

Yeats shook his head in sheer admiration, entranced, mixed emotions flooding his mind: pride in the play and in her portrayal of the old woman. And most of all there was love, obsessive, suffocating love for his Cathleen, for Maud Gonne. She was so striking and her interpretation of the role so hypnotic that tears misted his eyes throughout the performance, tears which were visible on the faces of almost everyone in the theatre as she played the role to perfection. And beyond.

Slowly, intensely, the play built to a climax in which Michael is torn between his marriage and the nationalist cause, Maud's voice bewitching.

It's a hard service they take that helps me ... many a child will

*be born and there will be no father at its christening to give it
a name ... They that have red cheeks will have pale cheeks for
my sake, and for all that they will think they are well paid.*

She turned and left the room and, from outside, her
voice could be heard singing:

They shall be remembered forever,
They shall be alive forever,
They shall be speaking forever,
The people shall hear them forever.

There was a magnificence, an almost unnatural power
in Maud's performance as Cathleen succeeds, luring young
Michael away, leaving his mother distraught, pleading with
him, and his bride-to-be, Delia, calling his name.

Why do you look at me like a stranger? she says, as Patrick
shouts from outside that the men of the village were all hur-
rying down the hillside to join the French.

Delia put her arms around Michael and he appeared to
weaken as she and Bridget continued to plead with him not
to go. And then the old woman's voice again from outside:

They shall be speaking forever,
The people shall hear them forever.

At that moment Michael's brother rushes in, the family
asking him if he had seen an old woman leave the cottage.
He looked bemused.

*I did not, but I saw a young girl and she had the walk of a
Queen.*

And then, dramatically, the old woman walked onto the stage again, throwing off her cloak, transformed into a young woman that young men were willing to kill and die for her.

The audience sat in awe-struck silence. Maud Gonne had become the personification of Ireland.

Mesmerising and magnificent, Maud stood centre stage, her arms wide, embracing the whole audience as again she uttered the final lines:

They will be speaking forever,
The people will hear them forever.

Then there was an eerie, stunned silence, interrupted only by muted sobs from women in the audience. A strange emotional silence and then an almost instantaneous explosion of noise as the whole theatre rose to its feet, a tumult of sound, tears and emotion, continuing rapturous applause until the doors at the rear of the hall were opened and people began to disperse. And through it all Maud Gonne remained where she was, centre stage, arms still raised wide, living for the applause, almost detached recognition of the acclaim on her face.

It was electrifying, intense and inflammatory. And a stepping stone towards Irish nationhood.

Later, when all was quiet, the audience gone and the players preparing to leave, Arthur Griffith was still in his seat, almost central in the front row. He was quiet, staring up at the now vacant stage. He turned to Yeats as he approached. There were tears in the journalist's eyes. 'I am overwhelmed. Willie. That was the very soul of theatre. Now at last I believe that nothing but victory on the battlefield would strengthen the national spirit more than the creation of an Irish theatre. We must work for it.'

Yeats too was overcome. His words were quiet, almost to himself. 'It was unforgettable, Arthur. Quite unforgettable. She is a goddess. She made Cathleen seem like a divine being, fallen into our mortal world.'

Lady Gregory took his arm; there were tears in her eyes. 'Now I see what she has, Willie. Not only is she the most beautiful woman in Ireland but I see now why she inspires the revolutionaries here. In her the youth of the country must see all that is magnificent in Ireland.'

Others came to congratulate him. Constance Gore-Booth, now Countess Markievicz, had sat with Augusta Gregory throughout the performance. 'I cannot say enough, Willie. It was a religious rite as much as a play, a kind of gospel.'

Griffith stood up to join them. 'How did you write such a masterpiece, Willie?'

'Praise should not just be given to me, Arthur. I was at Lady Gregory's and had a dream one night. Augusta helped me turn that dream into a play.'

Griffith face was suddenly solemn. 'Many left here terribly disturbed, Willie. One journalist friend asked if such sentiments are justified. Should such plays be produced unless one is prepared for people to go out and shoot and be shot?'

Another friend of Griffith's, a fervent nationalist poet and teacher of Irish, Patrick Pearse, had sat with Griffith and was overwhelmed by the play's intensity, shaking Yeats' hand and complimenting him. 'It's the most beautiful play that has been written in Ireland in our time, Mr Yeats.'

BUT THE nationalist fervour the play created caused a split that became evident later that evening, when Maud had invited several guests back to her new home in Coulson Avenue. The mild-mannered Griffith, roused by the ideals of the play, was urging Yeats that they had to build on its sentiments, arguing that the role of the theatre was important in nationalist ideals.

'But in which way, Arthur?' Yeats was wary of Griffith's aims. Despite the play's nationalistic intensity, his ideas for the direction the theatre was to take remained unchanged. 'Lady Gregory, John Synge and I want a national theatre for art alone. We must not be split on this.'

'Yet Arthur and I need drama to be a reason for political ends.' Maud leaned forward as she spoke. 'As *Cathleen ní Houlihan* was. And is. We should stage plays and act only for those opposed to the British government in Ireland.'

Yeats raised his hand, palm towards her, with the intensity of his feelings. 'No. I cannot and will not agree.' He was emphatic. 'I will not accept that plays with only a propagandist or nationalist message should be produced by the Society.'

The evening dissolved into uneasy disagreement which marred the play's success, Maud unable to hide her anger. Yeats, meanwhile, was disillusioned by her failure to support the theatre he wanted, though getting her assurance that she would continue her role for two more scheduled performances, crowds being turned away before each one.

12

‿○‿

'DID YOU live with him in Paris?' Kathleen Gonne's voice was accusing.

'Certainly not. I saw him a lot, but nothing else. He is a man of honour.'

Kathleen raised an eyebrow. John MacBride's advances towards Maud had been reported back regularly to her by a slighted Arthur Griffith.

Maud saw the scepticism in her sister's face. 'He'll do nothing improper. He is quite old-fashioned. I even had to persuade him to let me have tea with him in his apartment.'

'And?' Again a raised eyebrow.

Maud shrugged. 'We talked. Of how to free Ireland and other things.'

'And?' Her sister was persistent, sensing there was more to the relationship than Maud had admitted.

Maud nervously lit a cigarette, inhaling deeply and staring defiantly at her sister. 'He wants to marry me.'

Kathleen sighed. 'I thought as much. I hope to God you're not considering it.' She shook a finger at Maud. 'Willie Yeats is the man you should marry. He's besotted with you and cares deeply for you.' She leaned towards her sister. 'Listen to me, Maud. Willie is so right for you.'

'Perhaps, Kathleen. He tells me he loves me but it's not enough. I am tired of his proposals.' She stared at her sister. 'I need someone who agrees with my beliefs completely. I'm getting older and tired of fighting on my own and in John MacBride I have found a man who has a stronger will than myself, yet at the same time is thoroughly honourable. I trust him.'

Kathleen stared hard at her sister. 'Willie has those beliefs, Maud.'

Maud frowned at her sister, standing up and adopting her familiar lecturing stance, feet apart, one hand on her hip. 'But he thinks of different ways of achieving them. Through the theatre and culture and politics.' She inhaled deeply, letting out a stream of spent smoke and staring at it as it settled over one of her caged birds. The canary chirped and fluttered in discomfort. She clucked at it comfortingly before continuing. 'John is with me in knowing that only the gun and the bullet will rid Ireland of British rule.' She turned pleadingly to her sister. 'Can't you see the logic? Marriage to John will not change my lifestyle. We both believe in revolution. Don't you think the name Madam MacBride would count for something?' She sat down abruptly. 'And I have to think now of Isoeult's future.'

Kathleen remained silent, sitting impassively as Maud continued to defend her decision. 'I love Willie dearly as a friend, but with John there is an excitement and joy in life which I thought had gone forever. I will be happy with him.'

'What does Isoeult think?'

Maud shrugged. 'She cried. She said she hated him.'

'And your other friends?'

'I know people are prejudiced against him.' She glared at her sister, suddenly angry. 'Like you, they are all against him, none of them wish me the happiness I want.' Her voice became bitter and she threw her cigarette into the fire. 'Even Arthur, who claims John is one of his best friends, is against it. He has written to me.'

She opened up a letter and read to her sister. 'Queen, forgive me. John MacBride is one of the best friends I have. You are the only woman friend I have. For your sake and the sake of Ireland, to whom you belong, don't get married ...' Maud's voice trailed off, there were tears in her eyes as she looked at her sister. 'He says I am too unconventional and a law unto myself and John is full of conventions.' She laughed scornfully. 'He says we have little in common but our national politics.' She sat down and grasped her sister's hand. 'Why, Kathleen? Why? Even John's brother is against it. He said I am used to money and John has none; that I am used to my own way and listening to no one. He thinks these aren't good qualities for a wife.'

She looked suddenly vulnerable, again near to tears. 'And others criticise. They accuse me of hero worship.' She gestured dismissively, sudden uncertainty in her manner. 'I even heard our dead father talking to me. He said "Lambkin, don't do it. You must not marry him!"'

Kathleen made one more attempt to dissuade her. 'Arthur is soft on you himself, Maud. Have you ever considered him?'

Maud shook her head irritably, standing up and staring out of the tall windows her hands clasped in front of her, unable to meet her sister's gaze, her voice barely audible as she dropped her next bombshell. 'I have decided to convert to Catholicism.'

She raised her hand towards her sister as Kathleen sat up in her chair, her mouth open in disbelief, a protest on her lips. 'I want to look at truth from the same side as the man I am going to marry.' She smiled wryly. 'And there will be some political benefits in converting, of course.'

Kathleen was shocked. 'That as much as anything will hurt Willie terribly. You know that.'

Maud's demeanour suddenly changed, suddenly apprehensive. 'I know. I will go to see him this afternoon. He must hear it from me first.'

DEVASTATION. AN abyss of despair as his mind shattered into a thousand pieces, the room wavering and swimming before his eyes as her words refused to sink in. And then the terrible realisation. At last he found his tongue.

'Why Maud? For God's sake, Why?' He fought to hide the terrible fury and hurt; hate towards MacBride mixed with terrible fear that he was losing the woman he loved so much for so long. He shook his head, hardly aware of the torrent of protest which poured from him. 'If you convert you will do great harm to the religion of all free souls growing up in Ireland.' His hands trembled as he struggled to light a cigarette. 'The priests will walk all over you.'

'No, Willie. That's not true. I have often longed to denounce the priests and could not because I was a Protestant. But now I can.' She was sitting near an electric lamp covered by an ornate shade, a pearl necklace at her throat: a perfect profile in silhouette. She looked so beautiful that his love was near to hate. She recoiled as he leaned over her, sudden, intense anger reddening his face as he shook a finger. It was only the second time he had shown such anger towards her.

'Your influence in Ireland is largely because you come to the people from a superior class, those with a more refined

life. You are surrounded by romance and yet you put yourself away from that easy life to devote yourself to the people.
But if you do this, if you convert to Rome, they will never
forgive you. Trusting your soul to their faith will bring you
down in their eyes.' He turned from her, staring into the fire.
'You and I were chosen to uplift this nation.' He turned back
to her, his voice thickening with emotion. 'I appeal to you,
Maud. Please come back to yourself, to the proud, haughty
solitary life which made you seem like one of the golden
gods.' He sighed deeply and sat on the sofa beside her, taking her hand in his, his voice now at its most mellow and
eloquent as he tried to dissuade her from her betrayal. 'It is
not the priests who should lead the people. The priests soft-
en the will of our young men, even break their pride. You
have said that yourself.' He shook his head despairingly.
'Please don't do this Maud. Don't convert. And don't marry
this man. It would be your own soul that you betray.'

He stopped abruptly, his attempts to persuade her to
change her mind meeting with no response. She stared at
him, her head held high, defiant, but unable to answer him.
She stood up to leave, ignoring his attempts to prevent her,
pausing for his few sad parting words. 'We have so much
between us. Our ideals. Our mystic marriage. Now all we
have done together will be finished. I thought we had an
understanding to be together in old age ...' His words dried
in his throat as he fought back tears of anger and hurt as the
door closed quietly behind her.

For several days the hurt and betrayal made it impossible for him to do more than walk the streets, his despair
hanging over him like some black, suffocating cloud. The
headlines in the *United Irishman* glared at him from the
news stand: 'Maud Gonne to marry'. He picked up the

paper with shaking hands, hardly able to read the rest of the article; '... formally received into the church ...'

THE APARTMENT on the Avenue d'Eylau was to be given up and when she had finished packing she made one request before leaving to be married. She visited Kathleen, sudden concern creasing her sister's features when she spoke. 'Look after Isoeult for me, whatever happens.' She grasped Kathleen's hand. 'I fear we may not return. Please God what we do is right ...'

Her cousin feared the worst as Maud refused to say more, handing May a brown envelope, in it her last will and testament.

The wedding, at her parish church, Saint Honore d'Eylau, was on 21 February 1903. The flamboyant and colourful dresses which added to her great presence had been discarded for this day. They were a formal couple, she in a high-necked white blouse, ruffs at the wrists, heavy beads around her neck, and over that a suit of startling blue with a high-waisted skirt and grey boots; her husband-to-be in a high-collared starched shirt with a dotted tie, his moustache neatly trimmed, a handkerchief in his top pocket and a watch chain across his waist coat.

Throughout the day she had been quiet; as quiet and remote as she had been at her baptism several days earlier. An old friend, Canon Dissard, a fervent nationalist, had received her into the church in the chapel of the Carmelite Convent at Laval, where he was chaplain and where Isoeult would be staying while they were away on honeymoon. Victor Collins, a friend of John MacBride's, who had been Maud's godfather when she was baptised, was also the best man at the wedding, and the Chaplain of the Irish brigade,

Father van Hoek, had been invited to conduct the marriage service.

The church was decorated with flags, that of the Irish Brigade in the Transvaal alongside the flag of the Daughters of Erin. Although it was a quiet ceremony, only a few friends present, to Irish nationalists everywhere it was a union of heroes, and dozens of letters of congratulations, telegrams and gifts had been arriving all day, from Ireland, America and England. It was the approval she craved.

After the wedding there was the civil ceremony in the British Consulate, a small flicker of concern crossing Maud's face as they approached the building, her new husband still a wanted man in Britain and Ireland. 'Will you be safe here, John. The British ...'

MacBride put a finger to his lips. 'I'm armed, Maud. I won't let them try any tricks.' His hand was close to the revolver in his pocket throughout the ceremony.

Even on that day her rebellious spirit was with her; at the wedding breakfast she gave the final toast: 'To the complete independence of Ireland.'

The night of their wedding was spent in Paris, Maud slipping away early from her new husband and their friends to retire to their room, already in bed when he came to her. Her eyes were closed, feigning sleep, aware of every movement, every step in the room, a nervous tension making her feel nauseous as she waited for the moment she had been dreading since first accepting his proposal.

Quickly he was beside her, his hands on her, caressing her body through the folds of her nightdress. She returned his kiss tight lipped, attempting love, but unable to yield any passion as he kissed her neck and she turned her head away, her eyes closed, her body rigid, as demanding hands pulled at the long nightdress. He was strong, seeking his rights, moving over her as she acquiesced to him, muted protests taken as sounds of pleasure.

She prayed to her new Catholic God, to her country, to any deity who could help her through these moments, and she thought of Willie Yeats and his gentleness, and the hurt she had caused him. Then it was finished, quickly, thankfully, and she felt a wave of disgust sweep over her.

'Don't I please you, Maud? You didn't seem to be enjoying our love?'

She muttered soothing words to him, her hand lifted to his cheek gently placating him before turning from him. Soon she was comforted by sleep.

She had trampled all over his dreams. He was in London when the telegram arrived, only minutes before he was to give a lecture on the Irish theatre. Unable to face his unhappiness, a telegram was the only way. It told him simply that she had married Major John MacBride the previous day. Yeats tried to focus his mind, moving as if in a trance, stumbling through the lecture, unaware afterwards of what he had said, what questions had been asked, how they had been answered.

Now, with the sickening news, all his hopes and dreams of a new Celtic order, a castle of heroes together, were dead. Again he walked the streets for hours, not knowing where he was, his despair consuming him until, several days later, after nights of tortured sleep, he returned to Ireland to seek some solace in the company of Arthur Griffith.

He was beyond emotion now as he turned to his friend, questioning. The betrayal was more than he could understand. 'Why, Arthur? Why? Of all people? He will only bring her unhappiness.'

Despite the ending of his own slim hopes for Maud Gonne, Griffith was sympathetic. 'I warned her, Willie. Even her family warned her but her mind was made up. That is her way. I think it was hero worship. She sees him as a hero for Ireland.'

Yeats lifted a letter from the table. 'She writes to me. Good letters. Caring letters. But she just repeats what she said to me. Why? She says she is fulfilling a destiny.' He perched his reading glasses on his nose and read from the letter. '"I am at peace with myself ..." What can she mean?'

Griffith had no answer. Yeats continued. '"... I want to look at the truth through the same eyes as my country people, I do feel it is important not to belong to the Church of England ..."' Yeats stared angrily at Griffith. 'Such vain stupidity, Arthur!' He threw the letter down on the table, picking up another one, his voice desperate as he again read. '"Now that baptism and marriage are over, I am to abjure hatred of all heresies ... I said I hated nothing more in the world than the British Empire and I made my solemn abjuration of Anglicism ..."' Yeats slumped despairingly in an armchair. 'It's too much, Arthur. Her hatred goes so deep. It's too irrational. It will only cause her hurt in the end.'

Griffith shared some of his despair. 'Maud Gonne will always do what she wants, Willie, hate who she hates and love who she wants to love.' He put a sympathetic hand on his friend's shoulder. 'But I know she will always have a great love for you.'

'But not enough for the marriage I have always offered her.' The poet's tone was bitter as he buried his head in his hands, his muttered words hardly audible.

'Now we are finished forever.'

119

13

THE HONEYMOON was in Algericas, the day trip to Gibraltar planned beforehand; even on their honeymoon the nationalist ideal was foremost in their minds, she the decoy for the police who continually shadowed them, giving MacBride and his friends, ex-members of the Irish brigade, the opportunity to carry out their mission.

Maud was pale and tense, sitting with her husband and two others who would help his escape. It was a moment she had imagined, a destiny she was born to.

She questioned her husband over and again, every detail covered. They could not afford to fail; their country's destiny was in their hands as they made the final run through the plan, Maud the instructor. 'When I step out and wave a banner at the royal carriage, that will be the sign. All the police attention will be on me. You then get close from the other side. Draw your gun only at the last minute!'

MacBride nodded, pouring himself another drink. 'Two shots, that's all, then I will be away in the crowd. But then, what about you, Maud?'

She waved a hand. 'Don't worry about me. When they hear the shot, when they see King Edward is dead, they will not be interested in a mad woman at the edge of the crowd.' She moved the bottle away from him as he went to refill his glass. 'We have to get ready. He will be arriving in a few hours.'

She went ahead of them to a crowded Gibraltar, people in the streets already waiting patiently for the royal procession, as the plan, conceived in Paris and now to be carried out as a brief, perhaps final, interlude in their marriage, neared completion. An hour before the carriage was due she was in position, standing nervously on an unusually cold morning waiting for the King of England, the man she had danced with at court, the man who had sought her favours, to pass in procession, the cheers of the crowd announcing his approach as her eyes searched the crowd opposite for her husband. Then, as the carriage drew level with her she thrust herself forward, beyond the line of helmeted police, raising her banner high, only to be pulled roughly back. She fought against pinning arms, trying to draw attention to herself before being forced further back into the crowd. Falling again, she quickly struggled to her feet, standing tall and again waving the banner high overhead, shouting to make herself heard above the tumultuous cheers before dropping the banner and backing away, her hand to her mouth as she waited for the shots which signalled the end of the Empire.

But there was nothing. No sharp crack of a pistol, no sudden screams of disbelief, no death of a king, her own king.

There was no panic, no sudden pounding feet of police to the scene of the crime. Nothing except the continuing cheers of the crowd as the open landau moved slowly on its way and the crowd dispersed. There was no assassination; England still lived.

Maud Gonne stood silently, her heart in her mouth, fearing the worst. Captured and imprisoned. It could be the only reason for failure.

But there was another reason, and it was unacceptable.

There was betrayal when she returned to the hotel in Algericas, a glassy-eyed figure sprawled in a chair, attempting to focus, forcing himself up. 'Maud? Is that you? It didn't work this time, I'm afraid. Not quite ready, you know. We decided the time was not right. Too risky ...' He collapsed back into the chair, staring drunkenly at her, sighing apologetically. 'We were followed. The police; they were onto us. They wouldn't have let us into Gibraltar. And they could have connected you with me. I couldn't let that happen, Maud ...'

She stared at him with anger. This was not the selfless, unquestioning loyalty to the cause which she demanded. There was sudden disgust that this drunkard had lost the chance to bring England to its knees. She turned her back on him, unforgiving in her anger. He had failed the first real test she had presented him with. Terrible doubts seared her mind.

No more was said of the failure as she bottled her anger inside her, returning with her husband to Paris the following day. Their marriage was barely a week old, Ireland's cause the basis for that union. And already he had failed it.

IN THE long, hot summer of 1903, Yeats, once more at Coole, was taking his usual after-dinner walk with Lady Gregory along the path through the trees by the lake, as small, blossoming clouds played hide and seek with a haunting full moon.

Lady Gregory had other guests that week, among them his brother Jack, and a self-confident, intense and expensively-dressed Irish-American lawyer. John Quinn was a newcomer to the special world at Coole and, soon was an admirer of its beauty, entranced by the magic of the place. He was overawed by the easy after-dinner conversation which was an intrinsic part of Coole, talking poetry and philosophy with his new acquaintance, Willie Yeats, well into the night.

Quinn was the son of Irish Catholic immigrants, his a classic Irish American success story. He had studied law at Georgetown University at night school and then won a place at Harvard, joining an eminent New York law firm on graduating. By the time he was 36 he had his own law firm and enough private wealth to enjoy his passion for the land of his ancestors. This, his first visit, was prompted by seeing John Yeats' paintings, and then writing to Lady Gregory and Willie Yeats about them.

Lady Gregory and Yeats sat on the jagged grey rocks which lined the banks of the lake, staring out to where, in a mass of gossamer, wild swans were collecting. She waited patiently for him to tell her about Maud. He began hesitantly. 'She came to see me, early this month in London. She looked terrible. But I didn't feel sorry for her.' He shook his head sadly. 'I was secretly pleased, especially when she told me that she had found out that Millevoye had taken his new girlfriend to see Isoeult. She was so angry about it. But now, I'm afraid, she talks like a real convert and they are always the worst. She says the ritual of the Catholic church is beautiful and inspiring, and prefers the Pope as head rather than the King of England.'

Yeats stopped again as an owl hooted and drifted ghostly overhead. When he continued there was anger and hurt in his voice. 'But she is still the revolutionary. I don't know whether to admire her or despair, Augusta. She told me that on honeymoon in Gibraltar they had planned to assassinate the King and it was such a failure that she now has a personal vendetta against him.' He shook his head as he remembered. 'And after that there was the King's visit to Dublin.'

Maud had tried to get public support against the visit of Edward VII to Ireland, both Yeats and Lady Gregory supporting the opposition at a meeting of the National Council of Cumann na nGaedheal when a resolution against the visit was passed. The Daughters of Erin posted up copies of the Coronation Oath which repudiated the basic doctrine of the Catholic religion and linked the monarchy only to the Church of England.

'There was a meeting at the Rotunda about the visit and she stood on the platform and asked if the Irish Parliamentary Party intended to make a speech of loyalty to the King when he came to Dublin, if the country did indeed intend to welcome the English king to the Irish capital? She created absolute chaos, loyalists storming the platform and I was worried for her safety, but the nationalists protected her and carried her away.'

He smiled ruefully at another typical Maud Gonne demonstration. 'She is right, of course. They come here with promises of land reform and whispers of Home Rule. But where is it?" He glanced at Lady Gregory, knowing how intensely she disliked the woman he praised.

O N 8 October, 1903, John Synge's, *The Shadow of the Glen*, written for the Irish Literary Society, was premiered in the Molesworth Hall in Dublin. And again there were problems for the National Theatre Company, the play too extreme for the conservative Irish theatre-going public.

Synge's story was simple but the theme and dialogue outraged many in the first-night audience. It was about a young wife trapped in a loveless marriage to a peasant farmer. She lets a tramp into the house while she herself awaits her lover, her husband pretending to be dead. When the lover arrives, the husband reveals his deception and gives the lover the choice of running off with Nora, his wife, or remaining with him as a friend. The lover chooses to stay but when the tramp offers Nora the chance of sharing his life on the road she chooses freedom rather than a stifling marriage:

> I'm thinking it's myself will be wheezing that time with lying down under the heavens when the night is cold, but you've a fine bit of talk, stranger, and it's with yourself I'll go.

There was near riot, Maud Gonne staging a dramatic walk out when Lady Gregory called the police. The following night was chaos again, Trinity College students, who approved of the play's sentiments, singing 'God Save the King' in defiance of the nationalists in the audience who booed and objected when the police were again called.

Yeats was furious, calling for a public debate in order to preserve free speech, more incensed when several days later, he received a letter from Arthur Griffith. He scanned through it before passing it to Lady Gregory. 'Even Arthur disapproves.' Yeats sighed. 'They want something more romantic. It's the same old argument, art versus propaganda. And he says he doesn't like the direction in which the theatre is going; that Irish women are the most virtuous in the world and the play is nothing more than a farcical libel on the average, decently raised, Irish peasant woman.' Yeats laughed ironically. 'He tries to soften it by saying that though I am the greatest living Irish poet, Synge and

I, perhaps because we live so much outside Ireland, are difficult to understand and appreciate.'

He paused, a sad expression on his face. It was only shortly before the premiere that John Synge had told them he was ill with lymphatic cancer. 'But John, even though so ill, has responded, reminding Arthur of his preface to the play.' Yeats read from the programme. "'Anyone who has lived in real intimacy with the Irish peasantry will know that the wildest sayings and ideas in this play are tame indeed when compared with the fantasies one may hear in any little hillside cabin ...' He looked up. 'And now this!'

He picked up a copy of the *United Irishman's* review, reading Griffith's comment aloud. 'The best and truest writings of our greatest living poet, W.B. Yeats, are understood and appreciated by people. The poems and essays which they do not understand are those touched by foreign influence, from which Mr Yeats has not altogether escaped, having lived long out of Ireland. A nationalist is one who is ready to give up all that he may preserve his country.' Yeats looked up at Lady Gregory. 'Aren't they the sentiments of *Cathleen ní Houlihan?*'

Lady Gregory waved a hand. 'Don't let it bother you so. We just have to accept that Maud and Arthur will always want to use Irish drama for their own nationalist cause.'

Yeats looked at her, lips firmly set. 'If that is what they believe then we can't work with them. There will have to be changes. We can dissolve the Irish National Theatre Company and make a new company, call it the National Theatre Society with John Synge, you and I as directors.'

Once the decision was agreed he wrote to Maud, her reply coming a week later. He showed it to Lady Gregory. 'She agrees, and says it will be best for her to cease to be the

Vice-President of the Theatre Company since it is a great disappointment to her and all the nationalists interested in it. And Arthur, as, of course, you might expect, agrees with her.'

He glanced at Lady Gregory. 'She will always try for the last word. She reminds me that the creation of the National Theatre Company was originally due to the Daughters of Erin and Cumann na nGaedheal, who financed the first performance, and that the Company was formed to help us control the influence of the English theatre and music halls.' He looked up. 'She acknowledges we have given it great financial help and London publicity,' he shrugged, 'but continues that nationalists are fighting an up-hill battle against overwhelming odds and it is hard to see the theatre being taken possession of for another purpose by people who are not militant nationalists. It has since been taken from them by someone she looked upon as a friend.' He shook his head in annoyance. 'Me!'

He glanced back at the letter. 'Maud says the Nationalist ideal is a religion to her and a theatre company, unless it served the nationalist cause, is of little importance. So they will form another interest to combat English stage influence and won't have writers like Shaw who look to England more than to Ireland.' He stared sadly at the letter for some time before reading Maud's final lines. 'The letter concludes that we are in a life and death struggle with England, most of the men and women who started the national theatre are in that struggle and have not time or energy for a purely literary and artistic movement unless it serves the cause directly.'

He looked up. 'She has added her letter of resignation and says she will now support the Cumann na nGaedheal Theatre Company.' There was a great sadness in his voice. 'She distances herself from me even further.'

14

JOHN MACBRIDE was a hero without money, jealous of Maud's fame, of her friends and of her wealth, giving her the freedom to indulge her own revolutionary ideals which, it became increasingly obvious, were the most important things in her life after her daughter.

Arthur Griffith's prediction was coming true. They had little in common, his insular, Catholic view of the role of his wife in their marriage incompatible to those of a wife who took for granted the right to choose her own way in life.

Perhaps because of these irreconcilable differences, perhaps because of his drinking, their sexual marriage had finished soon after the honeymoon and the debâcle of the failed assassination attempt. But now she was pregnant with his child.

Even then everything she did seemed to annoy him and Isoeult, now eight years old, who had never accepted him as a replacement for her own father, hated him more than ever, the child's hate adding to Maud's disillusionment with him and the marriage. And as these feelings could not be hidden, so his drinking increased; drink to try and hide his frustration when continually rejected by her.

Gradually, with each disagreement, his resentment

turned to long sessions of verbal abuse which eventually turned brutal when, on Christmas Day, his control broke. It started outside their home, a fight which had been little more than a pub brawl, a garrulous disagreement between two hopelessly drunken men which continued when he arrived back at their Paris home.

'Stop it, John. Stop fighting, please?' Maud pleaded with him, begging them to stop but MacBride ignored her, pushing her away as he continued the fight whilst staggering through the door.

Maud screamed again, this time in terror as he pulled a pistol from his jacket pocket, throwing herself at him and hanging onto his arm in an attempt to take it from him. He pulled himself free, pushing her away, slamming her across the head with the weapon, trembling with fury, kicking her repeatedly as she cowered on the floor, doubled up, arms crossed over her pregnant stomach.

She moaned with relief as MacBride turned again to the fight, waving the pistol as he stumbled to the door, shouting after his former drinking partner, by now fast disappearing down the stairs, before staggering to the bedroom, ignoring his wife as he slammed the door behind him.

Maud Gonne sat back against the wall, tears pouring down her cheeks, great sobs racking her as she cried for herself, her marriage and her child, her thoughts turning, yet again, to the only man who could help her; the man she now knew she should have married. She cringed in fear as, only minutes later, the bedroom door opened and a contrite John MacBride came to her, kneeling by her as she recoiled from him.

'Why do you make me do it, Maud? Why do you drive me to it? I can't live with your rejection. You give me no love, you refuse to satisfy any of my needs as a husband or as a man.'

She looked at him despairingly. 'You know I can't help it.' She fought back tears. 'You know how I hate the sexual thing. Please let it be.'

He shook his head despairingly. 'Even if I do drink too much I have a right too, Maud, to drown my sorrows when you refuse to honour your marriage vows.' He slumped against the wall beside her. 'I loved you so much. You were my goddess. Now you're nothing but an ice queen.'

She closed her eyes as he smoothed the bruise on the side of her face.

'I am sorry, John.' She rested her hand on his arm. 'Perhaps in time it will be better. Just give me time.'

But she knew there would be no time. The marriage was already over.

WILLIE YEATS, accompanied by his father, had sailed from Liverpool in October of 1903 on the liner *Oceanic* for his first lecture tour to America. A famous figure on the British lecture circuit, John Quinn was now actively promoting him there.

They stayed with Quinn in his splendid home in New York, tastefully decorated with paintings by both John and Jack Yeats. The tour, in which he lectured on the Intellectual Revival in Ireland, was strongly supported by the Irish Americans with publicity throughout North America. It took in all the leading universities, among them, Yale and Harvard, the City University of New York, Amherst, Bryn Mawr, St Louis, Purdue, Notre Dame, Berkeley, Stanford and Toronto. They were all in cities with large communities of Irish Americans, most of them Catholic and with an ingrained anti-British bias. They took to him and Yeats, amazed and pleased at the reputation he had established there, in turn liked them and America. He was stimulated by the country, small incidents intriguing him. At Notre Dame he enjoyed the company of the Irish priests who were proud of their success in getting non-Catholics to attend their college, sitting into the early hours with them telling Irish ghost stories.

During the visit he met the President, Theodore Roosevelt, although, when lunching at the White House, he was shrewd enough to realise the President was using him to demonstrate his sympathy with the large Irish-American vote.

At the end of the tour almost 4,000 people attended a lecture at the New York Academy of Music. It was a triumphant occasion as, dressed stylishly, wearing a pince-nez and a huge, floppy bow tie, with his handsome, fine-chiselled face and heavy shock of black hair now sprinkled with grey, he captivated his audience, his gestures carefully managed, emphasising each sentence with his hand.

Willie Yeats had become an inspiring speaker.

He had earned $3000 and was established in the United States. But when he returned to England, it was without his father, who liked America so much that he stayed on, taking an apartment in New York.

O N 26 JANUARY, 1904, when she was 37 years old, Maud's son Sean was born in Coleville. She was overwhelmed with joy at once more having a son and, with the hundreds of messages of congratulations and goodwill which had come from all her Irish nationalist friends and others, many with the same message; her son was the offspring of heroes.

She was happier than she had been for years and, when she was well enough to travel, she left Paris for Ireland where John O'Leary had agreed to be godfather at the child's baptism in Dublin.

In the summer of that year Yeats was spending another of his working visits in the peace of Coole. There were dark, mountainous clouds obscuring the moon on one of their late-night walks, when he again confided his fears for Maud to Lady Gregory. The birth of her son by MacBride had made him more bitter and now he looked thoroughly despondent as he opened his mind to Lady Gregory. 'The Maud Gonne I used to know is gone forever. It makes me so sad, Augusta. She faces a terrible and bitter time if she continues as she does, with him and her revolutionary ideas.'

Lady Gregory's voice was gentle and full of emotion. And more. 'You must try to put her from your mind, Willie. You must write, spend the summer doing beautiful things.' She stopped walking and turned him to face her, her eyes firmly on his. 'There are others who care for you. Others who would marry you and give you the security and peace of mind that you need. One especially, Willie.'

He stared at her, his eyes suddenly moist, emotions overflowing as he squeezed her hand, acknowledging the proposal but making no comment. Taking her arm, they strolled slowly back to the house, Augusta giving him news which she knew would cheer him. One of the helpers at the National Theatre wanted to be more involved. Annie Horniman had been introduced to the theatre by Lady Gregory and had already shown a romantic interest in Yeats. An emotionally intense, plain but energetic woman, she dressed in flowing pre-Raphaelite silk dresses, a huge locket often around her neck, her hair parted severely in the

centre. The elder child of the Horniman's tea-trading family, she had been designing stage sets, making curtains and
costumes for plays and even spending some time as Yeats'
part-time secretary.

Unfortunately, although the critics were impressed by
her costume design, Yeats hated them and had little time for
Annie. He was hardly listening as Augusta continued. 'She
says we should have better conditions to work in and has
offered to spend money on hiring or building a little hall
where we can perform in comfort.'

She paused and took his arm again. 'She is 43 and lonely, Willie, and looking for a purpose in life. Just as I was
when we met. And one interest would be in supporting the
theatre. We have found somewhere, the old Mechanics'
Institute in Abbey Street, and another building next to it in
Marlborough Street.'

Yeats looked at her almost in disbelief. 'Refurbishing?
Redecorating?'

Augusta nodded, smiling at the expression on his face.
'She will give £5,000, some to refurbish it, the rest for an
annual grant towards wages.'

Yeats frowned, still looking for another motive behind
such generosity. 'But she doesn't like my politics and she's
English. Why should the National Theatre come from an
Englishwoman?'

Lady Gregory's hand was on his arm. 'It's a gift horse
we can't ignore, Willie. She wants portraits painted by your
father to hang in the vestibule. You, myself and others. It's
possible we could even open this winter.' She glanced up
quickly at him, her voice teasing. 'And anyway, Maud
Gonne was an Englishwoman. You had no such objections
when she gave her help ...' Her expression changed. 'There

is a problem. She is a business woman and will not have any cheap seats. You can imagine what Arthur Griffith will say; it will stop the poorer people attending!'

The theatre was once the Mechanics' Institute and Evening School and, since then, had been used as a morgue and coroner's office. It was a place where the coroner's jury would sit and give their verdict on the fate of sailors and women dragged from the river or murdered down on the quayside. More recently it had been used as a cheap music hall and needed much work to restore it. But an eminent architect who was also a keen theatre enthusiast, Joseph Holloway, was commissioned and within weeks the renovations were underway.

But not without problems. During the second week, workmen cleaning out a rubbish pit found human bones. At first the police thought they were from a murder until the old caretaker remembered that when it had been a morgue, some six years previously, a body had been lost and could not be found for the inquest. The police were satisfied they had found the missing body and, after an inquest which was six years late, the work was allowed to continue.

The Irish National Theatre was becoming a reality, the realisation of a dream. When the new Abbey Theatre opened two days after Christmas in 1904, the house was packed for performances of *Cathleen ní Houlihan* and *On Baile's Strand*, a play by Augusta Gregory based on Irish folk tales, in which the mistress of Cuchulain, the mythological Irish hero, sends her son to fight against him.

Willie Yeats stood in the wings, moved almost to tears by the reception given to his players, waiting until the last ripple of prolonged applause had died away before walking onto the stage himself. His address was brief as he thanked those who had made the new theatre possible, especially Annie Horniman for giving the Irish Literary Society the possibility to produce plays in the only theatre, in an English-speaking country, free to put on what it thought worthwhile.

BUT WITH success there was sorrow as, in the same year, yet again Maud Gonne came between him and someone he cared for. It was to be the end of another intense love affair, a necessity while it lasted. The tour to England had been another opportunity for he and Florence Farr to be together. They were staying in the Adelphi Hotel in Liverpool and one evening, as they lay together in each other's arms, resting after the strenuous lovemaking he demanded, he turned, leaning over her, stroking her lustrous dark hair, usually held back by pins but now flowing in shining waves over the pillow. His voice was unusually tender.

'I love being with you, my darling. You will never know how good it is to be so close to somebody I am able to talk to; to love the way I do.'

Her response sent a sudden wave of guilt and concern through him as she turned on her side to face him, her face serious. 'But that's all it will ever be. You can't put her from your mind, can you? Even in our bed you still think of her.' There was sadness in her expression. 'I'm sorry, Willie. I have enjoyed our love, our closeness, but there's no future for us. I don't want to be a mistress in someone else's shadow. If that is all you have to offer me it isn't enough.'

He stared sadly at her. She had been a friend for so long, from even before he had known Maud, a friendship which had moved easily into a caring, undemanding love affair.

'You do mean so much to me. You must know that. You have such warmth and I love your beauty, and admire your greatness as an actress. I need someone to share my passions with.'

'Just someone, Willie? It's not enough.'

Yeats watched her dress. She had helped him through his misery, her body a refuge for his hurt and his needs. He loved her for it yet now there was some relief that it was over.

She leaned over him and kissed him gently before leaving the room.

MAUD HAD betrayed him, married someone else, despite her repeated avowal that marriage was not for her. But even the betrayal of her conversion to Catholicism had not stopped his devotion to her and he was still the one person she could turn to. Always her friend.

It was only two months after the marriage when she admitted it had been a mistake. Now she wanted her freedom again.

She had been playing tennis with Constance Markievicz, unsullied and lovely in a white tennis dress, when he called to see her in answer to her summons. His concern showed as she sat beside him, and confided her reasons for the breakdown of the marriage. Her husband's drunkenness and brutal behaviour had become intolerable and her revulsion to the sexual side of their marriage had increased.

'Perhaps that was the reason for his drinking.' Yeats' sarcasm went unnoticed. 'Although if he was an habitual drunkard he would be in good company with half the population of Dublin; of all Ireland, in fact.'

'I know that, Willie, and I do feel some guilt. Perhaps because I was so frigid towards him drink was the only answer.' There were tears rolling down her cheeks as she continued, unable to face her friend. 'But it got worse. When I got back to Paris from Ireland after Sean's baptism, the whole household was upset. He was continually drunk. It was hell. Hell! He attacked me and I feared for Kathleen who was staying with us, and for Isoeult. She's only ten. And on top of that I think he's been unfaithful.' She gripped his arm tightly. 'I have to separate from him, Willie. I know how it will affect my support in Ireland but I have no choice.' She stopped, sudden tears flooding her eyes. 'I hoped it would be by mutual consent but he won't agree.'

She fought to control sudden deep sobs, no longer able to hide her despair. 'I know I brought it all on myself.' She tried to laugh but it was a hollow laugh. 'I married a hero I had created but there is nothing left. Now I am fighting a man without honour or sensitivity who is sheltering himself behind the nationalist cause.' She stopped, her voice now quieter. 'He is insanely jealous of all my men friends, Willie. He has even threatened to kill you and before he left the house he took all your poetry books; they always annoyed him. When you went to Coole he said he was glad "weeping Willie" had returned to solitude. Don't let it bother you though, Willie. There is a lot of jealousy there.'

Yeats dismissed her fears, his voice quietly sarcastic. 'Don't worry, Maud. His words are as empty as his pistol.'

'But he has powerful friends, Willie. He is trying to turn the nationalists in Ireland against me, and John O'Leary is supporting him.' She smiled ruefully. 'Only the Daughters of Erin are on my side.' Her eyes pleaded with her friend. 'Can you help me?'

He looked sympathetically at her, wanting to help. 'I will speak to Lady Gregory and John Quinn. They will help find you a lawyer. The best one in Paris.'

The divorce action divided nationalist Ireland, Yeats helping her continuously with advice and support, the dispute dragging on until late in the summer of 1905. When the case was finally heard MacBride contested the petition for a separation, arguing for custody of the baby, his lawyers trying to defame Maud, MacBride claiming she was English, not Irish, and therefore the case should not be tried according to Irish law. And there were other claims, that she was credulous, believing in reincarnation, addicted to morphine and had committed adultery with all his male friends.

Her expression was infinitely sad when she told Yeats of the hearing. 'He is a broken man, Willie. He went to Dublin. It was stupid of him, he could have been arrested, and at the hearing it was terrible. He broke down and cried.' She looked terribly upset. 'For what might have been, I suppose.'

Finally a judicial settlement was reached, her separation granted on the grounds of drunkenness, Maud retracting the most damning evidence of cruelty and infidelity she was prepared to use against him. But, as she was a Catholic and had married an Irishman she could not be granted a civil divorce, the separation giving her custody of Sean with one day a week visiting rights for MacBride.

It was a settlement which came with a heavy price, yet one which would give a new beginning to her fight for Irish freedom.

15

Iᴛ ᴡᴀꜱ cruel and unjust. MacBride had strong allies, the Irish Americans in particular, to whom he was still a hero, with articles published in the Irish-American press saying Maud was not of Irish origin but the daughter of an English colonel. This was followed by MacBride's friends in Cumann na Gaedheal arguing that, as she was English, she was not eligible as a member. It was a devastating blow to Maud who protested the unfairness of this as she had created the organisation and had even drawn up its rules and objectives.

In her defence she wrote to John O'Leary, sending him family records to show her Irish descent before finally and philosophically accepting the decision. Her work for Ireland was for Ireland's sake, not her own.

Then, to add injury to hurt, she was replaced as Vice-President by John MacBride, her expulsion also preventing her remaining part of the breakaway theatre company the militant nationalists were forming.

At this final blow she was bitterly hurt, voicing her anger to Arthur Griffith.

'Why, Arthur? Why? I have worked for Ireland, for the poor and for the country itself. Why do they do this to me now?'

Griffith shook his head slowly. 'It was inevitable Maud. Your accusations against John MacBride ...' he shrugged. 'Your demands for a divorce. You insulted a national hero, a man who had become a role model for our young people and a saint for Ireland to many others.'

'He was not a hero to me, Arthur. He beat me ...'

Griffith broke in. 'He tells me he had his reasons. I don't want to go into them Maud, but others hear the same story from him. You were not a wife to him ...'

Maud was quiet for a few moments, staring at him, taking in what he had said. Her fists were clenched at her side when she spoke again. 'And yet they use the excuse that I am not Irish, that an English woman cannot be a member of Cumann na nGaedheal. What about the hundreds of other English women in this country, wealthy women who do other things with their time, women who are working for the poor. And for the rights of the people. Women like Lady Gregory who do not get abused like this.'

Griffith looked apologetic. 'Lady Gregory fights only for artistic ends. She is not a politician, Maud. She and Willie Yeats may want to use Irish drama to promote nationalism but you and I have political aims which their theatre can never give us.'

'Except for *Cathleen ní Houlihan*.'

He inclined his head in acknowledgement. 'Except for *Cathleen ní Houlihan*. If it is the only thing the Abbey does for this country's freedom, it could be the most important.'

Maud sighed, near to tears. 'But I started Cumann na nGaedheal, Arthur, with you. It isn't right that I should be thrown out now.'

He paused, his voice quiet but pointed when he continued.

'In the eyes of many people the end of your marriage has compromised your political ideals.' He hesitated before continuing. 'Times have moved on, Maud. We were a moderate organisation but your ideas were sometimes too extreme and we attracted rebels and extremists ...'

She broke in quickly, not letting him finish. "Then we must move on. Perhaps Cumann na nGaedheal, as it was, has served its purpose. Perhaps we need a new, non-violent separatist organisation ...'

It was Griffith's turn to interrupt, smiling his agreement. 'I've had the same thoughts for some time. A new movement and a new name ...'

She broke in. 'Just us, if necessary. Back to the ideals of the Gaelic League. That's where it all started.'

'And use their motto. We ourselves, *Sinn Féin*! That's all it would be at the start, Maud. And our aim will to be to seek Home Rule but within the monarchy.'

She stared at him, wide-eyed, sudden fresh enthusiasm coursing through her. 'But we won't be alone, Arthur. There will be many who will help; the Daughters of Erin and Constance. She would certainly agree to be one of our executive members.'

Griffith nodded. 'The *United Irishman* could take the new name. I really believe that such a policy will eventually be accepted by all Ireland.'

Maud was suddenly energised again. 'It's a new start, Arthur. Let us pray that its ideals never change.'

THE SUMMER of 1906 at Coole was again an escape, a respite from Maud and the effort he had put into helping her. It was time now to write, to catch up, to rest and walk in the woods he loved, or go fishing, often in the preferred solitude of his own company; time to reflect; gaze over the still waters as poetry formed in his mind.

It was another productive summer, halcyon days of peace and tranquillity, every whim tended to by Lady Gregory. And there were other visitors, Bernard Shaw among them, irritating Yeats with his new interest in photography, particularly when Shaw coerced him to take one of Lady Gregory, Robert and himself posing beside her new Daimler motor car, or when he took hours over portraits of the lake framed by overhanging trees. He appealed to the poet's vanity though when he also took his portrait beside the lake.

Augustus John was another visitor that summer, Lady Gregory having commissioned him to paint Yeats' portrait, the result a likeness Yeats was unhappy with; in his mind the artist had made him look like a melancholy English bohemian.

Yeats' workroom had again changed, his bedroom taking the place of the drawing room at the back of the house. It was a place of isolation, the hall outside lined with thick rugs to prevent any alien noise interrupting his concentration. But the daily routine remained unchanged, dinner the occasion it had always been except that the choice from the cellar of great wines was by now greatly reduced, much to the disapproval of Lady Gregory's son, Robert, when home for his summer holidays. It increased Robert's resentment of Yeats' presence, aroused for other reasons, particularly his sitting at the head of the table at meal times and his taking over the management of the estate. But such resentment was short lived, Yeats' easy manner soon winning Robert over as a friend, a fellow fisherman and the curator of the great estate.

At Coole there was time for Yeats and Lady Gregory to think about the future and, as had become their habit, discuss their business affairs when strolling together after dinner along the familiar path through the woods by the lake; two minds in harmony.

The demands of managing the Abbey were great and increasing, attendances were down and they often played to half empty houses, with just a sprinkling of people in the pit and stalls. Change was needed, particularly since the breakaway formation of the Theatre of Ireland under the patronage of Cumann na nGaedheal. Now, with John Synge ill and Annie Horniman no longer interested, Lady Gregory argued that it was time to run the theatre themselves and remove the unwieldy board which so often involved them in time-consuming meetings. There was no dissent from Yeats when she suggested making it a limited liability company, herself, John Synge and Yeats remaining as directors.

Yeats shared Lady Gregory's enthusiasm. It was now the Abbey Theatre Company, not merely the National Theatre Society.

But the changes brought disagreement from a number of the actors, some demanding increased pay, others choosing to leave in protest at the takeover, to join the Theatre of Ireland of which Edward Martyn was president and Patrick Pearse one of the board members. As a rival it would be a threat to the Abbey's takings.

Even Annie Horniman, who was still subsidising them to the extent of £400 a year, had begun to fall out with some of the players. The final straw was when she was ignored by the manager when she commented on the behaviour of some of the actresses when on tour in England. She had been unable to sleep until the early hours as members of the group threw noisy parties in their rooms.

She wanted the manager replaced, furious that he had told her not to interfere in something she was financing, Yeats giving her little sympathy. She consequently accused him of thinking she cared little for dramatic art and that he made her feel like an outsider.

Yeats told Lady Gregory of Annie's concern, staring at her pensively. 'But I am still in her debt while she subsidises my work. She has guaranteed £1,500 to sponsor publication of my collected works, promising me it will be a beautiful set of books, in eight volumes. She says she is doing it to show people, especially among my twittering imitators in Ireland, what my real status is.' Yeats looked pleased and rather smug.

'She's very generous to you, Willie. You'll have to be careful.' She looked at him, nodding her head slowly and smiling. 'She is after you, you know. I think she is madly in love with you. Can't you see it?'

He smiled in return and shrugged. 'You may be right. She has written to me inviting me to go touring with her. And to help her set up a theatre group in Manchester or Liverpool when her subsidy finishes next December.'

'You have refused?' It was a command rather than a question. She showed sudden concern.

'Of course. Her anti-Irish feelings annoy me.' He took her hand. 'My true loyalties are here, with you Augusta, and to the Abbey.'

He read from the letter Annie had sent to him. '"My dear demon!"' He laughed. 'Why she calls me that I will never know. She says my work is too valuable to the world for her to allow any loyalty to the theatre on her behalf to cramp it.' He took out another letter. 'Here she says they sacrifice me and my work to keep me a slave to them because I am touched by the vampire, Cathleen ní Houlihan and that I am victimised by you.'

He smiled at Augusta. 'I wrote back that her proposal was totally unsuitable and that I am too old to change my nationality. I may have accepted her money but I won't prejudice my artistic independence.' His face was suddenly solemn. 'I will write for my people, whether in love or hate of them matters little. Probably I shall never know which.'

A NUMBER of small plays had been produced at the Abbey since the opening night but now there was the first major production. In October 1906, uncaring of his own reputation, Maud Gonne was on Yeats' arm as they entered the theatre for the opening night of Lady Gregory's play, *Gaol Gate*, a tragedy about patriotic self sacrifice.

There was an immediate response from a small group in the audience when they saw Maud on Yeats' arm and began to hiss and shout, 'Up John MacBride', at the woman they had once cheered. They had turned against her. Yeats was bewildered, his face strained as the noise drowned out any attempts by the actors to start the play.

Maud Gonne stood facing them, tall and dignified, unperturbed and smiling in acknowledgement. She was a legend to many of the younger people in the audience but to others she had tried to bring down a national hero and then made it worse by attempting to divorce him.

Yet she was magnanimous in her defence of those who protested against her, turning to Yeats as the noise gradually subsided. 'Don't worry, Willie. I'm not offended and, after all, you have to admire them. They are only defending their hero. Surely they are the true nationalists?'

If they thought that noisy occasions at the Abbey were over, they were soon to be disillusioned. In January of the following year there were more riots when John Synge's play, *The Playboy of the Western World*, was presented, a comedy in three acts which some saw as yet another insult to Irish womanhood.

It was a story of Christy, a witty and talkative young man who, by claiming to be his father's murderer, fascinates the girls in a small community in the west of Ireland.

Even Yeats and Lady Gregory had reservations about the play, Augusta complaining about the language used and that there were too many scenes of love and violence together which many would see as titillating. But Synge was unrepentant, resolutely firm in his disagreement and refusing to change anything. 'I don't agree, Augusta. I've used very few words I have not heard among the country people in my own childhood, or the peasants of Kerry and Mayo. Or the beggars of Dublin, for that matter.'

During the premiere it was in the third act that the trouble really started, with the playboy's words:

It's Pegeen I'm seeking only, what'd I care if you brought me a drift of chosen females, each standing in their shifts.

It was the signal for some of the audience to start booing, objecting to the mention of women's petticoats, which they saw as immoral and improper. Even the critics condemned the play, calling it a libel upon the Irish peasant men and, worse, Irish peasant women, and an insult to the people in the west, people who should have been portrayed in an idealised light.

During the second night's performance the interruptions

by the nationalists were more prolonged, the second act almost inaudible, the arrival of the police enraging the nationalists still further. The performance finished before the end when Yeats took the stage, calming the uproar and announcing the theatre would open the following Monday for a debate about the play.

Still the protests continued, Annie Horniman appalled, her hatred of Irish politics showing and even Maud attacking Yeats, calling to see him and berating him for bringing in the police. 'Why did you do it, Willie? Those who protested are true nationalists.'

'With a narrow outlook.'

She waved her arms disparagingly. 'Why don't you forget the Abbey, Willie, and get on with your poetry. The theatre just brings you jealousy and petty quarrels and arguments which you, a great writer, have no need to be involved in.'

Yeats was stony faced. 'I don't need your criticism, Maud. Not now. It's bad enough Arthur criticising my choice of play.'

Maud raised a questioning eyebrow as Yeats picked up a copy of the new paper, *Sinn Féin*, and read it aloud: '"This story of unnatural murder and lust told in foul language, was told under the protection of a body of police and concluded to the strains of 'God Save the King.'"' He looked up at her. 'That is not true, Maud. And from the man who founded the Sinn Féin movement ...'

Maud bridled, interrupting him angrily. 'I started the Sinn Féin movement, Willie, no one else can claim that, even though Arthur has worked hard for it.'

Yeats shook his head dismissively. 'I'm disappointed with him. Not just a fanatic; now he's a bigot. I hope you

will come to the meeting to face him and the other protesters. I want once and for all to let everyone know that this is
not just a theatre for nationalist propaganda.'

On the following Monday the Abbey was packed, all the
Dublin literary élite attending, with the exception of John
Synge himself who was now gravely ill. Yeats, wearing full
evening dress, was both brilliant and brave. 'The author of
Cathleen ní Houlihan addresses you. We have put the play
before you to be heard and judged as every play should be
heard and judged. Every man has a right to hear it and con-
demn it if he pleases. But no man has a right to interfere
with another man hearing a play and judging it for himself.
The police were brought in to protect freedom of speech.'

He continued eloquently to defend the play, pointing
out that it was a masterpiece and that those who rioted
against it were not the rural dwellers depicted in the play
but their offspring and grandchildren. It was a portrait of a
harsh and violent way of life which they preferred to view
in a melodramatic and sentimental way.

When he had finished other speakers took the stage,
Yeats shaking his head in disgust as one after another had
their say. Their objections were trivial, aimed at profanity
and blasphemy in the play and accusing it of being an insult
to the people of the west.

But one speaker made his point majestically; John Yeats
was as dramatic as his son, striding up and down the platform as he spoke, grasping the attention of the audience.
'Of course I know Ireland is an island of saints ...'

There were cheers and shouts of agreement, rapidly fading away as he continued. 'But thank God it is also an island
of sinners; of plaster saints.' There was a stunned, embarrassed silence; little further dissent.

The following morning Yeats joined Lady Gregory for breakfast, opening his copy of *The Irish Times* and nodding his agreement at the article on the debate, reading aloud to her, one of the players interviewed for the article commenting that they had never witnessed a human being fight as Willie fought that night, nor ever knew another with so many weapons in his armoury.

The paper was complimentary about the play; reassurance for John Synge who, only recently, had threatened to resign after complaining that plays by Yeats and Lady Gregory were being shown to impresarios in preference to his.

THE GREAT, white-bearded Fenian, John O'Leary, died later that year and it was a time of reconciliation as Yeats sympathised with Maud and his new adversary, Arthur Griffith. O'Leary's brand of nationalism would be replaced by the new movement, Sinn Féin, and with new leaders, Arthur Griffith and Maud Gonne.

It was several months after the first staging of *The Playboy of the Western World* while working at Coole, that Yeats received a letter from John Synge. Yeats stared sadly at Augusta. 'He has to have another operation and asks me to complete his play, *Deirdre*, if anything goes wrong.' He shook his head sadly. 'The operations were not a success. The tumour can't be removed. He writes as if there is not much hope.'

She looked at him, tears in her eyes. 'I will complete *Deirdre* if he leaves us, Willie. It is the very least I can do for him.'

16

Paris, in the December of 1908, was resurrection. And with it the magic, emotional, sensual moments Yeats had been living for. The hurt, the bitterness, the betrayal, all to be eclipsed from his mind.

Maud seemed terribly pleased to see him, tearful when he held her, as if she feared he would refuse her invitation to visit. Her apartment was warm in that cold winter, a depth of luxury there, the children asleep in their rooms, the menagerie reduced to a few caged bird, and Minnaloushe, her black Persian cat which stared at Yeats from the depths of a comfortable velvet armchair beneath the window. There were red drapes on the wall and deep green plants in pots around the room.

They sat on the floor, staring into the roaring fire, their backs against the couch, a warm sensuality pervading the room. Near them was a half empty bottle of wine, the soft candlelight casting flickering shadows, bringing a gentle intimacy which the recent tension between them had prevented.

Eyes half closed, dreaming, wondering, Yeats stared into the fire. Their conversation, interrupted only by long, easy silences was not that of adversaries, nor of man and wife nor of brother and sister but that of confidants, soul mates gradually opening their minds to each other. And their hearts.

They were at peace together. She asked him about the theatre, the strain it had put him under still showing as he replied. She placed her hand on his, turning to him, pulling her knees under her and smoothing her cream dress as she spoke, her voice soft and low. 'It's a millstone you don't need. You know how I feel about it. For the sake of Ireland your writing must come first, Willie.'

Another long silence as he rested his head back against the sofa, slowly nodding his agreement. 'There are too many jealousies and arguments.' He stared deep into the glowing coals, his voice wistful, full of longing. 'And my writing has such a special purpose. It's for you, Maud. It always will be.' And then there was melancholy in his voice. 'Everything else done without you seems so pointless.'

Glances exchanged. A sudden trembling. And then a movement; imperceptibly closer.

'I saw you in another dream, Willie. It was a place of dazzling brightness and you seemed worried about something. You needed help. It was a vision I didn't understand. You were terribly upset.' She paused, wide, brown eyes full of concern. 'But I was able to calm you and, on another night, I tried again to reach you. We went together where there were stars and sea. We seemed to melt together like one being. Then a clock struck and we separated. That made me sad ...' She hesitated before continuing, looking away from him. 'We were happy together and you said the spiritual vision would increase sexual desire ...' She stopped abruptly, as if she had said too much, a slight frown crossing her face. 'But there was nothing physical in that coming together.'

He turned his head and caught her gaze. The puzzled frown was still there. And then something more, as he reached out and took her hand, unable to control a tremor that ran through him as he moved closer to her, waiting for rejection but there was none. He lifted his other hand, still holding her gaze, their eyes hypnotically together as he stroked her hair. A gentle caress. Then his hand moved around her shoulder. Resting there. And then slight pressure. Still no rejection as she leaned her forehead against his and he pulled her to him, their movements slow, dreamlike in the half light from the wintry moonlight through the drawing room window, the flickering white light of the candles and the warm red glow of the burning coals in the fire place.

He kissed the back of her neck, tentatively at first, and then her cheek and then, as she turned her face to him, he kissed her on the mouth. It was gentle at first and then with the passion and skill he had discovered with Olivia and honed to ability with Florence. Daring, frightening, electric at first, and then pure. No longer the bumbling suitor. She moaned, quiet protests, unused to the searching, gentle sensuality of his lovemaking but giving herself to it, acquiescent as he continued, her whispers ignored, objections fading as he fumbled with the clasp of her dress, slow and determined in his need, now with a familiarity of a woman's armoury, the hooks and eyes and buttons and laces, his hands working patiently as they exchanged long, dizzying kisses, she following his lead. Learning, her tongue, tentative at first, tasting his. Then, in a sudden release of need, surprising even herself, she quickly threw

the dress aside, getting to her knees to discard the petticoats, before lying down again on the soft warmth of the
rug, her arms and body open to him.

There was no false modesty, their eyes locked, her hand
touching his cheek, stroking, as he quickly shrugged off his
clothes. It was a lifetime of dreaming, of fantasy realised as
he explored her body with his eyes and his hands for long
measured moments, drinking in the beauty of her smooth
swelling curves, the silken hollows, the shadowy deep
declivities enhanced in the flickering candlelight as the fire
died away unheeded. He stared into her melting brown
eyes which gazed unflinchingly at him, her only response
an almost imperceptible raising of an eyebrow, questioning,
inviting, before the fervour of his kisses increased.

Kisses of terrible intensity. Of a passion and need built
over decades of longing. He touched her and she lifted to
him, a frown of amazement, of curiosity as he gave her
pleasure she had never before experienced. Long, sensitive
fingers were gentle as he explored the intimacies of his goddess, his lips following the curves of smooth shoulders,
then back to her lips, her eyes and then her throat, burying
his face in her hair, before his mouth caressed her breasts,
savouring their soft, ivory beauty, his eyes lifting to hers
again, waiting, still in a dream, for her sign of readiness.

Her eyes were hypnotic, glazed, half closed as she
smiled, her arms guiding him. He moved over her, and it
was surprisingly easy, his concern for her fears, her pain, his
readiness for failure unnecessary. She was ready.

Movements never to end, slow, his eyes fixed on hers,
her smile now gone, her mouth open, breathing deeply,
moaning gently, head tossing from side to side on the thick
rug, trapped in a pleasure she had never known before.

Until the need was overwhelming.

It was a stanza from his poetry; long, pulsating. Dreamlike yet earthy. Demanded by both of them. She moved for him, with him as the poem reached its searing climax. She knew and whispered to him. 'Yes, my darling. Yes.' And then the frustration of decades boiled over, her response, her readiness, surprising even herself.

And then, after resting, control over his breathing regained, the question. 'Marry me?'

She smiled and put a finger to his lips as he took her in his arms, her head on his chest, stroking her hair, unspeaking, at peace together at last until they fell asleep in each other's arms, only to wake in response to the other's needs throughout the never-ending night.

For both of them, at last, there was true union, created through love but welded by need. He knew it might not last, feared even then that the dream might never happen again. But for the next few days, until he left Paris, their mystic union had became a glorious, physical and spiritual closeness.

L EAVING HER was almost too hard to bear, and the letters which followed tore his dreams to shreds.

There were several of them, the first later that same month. It was as if she was purging herself, writing to re-script what had happened. He read and re-read them, his fingers tracing the words.

Dearest. (*It was the first time she had addressed him with such fondness. Sentences, words, jumped from the pages at him.*) It was so hard when we parted yesterday but I knew it would be just as hard today. Life is so good when we are together and we are together so little!

I tried to reach you in a vision again last night ... I shall try to make you strong and well for your work for, dear one, you must work or I shall begin tormenting myself, thinking perhaps I helped to make you idle and then I would feel we ought not to meet at all and that would be so awful!

It is hard being away from each other so much. There are moments when I am dreadfully lonely and long to be with you. One of those moments is now but, beloved, I am so glad and proud of your love and that it is strong enough and high enough to accept the spiritual love and union I offer.

I have prayed so hard to have all earthly desire taken from my love for you and, dearest, loving you as I do, I have prayed and I am praying still that the bodily desire for me be taken from you too. I know how hard and rare a thing it is for a man to hold spiritual love when the bodily desire is gone and I have not made these prayers without a terrible struggle ...

He stopped reading, dropping the letter on his desk, bewildered, finding it difficult to continue, apprehensive, frightened of what it might say. He lit a cigarette with trembling fingers. Marriage, the proposal he had proffered during their brief days of love together seemed irrelevant. He continued reading.

That struggle is over and I have found peace. I think today I could let you marry another without losing it for I know the spiritual union between us will outlive this life, even if we never see each other in this world again.

Despair flooded through him like a suffocating cloud but even though he wrote back to her immediately, pleading, there were more letters, throughout the early months of the following year, each one adding to his misery as she continued to reject their love, denigrating his feelings to some passing need. An irretrievable sadness began to sweep over him. And then, sudden hope:

I think of you very often and wish you were back in Paris. I miss you very much. (*But any hopes this may have raised were cruelly dashed in the next letter.*) I always feel that marriage for you would be a mistake ... I have always felt this. (*And then another letter, a letter to quash all the love and desire in his letters to her.*)

Beloved. I write to you things I wanted to say and could not. Last night I was with you in happy dreams ... I pray with my whole strength that suffering and temptation be taken from you as they have from me and that we may gain spiritual union stronger than earthly union could ever be. I was full of human passion and weakness, Willie and even your arms are not strong enough to save me.'

(*His feelings of terrible loss and despair were complete as he read on.*) I belong to you more in this renunciation than if I came to you in sin.

(*And then, perhaps finality.*) Dearest. It is hard to be parted and yet perhaps it is better for both of us until we grow very strong. The love whose physical renunciation we obey will reunite us in another life. The love you have given me is so wonderful, so pure and unselfish, I want to keep it always bright and shiny ...

The letter fluttered from his hand as he collapsed into a chair. He could never accept such self denial. It was the end of all his dreams, his hopes.

HER REJECTION of his love; the brief taste of sensuality and passion with her, their happiness together, had brought him near to mental breakdown. Now care and love for others, those who also gave him love and support, helped him through his despair.

The letter confused him at first, the writing unfamiliar. Then came deep, quickening fear. The letter was from Robert Gregory. More even than family, another one dear to him was in need.

Augusta Gregory had suffered a cerebral haemorrhage and had nearly died. Yeats left immediately for Coole, Robert meeting him at the door as he climbed from the cab, her son's voice distressed as they raced up the stairs to her room. 'She's no better, Willie, but no worse, thank God.'

She was in her bed, propped up on pillows, her face pallid, her eyes closed. Yeats sank to his knees by the bed, his voice breaking as he took her hand. 'She was a mother, a friend, a sister and brother to me.' His voice fell to a heartbroken whisper. 'I can't think of a world without her.' He kissed her hand, then looked up, startled as it moved to stroke his face. She was alive and smiling wanly at him, her whisper hardly audible. 'I almost slipped away, Willie.'

There were tears welling in his eyes as he leaned over and kissed her cheek. 'I knew you wouldn't leave me. We can't lose what we have together, our Irish dynasty.'

She smiled weakly, her voice strengthening, life flowing back into her even as they talked, she apologetic about the latest difficulty at the Abbey. He put a gentle hand over her mouth to prevent her worrying but she insisted, her hand clinging to his as Robert, unnoticed, quietly left the room.

When the King died in May all the theatres in Britain had closed as a mark of respect but the Abbey had remained open, Yeats in England when it happened. 'I did send a telegram, Willie. I told them to close out of courtesy.'

'I know. It arrived too late.' He shrugged. 'Don't worry about it.'

A new manager, Lennox Robinson, had recently been appointed for the day-to-day running of the theatre. He had accepted that the Abbey, from the beginning, had been a purely artistic venture, its policy to ignore politics and, at the time of the King's death, thought the directors had decided it must remain open.

'Annie Horniman sees it as an insult to the crown and has threatened to withdraw her subsidy. She wants Lennox dismissed. I explained it had been unintentional but she wasn't satisfied and wants an apology.' Yeats' face showed his irritation. 'And now Arthur has become involved. He has written in his paper that it has to be seen whether I will permit myself to be whipped in public by apologising in return for English money.'

Augusta Gregory lifted her hand, her voice weak. 'You have to stand up to her, Willie. You have to show her the Abbey is politically neutral and ignored politics in staying open. And show Arthur and Maud and Sinn Féin it is not a mouthpiece for their propaganda; remind them that the British national anthem has never been played there.'

Yeats nodded. 'Annie has written to me. Dear demon again! Does she really see me as that? She says she will sell the lease and contents for a minimal sum if we take it over by December. She suggests about £15,000.' He laughed dryly. 'Then she becomes sarcastic, and says we can then sell six-penny seats.'

'She has probably had enough, Willie. Especially after you turned her down. She told me she has lost over £10,000 and that you are ungrateful!' With an effort she lifted her head. 'Can we raise the money, Willie? We did it before.'

'I think so, Augusta. Bernard Shaw and I could give lectures and we ...' he paused for effect, unable to control his excitement over his latest news, '... we've had an offer from America for the Abbey to perform there with all expenses paid. It couldn't have come at a better time.'

There were tears in Augusta's eyes, her voice tiring now. 'It's taken ten years Willie but, with John Synge, we have preserved the Abbey's independence and made it a part of Irish life. It is we who stopped Irish writing being provincial and narrow.'

He squeezed her hand in acknowledgement, his face suddenly solemn, unsure how to break further bad news. Tired eyes opened wide in alarm. 'It's John, isn't it?'

He nodded. 'I'm so sorry, Augusta. The cancer has finally taken him. He was very brave. He told his nurse it was no use fighting death any longer and just turned over and died. He was only 38.' Yeats looked immensely sad, Lady Gregory closing her eyes as if in silent prayer. When she opened them she took both his hands in hers and they sat quietly together for long moments of quiet thought for a man they had both loved and admired. Yeats was the first to speak.

'I don't think I ever really knew him, although I liked him a lot. He was such a drifting, silent man, full of hidden passion. In all our time together he never spoke freely to me. And although such a dramatic genius, he was worse treated by his country than any other writer.'

When Augusta spoke it was so quietly that Yeats had to lean towards her. 'Yesterday you could have asked him his wishes and heard his thoughts. Today, nothing! This sudden silence is so awful.' There were tears in her eyes as she looked at her friend. 'You did more than any for him. But without him we may not have got started. Our theatre owes him a huge debt.'

B UT AT the theatre which John Synge had helped to establish, there were still more battles to be won. Bernard Shaw's one-act play, *The Shewing of Blanco Posnet*, set in a small town hall in America, was premiered at the Abbey in August of 1909. As it had been banned in England, Griffith and Sinn Féin objected to it being staged in Ireland, the English censor at Dublin Castle deciding to ban it on the grounds of blasphemy, threatening a fine and a withdrawal of the Abbey licence if a performance went ahead.

But Yeats and Lady Gregory, now fully recovered from her illness, refused to accept the ban, writing to the censor to argue that the decisions of the English censor should not be brought to Ireland, copying the letter to the press. It was another shrewd move by Yeats which gained free publicity for the play.

But there had to be compromise, Shaw modifying the play, removing some of the offending passages but refusing to withdraw those denigrating the army and the words 'dearly beloved brethren', which the Irish censor thought would shock a Catholic nation since the words were associated with a religious service.

The premiere was a sell out, ticket prices at their highest yet, the play taking place during Horse Show week, many of the more affluent people visiting Dublin for the show also taking the opportunity of seeing the play. With the growing fame of the Abbey, coupled with Shaw's and Yeats' reputations, there were critics in the audience from America, Italy, Germany, Austria and England, messengers waiting outside to rush copy to the telegraph office.

Then, despite the growing expectation in the theatre as the curtain rose, there was a sense of anti-climax. Nothing in the play gave reasonable offence to anyone, and at the final curtain Shaw and Yeats appeared on stage to receive the applause of an enthusiastic audience. Even Arthur Griffith was satisfied, critics commenting favourably, the success of the play helping heal the rift with Griffith and Sinn Féin which had begun with the premiere of *The Playboy of the Western World.*

One critic whose opinions still mattered, however, was Annie Horniman. With her deep hatred of Irish nationalist politics, she was infuriated. As the play had been banned in England she saw its production in Ireland as a political act. Her association with the Abbey was now nearing open conflict.

YEATS HAD first met Mabel Dickinson in the spring of 1908 at a society lunch in London and had written to her several times. She was a young, single and middle class Protestant like himself. A medical masseuse and physiotherapist in her mid twenties, she was blond, with a full and sensuous body, always appearing ready for sexual pleasure and pleasing. Since that first meeting, she had become one of his secondary fantasies.

Mabel had been commissioned to develop physical fitness exercises for the Abbey players. Since his break up with Olivia, his continual rejection by Maud and the loss of Florence Farr, the few times he had met Mabel since that lunch had only served to increase his interest in her.

There was longing and sorrow and need in the letter which finally asked her to meet him. He wrote of his distance from Maud: '... with Maud I talked about things which have drifted away ... I shall be returning to London on Monday ... I am hoping to see you ... For the moment I am tired of modern mystery and romance and can only take pleasure in clear light strong bodies, having all the measure of manhood ...'

His needs were transparent and she was available; he, aroused by her physical beauty and sexuality, she, impressed with his fame and gratified by his greed in bed. It was an exhausting and physical love affair, all the frustrations Maud had created taken from him. But always without the love and sensuality he craved. Mabel's was a sexuality which in the end would bore him.

17

IT WAS a tall, rambling, house with gardens running down to the beach at Coleville in Normandy. Maud had bought Les Mouettes with a legacy from a great aunt and in May of 1910 invited Yeats to visit her there. The house contained the now familiar menagerie: birds, dogs, rabbits and doves and, outside, a well-tended flower and vegetable garden.

The beach was wide and stretched for miles, no other soul in sight except for Maud's daughter, the weather unnaturally warm for the time of the year as, one morning, soon after his arrival, they walked along the shore, Maud's arm through his, a parasol in her other hand shielding her from the hot sun. Isoeult, now sixteen years old, was walking barefoot in the surf some distance ahead of them.

Yeats' eyes kept returning to her; she was growing tall, a beauty not unlike her mother, nubile and, to him, innocently erotic with her clear complexion, large brown eyes, sensual lips and wide mouth. Almost absentmindedly he spoke to Maud. 'She's so beautiful. Like you, Maud. And precocious.' He laughed, sadly. 'When I arrived she flirted with me quite scandalously and told me that some day we would be married.'

She laughed with him, her expression becoming serious

as she tightened her grip on his arm. 'It's so long since I heard from you, Willie. I felt we were drifting apart.' She looked at him slyly, a slight smile on her face. 'Perhaps you have found someone else? It must be something, or someone very interesting to keep you from writing to me or visiting me for so long.'

He shook his head, laughing. Isoeult was a figure in the distance, at the tide line, as he slipped his arm around Maud's waist and attempted to pull her to him. 'I've been busy Maud, but I've missed you. I hoped so much that you would come back to me.'

She pulled away quickly, moving his hand from her waist, laughing. 'Willie Yeats. That's enough. There's no need for that.' She frowned disapprovingly. 'You know that I live only for her.' She gestured towards Isoeult. 'And for my son.'

She glanced at him, softening the rebuff. 'But we have children, Willie. They are your poems which make the world a better place, just as you and Lady Gregory have a child; the theatre, which needs so much looking after but which ...' she shook her head sadly, '... you know how I feel; it has prevented you writing many beautiful poems.'

He sighed and stroked her cheek with his hand. 'I fear for you and for myself, Maud. Because you are all I want. You have never looked more beautiful and I have never been more in love with you.' He stood staring out over the sea, his voice almost a whisper. 'I suppose I should look elsewhere for my needs.'

She looked at him over her shoulder as she walked on, a gentle and questioning smile on her lips. 'But we will still have true friendship, won't we, Willie?'

'Of course, my darling. It can only get deeper.' He

strode after her, long legs eating up the ground, taking her arm. 'There is something I have to tell you.' He hesitated, unsure of her response. 'The Prime Minister, Mr Asquith, has recommended me for a pension from the civil list. £150 a year. Lady Gregory and her friends had a hand in it. They say for my services to literature, for being Ireland's greatest living poet.' He looked at her, waiting for approval but there was none as he continued. 'I suppose I am now to be recognised as an eminent man of letters, but it has brought problems. My father has written to me. He thinks it will solve my money problems but tells me it has angered the Anglo-phobic Americans. And I hear that even some nationalists in Ireland disapprove. They call me pensioner Yeats.' He laughed, but there was no sign of pleasure in his voice.

HE WAS floating on his back, only yards from the shore, his mind preoccupied with his work, his eyes fixed on a sky blotted with a few cotton wool clouds. He turned his head as he heard a slight noise above the low murmur of the surf. Some yards away from him, walking slowly along the tide line, barefoot, wearing only her bathing costume, arms bare, skin flawless, long hair hanging halfway down her back, Isoeult was talking softly to herself.

He stood up in the water, staring, suddenly captured by her beauty as she caught sight of him, blushing slightly, suddenly embarrassed.

'That sounded like poetry. Was it?'

She blushed again but her eyes were challenging. 'I wrote it myself ...'

'It sounded as beautiful as you are, Isoeult.' He felt a sudden pang of arousal, sexual, a passion carried over from her mother stirring inside him.

He turned abruptly from her, diving into the breakers, swimming strongly from the shore, furious and disturbed by her effect on him. He thrashed wildly until stopping for breath, floating on his back, staring again at the few lonely clouds which disturbed a deep blue sky.

There was a splashing nearby. She had followed him into the water and, despite a pang of guilt at her naïve unawareness of his sudden lust, he swam strongly towards her until, only yards away, he dived beneath the surface and swam past her, pushing her gently, coming to the surface to laugh at her pretended fright. She screamed in pretended alarm, backing away, hands crossed in front of her, eyes searching desperately for where he would surface, and then the shrieks of laughter and fear again as he pulled at her, sudden excitement flooding through him as his hands grasped her leg, the skin smooth and soft, slipping through his fingers as she kicked madly away.

He was a strong swimmer and continued the game, disappearing under the water and pulling at her, his hands lingering on soft, smooth skin, unable to resist the temptation, gentle caresses amid great shrieks of laughter.

And then it changed as she turned in the water, suddenly tight against him and he could feel the fullness of her body against is. The arousal was now intense and obvious, a need which she saw in his eyes. It was time for the dangerous game to end.

Frightened of his emotions, he allowed her to gently push him away from her as high, firm young breasts, water stiffened nipples pushing against the dark fabric, fought for his attention. He took his eyes away, sudden guilt sweeping over him at his almost incestuous passion as he followed her back to the shore.

They returned to the house and for the rest of the morning he ignored her. But the memory of her young body against his refused to go away as he fought to remove from his mind feelings which once were solely for Maud.

WILLIE YEATS was now an established guest at social occasions and dinner parties, one of these at Olivia Shakespeare's house in Brunswick Gardens, close to Kensington Palace. It was there that he met one of his greatest admirers, a friend of Olivia's daughter, Dorothy. Ezra Pound was a graduate of the University of Pennsylvania, who had read and admired Yeats work. Twenty years younger than Yeats, he had a mass of golden brown hair crowning a pale face, an auburn beard and piercing grey-blue eyes.

The young American poet was visibly excited. Later, after he had left, Olivia spoke to Yeats. 'He was so pleased to meet you, Willie. He said he would be writing back to his American friends to say he had sat on the same hearth rug as Willie Yeats. And I think Dorothy may even be in love with him.'

Olivia took him by the arm and led him across the room to where Dorothy was sitting, in conversation with another woman of the same age. She was beautiful, with piercing brown eyes and a stiff, clipped English accent, her clothes feminine and fashionable, an evening shawl over her shoulders, her long pendant earrings and dark complexion giving her a gypsy-like appearance.

Olivia introduced her to Yeats. 'Willie, this is Dorothy's friend, Georgiana Hyde Lees.'

Yeats leaned over her, taking her hand. He bowed

slightly, kissing her hand flirtatiously. 'How do you do, Miss Lees?'

She nodded graciously. 'I am so pleased to meet you, Mr Yeats. I admire your writing very much. And please, do call me George.'

She took in his appearance at a glance. He was wearing a tie loosely knotted like a cravat and a velvet jacket, his hair long and slightly greying, flopping over his face as he leaned over her.

'George it is. And thank you Olivia, for introducing me to such a lovely friend.'

Olivia raised an eyebrow and smiled. After a brief conversation, Yeats excused himself politely. There were other people of importance he wished to meet. 'You must excuse me, ladies, if I can drag him away from his bridge game I wish to talk to Winston Churchill.'

As he left the room Georgiana turned to her friend, an amused expression on her face. 'You arranged that, didn't you, Olivia?' Olivia said nothing, smiling enigmatically. Georgiana's expression remained serious. 'It doesn't matter. I think I would marry him, if asked.'

Olivia nodded slightly, still smiling. 'I think you might. He certainly likes you. I could see it in his eyes.'

Time had passed but the old familiarity and closeness was as if their affair had never finished. Now based on a deep friendship and the familiarity of former lovers, when he returned to the room he caught Olivia's eye, seeing something there and, later that evening, took her back to his rooms. It was as if their intimacy had never ceased.

EZRA POUND was to become a close friend, Yeats admiring much of the American's work, the younger man encouraged by praise from the famous Irish poet and soon becoming established at Yeats' Monday meetings at his rooms in Woburn Buildings. Here, Pound frequently dominated the conversation, his comments always shrewd and constructive. He rapidly became at home among the writers and poets, adopting their bohemian dress sense. Those in attendance on these social occasions included most of the literary figures of the day: Bernard Shaw, D.H. Lawrence, Ford Maddox Brown, John Masefield, occasionally Oscar Wilde and Robert Bridges.

James Joyce was one of the earliest visitors, Yeats laughing at the younger man's arrogance when he told Yeats he had met him too late; the poet was too old to take advice. But he helped Joyce, introducing him to the many publishers and editors who attended the meetings.

THE ABBEY Theatre was continuing to be mentioned in the American newspapers and a New York agency had offered backing for another tour. At the end of January 1912, Lady Gregory and Yeats joined the company. It was his third visit to America and there was another reason for travelling: his father was ill and short of money. On arrival Yeats stayed at the Algonquin Hotel, working first with John Quinn to sort out his father's finances before joining the tour, during which he lectured on the Abbey Theatre as a part of Irish life.

But the negative comments which had appeared in the press about *The Playboy of the Western World* continued to cause difficulties. American Gaelic Societies attacked the play as containing both blasphemy and political treachery and, soon after Yeats had returned to England, during a performance in New York, the stage was attacked and the sets wrecked, though President Roosevelt had attended on the previous evening.

Worse was to follow. In Chicago, Lady Gregory received threatening letters, the final straw coming in Philadelphia where the whole company was arrested, local Irish societies demanding they be held on bail for days, to be released only when John Quinn intervened.

But again, Yeats was secretly delighted. They had received all the publicity they could have hoped for and the tour ended with a farewell dinner organised by Quinn.

On his return to Europe, in early April, Yeats again visited Maud at Coleville, the first evening, over dinner, telling her about the problems during the tour. Maud had news of her own. 'You know about John Quinn and Lady Gregory?'

Yeats stared at her, unsure what she meant. Maud laughed, a mischievous look on her face. 'Your precious Lady Gregory is not as aloof as one might think. They're in love, of course. After you left she had a passionate affair with him and stayed at his apartment.' She raised an eyebrow teasingly. 'You didn't know, Willie? She must have been worried at what you might say. But she said it was like a dream, a wonderful dream.'

Yeats felt an almost childish jealousy. 'How do you know?' His question was almost aggressive.

'I've had a letter from John. He is in raptures. She writes him long passionate letters.' She looked at Yeats with concern at his reaction. 'Be pleased for them, Willie. They are very much in love.' She laughed again. 'Don't tell me you were not tempted yourself? Were you? You've had the opportunity and I know your needs.'

Yeats blushed, a sudden child-like naïvete showing through again. 'I could, I suppose, have married her.'

'And?'

He stared pointedly at her. 'No one could take your place, I suppose.' He waved a disparaging hand, refusing to be drawn any further.

Still she teased him. 'And I hear you've also split with your other friend, Mabel? What was she to you?'

Yeats glared at her, showing his anger at her persistence in humiliating him. 'She was there for me, Maud. It meant nothing.'

She smiled teasingly again. 'Is it true she is a masseuse, Willie? Very apt.' He stared stonily at her as she continued. 'You loved her?'

'No, not love. She was good company and gave me the physical release I needed.' He looked at her sadly. 'But without what you could give, Maud.'

'Do you still see her?'

He shook his head angrily. 'When I was at Coole she sent me a telegram to say she was pregnant.' He smiled ruefully. 'I was very convinced.'

'And was she?' There was a sudden edge to Maud's voice.

'No, but it worried me. I thought she wanted marriage but I could not have married her. A mistress cannot give one a home, Maud. Perhaps I'll never marry and have a home.'

Still her questioning continued. 'So it's over with her?'

'It's over. I wanted to do the right thing even though I didn't love her. I panicked. I dashed back to London and met her outside the Victoria and Albert Museum. Then she told me it was a false alarm. I got angry and we had a terrible quarrel.' He laughed bitterly as he remembered his last meeting with Mabel. 'We must have been some sight.' He became quiet, his face sad.

She stopped teasing him, her heart suddenly going out to him as he continued, his words full of sadness. 'I'm so depressed, Maud. All my old friends are leaving me and I seem to be in constant trouble with women. Mabel has deserted me and I've quarrelled with Annie Horniman and poor Florence has cancer and has gone away to run a girls' school in Ceylon. My eyesight is failing, it stops me reading and even going to the theatre is not what it was. Dining out with people sets my nerves on edge and I find it hard to be famous yet get so nervous when alone.'

He sighed again and Maud fought to suppress sudden laughter at his misery. She hid her face behind her hand as he continued. 'I'm almost 49 and yet I have no child to carry on the family line, even though Lady Gregory and others introduce me to so many well-off and attractive women. Even Eva and Constance are out of reach now. Constance had taken up politics. She thinks the life of the great families in Ireland are irrelevant to the country's needs.'

'She was always a socialist, Willie.'

'And now she has joined your Sinn Féin.' He shook his head despairingly. 'Even Olivia thinks I should marry. They all seem to think there is no hope for you and I together ...'

She took his hand sympathetically. 'I will pray hard for you at mass, dear Willie.'

'Is that all I can hope for?'

She turned from him, refusing to answer. He sat down, pulling her down beside him. 'I wrote something for us, Maud. I call it "A Memory of Youth".'

We sat as silent as a stone,
We knew, though she's not said a word,
That even the best of love must die

And had been savagely undone.

He had almost completed the third and last verse when she cut across his words. There was sadness in her voice. 'Is that us? Are we really that sad?'

He held her hand as he completed the last few lines. When he had finished he had a surprise for her. 'I brought you something back from America. I hoped you would wear it.' He took a small box from his pocket, handing it to her. She stared at him, a slight frown crossing her face before opening the box and staring at the small ring. It was in the shape of a shamrock, each of the leaves outlined in small diamonds. She looked back at him, questioning, about to speak when he put his finger to her lips. 'It is a proposal, yes, Maud. But whatever your answer, wear the ring for our special friendship?'

She smiled gently, kissing him on the cheek before slipping the ring onto her finger. 'I will wear it always, Willie. For our special friendship, I promise you that.'

That night she had a gift for him. It was a framed photograph of herself taken the previous year in Paris, set against a staged background. Yeats thanked her, smiling as he read her personal motto below her signature: 'Onwards always till liberty is won.' No matter what the future held, her politics would always come between them.

18

IT WAS again a time of poverty and sadness and despair. But a time which cast another stepping stone towards a new Ireland. In 1913, labour disputes were increasing after industrial disruption by James Larkin, an ex-soldier from the King's Liverpool regiment and the son of Irish emigrants. In Ireland he had founded the Irish Transport and General Workers Union and was its General Secretary, James Connolly one of the organisers.

Larkin's activities eventually led to a strike in an attempt to force employers to improve working conditions. This, in turn, led to a lock-out by employers who were supported by the newspapers and the church, which preached to the wives of the workers that Catholic mothers should not allow their children to be fed in the houses of English sympathisers.

Griffith and Sinn Féin opposed Larkin. To them he was a trouble maker, unpopular with both the employers and rival trade unionists, frequently having to appear in disguise at meetings during the lockout. Eventually, when Larkin was arrested for incitement to riot, Connolly took over leadership of the Union.

Tens of thousands were in dire poverty and facing

starvation: in Dublin whole families lived on less than one pound a week and when English trade unions withdrew their support from non-union workers, things became worse, many without an income at all. Children were starving, their death rate among the highest in Europe, tuberculosis being rife.

Yeats was furious at the employers, writing to the newspapers and supporting Maud's appeal to Dublin Corporation and MPs to extend to Ireland the School Meals Act, which guaranteed meals for children attending school. As soon as she heard about the strike Maud had rushed back from France and, with Constance Markievicz and the Daughters of Erin, set up soup kitchens to feed the starving. She had even travelled to London to lobby the Irish Parliamentary Party for support.

She had also arranged for bundles of clothes to be sent from France, her generosity without any concern for things she treasured. To provide food she had sold the last pieces of her jewellery collection, a diamond necklace and a ruby brooch which had belonged to her mother.

But she never parted with the ring given to her by Willie Yeats.

As the lockout continued violence had become widespread, the Royal Irish Constabulary often brutal in suppressing demonstrations by the strikers. To protect them against this, Connolly had formed the first fledgling army of a new Ireland, the Irish Citizens Army, with its headquarters at Liberty Hall, also the headquarters of the Irish Transport Workers Union.

It was a makeshift army, unarmed, with little experienced military leadership, and they drilled with wooden broom handles and hurleys. But it was the nucleus of an army of rebellion.

For almost a year the lock-out continued until, by the early months of 1914, even the most fervent could see the strike was doomed, the demoralised strikers drifting back to work. Later that year the mood changed when the Government of Ireland Act, paving the way for Home Rule, was put into the statute Books.

It was a time of celebration, bonfires lit and even 'God Save the King' sung by nationalists. But then hopes were dashed when further discussions on Home Rule were postponed until the Great War in Europe was over. No decision had been taken over the fate of the six north-east counties, and Winston Churchill, the Secretary of State for the Colonies, suggested partition.

The mention of the loss of the six counties was too much even for the usually moderate Arthur Griffith, whose articles in his newspaper declared that: 'Any Irish leader who would connive at Home Rule which yields even a square inch of the soil of Ireland would deserve a traitor's fate.'

It was a catalyst for revolution which the extremist nationalists and even those in Sinn Féin needed, a secret Supreme Council of Sinn Féin being formed which resolved to turn England's involvement in the war into Ireland's opportunity.

In the north, thoughts of partition had aroused other loyalties and an Ulster Volunteer Force, who had already formed their own provisional government, was being raised from among the Orangemen. Yeats, among others, was unconcerned, believing it should be ignored and that, as the Nationalists had agreed on a united Ireland, there was no reason or possibility of the north being allowed to opt out.

Others, however, refused to share his optimism, there being little chance that the British Army in Ireland would fire on the northern unionist Protestants who had already brought in ammunition from Germany, prepared for any efforts by the nationalists to take the six counties by force.

This was implausible as the south had only Connolly's Citizens Army and their makeshift weapons. But then another force was formed, the Irish National Volunteers with the Sinn Féin Volunteers, who chose as their emblem the letters FF for Fianna Fáil, the legendary warrior band. They would fight, if need be, against the Ulster Volunteers, for an Irish Republic independent of Britain.

Founding members included a leading member of the Gaelic League, Professor Eoin MacNeill, who was appointed president and who wanted to form a force strong enough to claim Home Rule after the war. He recognised though that only if there was a real chance of military success would physical force be justified. Other members included Michael O'Rahilly, a wealthy early member of Sinn Féin, along with Patrick Pearse and Eamon de Valera, another young university professor. Pearse was a great orator, his fanaticism inflammatory, proclaiming that 'the Volunteers may make mistakes in the beginning and we may shoot the wrong people, but bloodshed is a calming and satisfying thing. There are things more horrible than bloodshed; slavery is one of them.'

Maud Gonne was a fervent supporter of the Volunteers, strong in her conviction that the British Empire, as it existed, would soon disappear. Together with the Daughters of Erin she formed the women's organisation of the Volunteers, the Irish Women's Council, Cumann na mBan, for which Maud and Kathleen, the wife of Tom Clarke, another member, had designed a flag, a tricolour of orange, white and green which was to become the flag of Ireland in coming times.

The new force would not go unarmed. Roger Casement, a supporter of the Nationalist cause, and Clan na Gael in America, together with Anglo-Irish supporters were already raising money for arms, Casement's friend, Erskine Childers, even then in Germany buying weapons.

The new Volunteers were, however, without the approval of the Irish political leaders. John Redmond, the leader of the Irish Parliamentary Party, had promised that British troops for the war in Europe could be raised in Ireland, seeing joint action against Germany as a uniting force for all Irishmen and pledging an Irish Volunteer Force to support the war. He claimed, justifiably, that most Irishmen supported England and that thousands of young Irishmen had already enlisted, a larger proportion than from any other part of Britain.

Redmond had encouraged them, telling them it would be a disgrace if young Ireland remained at home to defend its shores from an invasion and that they should prove on the field of battle the courage that had distinguished the Irish race through all its history. But there were other reasons: enlistment gave the families of the soldiers some relief from poverty, the recruits getting a separation allowance for their wives.

Over 100,000 of his volunteers, already recruited into the British Army, were serving in a number of Irish regiments: the Irish Guards, the Leinster Regiment, the Royal Irish Fusiliers and the Royal Irish Rifles. By the end of the first year of the war, seventeen Irish volunteers had been awarded the Victoria Cross, the highest award for valour.

SLOWLY, LIKE a mirage, the *Asgard*, a sleek white motor yacht, emerged from the heat haze over Dublin Bay in the midsummer of 1914, moving silently inshore, the boat's owner, Erskine Childers, at the helm, eyes searching for the reception party at Howth. Mooring ropes were thrown, the boat tied to the quay and the cargo quickly unloaded, 1,500 single-shot Mauser rifles with thousands of rounds of ammunition in wooden cases and oilskin-wrapped packages.

James Connolly looked around uneasily. It was not against the law to import arms and news of the cargo's imminent arrival had been hard to conceal, a large crowd of the Volunteers and the Citizens Army waiting to help unload and lay claims to their own right to arms. Amongst these was Michael O'Rahilly, who loaded his large, expensive motor car with cases of guns and ammunition, others passed from hand to hand to be loaded onto carts, into taxis or even carried over shoulders for dispersal through the city.

Arthur Griffith and Patrick Pearse stood beside Connolly, who voiced his concern at the attention they were attracting, gazing intently along the quay. 'I don't like this at all, Arthur. We'll have the police and soldiers here soon.'

Griffith stiffened as he stared beyond the crowd. 'Too late, my friend. Dublin Castle is already with us!'

They stared in dismay at the squad of soldiers and police who had moved slowly forward to stand, uncertain of their role, at the entrance to the quay. Connolly moved quickly in an attempt to quieten the murmurs of apprehension and anger among the Volunteers, his advice ignored as, within minutes of their arrival the troops were mocked by the crowd which now moved slowly towards the uniformed presence, the troops standing their ground as the police fell back and then, outnumbered, quietly slipped away.

The Citizens Army and the Volunteers surrounded the loaded wagons and cars as they moved from the quay. The soldiers moved forward and walked in front of them. Some of the nationalists slipped away over the fields to their homes, others marching in formation towards Dublin, rifles over their shoulders, the troops jeered at by a hostile crowd, stones and missiles raining down on them.

Then tragedy. There was a shouted command, the troops stopping and lining up against the newly-armed nationalists, an officer stepping forward, his hand held high for silence. And then the first shots in the war for independence were heard as the signal was misunderstood, and a nervous soldier opened fire.

There were shouts, cries of alarm, followed by a sudden hush as Connolly's worst fears were realised. The nationalists pushed forward menacingly only to scatter in disarray as they were met by a volley of shots from the retreating soldiers who quickly dispersed as the volunteers made use of their newly-acquired arms. Then silence but for the cries and moans of wounded men.

Three of their company lay dead, another 38 wounded, some of the wagons which had carried the weapons now requisitioned to transport the wounded to hospital, the dead to their families.

'It's the start, Arthur.' Pearse turned to Griffith. 'Now we are armed. There will be no end until Ireland is free.'

IN SEPTEMBER of that year Yeats travelled to France to again visit Maud at Coleville, changes obvious as soon as the taxi dropped him at the front of the house. The orchard and lawns had been given over to growing potatoes and other vegetables for the war effort.

Maud had been working with the wounded in France, her letters to him full of outrage and despair at what was happening at the battle front. Now he was able to see for himself how much it had taken out of her. He held her briefly when she ran down the steps to meet him, looking at her sympathetically. 'Is it that bad, Maud?'

She nodded. 'It's so awful, Willie. And no escaping it. After the Zeppelin raids the little French houses looked like the ones I saw in the west after the English had used battering rams and fire. We were in Argeles, in the Pyrenees, well behind the front line. We had a small house where I nursed some of the poor, wounded young men brought by train from the front, although many of them died on the journey.' There was terrible sadness in her voice. 'We made them well just so they could return to the slaughter.' She grasped his arm. 'You have no idea what it is like; the maiming and killing ...'

He held her arm, muttering his sympathy as he walked with her along the beach. 'And the children?'

She smiled. 'They were wonderful. A great help. Isoeult and I have been given the rank of lieutenant and Sean is a messenger boy. We can travel with the army and nurse as required.'

Yeats raised old doubts. 'Shouldn't Ireland be helping more?'

She shook her head vehemently. 'No, Willie. No. Ireland will have nothing to gain and should avoid this war. It is sheer brutality, all the young French intellectuals killed in the trenches. Believe me, it's not the war of nationalist

Ireland, although thousands of Irish soldiers have been killed already.' She paused, huge eyes suddenly tearful. 'All those young men dying needlessly. It's such madness, race suicide for all the countries involved; only the weaklings will be left to carry on. Even the leaders hardly seem to know what they have entered into and certainly the people don't.'

She looked terribly sad. 'Kathleen's son has been killed. He was only 21. And yesterday I learned that Lucien Millevoye's son has been killed.'

She could no longer hold back the tears as Yeats comforted her, his arm around her, holding her to him. She rested her head wearily against his shoulder. 'Where will it end? The only thing worth working for now is peace.'

He buried his head in her hair, consoling her. His own news was almost as sad. 'Robert Gregory has joined up. Augusta and I worry about him.'

Maud shook her head in sorrow. 'I'm sorry for that. War seemed so remote from his life. Augusta must be suffering.'

There was a frown on his face. 'Sometimes I feel I should support the war effort. Even write a war poem. All the newspapers and even poetry magazines are full of them. Kipling and Housman and others.' His frown deepened. 'But I have little feeling for writing about this war.'

He shook his head woefully. 'The Irish party and the government offered me a knighthood if I helped get Irishmen to enlist. Can you see it now? Sir William Yeats.' He smiled sadly at her. 'And you could be Lady Yeats, Maud. It has a ring to it.'

She pulled away, staring at him anxiously. He smiled at her. 'Don't worry. I refused it. I may have my doubts about enlistment but I believe in Irish independence and I had no choice but to turn it down. You must not say anything though, the nationalists would become too wary of me. I don't want anyone to say I left their cause for a piece of ribbon.' He shrugged. 'Even though I was told it would lead to a peerage.'

'An English Lord, Willie? Surely not?' There was no humour in her smile.

19

THEY WERE intellectuals and would-be martyrs, educated and indoctrinated by the nationalist Irish Christian Brothers. Idealists, a tiny, inconsequential minority in the country determined that armed rebellion would lead to an independent Irish republic – a return of the four green fields to its own people.

On 20 January 1916, the inner core of the military council of the IRB met in their inconspicuous headquarters. The hard-liners, the old Fenians and the new, eager, idealistic younger men, were planning rebellion.

The shop front in Parnell Street was narrow, the windows sparsely furnished with cartons of cigarettes, the shop deserted whilst the small back room was filled with people.

Around a table sat the revolutionaries. Their leader, Patrick Pearse, the son of an English father and born in Dublin, saw himself as the founder of a new Ireland. A barrister by profession, he had given up his calling to advance his own educational ideas, opening a school, St Enda's, in an old mansion in the hills above Dublin, the school motto being the old Celtic slogan: 'I care not if I live but a day and a night, so long as my deeds live after me.'

At the school Pearse was a quiet, gentle and sensitive

man, a poet and a teacher dedicated to his work, interested only in instilling the values of Irish society and insisting that Irish be taught alongside English at the school. James Joyce was one of his early students of Irish.

Pearse was a great speaker, sharing with his friend Willie Yeats a love for the heroic fables of Ireland while at the same time deploring Yeats' rejection of Christianity. And, although a friend, Yeats in turn rejected Pearse's philosophy that a new country would only rise again through a baptism of blood. Yeats openly disagreed with the sentiments Pearse espoused in the obituary at the funeral of an old Fenian friend, Jeremiah O'Donovan Rossa:

Life springs from death and from the graves of patriotic men and women spring living nations ... the defenders of this realm think they have pacified Ireland ... but, the fools, the fools, the fools! They have left us our Fenian dead and while Ireland holds their graves, Ireland unfree shall never be at peace.

To Pearse's left at the meeting sat Tom MacDonagh. Once a student for the priesthood, he was now an assistant professor of literature at University College Dublin and a poet, who had helped Pearse found St Enda's. MacDonagh was a commandant in the Irish Volunteers and had only recently been co-opted onto the military council

Further down the table sat the elderly Fenian, Tom Clark, the owner of the small tobacconists and the link between the IRB and Clan na Gael in America, a man who had spent many years in prison for his part in a bombing campaign in mainland Britain. Beside him sat James MacDermott and James Connolly was further along, not strictly a council member but another co-opted for the occasion.

Facing Pearse was Constance Markievicz, whose clipped Anglo-Irish drawl and melodramatic gestures still made some of the others uneasy. Unlike the simple clothes of most attendees, she was elegantly attired, on this occasion wearing a crocheted shawl over a long-sleeved white blouse, worn with a thick choker.

Only two of the inner core were missing. Ill with consumption, Joseph Mary Plunkett was another poet and idealist, and the son of a papal count. The other noticeable absentee was John MacBride. He was one of the leading activists in the Irish Neutrality League, working to stop British recruitment efforts, and this position resulted in his appointment to the Supreme Inner Council of the IRB.

MacBride was not told of the meeting. At one time his advice and comments had been constantly sought. Now, when an uprising was planned, MacBride was not party to it. He was the only member of the inner council with any experience of soldiering, one whose advice and comments would have dampened their belief that the revolution could succeed, that the people of Ireland would rise up and support them. He would have scorned their martyrdom and the zealots had no wish to hear his cautionary words. There were other reasons for his absence. His over fondness for drink was well known and since he was under constant surveillance by the G men, MacBride could not be allowed to draw attention to their meetings.

The arguments, the passionate, emotional and angry appeals for rebellion lasted three days. When agreement was reached Pearse gazed around at his friends before lowering his eyes and quietly reciting from his poem, 'the Fool'.

O wise men riddle me this: what if the dream comes true?
What if the dream comes true? And if millions unborn shall
  dwell
In the house that I shaped in my heart,
The noble house of my thought?

When he had finished there were several whispered amens before a long silence.The date for rebellion was set for 24 April, Easter Monday.

Unaware of that meeting and its outcome, John MacBride felt the atmosphere of unease, of strange expectancy which seemed to hang over the city before Easter. There was conjecture about an uprising, in public houses and churches, in journalists' meeting places and even among the work mates of those suspected of being involved.

MacBride's job as Water Bailiff for Dublin City Corporation paid well and on 21 April, Good Friday, after checking and auditing the harbour fees collected that week, he closed and locked the door of his office on the quays. That evening, while out with friends, more rumours were fed to him and, despite the fact that the previous night both Pearse and Plunkett had assured him no rebellion was planned, his belief that something was about to happen was so strong that the following day he called to see his old friend Eoin MacNeill. MacBride, an early member of MacNeill's Gaelic League, sought assurances. 'There's something afoot, Eoin. What is it?'

MacNeill held his hands wide. 'John, I swear I don't know. I even spoke to Pearse earlier this week and he told me nothing is happening.'

MacBride looked grim. 'You know about the latest

arms' shipment?' He shook his head in disgust, continuing without waiting for an answer. 'Casement was arrested in Kerry when he landed from a German submarine. His ship, the *Aud*, was seized by the British navy, and is at the bottom of Queenstown Harbour.'

'I know ... dear God, John. If they really are planning anything, without those arms it would be suicide.' He shook his head in consternation. 'When I was told the government were about to raid the Volunteers to disarm them I agreed to go along with rebellion; I told Pearse the Volunteers would help.' His expression was grim. 'But then, when I heard this morning that the arms had been captured, I arranged for a notice to be put in the Sunday papers, cancelling all orders. I said there was to be no parading, no manoeuvres or any other movements. But, just in case, I have passed the word for all the Volunteers to prepare for their own defence if anything should happen. You can be sure the British will come down on any uprising without mercy.' His frustration was evident. 'I'm trying to save their lives but I know many will disobey and fight. Now I'll have to do all I can, short of informing, to stop any uprising.' He sighed. 'It's hard to believe the military council will order rebellion in the face of certain defeat. It's just more of their romantic nonsense; shedding blood is a cleansing and sanctifying thing. Surely nothing will happen ...?'

But rumours continued to spread that arms were being landed and that German soldiers and the International Irish Brigade were coming to help. The news was out that Casement's boat had been taken, Casement himself arrested and in gaol. But it was too late and the rebels' decision could not be changed.

Early on Easter Monday MacBride visited John

MacDonagh in another attempt to find out what was happening. MacBride's heart fell as he saw his old friend, a married man with two children, armed and in uniform. He was in charge of number 2 Battalion of the Irish Volunteers, detailed to take a party of over 100 men to occupy one of the strategic positions in the city. MacNeill's warning had been ignored. MacBride swore loudly. 'But you have no hope. There's no strategy to it. There are too few of you.'

MacDonagh shrugged, staring at him questioningly. 'Are you with us?' He answered his own question. 'You have the experience, John. We could do with your help.'

MacBride sighed despairingly. 'It's so bloody stupid. I've faced death often enough with the Irish Brigade but, believe me, never with such certainty.' He took his friend by the shoulder. 'If we don't win or die in battle then the British will surely do for us.' He stared resolutely at MacDonagh. 'You do know that?'

MacDonagh merely nodded. MacBride closed his eyes and breathed deeply before shaking his head resignedly. 'Where do we go?'

'Pearse wants me to take charge at the Jacobs biscuit factory. Men are already on the way there.'

MacBride left without further comment, rejoining MacDonagh after collecting his hidden weapons and changing into the uniform last worn with the Irish Brigade in the Transvaal.

A short time later, on an unusually warm spring day at noon, MacDonagh and MacBride joined the nationalist officers and troops of the Citizens Army and the Irish Volunteers, a tiny force of only 1,600 men who had assembled at the Liberty Hall and who, together that day, created the new Irish Republican Army. Rebellion was to begin.

20

PATRICK PEARSE, a single man, devoted to his mother and sisters, wearing the full uniform of the IRB, over that a khaki greatcoat and armed with sword and pistol, left his home even as one of his sisters hung onto his arm, begging him not to go. His intention, to sacrifice himself for Ireland, was to her, as to others, just futile martyrdom.

He gently prised her fingers away, setting off on his bicycle to Liberty Hall, there to take his place on the steps under a huge banner prepared by the Daughters of Erin which proclaimed 'We serve neither King nor Kaiser'.

Next to Pearse stood James Connolly and other commandants of the rebels, including a tall, pale-faced young bank clerk, Michael Collins, a member of the IRB, who had returned from working in London to join the fight for freedom. Behind Collins stood the tall, austere and bespectacled Eamon de Valera.

Some of those present wore full uniform, others only battle dress tops, many carrying old rusty bayonets and swords, the commandants marked by the breeches they wore and the bandoleers across their chests which bulged with ammunition. Connolly stared at the makeshift army, shaking his head, a grim smile on his lips as he muttered under his breath, 'We're all going to be slaughtered'.

'Is there no real chance of success? None at at all?' One of the Volunteers standing nearby had heard him.

Connolly clapped him on the back and shook his head. 'None whatever.' The questioner nodded dumbly, offering a quiet prayer: 'Jesus, Mary and Joseph, help us.'

There was another arrival before the ragged army marched off, the same car which the O'Rahilly had driven from the quay-side at Howth loaded with weapons from the *Asgard*. Now it was driven by O'Rahilly's American-born wife, Nancy. They had travelled overnight from Kerry to reach Dublin in time for the uprising. The O'Rahilly climbed out and grinned at Pearse. 'I helped to wind the clock; now I want to hear it strike.' He stood beside the car with his wife handing out the single-shot rifles; weapons which would be no match for the machine guns of the British army.

Soon they were ready to leave, lorries loaded with provisions following behind as they marched through the city to take up their positions, 24 public buildings, bridges and factories, some without any obvious strategic importance but seen as symbolic.

MacBride and MacDonagh followed as Pearse led his contingent to take the Post Office in O'Connell Street, ignoring puzzled Dubliners as they marched to martyrdom, some of the small army singing rebel songs to keep their spirits up. It was not an unusual sight, as they had been parading for months past.

Rebel songs rang out bravely, as others chanted, in time to their steps, lines from *Cathleen ní Houlihan*, the play which had ignited the torch. Trams gave way to them as their hobnailed boots rang on the cobbled street. This was part of a wonderful play with John MacBride now an actor in it.

And beside them on their day of glory went the women of Inghinidhe na hÉireann, marching to serve as nurses, load rifles and, if necessary, shoot if the time came. Soon there were more onlookers than rebels.

The General Post Office, in O'Connell Street, was a building of symbolic importance only, in the centre of the main shopping area and easily surrounded. They stopped when Pearse's contingent of 150 men reached it. There was a sudden order followed by a ragged dash inside, some with revolvers and swords raised over their heads.

For Pearse, martyrdom was assured as he marched into the building, beside him Clarke and Connolly and the ailing Joseph Plunkett, who had left his hospital bed that morning only hours after an operation. Pale and emaciated, blood seeping from bandages which covered his throat, he strode forward, sword in one hand, a revolver in the other, a defiant hero.

A few shots in the air and the postal workers fled the building as flags were raised, one with the harp on a green background, and the words 'Irish Republic', with the other the new tricolour of orange, white and green.

MacBride and MacDonagh watched as Pearse stood on the steps and declared himself the President of the Provisional Government and Commander-in-Chief of the Army of the Republic. Shouting to be heard above the noise of the traffic and listened to by a slowly gathering, curious and largely apathetic crowd, he read a declaration of independence:

We hereby proclaim the Irish Republic as a sovereign

independent state and we pledge our lives and the lives of our comrades-in-arms to the cause of its freedom ... In the name of God and of the dead generations from which Ireland receives her ancient station of nationhood ... Ireland, through us, summons her children to her flag and strikes for freedom ...

His final words were lost to the jeers and laughter of the crowd as he continued, claiming that gallant allies in Europe were supporting Ireland, many in the crowd shouting back derisively, aware that the flower of Ireland's manhood had been fighting those allies for almost two years.

MacDonagh spoke to MacBride, almost apologetically, at his friend's ignorance of what had been planned. 'We had the declaration prepared for a long time. Tom Clark was the first signatory, I was one, Pearse, Plunkett and Connolly were others.'

'You know what it means?' MacBride, unaware until now of the declaration, looked terribly sad. 'Pearse has signed his own death warrant. And possibly that of all of us.'

As Pearse and the other rebels disappeared inside the Post Office, MacBride and MacDonagh strolled casually to the Jacobs Biscuit Factory behind Dublin Castle which was to be their stronghold.

By now the other revolutionaries, members of Sinn Féin, with detachments of the Irish Volunteer Force and the Citizens Army, had seized other positions and barricaded streets. Eamon de Valera's squad had taken Boland's Flour Mills, their strategy being to guard the road from Kingston Harbour from which the British reinforcements would come.

Countess Markievicz, a lieutenant in the force, wearing a wide-brimmed, feathered hat perched incongruously on her head and waving a pistol, had led her squad to establish a position on St Stephen's Green, watched by a mocking crowd. Another group had taken over the Irish School of Wireless at the corner of Lower Abbey Street and Lower O'Connell Street, from where they would alert the world to the start of the new republic.

The Four Courts had been occupied and another group had attempted to blow up the magazine in Phoenix Park, a seventeen-year-old boy becoming one of the the first casualties of the rebellion, shot dead as he ran to give the alarm. Another early casualty was an unarmed policeman at Dublin Castle, shot as the rebels tried to force their way in.

Any sympathy the civilian population may have had for the rebels rapidly ebbed away when news spread that, on St Stephen's Green, a civilian had been shot as he tried to retrieve his cart which had been taken as a barricade. Now the mood of the crowd turned rapidly to hate.

The occupation of the biscuit factory was unopposed, the only opposition coming from departing workers saying that even in a republic people had to eat.

MacBride quickly organised the ragged army, heavy bags of flour and boxes of biscuits used to block the windows, anything else which could be moved set up as barricades behind the doors, with small spaces left for weapons to fire through, and those behind the weapons strong in their belief that they were invincible, their cause just, and that if they were to meet their end it would be quick and painless.

The Cumann na mBan women, some in their Daughters of Erin uniform, some wearing Red Cross and nurse's uniforms, busied themselves preparing meals, the store of biscuits in the factory supplementing the tins of stew, bread, biscuits and potatoes, stockpiled for a long siege, which had been unloaded from the accompanying wagons.

It was not until dawn next day that the first armoured cars came, the roads facing the factory lined with British troops, as the action to remove the rebels started, at first no more than a sporadic exchange of gunfire until on the third day it changed. More troops came, soldiers from the barracks throughout the city, others shipped from Liverpool and Aldershot, among them Irishmen of the 3rd Royal Irish Rifles and the 10th. Royal Dublin Fusiliers, men who now moved against their countrymen and the self-styled republic.

There was fear and apprehension, the tension inside at times almost unbearable, the smokers quickly using up the supplies of cigarettes which had been provided for them. MacDonagh and MacBride moved among the men, making morale-boosting speeches as the wounding and killing started, the walls of the factory pitted with small arm's fire, the armoured cars sending regular spats of machine gun bullets towards the factory through the thin slits in their turrets. Soon the walls became holed and crumbling from shell and mortar fire, the men inside still resolute at their posts. It had become a war of attrition which only one side could win.

MacBride, an experienced marksman and already showing himself to be an effective sniper, stared out from a barricaded window on the first floor of the building, ducking as an artillery shell exploded nearby. There were screams of pain as the bombardment increased, bursting artillery shells raising choking clouds of masonry dust.

By now the army stranglehold was tight around the

building. Encircling troops in armoured cars, field guns beside them, made it difficult for reinforcements to reach the defenders, if reinforcements had been available. After four days the spectre of impending defeat was facing MacBride and MacDonagh: a number of their men were dead, many more wounded, parts of the building smoking, small fires catching hold. The army had cut off the water supply and women were trying to douse the flames with blankets and bucketfuls of flour and milk, others struggling to move the dying and wounded, setting up a makeshift hospital on the ground floor. Food was running out and the runners, young boys and members of the Daughters of Erin, the only link to what was happening in the rest of the city, were now unable to get in or out.

The brave, foolhardy men who had sung their rebel songs were now reduced to silent incomprehension as the heavy guns gradually and systematically pounded the building, reducing parts of it to rubble. At night the moans of the dying and wounded were almost as frightening as the sounds of the bombardment by day.

It was not planned to be like this. It was to be a defiant stand which the people would cheer, the country rising in support to see the British troops marching to the boats back to England. MacDonagh stared out from behind the sacks of flour which guarded a blown-out window, staring at the troops waiting patiently behind their tanks. 'Gobshites! Fucking gobshites. They know they only have to wait.'

He slumped to the floor, his back to the wall, lighting two cigarettes and passing one to MacBride. 'The news is bad, John. The last runner to get in says that the people have refused to sympathise with us. They just stand and watch. And now even the churches are against us.' His bewilderment showed. 'Why don't they support us? For their country? With the people behind us we could win.'

If the people were not with them it was over. MacBride spoke his thoughts aloud. 'With what is happening to the city, the killing of innocent civilians, it's just too much for them to accept. We can't win, Tom, but we must fight on. Even if only as an example to those who will follow us.' He sat back, his eyes closed, his face turned ruefully towards the roof of the building. MacBride's military training had helped them hold out, organising the men into shifts, ensuring those not watching at the windows were given the chance to get some sleep, though, with fear, sleep was almost impossible.

The first elation of rebellion had long evaporated and, in the makeshift hospital, a priest was hearing confessions, 'Jesus, Mary and Joseph, pray for us; Jesus, Mary and Joseph, hear our prayers,' a solemn accompaniment to the sound of gunfire and the rumble of heavy artillery.

John MacBride had his own prayer, to the wife he thought had loved him as he loved her. 'Maud, why did you forsake me? Why aren't you here? To see the hero in me? Because I have been a hero to Ireland.'

By now the British artillery had devastated the centre of Dublin, shelling from a royal navy gunboat on the Liffey, reducing much of the city near the Post Office to rubble, parts of O'Connell Street and Eden Quay in ruins.

For six days the city was at a standstill. The rebels held the British army at bay, the barricades in the streets unmanned as the rebels took to the buildings, many of which were on fire, even the most fervent among them knowing it was hopeless, the rebellion collapsing as the army slowly recaptured the outposts. The brave band in the middle of St Stephen's Green were the first to fall to the might of armoured cars and massed troops, Constance Markievicz kissing her revolver symbolically before surrendering.

Six days after they had first taken the factory news reached them. Pearse had kept the British army at bay but now the Post Office had been taken, the machine guns and eighteen pounders from the river had been too much, soldiers and marksmen on the roofs of surrounding building, picking off any who raised their head. But they had not given up easily: the survivors had tried to flee and set up headquarters elsewhere, Michael O'Rahilly, among others, shot down by machine gun fire in Moore Street, Connolly wounded, shot in the left ankle.

Pearse had made the decision: the myth could only survive if he was to die a martyr. His death, and that of the others, would redeem his people. His would be a Christ-like passion. He surrendered his sword to the British at 3.30 on Saturday 29 April, on the steps of the Post Office.

MacDonagh and MacBride stared at each other, no words necessary. Theirs was the only stronghold left but now it was over. The word to surrender had been passed to them by a nurse who had helped in the Post Office. MacBride watched as she appeared, her escort, a British officer, standing back when she was near enough to be heard. There was a sudden strange silence as she passed the order from Pearse: surrender and pray!

There could be no escape. And now their fight was not for Ireland but to hold a half-demolished building of little significance.

'It's over, John. Especially if it saves lives. We must do what Pearse says.' He clasped his friend's shoulder. 'But there will be no mercy.' He laughed wryly. 'At last they will have a reason to get me.' He stared out of the window to where the British troops stood in rows behind their armoured vehicles, waiting, a strange silence hanging over the building. 'There is no other way. If we surrender we can make our case and die, if needs be, as martyrs. If we fight on we will die anyway, in the rubble. And that will be no martyr's death.'

'Then surrender it is ...' MacDonagh threw his cigarette away and embraced MacBride. 'I'm proud to have fought beside you, John. Perhaps we have given others hope for freedom in the future. Let us pray that there will be no turning back by those who come after us.'

MacBride's thoughts turned again to Maud, his love for her and his failing. Gibraltar had been hopeless, ill-conceived, carried along on a dream of nationalist fervour. As was this doomed uprising. But perhaps now she would see him as other Irishmen saw him. If necessary, his would be a brave and heroic end.

Quickly the word was passed among the remaining defenders, the women leaving the building first, allowed to pass through the cordon of soldiers, followed a minute later by the dead and wounded on makeshift stretchers and then the remaining rebels, MacDonagh and MacBride in the lead, a large white handkerchief fixed to the barrel of a rifle held in front of them as they slowly stumbled into custody before being marched away, four abreast, through streets crowded with angry Dubliners.

The general public were against them, particularly the women whose men even then were fighting alongside British troops in the war in Europe, at Verdun, Ypres and the Somme, dying alongside British comrades. Now these same women were bitter at the destruction of their city: the same Dublin housewives who had made tea for the soldiers spat at the rebels, cursed them as they were marched past, pelting them with eggs and tomatoes, rotten fruit and meat, even broken paving stones, cobbles and rubble from ruined buildings.

When they reached the Post Office all the prisoners were assembled. MacDonagh, MacBride and the other leaders, disillusioned and bitter at the insults thrown at them by their countrymen and women, were identified by the government G men and pulled from the crowd, Connolly lying wounded on the ground, dragged roughly to the front.

At the end of the uprising, 64 of the rebels were dead, some of them still lying, covered with rubble in the obscurity of shell-pocked buildings. With them, 134 police and soldiers and 220 civilians had died, many others wounded.

21

THE LEADERS knew, when the rebellion was crushed, that the cruel terror of revenge and execution would soon follow. There was to be no mercy, their fate predetermined.

The Crown Prosecutor and the British Commander-in-Chief were merciless, convinced that the uprising had been German-supported, the court martials over quickly, the defending officer British, the sentences British.

Now their final act for Ireland was to die as bravely as they had fought; their's to be a sad, quiet death, dignified only by their bravery. Before the end they were allowed to write last letters to their families, sad, lonely letters, the poets among them completing their final lines before their end came.

Patrick Pearse's letter to his family was that of an idealist, of a willing martyr:

> This is the death I should have asked for if God had given me the choice of all deaths; to die a soldier's death for Ireland and for freedom.

His final poem, 'The Wayfarer', written on the eve of his execution, was beautiful and heart rending.

The beauty of the world hath made me sad,
This beauty that will pass;
... Things young and happy,
And then my heart hath told me:
These will pass,
Will pass and change, will die and be no more.
Things bright and green, things young and happy;
And I have gone upon my way
Sorrowful.

Four monks from the Capuchin Friary in Dublin's Church Street were allowed to attend the last hours of the condemned men, giving them absolution, communion and the last rites, praying with them to the end.

It was bitterly cold at 3.30am on 3 May, just before dawn broke, no drummers drumming, just an eerie quiet as Patrick Pearse, Commander-in-Chief of the Army of the Republic was the first, one of the priests beside him as he was led out into the yard at Kilmainham Gaol, facing the six men who knelt and six who stood behind.

Pearse stood alone, a sad poet, oblivious of the cold, unaware of the half light, waiting for the order which was hardly audible. The governor of the prison watched as the order was given by Captain William Clewes-Porter, the English Officer-of-the-Day.

The would-be President of the new Republic of Ireland died instantly.

Blindfolded, hands strapped behind their backs, a small piece of white paper pinned over their hearts and still wearing the clothes they had worn during their short-lived battle for freedom, one at a time they were led before the firing squad.

It was a painless, easy change from life to death as two more died that morning, one of them James MacDonagh, the other Tom Clark.

Four more met their end the following day, among them William Pearse, the younger brother of Patrick Pearse, guilty only of following in his brother's footsteps and acting as a messenger boy.

There was a solitary, flickering candle in the cold damp of the prison chapel. A sad, old monk and an armed guard: there were few to witness the wedding of Joseph Mary Plunkett. In an unlikely act of compassion he had been allowed to marry his fiancée, Grace Gifford. But that was the end of compassion. Immediately after the priest had pronounced them man and wife and they had exchanged sad vows, ''till death do us part', they were allowed a brief embrace before he was led to his execution, a short lifetime for his wife, who clung desperately to him before she was pulled away in helpless, unredeemed despair. Silence followed, like an eternity, and then a sudden volley of shots were heard before Grace Gifford collapsed into the arms of the old priest.

Like Michael Gillane, her husband had sacrificed his bride and chosen death for Cathleen ní Houlihan and her four green fields.

John MacBride, who had not been part of the plan for rebellion, was composed and quiet when, on the third day, his time came, only a few words to say to Father Augustine, the monk who attended him. 'I'm sorry for the surrender Father. There was little more we could do.' They prayed together before he emptied his pockets of all he had, asking the priest to use any money for the poor of Dublin, handing him his rosary to be given to his mother.

After hearing MacBride's confession and giving him communion, the priest took his hand in his own as he comforted him, assuring him he would be with him to the end.

'I need no comforting, Father.' MacBride's smile was rueful rather than bitter. He had chosen his fate. He turned to face the soldier who prepared to strap his arms behind his back. 'I don't need that.' He pulled away. 'You have my word I will remain perfectly still.' His voice was quiet and composed.

The young soldier was taken aback, confused, an older, more senior man stepping forward, his voice firm but polite. 'I am sorry. They are orders.'

MacBride shrugged, repeating the request as the young soldier raised a blindfold. Again a refusal. A mild smile played on MacBride's lips as he turned to the priest. 'You know, Father, I have often looked down their guns before. I have no fear now.'

He was led into the execution yard, a soldier at one side, the priest on the other. He felt the target being pinned over his heart and responded to the final prayers recited with him, before the priest was taken by the arm and led aside to stand next to the prison governor and doctor.

John MacBride's last thoughts were of Ireland, of Maud Gonne and of his son. He heard a quiet command and pulled himself erect. And then there was nothing. It was the heroic end he had wanted to show her.

On 8 May four more were shot, among them Sean Houston, a young rebel whose last letter to his sister, a teacher and nun, was of his thoughts for Ireland: '... teach the children the history of their own land and that the cause of Cathleen ní Houlihan never dies.'

On the final bloody day of executions James Connolly

was one of the last two to face the firing squad. The priests had begged that Connolly be allowed to live, arguing to the British Commander-in-Chief that the execution of a wounded man, his ankle fractured by a bullet and suffering from gangrene, was an outrage, an act against humanity.

Their pleas and prayers were to no avail. James Connolly was carried out to his death on a stretcher before being strapped to a chair, meeting his fate without a murmur.

Inquests were held immediately each batch of men had been shot. They were perfunctory, the witnesses signing that the executions had been carried out humanely and with dignity, the medical report on James Connolly revealing that only nine of the bullets had reached their target. The shooting of a wounded man, strapped to a chair, had not been easy for some.

There would be no shrines to martyrdom, no burial in consecrated ground. Immediately after the inquests theirs was a grave inside the prison walls, their shroud a cloak of quicklime.

Eamon de Valera, the young physics teacher and almost reluctant but courageous commander at Boland's Mills, was the next rebel condemned to face the firing squad. He was a fortunate one. On the evening before the sentence was to be carried out there was a reprieve, his sentence commuted to life imprisonment, his American citizenship a strong reason for the sentence being reduced.

The other leaders, Constance Markievicz among them, also had their death sentences commuted to penal servitude for life, the 65-year-old Count Joseph Plunkett sentenced to ten years, they and the prisoners marched to the cattle boats for the journey to prison in England. Among them was Michael Collins who had fought at the Post Office.

In Ireland the reprisals continued, widespread house searches bringing a change in public mood, outrage at the victimisation of innocent people and the arrest of many nationalists who had nothing to do with the uprising. But those who 'stabbed the Empire in the back in war time' were seen as traitors. There were 400 men gaoled, among them Ioein MacNeill, who had done all he could to prevent the uprising and knew no details of it but was now sentenced to life imprisonment in Dartmoor, hundreds more sent to detention camps in Britain.

But opinions were changing in Ireland and England, the contempt for the rebels changing to sympathy. The uprising had little support but the executions brought widespread condemnation, even revulsion, and in America a surge of anger swept through Irish Americans.

The British government had made a tragic mistake. If gaoled the leaders would have soon been forgotten but the executions had created martyrs, Bernard Shaw being one among many who were outspoken in their criticism of the British government: '... the men who were shot in cold blood after their capture or surrender, were prisoners of war. An Irishman resorting to arms to achieve independence is doing only what an Englishman would do if invaded by the Germans ... It was intensely incorrect to slaughter them ... The military authorities of the British Government must have known that they were canonising their prisoners.'

The martyrs had cast more stepping stones towards freedom, and Home Rule would not now be enough. Only a republic, if necessary to be achieved by bloodshed, would suffice.

WILLIE YEATS was in England when the news reached him. Stunned at the brutality and speed of the executions, deeply moved by the courage of the executed men, he returned immediately to Dublin. He walked slowly past the Post Office, gazing at the rubble which littered the ground under the six great columns, staring up at the empty windows, above them the flagpoles from which the new tricolour had so briefly and bravely flown. He searched for the ghosts of heroes as he stared into the ruined, scorched depths of the building, to see for himself the results of the emotions which drove Pearse to this place, to the ignominy of surrender and the ultimate price.

He walked blindly on, along Henry Street and into Moore Street, staring at a doorway. The story was already one of legend. When the garrison had tried to make a break for it, Michael O'Rahilly had led the charge up Moore Street. One of the first to be gunned down, he had slumped into the doorway while others were caught in a hail of bullets as they fled into the nearby warren of streets, others gunned down as they tried to scale the barricades they themselves had erected only days earlier.

Across the wooden panelling of the door an inscription was written in blood. The O'Rahilly had died alone. Hurting. In pain. And yet he had immortalised himself, poetry in his own blood, in letters which tailed away at the end.

Here died The O'Rahilly. RIP ...

Slowly, his melancholy deepening, Yeats continued his painful pilgrimage, past the flour mills and biscuit factory, finishing his journey at St Stephen's Green, the only place which showed little evidence of the rebellion. He struggled to express his emotions, and though there was a glimmer of words, brave words, names and praise, the form was still to come.

THEY WERE unusually quiet at first, Yeats standing by the window of Lady Gregory's Dublin hotel room, his clothing in disarray, black hair hanging limply over his forehead, a cigarette held in trembling fingers. She waited, wanting to give assurance, knowing he needed the humility of silence to compose himself. When he did speak it was as if to himself; she had to lean forward to hear. He waved his hand, gesturing at the streets outside. 'I had to come. I had to see where it happened. They were good men, naïve patriots, ready to die for their beliefs and blinded by their fanaticism. Yet the rest of the country were not behind them.' He smiled sadly. 'But what men they were, Augusta. Just poets and schoolmasters perhaps, and unfit for practical affairs, a small band of unrepentant, middle-class intellectuals who provoked themselves into action against their better judgment. Good men, throwing their lives away in a forlorn hope.' He shook his head, an expression of disbelief, almost of surprise on his face as he turned back to her. 'I had no idea that anything could affect me so much. It makes me so terribly pessimistic about what is to happen in the future to this country.'

He stared at her intently, as if seeking absolution. 'I was safe in London while they risked their lives. But I was a part of it. I helped rouse their feelings for the uprising they wanted.'

He pulled on his cigarette, his eyes sad, the hand removing the cigarette from his mouth still trembling uncontrollably. 'Did I help to create the emotion that drove them to their deaths: Pearse and MacDonagh and the others? Even Maud's husband, MacBride?' He paused, the enormity of the events still beyond him. 'Did you know that Cathleen ní Houlihan was to be played on Easter Monday? Instead, all the play's prophecies came to pass in the streets outside. And Seamus Connolly, one of the actors, was, I am told, the first man to be shot, his fiancée, Helena Mooney, one of Maud's Daughters of Erin, standing beside him in the attack on Dublin Castle.' He paused again, overcome with emotion and self-tormenting guilt. 'But this will change Ireland.' His self-control suddenly broke, tears flooding down his cheeks as he threw his cigarette into the grate. He whispered to her. 'There is great beauty in it. And a poem, a great, heroic poem to commemorate them.'

Lady Gregory joined him at the window, her hand on his arm, consoling him. 'The British are handling it badly, Willie. The house searches, the arrests, the internments. They have changed people, making the whole country support what those men died for.' Her face became grim. 'What will happen to Roger Casement? He's been condemned to death. Has he any hope?'

Yeats shook his head despondently. 'I have written to Asquith asking for clemency but as yet there's been no reply. His trial was unfair, the sentence unjust.'

They fell silent as they thought of another patriot they had both admired. After his arrest, Casement had been charged with high treason outside the realm. His defence was that he was an Irishman, his plea from the dock both recklessly brave and emotional: 'The facility of preserving, through centuries of misery, the remembrance of lost liberty, this surely is the noblest cause ever man strove for, ever lived for, ever died for. If this be the case then I stand here today indicted ...'

Augusta Gregory held Yeats' hand. 'If he is hanged it will create further propaganda against Britain. Public opinion has changed so quickly: now they have a new generation of martyrs. Remember the words of Cathleen ní Houlihan: "they will be speaking forever, the people will hear them forever."' She lifted a cautionary finger. 'But you must not commit yourself too publicly to their cause, Willie. You have much to lose, your Civil List pension and your English friends. There are other ways you can help.'

He nodded and smiled sadly, his thoughts suddenly elsewhere. 'Soon I must go to Maud in Normandy. She has written to me; her grief and anger are so tangible.'

22

THE HEADLINE was on an inside page of *Paris Soir*. Maud stared at it, refusing to believe.

The names of those executed were listed in order of their execution. For some time she sat quietly, tears streaming down her face as she remembered again the way she had maligned him.

She called Isoeult, her voice sad but detached as she told her. 'John MacBride is dead.' There were a few consoling words, Isoeult holding her mother before leaving to be with her own thoughts, as Maud sat with her son and told him of his father's death. 'He died for his country, Sean. No matter what he did to us, now we can be proud of him.'

Sean took the news quietly. Since the separation, a true father-son relationship had never been allowed to develop.

Some days later, when she took Sean back to the Jesuit school, Saint-Louis-de-Gonzague, in Plessy, Maud was moved to tears when the Director told the whole school, at morning assembly, that although not fighting on the same side as the French, Sean's father was fighting for the freedom of a small nation. MacBride's name was included in the roll of honour read every morning for pupils' relatives killed in the war.

From that time on, Maud Gonne-MacBride dressed only in black.

It was several days later that she was composed enough to continue her letters to her closest friend, Willie Yeats. 'I read the paper's account of Major John MacBride's execution. He has died for Ireland ... he has left a name for Sean to be proud of. Those who die for Ireland are sacred. A tragic dignity has returned to Ireland.'

The letter was short and sad, and when she had finished it she stood in her room, staring out of the window across Paris, before sitting down again at her writing desk. As she wrote she purged her mind of the hurt and accusations she had hurled at MacBride in her efforts to get custody of her son. The letter was addressed to the editor of the Paris edition of the *Daily Mail*. The account in the paper had been defamatory, that the Transvaal Boers had been glad to get rid of MacBride because he was a horse thief. There were tears of anger in her eyes as she wrote.

I separated from my husband for personal reasons but I do not want the memory of him to be dishonoured ... he was in the Transvaal long before the Boer War ... He had grouped together his fellow countrymen who were working in the mines in a patriotic Irish Association ... At the end of the Transvaal war Major MacBride came to Paris and received unanimous praise. General Botha thanked him publicly for the service he had given.

When the letter was finished another decision was taken. Now that her husband was dead, although officially banned, she would risk returning to Ireland to live. She had been out of the country for two years.

It was August. She ran to meet him when his car pulled up in front of the house in Coleville. He held her to him as they remembered old friends who had died.

'I had a vision, Willie. I saw Dublin in darkness, ruined houses in O'Connell Street and figures lying by the quays and O'Connell Bridge, dead and wounded or dying of hunger. It was so clear it has haunted me ever since.' There were tears in her eyes. 'They fought and died with such dignity.'

Yeats thought again of those who had died. 'They weighed so lightly what they gave. They told me Pearse said that yet unborn generations of Irishmen would remember them more than those present today.' He shook his head sadly. 'He was a sad and romantic writer of nationalism with an almost mystical belief that bloodshed was necessary to save Ireland.' He stared hard at her. 'You had such a conviction, Maud.'

She ignored the implied criticism. 'But what they did was full of beauty and romance.' She turned tearful eyes to him. 'I think now that MacBride, by his sacrifice, has atoned for everything he did to me.'

He took her hand as they walked along the beach. 'You know about Roger Casement?'

She nodded sadly. Casement had been the last to be executed. On 2 August he was received into the Catholic church and the following day stripped of his knighthood before being marched to the execution shed at London's Pentonville Prison and hanged.

It was mid-morning the following day, the only sound that of the gulls and the soft waves breaking on the shore at high tide, the house shuttered against the heat of the day as he sat at the edge of the dunes, watching her walking in the light surf, a thin, white dress clinging to every contour of her body. Again he felt his arousal as the wind pressed the dress tight against her, full, high breasts perfectly outlined, firm thighs straining through the clinging sand. He was bewitched and aroused, Isouelt's beauty so like that of her mother. It was hard to believe she was now 21, grown into a woman since he had last seen her. He remembered the previous night, walking with her on the darkened beach. The sweet stolen kisses. The guilty excitement, her body tight against his, her response to his kisses. Flirting. Teasing.

He looked up, startled, no longer alone. Maud was speaking to him. 'She is very lovely, isn't she, Willie. And such a help to me and Sean. As you know.' She smiled, reaching out her hand to help him to his feet as he tried to hide his sudden embarrassment.

'She has changed so much, Maud. Grown up so quickly. When she was staying with May, in London, she came to see me. When I opened the door to her it was as if I was looking at you so many years ago. So beautifully dressed.' He frowned. 'I tried to get her to stop smoking but she said it was the fashion and who was I to talk, forever with a cigarette in my mouth!' He sighed softly, a touch of bitterness in his voice as he glanced sideways at Maud. 'It makes me sad as I could have had a daughter of her age. It means that I am beginning to get old.' He took her hand with an easy familiarity. 'Perhaps now is the time for us to marry, Maud. She could be my daughter then. And you could give up politics.'

She smiled gently, turning to him and stroking his cheek with her hand. There was a terrible closeness between them which somehow made yet another rejection even harder to bear. She stared at him. His profile was sharp in the sunlight, the tall angular figure had filled out and he was still as handsome as ever.

His need made his voice break, his loneliness surfacing. 'I'm 51 Maud. I want a wife and home and children. Marry me now. Now MacBride has gone, marry me and let us put all violence behind us.' He smiled sadly. 'Even Augusta still says we should marry. But only if you renounce all politics and work for Ireland in different ways.'

Her eyes were moist as once more she refused him, just as she had so often in the past. 'You have been asking me that for 25 years now, Willie.' She smiled gently at him through tears, tears for herself and for the almost child-like hurt on his face. There were tears in his eyes also as they clung to each other desperately on the shore.

'Dear, dear Willie. I can never marry, though I do care so much for you. I have to think of Sean; I want him to be brought up in Ireland where I feel my place is, as Madam MacBride. He's thirteen now and clever: he's even able to criticise my politics.'

Yeats smiled. 'We can all do that, Maud.' He paused, his voice quieter when he continued. 'You say you cannot marry me, or anyone. But I want a family of my own.' He stumbled on, holding her away from him, unsure of her reaction to his next question. 'Would you object if I proposed to Isoeult? Now she is 21?'

She stared at him, open mouthed, incredulity spreading over her features. 'Willie! She would never take you seriously. She has flirted with you since she was a little girl. And you're just infatuated with her.'

He looked so embarrassed that her heart melted for him when he replied. 'But I feel with her something of what I felt for you ... at first, anyway. And she is the same age as when I first met you ...' he finished lamely.

Maud's reply was gentle. 'It would never happen. She is beautiful and talented but you have seen how moody and difficult she can be. She wouldn't be right for you.'

Yeats sighed. It would have been a way of binding himself even closer to the family. 'I suppose I have been a success with her as a father.'

Maud nodded. 'That you have, Willie.' She felt terribly sorry for him. 'Ask her anyway, if you must, but don't let your hopes build up. And be sure of what you want.' She leaned forward and kissed his cheek as he fumbled in the pocket of the jacket slung over his shoulder.

'It's finished, Maud.' He pulled several sheets of paper from his pocket, starting to read as she took his arm and they followed in Isoeult's footsteps along the edge of the tide. She remained silent as he read, her pace slowing almost to a stop several times, the tears in her eyes overflowing as he recited the litany of names, his voice deep and slurred with emotion.

> *I write it out in verse*
> *MacDonagh and MacBride*
> *And Connolly and Pearse*
> *Now and in time to be,*
> *Wherever green is worn,*
> *Are changed, changed utterly:*
> *A terrible beauty is born.*

She stood, neither complimenting him nor criticising as he continued the poem.

> *... A drunken, vainglorious lout,*
> *He had done most bitter wrong*

To some who are near my heart,
Yet I number him in the song;
... He, too, has been changed in his turn,
Transformed utterly:
A terrible beauty is born.

She stared at him as he repeated the final words, 'a terrible beauty is born', tears blinding her eyes, her voice trembling with emotion. 'It will be the greatest war poem ever written, Willie. So many beautiful lines. Even MacBride is elevated to a hero. What will you call it?'

'"Easter, 1916".'

She nodded. 'It is enough. It will be eternal.'

23

FOR NINETEEN years he had spent long, idyllic summer months seeking inspiration as he relaxed in the peace of Coole. For nineteen years he had walked by the lake shore near the great house and fished in those waters.

Now, in September 1916, after the trauma following the uprising, an explosion of work helped thrust the guilt and sorrow from him, allowing him to enjoy the delights of the autumn which so many of his friends would never again enjoy.

The sun was strong and low in the west and his concentration such that he was unaware of Augusta until she was only a few yards away. She stood on the bank, a silent communion between them, two friends at peace together as she watched him casting his line into a deep pool beneath the far bank.

Yeats gazed out over the still lake, with the drifting clouds mirrored in it. A flock of swans rose slowly and heavily from the water, frightened by some unseen intruder, leaves of gossamer feathers moving gently with the wind to show where they had rested. Augusta glanced at Yeats and smiled as she opened the sheets of paper he had given her that morning. She read slowly:

The trees are in their autumn beauty
The woodland paths are dry,
Under the October twilight the water
Mirrors a still sky;
Upon the brimming water among the stones
Are nine and fifty swans.

'It's lovely, Willie. Beautiful. What will you call it?'

'"The Wild Swans at Coole". What do you think?'

'That's perfect.' A slight frown crossed her face. She read from the poem again. 'The nineteenth autumn has come upon me.' There was surprise in her voice. 'Has it really been that long since we first met?'

He smiled as he reeled in his line. 'It is. And I have watched the swans, even talked to them, walking or sitting here beside these waters. Nineteen summers of such wondrous thoughts.'

'Perhaps after all these years you need a home of your own, Willie.' She glanced at him. 'For when you are married. And Robert and I have found such a place, just a few miles from here, in Gort ...' She smiled, keeping him in suspense. 'It was part of the Gregory estates, a little castle, Thor Ballylee. It's old. Fourteenth century, and almost a ruin but it could easily be restored. There is a small cottage with it where you could live until it is ready. Room enough for you. And for a family ...'

The following day she took him to Ballylee. Willie Yeats was captivated. It was part of romantic Ireland, of poets and legends. An ancient stone tower, alongside it a bridge over a small river, a tinkling melody from the small stream feeding it. It had been waiting for him, for the romantic in him. The roof and the floors had long since fallen in but beside it, built against the walls, was the small cottage which could be a temporary home.

Lady Gregory had obviously thought about it for some time. 'There is an old ruined mill just along the river which has huge wooden beams, planks and old paving stones. You can use them all to do it up.' Her face was animated as she continued. 'And there are fine trout in the river. You will be able to fish here.' She shared his obvious pleasure. 'It could be ready for next summer, Willie.'

She took his arm as they walked around it. 'It is perfect, Augusta. And the first home of my own.' He smiled at her. 'And a gift for whoever I marry.' And then, dolefully. 'If I ever do!'

He stopped, leaning against the bridge, gazing down at the ford over the river, gurgling water falling over a small weir. He hesitated before he spoke. 'I need your advice, Augusta. Isoeult and I spend a lot of time together and she is very affectionate.' He looked away from her, suddenly embarrassed. 'I proposed to her but she laughed and said she would have to think about it.'

Lady Gregory's heart went out to him, he looked so dejected. She had seen him slowly falling in love with the young girl and knew Isoeult would be a more suitable wife than her mother, her interest being literature and without the terrible passion of her mother's politics.

Yeats' gained confidence when there was no obvious disapproval. He laughed.

'I think she was flattered and charmed but kept me waiting until I lost patience. I told her that if she didn't decide soon I would marry someone else. Then when I helped she and Maud return to England earlier this month, immigration officials took them aside at Southampton and they were interrogated as possible spies. When they were released they were forbidden to continue to Ireland under the Defence of the Realm Act. After all that, Isoeult got very upset and broke down in tears because she was ashamed at being selfish in not wanting me to marry anyone else and so break our friendship. And Maud, I'm afraid, is no help. She is in her own world, full of joyous, polished hate, the like of which I have never seen before.' He paused, gesturing. 'She seems shattered. So many of her friends are dead. She sold up everything in France and feels her place is in Ireland. For more revolution, no doubt.'

He slumped back against the rough stone wall of the bridge, sudden emotion overwhelming him, Augusta holding his head to her, tears in her eyes at his loneliness and despair. She smoothed his hair with her hands, holding him tight to her, kissing him on the forehead before lifting his face to her.

'Then we must find you a wife to go with this lovely place.'

He stared at her, waiting. 'Olivia Shakespeare tells me that she introduced you to Georgiana Hyde Lees ...' She stopped as the lowering sun behind the tower cast a sudden shadow over them. Augusta had already selected Georgiana, a gentle, unassuming young woman who would not threaten her friendship with Yeats. And she was a woman with money of her own.

Yeats turned away to gaze down at the river. Since Isoeult had refused him his own thoughts had turned to George. Unsure of Lady Gregory's opinion, he took some time before replying. 'You are right, as usual, Augusta. I did think of proposing to George when I returned to England. I've spent many sleepless nights thinking about it. And her.'

Augusta opened her arms in delight. 'Oh, Willie, I'm so pleased. You should marry her.'

His relief at her blessing was obvious. He turned back to her, suddenly animated. 'I'll go to see her mother and then propose to George.' He was suddenly downcast. 'But I have no money. She might think my pension and small income is not enough to care for her. After all, her family are wealthy, her father went to Eton and Oxford.'

'Don't think of money, Willie. Think only of her. Money won't worry her. I have already spoken to her mother about you and then she wrote to me. She was not at all happy about the idea though. She is worried about your intentions, knowing her daughter has feelings for you but she thinks you have little in common. She sees you as a man with a reputation who is 30 years older than Georgiana.' Augusta pulled a face. 'She even asked me to put you off the idea.' She glanced sideways at him. 'Georgiana is only 24, after all.'

'And I am twice her age ...' He looked quizzically at her. 'But you won't? Put me off, I mean?'

She shook her head, smiling gently at him. 'I have already written to her to try and convince her that you will make a good husband. I don't think there will be any more objections.'

Now that he had the blessing of the woman he trusted above anyone else, he accepted Georgiana's mother's invitation to join her and her daughter at their home two days later.

A T CHRISTMAS that year, as a goodwill gesture, the British government released many of the prisoners who had been held without trial in England, among them Arthur

Griffith who, in Gloucester Gaol, had organised a celebration of Yeats' birthday with readings from his plays and poems, pronouncing it as a day of national importance to Sinn Féin.

Michael Collins and Constance Markievicz were also released, together with Eamon de Valera, the sole surviving commander of the Easter Rising, who, on his return, was carried shoulder high through the streets of Dublin, Constance Markievicz's homecoming celebrated with her riding triumphantly on a float covered with flowers and the tricolour.

At Easter the following year the new republican tricolour flew again over the Post Office and shortly afterwards an Irish Assembly was held at the Mansion House in Dublin, at which Sinn Féin claimed that Ireland, as a separate nation, should have its own parliament with de Valera elected President.

It was yet another stepping stone towards independence, Sinn Féin finding support throughout the country, Griffith and Collins, working in partnership, selecting Sinn Féin candidates for the coming by-elections, though some were still in gaol. Eamon de Valera was one of those elected, his calmly eloquent election speeches calling for complete independence and liberty for Ireland.

Count Plunkett, whose son had been executed, also won a by-election after canvassing that, if elected, he would not take a seat in Westminster but would demand a parliament in Dublin.

But for many the pace of change was too slow. Some, like Michael Collins, were already critical of the way the executed men had bungled the uprising. He was preparing for rebellion, enrolling volunteers throughout the country and, with money raised from supporters in America, bringing in arms from Germany and America. Arms were smuggled through the docks labelled as machine spares, some consignments dropped from small boats on quiet beaches including guns in oiled packages, Smith and Wesson, Lee Enfields and Thompson sub-machine guns, other weapons brought from Irish troops serving in the British army and distributed by Cumann na mBan throughout the country.

Rebellion was nearing.

W ILLIE YEATS was married on 20 October, 1917, at the registry office in Harrow road, in London. It was a simple wedding, their friend Ezra Pound acting as best man, George radiant, noticeably younger than her groom, wearing a drop-waisted chemise dress, a border panel across the knees. He was less flamboyant than usual in a new suit with a waistcoat, silk tie and flower in his buttonhole.

If the wedding was a successful and happy occasion, the honeymoon was a near disaster.

Yeats fought to lift himself from the sudden trough of despair which enveloped him as soon as he was alone with his bride. He walked the grounds of the honeymoon hotel in Ashdown Forest, smoking incessant cigarettes, guilt sweeping over him. At this moment the marriage seemed a terrible mistake, his choice of bride, his third proposal in little over a year, also a mistake.

Before the wedding thoughts of Isoeult could not be forced from his mind. Now he suffered his betrayal not only of her but also of Augusta Gregory and his first and only true love, Maud Gonne.

Over breakfast on their first morning together, after a

night of clumsy and unsuccessful attempts at making love, as a wild storm raged outside, he stared dolefully at her, wondering if she, half his age, also thought it all a mistake. But to her his wretched sadness made him seem attractively vulnerable, more in need of her, as a wife, than ever.

It was almost a week later, a week of continuing misery and heart searching, that Isoeult replied to a letter from him. It was a thoughtful letter: she shared his sadness but gave him support, telling him she would also share his joy when all was well.

But to his bride the letter was a withering blow, her dismay as strong as his, thoughts of whether he loved her or not beginning to surface. She would fight for her marriage, however, and had a way to control him.

'Let me read the cards. They might cheer you up, Willie.'

He looked at her, shaking his head; even the tarot cards, predictions, if they were good ones, would not remove his misery. She smiled reassuringly, her hand on his. 'Then let me write for you. The mystics let me write what they have to tell me.' She took a sheet of writing paper, making him sit at the table beneath the window, holding a pen over the paper, her hand moving out of control as she stared deep into his eyes. 'There will be a message for you, written through me.'

He stared at her gloomily, desperate for reassurance as she faked a few sentences. In his confused state of mind he was easy to convince. She continued as if her hand was taken over and driven.

Words took shape, scrawled and hardly legible. He stared in amazement, just able to decipher what was written there.

'With the bird all is well at heart. Your action was right for both.'

He looked at her questioningly, pleading. 'Isoeult?'

She smiled and nodded as her hand continued to move over the page, the automatic writing continuing as he falteringly asked about his relationship with the women in his life. She had an answer to all his questions, answers that pleased him. It was as if a weight had been lifted from his mind, his depression rapidly lifting.

It was several hours before she stopped, Yeats' despair forgotten, his new companion now more than a wife as she became a communicator with the mystic world he had discovered with Maud.

He took the pen from her hand, gently pulling her to her feet and leading her across the room. He stopped, undressing hurriedly, almost pulling her clothes from her, before falling onto the bed. His fears had evaporated and their physical marriage was celebrated greedily.

Throughout the honeymoon the writings continued, he asking questions, she giving the answers she knew he needed. She used his interpretations, massaging and bending them to give him the peace of mind he needed. Or to manipulate him to satisfy her own needs.

It was to be the start of hundreds of hours of writing during their life together, interpretations which would take him from occasional depression and lethargy to his energetic, prolific self, George putting up with an almost daily barrage of questions which the automatic writing answered.

His life changed. Willie's comfortable bachelor untidiness was banished forever as George soon had his rooms in Woburn Buildings, now their home in London, almost unrecognisable. Married life was as he had hoped. He had someone to share his successes with as well as the disappointments, someone young and vital to care for him. More than a wife and lover, she was his confidant and, through her automatic writing, his mood controller whenever needed.

T HE FINAL seal of approval on his marriage was from Maud, his love for over 30 years, a love that would never, could never, change. She looked old and tired, world weary in her long, sombre black dress, dramatically dour in contrast to the vivid colours George chose to wear. Their meeting, over tea in his rooms in Woburn Buildings, went well. The conversation was relaxed and easy between George, Maud and Isoeult, with Sean sitting between them. Yeats' initial fears about the meeting were soon dispelled when Maud stood up and took him aside as Isoeult and George, their ages so much closer, were talking together animatedly.

'She's charming Willie. I'm sure we will be good friends. She's very beautiful and if she wears such bright colours all the time it will cheer up the grey walls of your new home in Ballylee.' She kissed his cheek. 'I'm so pleased you have chosen someone who won't break up our friendship.'

Her expression changed. She looked sad. Her beliefs had brought with them other problems needing to be shared. 'Sean joined the Fianna. I told him he was too young and wasn't ready, but he wouldn't listen to me.' She ruffled her son's hair as he joined them.

Fianna Éireann was the nationalist boys' movement which Constance Markievicz had planned while in prison, to prepare boys for enlistment in the IRA when they were older. Sean raised his head proudly. 'Boys died for Ireland when they were little more than my age, mother.'

'But the Fianna, Sean? Why that? It's just a breeding ground for young republicans to join the IRA.' She paused. 'And you know I have refused to join them. No matter what that may do for my standing in nationalist Ireland.'

'Why, mother? You say your life is for freedom for Ireland.'

Yeats remained a quiet listener. Sean's mother had been the boy's example. Maud sighed and shook her head slowly. 'Because it means violence, Sean. So much violence, just as you saw in France. Good, dear friends have been lost. I know now that violence will solve nothing.'

The boy would not be dissuaded. 'Please mother. Please understand. I have to find out for myself.'

'Why don't you listen to what Eamon de Valera says. He believes that the Irish republic can be achieved by non-violent means. He is a good man, Sean.'

'And Michael Collins is also a good man.'

'A good Irishman, yes, but he believes in violence.' She smiled. 'He will surely help make Sinn Féin successful. But most people don't want armed politics any more. There has been too much suffering. There will be a peace conference at the end of the war and violence surely won't be necessary for what we want to achieve.'

24

ROBERT GREGORY was dead. The letter from his mother came late in the January of 1918. Yet another tragedy, again someone close.

Quickly a war hero, he had already won the Military Cross and the Legion d'Honeur and was a major in the Royal Flying Corps when shot down, in error, by an Italian pilot over the north Italian front. His fellow airmen had buried him in Padua. Yeats handed the letter to George who sank to the floor beside his chair. Willie was lost in thought, in memories of a vibrant young man. He stared sadly at her as she read quickly. When she had finished her eyes brimmed with tears.

'I'm so sorry, Willie. I know how much you thought of him. And I'm so sorry for Augusta. You must go to her.' She glanced at the letter again. 'She wants you to write something for him. And an obituary. Will you?'

He ran his hand through her lustrous red-brown hair, nodding slowly, his voice full of emotion, a great sadness about him as he spoke 'Robert was everything. Painter, scholar, boxer, horseman, airman. And he designed costumes and scenery for the Abbey.' He shook his head in disbelief. 'He was a brave man. With a great love for Coole.' He sighed. 'I will write for him. And then, after Christmas, we will go to Ireland, to Ballylee, to see Augusta.'

It was several weeks before they left for Dublin where George met her husband's sisters, brother and colleagues at the Abbey. After that, before taking her to visit Lady Gregory and their new home in the west, they had a short fishing holiday in Wicklow, staying at the Royal Hotel in Glendalough. They were happy and life was good, spring on the way when, a few weeks later, he took his new wife to Galway.

Augusta Gregory had aged noticeably, still wearing mourning clothes, their arrival helping her find some of her old spirits, and going with them when he took his wife to Ballylee.

George was entranced, immediately offering her impoverished husband money towards its restoration, Yeats having already asked an architect friend to draw up plans for both the castle and cottage. Within days, using the remnants of the old mill and with the help of a local mason and a carpenter, Raftery, recommended by Lady Gregory, the conversion was underway.

It was an unnaturally cold early spring, the trees still bare, the lake calm, thin ice floating on the surface, when, the next morning, Yeats and the two women walked slowly around the edge of the lake. The older woman stopped, staring out over the water, an awful sadness in her voice.

'This is where he would often sit and paint. It could have been his future.'

Yeats linked his arm through hers, squeezing in sympathy as they continued their walk.

'What shall I do, Willie, now he has gone? I want to keep this house and keep the Abbey going but I feel so alone.'

She shook her head sadly, her despair inconsolable. 'I miss him so much when I wake in the morning and find he is no longer in the house.'

Georgie took Lady Gregory's other arm. 'You mustn't grieve any more, Augusta. He was a brave man and you will always have his children to remember him by.'

They walked slowly back towards the house, Augusta's arm through his, leaning heavily on him as they went down the steps to the lawn. She stared unseeingly over the old cricket pitch. Her voice was barely audible when she spoke. 'He loved playing here. He was such a good sportsman. Do you remember?'

Yeats placed his arm comfortingly around her shoulders. The cricket matches had been happy occasions at Coole Park, a game he could never play but would watch with others from seats under one of the majestic ilex trees. Those times seemed like yesterday, as he saw ghostly figures on the lawn, Robert captaining one side, W.G. Grace, the English cricketer, visiting Coole for the shooting, captaining another; Bernard Shaw fielding, paying the young son of one of the gardeners to run for the ball when it came his way.

They stood for long moments of sad nostalgia before continuing their walk, talking quietly, back up the steps and on to the walled flower garden and the collection of great trees, tall Irish yews and, alongside the path, the towering copper beech, its branches sweeping to the ground in a wide circle on which, deep into the wood, so many visitors to Coole had carved their names, Yeats, Synge, Shaw, O'Casey, Masefield, W.G. Grace, Jack Yeats, John Quinn and Augustus John, many of the visitors Lady Gregory had invited to her home. Yeats remembered the occasions, almost formal affairs, when new signatures were added, the laughter and jollity and even the mild jealousy when Augustus John demonstrated his agility by climbing higher up the tree than any of the others and carving his name on the top-most branches.

Now all the jollity had gone.

They continued their walk before resting on a seat beneath a spreading catalpa tree, a soft lullaby of bird-song floating from somewhere nearby as Yeats took a folded sheet of paper from the pocket of his jacket, standing before them, his breath frosty in the cold morning air, as he read the poem slowly. It was a memory of friends long gone, emotion and memories sometimes blurring the words, his eyes moving from one of his listeners to the other and then back to the paper. The poem paid his tribute:

I know that I shall meet my fate
Somewhere among the clouds above;
Those that I fight I do not hate,
Those that I guard I do not love;
The years to come seemed waste of breath
A waste of breath the years behind
In balance with this life, this death.

His voice slowed as the poem neared its end. He stopped, looking at them. 'I call it, "An Irish airman foresees his death".'

There was silence when he finished, George's arm around Lady Gregory as tears flooded down the older woman's cheeks. 'You never let me down, Willie. He will live forever in your poetry.'

He leaned forward, taking her hand in his and kissing

her gently on the cheek before they continued their walk, one arm linked through that of his wife, the other through that of the small, sad figure of Lady Gregory.

O N A damp, mid-February day in 1918, the harbour walls were barely visible under a heavy sea mist when the old lady shuffled up the gang plank, stooped, heavy garments hanging shapelessly, a plain shawl over her head, a cardboard suitcase tied with twine in one hand, a young, poorly dressed boy clinging to her other arm. The ferry from Holyhead was already crowded, people returning from visits to relatives, men bringing their hard-earned savings back to the poor they had left behind.

Passengers moved apart on the bench, a maternal figure beckoning the old woman to a space on the ribbed wooden seat beside her. The old lady mumbled her thanks, head down, fumbling with the beads of her rosary when any officialdom approached.

Throughout the journey Maud Gonne remained where she was, for four hours hidden behind the anonymity of the shawl in her Cathleen ní Houlihan incarnation before hobbling past officialdom when the ferry arrived at Dublin.

Exile from her fight could never be accepted.

I N APRIL 1918, Lloyd George's government made one of its biggest blunders, which united Irish nationalists as never before as it played into the hands of Sinn Féin.

After heavy casualties and horrendous loss of life on the Western front, conscription was introduced in Ireland for men aged up to 50, Lloyd George arguing that if Ireland wanted Home Rule after the war they should be willing to help win the peace. It was an ill-judged decision, the postponement of

Home Rule already the catalyst for revolution.

Yeats was in despair at the government's actions, outspoken in arguing that conscription would destroy all hopes of peace in Ireland and any remaining goodwill towards England. He, Lady Gregory, Maud and others signed a public protest against it.

At Westminster the Irish Party members dramatically walked out of Parliament and returned to Dublin to support Sinn Féin's protest, calling for all Irishmen to resist conscription by the most effective means at their disposal. The Catholic church joined them, decrying forced conscription as an offensive and inhuman law which the Irish people had the right to resist by all means consonant with the law of God.

The response by the British government to stop opposition to the new law was immediate and indiscriminate. On 17 May, almost the entire leadership of Sinn Féin and the volunteers, among them Constance Markievicz, Arthur Griffith and Eamon de Valera, were arrested in a well-planned round-up, accused of having been involved in traitorous negotiations, newspaper headlines reporting the discovery of a plot in which Sinn Féin was in league with Germany. There was no evidence to support the charges, except for a speech by de Valera in which he called for the volunteers to be ready to take advantage of a German invasion of England.

The situation in Ireland became increasingly tense, Griffith and de Valera, though in prison, elected to seats when Sinn Féin contested by-elections, demanding Home Rule and resisting compulsory conscription.

Maud herself had not escaped. She had bought a house in Dublin, at 73 St Stephen's Green, and was establishing herself again working for Sinn Féin, mainly as a journalist and in public relations with the foreign press.

On the day of the arrests she was accompanied by Sean and an English MP, Joseph King, visiting Ireland on a fact-finding mission. They were returning from a meeting at which they had tried to find a way to challenge the arrests. and had taken a tram before walking to her house when there was a sudden squeal of brakes. A police van pulled up beside her and a squad of policemen emerged. Maud fought like a mad woman, tigerishly, Joseph King restraining her son as she was thrown into the back of the van, cursing her captors while Sean ran along behind the van as it drove away.

She was back in England 24 hours later and in the hospital wing of Holloway Prison, sharing a cell with Constance Markievicz and Kathleen Clarke, the widow of her old friend Tom Clark, one of the martyrs of the Easter uprising.

Confined. Helpless. Maud's frustration showed, her friends increasingly resentful of her nerve-racking restlessness, Constance finally unable to stand it any longer. 'You're like a caged animal, Maud, prowling up and down.' Maud made no reply. Constance was right. After several weeks of the prison diet and prison regime, all their nerves were near to breaking point.

A hunger-strike had been ruled out as they knew the elderly Kathleen Clark would not survive for long, Constance sharing some of the meals she had sent into the gaol with her, Maud stubbornly refusing any, taking only her prison diet.

She had forced the others to refuse to sign a pledge not to discuss politics, which would have enabled them to receive visitors and news of the outside world. But for Maud, news did come. Early one morning she was summoned to the governor's office, refusing his offer of a chair. 'I have bad news for you, I'm afraid, Mrs MacBride. Your daughter has asked me to tell you that Mr Lucien Millevoye has died.' His voice took on a more considerate tone. 'He was something to you, I believe?'

Maud felt a sudden sadness sweep over her, sinking into the chair in despair. More of her past life had gone, another one-time friend and lover. She was helped back to her cell where Kathleen and Constance supported her in her grief, the sympathies of the other Daughters of Erin short-lived when Maud told them she had decided to apply for release. Kathleen was particularly vehement in her objections, as Maud had no grounds for applying before any other political prisoner, though Maud argued that she was not in Ireland during the war.

Constance was furious, telling her bluntly that if she did apply she need never come back to Ireland, grabbing the application papers from Maud's hand and tearing them to pieces. Her tone soon softened though, as Maud's health had begun to cause her friends concern, the terrible cough she had developed keeping them awake at night. Maud seemed to be fading fast and they now felt she should at least see a doctor.

Then came further bad news. Maud's sister Kathleen had died. She had faded slowly after the son she adored was killed in the war. It was infinitely sad for Maud, who had always been close to Kathleen. Kathleen's husband, Colonel Daniel Pitcher, had been a career officer in the British Army, had become ADC to the King and a captain commanding a flying squad in the Boer War, but these facts were never discussed by the two sisters.

Now Constance and Kathleen encouraged her application to leave. As Kathleen said, 'You have been kind, gentle and courteous through all this Maud, and even though I will miss you I will be glad if you get out of this place.'

Yet again Willie Yeats was there for her. Maud had written asking him to look after her children, though Isoeult was a grown, strong-willed and determined woman. When Constance wrote to him about Maud's condition, Yeats, having no wish to see her become a martyr, arranged for a Harley Street specialist to examine her, the diagnosis confirming her friends' worst fears. She had pulmonary tuberculosis and required treatment and a healthy environment if she was to recover.

Her friends worked for her, Yeats appealing to the Chief Secretary of State for Ireland for her release on medical grounds and, within hours of a strongly-worded telegram to the British government from John Quinn in America, warning of the effect on American opinion if Mrs John MacBride were to die in a British gaol, she was moved to a nursing home. She had been in the prison for over five months.

Sean was her first visitor, staring in dismay at his mother. Her face was wan, her once lustrous hair parted in the middle and hanging listlessly to her shoulders. She needed the attention of her family, and a few days later he smuggled her from the nursing home back to their refuge in Willie Yeats' flat in Woburn Buildings.

It was a short stay in London. Ireland was her home. This time, less than four weeks after leaving Holloway, and disguised in the uniform of a Red Cross nurse, she arrived back in Dublin, where the disguise was discarded when she took a cab from Kingston to her house in St Stephen's Green, which Yeats was using in return for the use of his London flat.

It was early morning and impatient hammering at the door brought Yeats stumbling down the stairs. His heart jumped as he stared in disbelief at Maud and, behind her, Isoeult and Sean.

His face was blank with shock and disbelief. 'Maud? How? Why ...' He glanced up and down the street, blocking her way as she made to come inside.

'No, Maud. You can't come in. You shouldn't even be in this country.' He looked wretchedly embarrassed and confused. 'George is ill. She's seven months pregnant and has the 'flu. I hope to God it won't turn to pneumonia.' He held his hands out to her, pleading understanding. 'I can't take the risk of them coming for you and disturbing her.'

Maud stood back, disbelief on her face which swiftly turned to a cold anger. 'We won't disturb her, Willie. We need somewhere to stay.'

'Not here, Maud. Please understand. If the police find out you are here they will raid the place. God knows what could happen to George.'

She pushed forward. 'I'm coming in, Willie. This is my house.'

He shook his head, holding her back. 'Not this time, Maud. Surely I have done enough for you? Surely you can try to understand?'

Her expression was cold. 'Is this what it comes to, Willie? Is this how you treat your friends, Ireland's friends?' There was a bitterness in her voice he had never heard before.

He closed the door on her, parting words shouted at

each other. 'You have a love of making mischief, Maud.'

'And you are an unpatriotic coward.'

Yeats stood, breathing deeply, his back against the door as Maud continued to hammer on it to be let in, ignoring the small crowd which by now had gathered on the pavement. Finally she gave up and turned away, beckoning the children to follow her.

It was the first time Willie Yeats' had rejected the woman he loved. And the first time he had little concern if it was the end between them.

25

T HE GREAT War was over and Maud felt mixed emotions. She had seen enough horror and death in France to wish it all to end, yet regretted the opportunities Ireland had not taken. Her life was returning to some normality and in December, when Yeats took his family to live elsewhere, she had moved back into her Dublin home. Her presence in the city had been tactfully ignored by the authorities but she was still in danger of deportation if she attracted attention. She had not spoken in public since her return but had been working for Sinn Féin on the campaign for school meals and the amnesty for nationalist prisoners.

On Christmas Eve the house was crowded with friends, nationalist friends from the theatre and her children's friends making it a special Christmas, one like those before the war.

But one close friend was missing, a friend she had thought about constantly during the evening, regretting the bitterness of their quarrel and wondering if things could ever be the same again.

It was late when the last guest had left. She was tired and sad when the door bell rang, staring in surprise as she opened the door to another, uninvited guest. He moved towards her and took her in his arms, her head against his chest. Tears filled both their eyes as she whispered: 'I hoped you would come. We're too much to each other to bear a grudge.'

'I wasn't sure whether I was welcome. But I had to come.' He held her at arm's length, smiling gently at her. 'You look better already Maud. Still too thin perhaps, and now with grey in your hair but still so lovely.'

She smiled sadly at his generous words, knowing the months in gaol had taken their toll. He closed the door behind him and then took her in his arms again, a gentle kiss returned, whispered words soft in his ear. 'I have missed you so much, dearest Willie. And I hate it so much when we quarrel.'

'And I love you, dearest Maud. I always will.'

She took him by the hand and led him into the warmth of the living room where there was low-lighting, aromatic Christmas candles burning in candlesticks dotted around the room, the tree sparkling in a corner, remnants of the party, empty glasses and wine bottles scattered everywhere.

Opposite the fire was a deep, comfortable sofa, the brown leather softened with age, and on it a pile of coloured cushions. They sank into it, his arm around her shoulders, her head against his chest. They lay back, both gazing into the fading embers of the fire.

There was comfort and ease between them, love and tenderness as they sat together in the soft firelight, the candles throwing flickering shadows over them. There were few words said, just contentment in being together, the familiarity of a lifetime's friendship. What they had seemed more than a marriage, it was a marriage of minds, a love beyond passion.

THE FIRST general election after the war had been held in December, the Sinn Féin party, outlawed by Britain, winning a resounding victory. Sinn Féin had fought the election on the manifesto that, if elected, they would again refuse to take their seats at Westminster but would form their own parliament, the Dáil Éireann, even though many of their candidates were in gaol, among them Countess Markievicz, the first woman to be elected to the British House of Commons.

The unfulfilled promises of Home Rule, the rising of 1916 and the handling of the conscription crisis could never be forgotten or forgiven and, in the following January, in another declaration of independence, Dáil Éireann met at the Mansion House in Dublin to establish an Irish Parliament, the Government of the Republic, Eamon de Valera, still in prison, elected as President. Count Plunkett was appointed Minister for Foreign Affairs, Arthur Griffith the Minister for Home Affairs and Cathal Brugha, an extremist who had remained at large when the arrests were made, the Chief of Staff and Acting President, whilst also given the role of Minister for Defence.

Constance Markievicz was appointed Minister for Labour and Propaganda, her priority, when free, to start propaganda and raise funds and moral support from the migrants who, with so many hopes, had left Ireland for a life abroad. Now, with their descendants, they could support Ireland's revolution.

Michael Collins, who, with his friend Harry Boland, had also escaped the May arrests, was appointed Minister for Finance as well as being the President of the Supreme Council of the IRB. Both Collins and Boland were absent from that first meeting, their names called in a cover up since, aided by Sean MacBride, now a fully-fledged member of the IRA, they were in England organising Eamon de Valera's escape from prison.

The Volunteers and the Citizens Army, which together made up the new Irish Republican Army, took an oath of allegiance to the Irish republic and the Dáil Éireann. Directed by Collins, the Irish Republican Army was now the official army of the republic, the IRB, which Collins also directed, remaining responsible only to itself.

THE BLOODY war for independence started in earnest when a consignment of gelignite bound for a quarry was ambushed by masked volunteers in Tipperary, two policemen shot dead at point blank range, their rifles and ammunition taken. It was the signal for an escalation in violence, post offices robbed to fund the new uprising, barracks burned down or bombed, much of the country now under military rule with permits required for movement.

Michael Collins, the 'big fella', in long overcoat and trilby, was the driving force behind the new rebellion, and was still bitter at the way the 1916 rising had been bungled. He moved between secret hideaways to avoid arrest, cycling through the streets, organising rebel brigades and building up his own squad of expert gunmen in Dublin. Information about any coming raids was obtained from inside Dublin Castle where, smuggled in by a detective who was a double agent, he was able to inspect secret British reports.

Collins' spy network was outmanoeuvring the forces of the British government.

But by the middle of 1919, moderates such as Arthur Griffith and others who had voted for Sinn Féin, were becoming increasingly unhappy at what was happening in the country, Griffith frequently having to intervene with Collins to prevent acts of murder and violence by the IRA, who did not fight alone.

Alongside were the women of Cumann na mBan, though Maud was reluctant to join them, supporting the moderate approach of Sinn Féin. After the killing she had witnessed in France she had no heart for the violence, with regular maimings, and bodies of informers often found under hedges, some labelled as spies, 'Killed by the IRA'.

Accepting there was no other choice but to fight, she now helped in other ways. She was still the leader of the Daughters of Erin and worked as assistant to Desmond Fitzgerald, the Minister for Propaganda, helping him launch the *Irish Bulletin,* the official paper of the new, illegal, Sinn Féin government.

A FEW months into 1919 Willie Yeats' daughter Anne, was born. It was a special time for him, living in his castle at Ballyfree, away from a Dublin full of soldiers and armed wagons as war approached.

One night at Ballylee, a great storm came in from the Atlantic, roaring over the woods at Coole Park as, his arm around George's waist, he gazed down at his daughter, asleep in her cradle. He whispered a few lines of a poem he had written for her:

> *I have walked and prayed for this young child an hour*
> *And heard the sea-wind scream over the tower,*
> *And under the arches of the bridge, and scream*
> *In the Elms above the flooded stream;*
> *Imagining in excited reverie*
> *That the future years had come*

Dancing to a frenzied drum ...

The small, innocent bundle brought him joy and hopes for their future, a future for which he had so many misgivings in a sad, troubled country. But for now there was to be a summer of rest, of contentment and the new magic of parenthood.

His study, a place of solitude and silence, was on the ground floor of the tower, its wide windows looking out over the river where he could watch otters playing on the river bank, moor-hens paddling through the reeds. On the same floor, an arched doorway led to the thatched hall between cottage and castle.

Their home was furnished with old Irish and English furniture, the seventeenth-century crib for the baby brought from a small shop on the quays in Galway, a large brass urn which Maud had sent him from Normandy by the archway.

Their home was still so new that the disadvantages were ignored. There was no plumbing, so water was carried from the river in buckets, drinking water taken from a well beside the road, warmth in the evening from peat fires in the huge, open fireplaces, oil lamps the only means of lighting and the nearest shops in Gort, some four miles away, reached by bicycle.

During the day, when the weather was fine, they would spend their time in the garden, George planting fruit trees and vegetables when she was not cooking or sewing or even painting and decorating the rooms they lived in, her husband writing whilst their daughter slept peacefully under the trees. At other times, seeking solitude, Willie would sit on the river bank, under the elm trees at the foot of the garden, hidden by a cobweb of branches, the only sign of his presence the faint pall of cigarette smoke which, on still days, would reveal his hiding place. He would write, watching the herons flying over the river or, at other times, cast for the lazy trout which hovered in the deep pool beneath the trees on the far bank. When successful, his catch was their evening meal.

At Ballylee they were a world remote from the butchery which was taking place in much of the country. It was here that a reluctant decision was taken – he decided to give up his flat in Woburn Buildings. With the decision came a sudden poignant sadness for Olivia and the love and friendship she had given him. He had lived there for twenty years. He composed some of his best work there but it was time to move on, until the rebuilding work was completed, and away from the terror of the guerrilla war in Ireland. He had the offer of a house in Oxford for the winter, away from the Irish troubles and the war which was surely coming.

And there were other reasons to leave Ballylee. More money was needed to pay for the repair to the first and second floors and complete the work on the roof. Again, John Quinn helped, arranging a lecture tour to America.

Yet Maud needed his help again.

STILL ONLY sixteen, slim, pale, hardly more than a boy, despite Yeats' warnings, Sean lied about his age and became a foot-soldier for the IRA. Maud had discovered it when he had accidentally discharged a rifle he had been cleaning in the attic.

Yeats' voice was both fatherly and critical in its concern.'Why don't you listen to me. You take no notice of my advice, Sean. Or your mother's.'

Sean shrugged slightly, pride mixed with defiance in his voice. 'They need people like me, Willie. Mother knows that.' Then, even more defiantly. 'I've already been put in charge of my own company, B Company of the 3rd Battalion.'

Yeats tried to reason with the youth, make him realise the dangers he was facing. 'It's too extreme, Sean. Collins' campaign of murder is a terrible thing. You shouldn't be involved in that.'

Sean smiled, lifting his head proudly. 'Michael Collins despises those who think moral force is enough. And I was there, with him, when Mick rescued de Valera from Lincoln Prison.'

Yeats felt despair at the depths of the youth's involvement, fearing there could only be one outcome. Sean continued, falling over his words in his eagerness to impress with his part in de Valera's escape. 'Do you know how we did it? Eamon used the chaplain's keys to make a master key; he made an impression in a tobacco tin of wax. Then he sent out a drawing of the key on a Christmas card and we sent a key back in a cake.'

The escape had been a high-profile publicity triumph and, after escaping, de Valera had been spirited out of the country to America to drum up the support of the millions of Irish descent there, receiving the welcome due to the self-styled President of the Irish Republic.

There was no way of dissuading Sean and, when the youth had left, a distraught Maud needed yet more help. This time it was for Isoeult. She had met a young poet, Francis Stuart, only seventeen, who was very much in awe of Yeats. He was at Rugby School preparing for his university entrance exam. Isoeult was infatuated with him, comparing him to Yeats. But Stuart was very immature and, because Isoeult was 25, he seemed to resent her sophistication.

Maud turned to Yeats for advice. 'They are threatening to elope so I think the only thing left is marriage. He has agreed to become a Catholic. But many advise against it. Even Lady Gregory says she sees nothing but disaster, his background is terrible. His father died in a lunatic asylum and his grandfather died of alcoholism.'

Yeats' feelings were mixed. Fatherly protectiveness towards Isoeult combined with a resentment, almost jealousy, that her friendship, her very dependence on him, could now be taken from him. For once he was unable to give Maud the clear advice she dearly wanted.

EARLY IN 1920 George and Willie Yeats sailed from Liverpool to America, where, in New York, they were met at the boat by John Quinn and numerous journalists. They were photographed as celebrities, she wearing a straw-coloured hat with a deep brim, a long, pale green buttonless coat with a fur collar and fur at the cuffs, pale green gloves, white stockings and fashionable raised heel shoes, a full cape around her shoulders. Yeats was greying and elegant in a soft trilby and huge double-breasted fur coat he had been given on one of his previous visits.

The lecture tour was exhausting but successful, taking in fifteen States and two Canadian provinces, through Toronto, Montreal, Washington, Pittsburgh to Chicago, from Oregon to California, Hollywood, New Orleans, Dallas and Boston. For much of the time, George stayed in New York with John Quinn and met Yeats' father, both taking an immediate liking to one another.

At each lecture Yeats gave a talk on the Abbey Theatre and then a reading of his own poetry, each preceded by how it came to be written. He would start with 'The Isle of

Innisfree', then the 'Fiddler of Dooney', 'The Wandering Aengus', 'The Cap and Bells' and then, the one to which they gave the longest applause, 'The Clothes of Heaven'.

In Oregon the Japanese Consul, Junzo Sato, who knew and admired Yeats' poetry, gave him a sword. It was wrapped in an ancient court lady's dress of pale blue, flower-embroidered silk and had been in the Consul's family for centuries. At first Yeats felt he could not accept such a gift, the Consul's hurt showing until George found a compromise. They would accept it on condition that he would tell them when his first child was born and it would then be returned to the family.

At the end of the five-month tour, his father took Willie to a huge rally of Irish Americans in New York at which the principal speaker was Eamon de Valera, now successfully raising funds for the republican cause. De Valera's talk emphasised that there would be no possibility of Ireland compromising for anything less than full independence. He had been trying to persuade the next presidential candidate to adopt a policy that the American government would recognise Sinn Féin's Irish republic.

Quinn introduced Yeats to de Valera as the one man of absolute genius he had known personally, and one of the most pleasant companions, as well as one of his best friends. It was a pleasant meeting, Yeats liking the president-in-exile more than he had expected, seeing him as energetic though rather charmless and pious, lacking in human sympathy.

26

WILLIE YEATS and his wife returned from America to find terrorism had increased. There had been brutal repression by the government troops, and in response the IRA had formed flying columns, Collins beginning to prove himself an organisational genius. Though there were only 3-4,000 armed activists, with no hope of military victory, their activities created political pressure for a truce and settlement as resignations from the terrorised police increased daily.

Gradually the IRA were taking control of the country, enforcing boycotts, women who consorted with the police having their heads shaved as a warning to others. Any Irishmen who joined the RIC faced having their knees blown away with a shotgun. Any Irish soldier who joined the RIC risked being murdered to discourage others. One victim, an ex-Irish guards soldier, was found executed, his body riddled with 26 bullets.

Many Irish policemen had been killed, often on the orders of Collins, others injured in the orgy of violence which in turn brought a frightful response from the RIC. The terror continued to increase until, by March 1920, the killing of policemen and ordinary citizens had become a regular occurrence, reprisals savagely brutal, the police now out of control. Frightened of assassination by any approaching civilian they began to take the law into their own hands, wrecking Sinn Féin assembly halls and the homes of known Sinn Féiners. This led to a further escalation of violence as the IRA got more recruits and became more practised at killing and punishing.

In April, Arthur Griffith set up Sinn Féin courts: Land Courts, Licensing Courts and Arbitration Courts which worked with the Volunteers in an attempt to stop the increasing lawlessness, as the British authority began to disintegrate. By June, Sinn Féin was overwhelmingly victorious in local county elections and by the late summer, the illegal government was more effective than the ruling government.

But still the awful savagery continued, shootings and armed raids met with retaliation on civilians as, from mid 1920, the police were augmented by replacements for those who resigned, recruited from among the ranks of demobbed men of the British army, the Black and Tans, ex-soldiers unable to find work in Britain, who were pouring into Ireland at the rate of 1,000 a month, their uniform a mixture of army and police uniforms, khaki coats and black trousers. With them came the auxiliaries, the police division of the RIC, ex-British army officers and sergeants, distinguished by their dark blue uniforms and Glengarry hats.

Their activities were uncompromisingly brutal, designed to quell rebellion.

L ATER THAT summer, Maud's cry for help with her children was repeated. It was again over Isoeult's marriage problems. And as always, when she needed him, Willie was there, responding immediately to her telegram.

His first thoughts were of what was happening in the country, the carnage which was reported daily in the newspapers. Maud looked at him disapprovingly. 'I don't think you, being away, appreciate the full horror of what is happening. You have to do something for Ireland, Willie. Let the people know.' Her hand was on his arm. She sighed. 'Life is becoming intolerable. The English try to batter us to pieces but they will never break our spirit. You really must use your influence in England to let the ordinary people know what is happening. The soldiers are murderers.'

'As are the IRA, Maud,' he replied quietly. He lifted his hands apologetically. 'What can I do? Collins has taken it upon himself to cause this.' He shook his head despairingly. 'God knows where it will end.'

Near Coole, the Black and Tans had flogged several young men and tied them to their lorries by their heels, dragging them along the road until their bodies were torn to pieces. Maud was in tears as she told Yeats the story, which she had heard from Lady Gregory. 'They said there was nothing left for their mothers but the head.' She composed herself before continuing. 'These men are just base riff-raff. They burn down homes, flog, torture and shoot unarmed men. Even a pregnant woman suckling a baby was shot at the gate of her house. But the Tans left Augusta alone, Willie, though they attacked her tenants and neighbours. Perhaps it was because of Robert's sacrifice for Britain.'

He sat down beside her. 'But that's not why you wanted to see me, Maud. What is it?'

'It's Isoeult. They are living in a house in Glenmalure but Stuart can't cope and after only three months his jealousy is terrible. He acts like the spoiled public schoolboy he is. It really is a disaster. Isoeult looks so thin, worn and tired. They row all the time and he beats her. He is selfish, though Isoeult pays for their flat and everything. He locks her out while he stays in bed all day and even burns her clothes with petrol.' She stopped, a sudden catch in her throat. 'And now she is pregnant.' She gave Yeats no chance to comment as she continued her accusations. 'He starves her into obedience or tortures her by not letting her sleep.' She took a breath. 'I hate him. And that upsets Isoeult. She is so besotted by him. She accuses me of shouting like a fish wife when I scream at him.' She attempted a smile. 'I suppose I do sound that way.' She sighed deeply. 'He sold her engagement ring and insults me. He calls my political views absurd.' She waved a hand disparagingly. 'I suppose that's all you can expect from an Ulster Protestant.'

She was trembling with anger and worry. Yeats took her hand. 'Calm down, Maud. I'll go to see them. It can't go on like that. Don't worry.'

She looked at him through tears of despair. 'Please, Willie. You're so much better at it than me.'

It was later that day when he visited Isoeult and Francis. The young poet, who admired and imitated Yeats, was unable to meet the older man's eyes.

Yeats' heart fell when he saw the young, vital woman he had once lusted over, had even proposed to. She looked withdrawn, her beauty gone. Yeats ignored Stuart's objections and arranged for Isoeult to go into a Dublin nursing home until fully recovered, after which she would live with Maud while waiting for the baby to be born, Isoeult promising Yeats that she would leave Stuart forever if there was any further trouble.

And only a few days after helping with Isoeult there were more problems for the adopted father of the family. Again Maud called for him. There were tears in her eyes when he asked, 'Is it Sean?'

She nodded. Yeats pursed his lips. 'I expected as much. He won't stop his involvement ...'

'His father's name goes before him, Willie. He sees it as his destiny but he's throwing away all his chances in life.'

And his mother's hopes for his future and possibly his own life, Yeats thought grimly to himself. Her voice was muffled as she spoke into his shoulder. 'The police stopped Constance Markievicz and a French journalist. Her car had a broken tail-light and when they realised who was in the car they sent for the military.' She moved away and sat down, clutching her hands in her lap. 'Sean was driving, it was after midnight, military law applied and he didn't have a military driving licence. They were all arrested.' She shook her head despairingly. 'Because of who he is I feared the worse. They took him to Mountjoy but he was released after a few days.' She looked up at her old friend. 'He missed his examination so a whole year's work is wasted. But Constance suffered most. She was court martialled and gaoled for conspiracy for having formed Fianna Éireann. They've given her two years hard labour in Kilmainham.'

He listened in silence, standing up and walking to the window and gazing out over the green. 'I'm sorry for her. It seems that was to be her destiny.' He sighed. 'But I'll talk to Sean again ...'

Maud stood up and came to him. 'Will you? He might listen to you after this. I'd be so grateful.'

'He has your fire in him, Maud. I don't know how we can change that. He has a strong character and remembers what his father died for. He knows his father is seen as a hero and has to live up to that.'

She held his hand tightly. 'I fear so for his life. I hear stories, things he has never told me. He even raided a hospital and rescued one of his men who'd had a leg amputated.'

Yeats had heard enough, interrupting her abruptly. 'I'll do what I can, if he will let me. But it was you who once said violence was the only way ahead.'

'That's cruel, Willie. He is my only son.'

He twisted the dagger. 'And could have been our son.'

She took her hand away, shaking her head slowly, meeting his eyes. 'That was uncalled for.'

There was silence between them for a few moments before he reached out and took her hand in his. 'It was a bitterness I thought I had lost. But it would have been wonderful, Maud.'

'But you love George, Willie.'

'I do. And my daughter.' He shrugged. 'What is done is done.'

HIS BITTERNESS disappeared when, in August 1920, his son Michael was born in England, his happiness suffering only when Maud had distressing news for him: Isoeult's baby had died. He held her to him when they met, the old comfort still there as she told him, her voice low and sad. 'It was from meningitis. The same as my Georges.' Her eyes were wild as she stared at him. 'There is a family curse that no Gonne daughter would ever find happiness in marriage. It was put on us by a priest from whom we had confiscated church land.'

He felt a terrible sympathy for her, aware of the sadness in her family. Her own marriage plus that of Kathleen, May and now Isoeult's had all failed. Yeats wondered what more sadness there was to be in her life?

BLOODY STEPPING stones to independence were still to be cast. In September 1920 the British Prime Minister, Lloyd George, introduced the Government of Ireland Act which granted Ireland the same status as Canada: that of a self-governing dominion of the British Empire with a parliament in Dublin but with partition, the six counties of Ulster excluded from the Act.

Now the war escalated to further levels of horror as the IRA resolved to fight on for full independence for all 32 counties of Ireland.

27

O<small>N</small> 1 N<small>OVEMBER</small>, 1920, at eight o'clock in the morning, eighteen-year-old Kevin Barry was hanged in Mountjoy Gaol.

At the front of a hushed crowd Maud Gonne, wearing her now-familiar black mourning clothes, stood beside Arthur Griffith. Barry, one of Sean's university friends, had been caught carrying a revolver, while taking part in an ambush in which one soldier was killed, another two fatally wounded. One of Barry's arms was dislocated under interrogation and torture, and was in a sling for three weeks until his court martial.

Despite pleas for mercy from both England and America, the first post-war British hanging in Ireland was carried out, a guard of soldiers and armoured cars training their weapons on the crowd of over 5,000 who prayed outside the gaol.

It was another mistake by the British authorities, many of Kevin Barry's fellow students immediately enrolling in the IRA.

After careful planning, the nationalists' retribution for the brutality of the Black and Tans and the execution of Kevin Barry was terrible: Sunday, 21 November 1920 became Ireland's bloodiest day.

In Dublin, Collins' flying squad of 35 hand-picked men had waged a war within a war on the English police in the G (Detective) Division of the Dublin Metropolitan Police. Collins himself had obtained their names and addresses from the records at the castle, his intelligence network now so efficient that he was aware of most of the authorities' actions before they took place.

Using this information, it was just after 9am when Collins' squad moved against their targets, assassinating twelve British G men living in hotels and lodging houses in Dublin, most of them still in their beds, some shopping, or walking in the park, some shot in front of their wives.

But the reprisals, although anticipated, were similarly terrible. That afternoon, at a Gaelic football match between Dublin and Tipperary in Croke Park, twelve civilians were shot dead as troops invaded the pitch, shooting indiscriminately. Later that day, Auxiliaries and RIC men shot three members of the IRA in the guard room in Dublin Castle.

The retribution continued as six republican prisoners were hanged, two at a time, whilst 20,000 stood in the streets outside Mountjoy Gaol. They had been convicted, on unreliable evidence, of the Bloody Sunday assassinations of 21 November. Other prisoners were spared the gallows but were subjected to dreadful beatings.

This further misjudgement led to more mass resignations from the police force, the guerrilla warfare now out of control until, by the end of 1920, almost 200 policemen and 50 soldiers had been killed, hundreds of others wounded.

The hostility to the Black and Tans was now so intense that they faced murder at every turn, people fleeing their homes whenever an ambush took place, hiding in the fields in anticipation of the inevitable reprisals. The anger of the Black and Tans spilled over into a bloody campaign, setting fire to houses and shops, throwing hand grenades indiscriminately, murdering innocent civilians, even children, and burning to the ground the creameries on which people depended for a living.

When Desmond Fitzgerald, the Minister for Propaganda, was arrested without charge in March 1921 and held in solitary confinement, Maud began working for Erskine Childers, who had taken over as Minister for Publicity. She was now a Senior Circuit Judge for the Sinn Féin Parish Courts and served on the executive committee for the White Cross, which organised relief work helping with money from the American Committee for Relief in Ireland.

Despite her recent illness, her energy was astounding as she worked with Griffith to help the victims of atrocities, feed starving schoolchildren in Dublin and tried to save the lives of those condemned to death by court martial, and despite all this, still finding time to work for the poor in Donegal.

But even with martial law and the threat of internment without trial, the war for independence had become a war which neither side could win; a time of fear, of hateful revenge as, in the first months of 1921, over 1,000 people were killed and half that number wounded. Throughout the country the rule of law was non-existent, daily incidents now so brutal that there was pressure internationally, and even in England, to end the killing.

In May 1921, there were elections for two Irish Parliaments, north and south, Sinn Féin winning resoundingly in the south, their candidates unopposed. It gave them a mandate for the southern counties. This prompted Lloyd George to capitulate. A meeting with de Valera took place in July, which Lloyd George had previously refused to attend until the IRA had handed in all its weapons. He ultimately proposed a truce between republican and crown forces, although still insisting on partition.

De Valera, with the backing of Griffith, Collins and Erskine Childers, agreed to the proposal, a conference arranged to work out a peace formula, de Valera travelling to Downing Street to begin negotiations.

A T THE house in Oxford, Yeats continued the Monday evening soirées he had started in Woburn Place, inviting selected undergraduates and lecturers to his home, sitting around the fire, some in chairs, others lounging on the floor while Yeats poured wine for his guests. He was taken by the charm and ambience of Oxford and had written a poem to commemorate these times which he called 'All Souls Night'. He read it to his guests at one of the evenings:

> *Midnight has come, and the great Christ Church Bell*
> *And many a lesser bell sound through the room;*
> *And it is All Souls' Night,*
> *And two long glasses brimmed with muscatel*
> *Bubble upon the table. A ghost may come ...*

Now these same guests gave him the chance to speak for Ireland, his chance to respond to Maud's plea, to let the people in England know what was happening in Ireland, to speak to the people who would influence the decision makers. Her poignant and vitriolic letters detailing the almost daily atrocities had been numerous. Yeats had finished reading her latest letter when he opened the next one. It was an invitation to speak at the Oxford Union, the motion for debate that the house would welcome complete self-government for Ireland and condemned reprisals.

It was 17 February 1921. He was the third speaker, resplendent in a suit and waistcoat, over it a scarlet gown, a large bow tie, as usual, at an angle: a tall and striking figure. By the time the case against the motion was completed the speakers had made him incandescent with fury. Seated at the back of the hall, George was both frightened at how far his words would go, and concerned for his health as he took his place behind the Treasury Box.

There was no slow build-up. He was immediately at his elegant and eloquent best, his words and emotions increasingly intense as he moved from the podium to pace up and down the aisle, striding between the 'aye's and 'no's, tearing into the previous speaker, occasionally standing, facing his audience, greying hair over his eyes. But he was always majestic in his manner.

He spoke with a strange, almost chilling power as he leaned towards his audience, strong jaw jutting forward with the fierceness of his words, which denounced the British policy of countering the IRA by its own acts of terrorism. There was hushed attention in the audience as he decried the atrocities of the Black and Tans: 'The horrible things done to ordinary law-abiding people by these maddened men, the Black and Tans and the Auxiliaries ... all this caused by drink and hysteria ...'

Not once during his furious oratory did he attack the British troops who had been a long time in Ireland, their morale and nerve destroyed. Such things had not happened when they had been in charge. He stood in the middle of the aisle, arms raised, dramatic and passionate. 'English law has broken down in Ireland, but the law has not. I am not a Sinn

Féiner but I think that Sinn Féin justice is real justice ... I don't know what lies more heavily on my heart, the tragedy of Ireland or the tragedy of England because of the horrible things done to ordinary people by these muddled men.'

Now in full flow, his delivery and timing were immaculate, his voice musical, sometimes melancholy, eloquent and savage by turn as he lingered over words before changing to harsh, uncompromising tones. It was magnificent oratory as he pleaded for his country, increasingly angry as he shook his fist, making his point aggressively.

When he finished, leaning breathless and exhausted at the Treasury Box, there were tears in George's eyes and in the eyes of others in the audience. They were stunned and silent, at first slow to respond but then the trickle of applause became a great tumult, an avalanche of cheers until the whole house, and even his debating opponents, were on their feet acclaiming him.

Yeats had made his point, the majority in the house now convinced that England was in the wrong, Ireland an exploited and despoiled country. His passion, his mastery of words ensured the motion was passed by an over-whelming majority. It was one of the greatest successes of one of the greatest orators of his generation.

Willie's triumph was complete when, one week later, he read and re-read Maud's letter thanking him for what he had done, her congratulations the supreme accolade.

28

IN OCTOBER 1921 the peace conference began in London. Arthur Griffith, almost fastidious in his tidiness, together with Michael Collins, an impressive figure in a new, pin-striped suit, were the main delegates, de Valera remaining in Ireland. He knew that, after two and a half years of awful bloodshed, over 1,500 deaths and widespread destruction, partition would lead to the tearing apart of Ireland. Now he chose to stay in Dublin, to argue from a position of strength if the negotiations failed.

Lloyd George was supported by Winston Churchill, the Secretary of State for the Colonies, and the negotiations were protracted, with neither side satisfied. On 6 December, Lloyd George threatened immediate war if the delegation did not sign the treaty. Since the choice was a war they could not win, or dominion status, the delegation chose the latter, though it meant accepting the right of Ulster to opt out of the agreement.

It was the price which had to be paid. At 2.20am, on 6 December at 10 Downing Street, years of stalemate were ended when the Government of Ireland Act was passed. Ireland was offered an Irish Free State.

Many, including Maud Gonne, were critical of the

outcome and of her friend Arthur Griffith's role in the negotiations. Maud's displeasure was softened by the fact that
Sean, who had accompanied the delegation as aid-de-camp
to Collins, at last seemed prepared to take a peaceful, political role in Irish affairs. On his return she reminded Griffith
that de Valera had said he would never accept such a compromise, she herself believing that a united Ireland had
gone forever, though Griffith continued to argue that the
best option had been taken if the Irish people wanted peace.

'It means we can now start to work for even greater freedom. Don't forget, Maud, even Willie Yeats said he never
thought we would get so much out of Lloyd George.'
Griffith paused for emphasis. 'And Mick Collins says the
treaty is not the ultimate freedom that all nations aspire to
but is the ultimate freedom to achieve it.' He shook his
head. 'I know he isn't happy with what we achieved, Maud,
but accepts it is the best for now. Mick even turned to me,
after he signed the treaty, and asked whether anyone would
be satisfied with this bargain?' Griffith looked grim. 'Will
anyone, Maud? He said he had signed his own death warrant. We had got a State but not the all-Ireland republic
which de Valera seeks.'

Maud's face also was grim. 'There are others beside de
Valera who are against the treaty, Arthur. All six women
elected to the Dáil, Constance among them, and even Sean.
Most of Sinn Féin and Cumann na mBan are opposed to it,
and the Volunteers, the IRA, are divided among themselves.
Willie is in despair about Ireland. He sees no hope of escape
from bitterness.'

From December to January, in meetings held at
University College Dublin, there was fierce and emotional
debate about the treaty, moderates arguing with extremists,

some in the IRA siding with Collins in support of the treaty but the Daughters of Erin, and others, were passionate opponents. To them the four green fields had to be sown together.

De Valera accused Griffith and Collins of settling for too little, that the treaty was a major setback to nationalist aims. But the Free States was accepted, a democratic decision unacceptable to de Valera. He rose to his feet, a tall gaunt figure, staring around the chamber in a hushed silence before resigning as President, denouncing the treaty and storming out of the house with his deputies.

After long, uneasy discussion as the significance of what had happened began to sink in, Arthur Griffith was appointed president of Sinn Féin, with Michael Collins as chairman of the Provisional government. The new constitution came into effect with two parliamentary houses, the Dáil and the Senate, the members of the Dáil swearing the oath of allegiance.

The flag-lowering ceremony was a sombre occasion as the Irish Free State army and provisional government took over Dublin Castle, Michael Collins, in full uniform, representing the new government, which took the title of Fine Gael, the Tribe of Ireland.

The anti-treaty party, informally known as Fianna Fáil, the Warriors of Ireland, with de Valera its leader, refused to recognise the new government, gaining many young recruits as de Valera talked of civil war as a means of achieving independence.

THESE WERE sad times, both for Willie Yeats and for Ireland. In February 1922 he heard his father had died in his sleep after a brief illness and, in Ireland, his worst forebodings were being realised as those opposed to the treaty turned to violence to destabilise the Free State government.

No one in Ireland would escape the terror, as slowly the disagreement between those for and those against the treaty slipped into civil war. A vicious circle of violence developed, Irishman against Irishman, the population living in terror as kidnap and murder became the norm.

Anarchy reigned as post offices were again robbed for funds, railway lines damaged, some of the IRA degenerating into little more than local bandits and racketeers.

IT WAS another Easter. Another occupation and bloodshed. On 13 April, 1922, an army of the anti-treaty IRA occupied buildings in Dublin, including the Four Courts, which they used as their headquarters. With them was the young, militant IRA member, Sean MacBride, now Assistant Director of Organisation, responsible for the purchase of arms in Europe. Lloyd George and Churchill issued an ultimatum. While a stand-off existed the provisional government was seen to be losing its authority. The Four Courts had to be retaken. If not, the treaty would be considered regarded as formally violated.

The provisional government had little choice but to agree, the British government supplying them with arms and sending a gun boat to Dublin. On 28 June, about three months after the occupation began, the provisional Free State government moved against the occupying anti-treaty force, Collins demanding that the irregulars surrender within twenty minutes, both he and Griffith accepting that if they had to attack the Four Courts it would amount to a declaration of civil war.

But for the anti-treaty IRA there could be no climb down. At seven minutes past four, the Irish civil war started when the Free State government ordered the taking of the Four Courts.

Yeats knew nothing of the attack until there was a loud knocking on the door of the house they had taken, just a few doors from Maud's home in St Stephen's Green. He opened it to find Maud on the step. He stared at her, knowing instantly that the worst had happened.

'They've attacked the Four Courts, Willie. And Sean is still in there. I just pray he is safe.' She looked at him in desperation. 'What can I do?'

He walked with her to stand among the crowds of onlookers across the river from the Four Courts. They watched helplessly as the Four Courts was systematically destroyed, gaping wounds appearing in the walls, Willie holding Maud back as she tried to make her way across the bridge. 'I have to go, Willie. I have to see him. I have to get him out.'

Yeats held her tight. 'It's impossible. You could be hurt or arrested with the rest of them.'

She turned tearful, frightened eyes to him. 'But I'm so frightened for Sean.'

Yeats' face was grim – the implications of what was happening were momentous. 'Fear more for your country, Maud. There can be no turning back now. This means civil war.'

For two days he kept a vigil with her as the Four Courts was slowly reduced to rubble, O'Connell Street and other parts of Dublin again in flames. But just as in 1916, there could only be one outcome and, on 30 June, after two days of bombardment, 180 of the garrison, in single file and under a white flag, walked out of the ruined and blackened building. Yeats grabbed Maud's arm, holding her back as her son appeared and was led with the other prisoners to police vans and taken to Mountjoy Gaol.

At the end of the fighting a large part of the city centre lay in ruins. Many buildings in central Dublin had been destroyed and the public archives of Ireland for centuries past were lost in the burned-out Four Courts.

When the final surrender came, 400 prisoners were taken and 60 people had been killed in eight days of savage fighting.

WILLIE YEATS had backed the new government. Despite his support of the nationalist cause, to him both sides were responsible for the terrible maelstrom of hate. He knew there was nothing to threaten the future of a country as much as a bunch of martyrs. And there had been martyrs enough in 1916.

There were pressing matters for his adopted family. And an old friend could save Sean, Arthur Griffith the one man who might even save the country from running with blood. Late in July Yeats escorted Maud and a delegation of women from the Daughters of Erin in an attempt to halt the escalation into full civil war, seeking a peace initiative with the leaders of the Irish Free State, Griffith, Collins and William Cosgrave.

Yeats was shocked at the appearance of his old friend. The neat, almost fastidious Griffith was a parody of his old self, his ruddy complexion now pale and drawn, the patriot exhausted by the terrible bloodshed of the past few years.

But he and the leaders of the Free State were adamant, Cosgrave particularly cold and unmoved by their pleas. A truce could only be agreed if their opponents laid down their arms, the ailing Griffith as emphatic as any, his voice weary as he spoke to his old friend. 'We are the lawful government. It is our duty to keep order. There can be no turning back.'

29

Thor Ballylee was a haven, just as Coole had been – a retreat from the bloodshed and tragedy of the Four Courts and the continuing demands of supporting Maud. After the meeting with the leaders of the Free State, Yeats took his family to a place he and George both loved. It was now midsummer, the countryside in full bloom, luxuriant blossoms along the river bank and, in the peace and calm of the evening, the gentle whispering noises of the river soothed them to sleep.

George's happiness was complete, her time spent decorating the house and working in the garden. In that quiet, rural place, happiness for all the family was complete. It was a castle for a poet and dreamer, a place where he could write out of doors, his son asleep under a tree, his daughter playing happily on the river bank.

The work on the castle was almost completed, with the ground-floor dining room, a bedroom up the narrow stairs and a room on the third floor, which was to be his study, all habitable.

In this new world of peace and calm he was able to return to his work, George's automatic writing still prompting and even inspiring him as his ordered schedule, first found at Coole, resumed once more.

It was a time of unnatural quiet at Ballylee. The civil war now raging through the country meant the end of a life they had become used to. During the first months of the war railway bridges had been blown up, roads blocked with stones and trees, communications completely broken down. There were no newspapers or post, the outside world hardly existed.

They were remote from the world until the calm was broken, when one night, in the early hours, there was a loud banging on the door, men demanding to be let in. Rooney, the Collie pup, yelped at them as Yeats stood inside the door, the only weapon to hand a hammer clutched in his fist. He shouted, threatening them, his heart thumping in his chest. There was a muffled conversation until, a few minutes later, he heard them tramping drunkenly over the bridge.

After that they had regular visits from both irregulars and troops of the Free State, the irregulars only coming at night. One evening in August as he sat smoking, sitting back gazing at a sky streaked with chalky clouds, there was a rustling in the bushes, a shadowy movement in the trees behind him. Yeats looked around, staring frozen at the line of men silhouetted against the evening sky at the top of the bank, one of them known to him, an irregular who frequently passed the tower. Yeats breathed hard, nodding to him as the anti-treaty man lit a cigarette. He spoke amiably to the poet.

'Your garden is looking good, sir?'

It needed an answer and Yeats replied hesitantly. 'It's this weather I suppose. Enough rain, and sunshine ...' The conversation was short lived. To enquire about the war, any interest in what was happening around them, would be dangerous.

The bridge beside Ballylee had survived longer than most. In late August, as a hot sun was losing its power and settled over the old elms, screams from outside brought Yeats running to the door as gunfire sounded along the river and George ran to gather up the children. He pushed them ahead of him as they fled up the stairs before staring out of a small, deep-set window. The gunfire came closer until he could see the opposing sides, some retreating to the far end of the bridge, the government soldiers hugging the walls of the tower, the rattle of rifle and pistol fire almost continual. There were shouted orders, a sudden abrupt scream of pain and, even as he watched, the uniformed government soldiers gave ground under a hail of bullets, retreating to shelter behind the walls of the cottage.

There was a lull in the firing, Yeats watching as one of the irregulars crawled slowly under the bridge, out of sight of the enemy, reappearing a few minutes later with a coil of wire in his hands.

Yeats blood ran cold as he realised what was about to happen, shouting to the men below. 'There are children here. Give me time to get them away.'

An irregular stared up at him, waving his hand. 'Take them higher up, they'll be safe there. We only want the bridge.'

Yeats ushered his family before him to the top floor, thrusting George and the children to the floor, lying over them as the explosion shook the old building, windows blowing in, glass, debris and dust showering the room and covering them.

Within minutes all was quiet again, the calm of Ballylee restored. Yeats stepped gingerly outside, motioning to

George to stay behind as he inspected the damage. The bridge was down, the rubble from the explosion damming the river which, even as he looked, was beginning to rise. There was a movement on the far bank, one of the irregulars turning, waving him good night and cheerily thanking him as they left, their objective achieved.

By the time he had brought his family down from the tower the opposing force's troops had gone and all was quiet. But the castle was now almost uninhabitable, the waters from the blocked river seeping into the cellar, the kitchen floor soon under water. It was time to return to Dublin.

The work on the castle had stopped for some time now. Raftery, their builder, had been shot and was in hospital and George wanted to find a permanent home in Dublin. The following evening, as they had their final walk that summer along the river bank, they were quiet, lost in their own thoughts, of the times they had enjoyed there, Yeats put his feelings into words as he took his wife's hand, a great sadness in his voice as he spoke for both of them. 'To go elsewhere, my dear, is to leave beauty behind.' Their home had been an escape, a place of serenity for eight eventful years.

THE LARGE Georgian house she had found was in Merrion Square and Yeats became the proud owner of another grand house; one of the most fashionable addresses in Dublin. But, unaware of what had been happening throughout the country, Dublin was not what they suspected. It had become a war zone, shots and explosions sounding continually as the republicans continued their war to undermine the Free State government. A hatred Yeats had not imagined was developing between the two sides.

Maud was their first visitor. She had again been work-ing as a nurse, the ground floor and basement of her house turned into a hospital for the republican casualties, Isoeult getting medical supplies from sympathetic doctors, Cumann na mBan women helping out as nurses.

Her visit was not merely a social occasion. Again she needed help. In July, after the Four Courts, Isoeult's hus-band Stuart had joined the IRA. He had travelled to Belgium to get arms and then joined the fighting in Dublin where he was arrested after helping capture an ammunition train loaded with Free State Arms at Amiens station. Now he was interned and was one of many prisoners who had gone on hunger strike. Now Willie Yeats was called on to intercede on behalf of both Maud's son and son-in-law.

ARTHUR GRIFFITH, the Prime Minister of the new Irish Free State, the man who, with Maud Gonne, had creat-ed Sinn Féin, now gave up in despair. The civil war had been the final crushing blow to his hopes and ideals for Ireland. In August of 1922 he collapsed and died of a cere-bral haemorrhage.

A few weeks later another leader of the new Irish Free State was dead. Michael Collins, who had carried Griffith's coffin on his shoulder, was killed in an ambush by irregu-lars when passing through de Valera territory in his own home county of Cork.

Willie Yeats and Maud had attended both funerals, Maud indescribably sad. Griffith had been one of her longest and closest friends. Yeats' own sadness was blunted by a wariness of the new leaders of the Free State, William Cosgrave and Yeats' friend, Kevin O'Higgins. They were young, resolute men, who would let nothing stand in the way of bringing peace to the country.

The first efforts made by O'Higgins, the Minister for Justice, were designed to stop the killing, making his intentions clear in his address to the first meeting of the Free State government after Collins' funeral. He told the assembly that the government could no longer tolerate a state of affairs in which hundreds of men took the lives of others. O'Higgins intended that the guerrilla war should be ended at all costs.

In a country whose economy was rapidly being destroyed, O'Higgins issued an Emergency Powers Act. It was blunt and brutal. The irregulars would be offered an amnesty for surrender before a certain date, or else any in unauthorised possession of a weapon would be shot.

The reply from the anti-treaty side was just as harsh – any member of the Dáil who had voted for the Act would be shot on sight.

O'Higgins' response was terrible as he ordered the summary execution, the following morning, of four of the leaders from the Four Courts. One of those shot, Rory O'Connor, who shared a cell with Sean MacBride, had been the best man at O'Higgins' wedding only the year before.

At the time of the executions Maud stood outside the gaol with broken-hearted mothers. It was the birth of another organisation, the Women's Prisoners Defence League, determined to improve the prisoners' conditions.

On 22 November, Erskine Childers, another old friend of Maud's, for whom she was acting as secretary, and who had sided with the irregulars as their leading anti-treaty propagandist, was arrested in Glendalough at his family home and charged with the unauthorised possession of a pistol.

Although a proven patriot and gun-runner, a hero of the war against the British and a member of the treaty delegation to London in 1921, it was not enough to save him from a government intent on making examples. There would be no favouritism: he was court martialled in secret and sentenced to death, along with seven other rebels. Despite Maud's desperate attempts to save him, Cosgrave refused clemency and Childers was executed on 24 November. He died a brave man, his last words to the firing squad inviting them to 'take a step or two forward lads, it will be easier that way'.

These ruthless attempts by the Free State government to restore law and order were an incitement to revenge and two members of the Dáil were shot, one of them killed. Yet again the new government felt examples had to be made and, after a final attempt to establish law and order, they took the awesome decision that all the men interned in Mountjoy Gaol for carrying weapons were to be shot without trial. After six months in power, the Free State government had executed 77 men.

O'Higgins was in despair. He shook his head wearily at a meeting of the Inner Council: 'What will happen to our country? We have practised upon ourselves worse indignities than those the British had practised on us since Cromwell and Mountjoy.'

O<small>N 6 D</small>ECEMBER a new Parliament was sworn in, a Cumann na nGaedheal administration, led by Cosgrave, taking the oath of allegiance, with a second chamber, the Senate, made up of a cross section of society, landlords, poets, lawyers and trade unionists.

The letters chalked upon the front door of the house in

Merrion Square announced simply, 'Senator W.B. Yeats'. Yeats stared at it, puzzled. Inside was a note. He read it slowly before passing it to George. He had been nominated for the Senate. The note was from his old friend, Oliver St John Gogarty, now a senator himself. And there was further news: he was to be awarded a Doctorate from Trinity College.

He stared reflectively into the blazing fire in the drawing room. 'To be a senator, to help save this country, will be the patriotic thing to do but it means I will have a bodyguard.' He smiled at her but inside he was torn with indecision. Maud's support for the anti-treaty republicans was growing all the time and he feared her response to him taking the position.

'You have to accept it, Willie. It will be a brave and patriotic decision and you will be taking risks for your beliefs. There will be objectors. What about Jack?'

Yeats shrugged. 'I doubt if he will speak to me.' His brother was a staunch republican who supported the antitreaty forces. George put his thoughts into words. 'And Maud ...? She will probably never forgive you.'

'I will have to try to get her to understand. Try to tell her again what I believe I can do for Ireland.'

30

MAUD HAD moved to a new home, Roebuck House, a small Georgian building in the Clonskeagh suburb of Dublin. Yeats visited her soon after his first appearance in the Senate, where his friend Gogarty had introduced him with great praise: 'Without his vision of Ireland in 1916 there would have been no Free State; without the poetry of Yeats, I and my colleagues would not be representatives of an independent state. His patriotism is pure, selfless and ideal.'

The meeting with Maud was intense, a turning point in their lives.

At first she was quiet, fearing Sean might yet face a firing squad. Yeats reassured her. 'Don't worry, Maud. His father's name, what you have done for your country, they will both stand him in good stead.'

She nodded, an almost confused expression on her face. 'My ideas have changed so much, Willie. My thoughts for the way ahead have changed. Now I deplore the military ...'

He stopped her, shaking his head vigorously. 'You advocated violence ...'

She stopped him, raising her arm angrily. 'We can all change. Perhaps I no longer believe in the violent approach but I don't support this government. They suppress the republicans so ruthlessly. Free State soldiers even raided this house when I was away. They ransacked it and burnt some of your letters and poems in the middle of the road.' She paused, near to tears, a tragic sadness in her expression. 'Why? Where is it leading? It's not Irish law that has broken down. When Arthur and I started Sinn Féin we brought real justice to Ireland for the first time in centuries.' Her face became grim. 'Now I have to support the anti-treaty side since the government started the terrible reprisals against the prisoners.'

Yeats was lost for words, lighting a cigarette and offering her one, trying to remain composed as he told her of his new appointment.

'Perhaps I have now become someone of importance, Maud. Dr Yeats and Senator Yeats! A pensioner of England and a senator of Ireland. How's that for a contradiction?'

She looked at him coldly. 'A member of Cosgrave's new government, Willie? Are you really willing to accept honours from traitors to nationalism? People who thought so much of you will say you are a pro-English traitor.'

'They can say it, Maud, but remember I turned down the chance of an English knighthood. And probably a peerage to follow. Have they such short memories?' Then he shrugged. 'I am told it is a reward for my writing although my old membership of the IRB must have helped, that and my work for the Abbey.' He laughed. 'Anyway, I couldn't refuse, I need the pay. I had to take it for my family.'

She looked at him scornfully for some time before replying. 'Who will you represent?'

'I'll be an independent. I'm learning to stay silent.'

She suddenly showed concern. 'Don't you see the danger you are in? De Valera has said that the senators themselves are the enemy. That includes you. And the anti-treaty IRA have orders to burn the houses of senators. Even the president's, Cosgrave's, has been burned.'

Yeats sighed. 'I know. George has insisted I have two bodyguards. I probably need them. Two bullets were put through my windows yesterday.'

She stood up, looking down at him coldly, her voice suddenly hardening. 'Why, Willie? Why you? Don't you see? The Free State is just a continuation of the old British Rule under a new name.' She paused, her hands on her hips, standing tall. 'I hate this government which you are a part of.' She had worked herself up into a rage and now her anger erupted, as she shook a finger at him. 'This means you and I are finished, Willie. Until you denounce this government, our relationship is over forever.'

Her stance was so melodramatic that Yeats suppressed an immediate urge to laugh, as she continued, in full, hectoring flow. 'You accept the legitimacy of a State which suppresses young republican soldiers still seeking to free Ireland from the contamination of the British Empire.'

He tried to calm her. 'Can't you see, Maud? I will be better placed to work for Ireland. I have already voted for things that matter to you. A pension for Arthur Griffith's family. You supported him when he was alive and together you created Sinn Féin. Now I have got support for his family. For your sake mainly, Maud.' He smiled resignedly. 'You don't seem to understand what I try to do for you.' He smiled wearily and recited from his poem 'Words':

I had this thought a while ago,
My darling cannot understand
What I have done, or what would do

In this blind bitter land.

He stood up, walking to her and reaching for her hand. She pulled it angrily away as his words had little effect. She looked at him almost with contempt, turning and striding to the door, and standing aside for him to leave. She stared hard at him, her words as he departed ringing in his ears. 'Forever, Willie.'

It was the parting of the ways. She and her son were now republican activists, her oldest and closest friend, Willie Yeats, part of the legitimate government.

But not even Maud Gonne could change his convictions. He had a role in helping create a new, free Ireland. He was married and had a son to carry on the family name – a long way from his humble beginnings. He was now an established figure, a man of influence with his castle in the west and an elegant house in the most fashionable square in Dublin.

He was a celebrity of some status, but his health was failing, George increasingly concerned. His blood pressure was high, his eyesight particularly bad and he was putting on too much weight. He was still a handsome man though, with a full head of white hair which still flopped over his eyes. He now dressed the part he thought befitting a world-famous poet and senator, a black velvet coat and silver-buckled shoes, a wide black ribbon retaining his tortoise shell glasses. And the social life of the once gauche young poet had expanded: he was a regular visitor to the great Dublin social occasions, a top-hatted, monocled visitor to the Horse Show and race meetings, now knowledgeable about horses and racing.

The house in Merrion Square became a centre for the

Dublin literary and even political scene, George running the home as well as acting as his business manager, editor and hostess, and sometimes also as his nurse.

Kevin O'Higgins, whose father had been murdered by the irregulars, and his young wife were frequent visitors to Yeats' home. Another genius from a poor, under-privileged part of Dublin, a shy, nervous little man in a cloth cap and steel-rimmed glasses, Sean O'Casey also often visited Merrion Square.

IN APRIL 1923 Isoeult came to Yeats for help. Again he felt nothing but despair for the family.

'Mother has been arrested, Willie. For being president of the banned Women's Prisoners' Defence League and for spreading anti-government literature. She's in Kilmainham Gaol.' Isoeult looked frantic. 'She's gone on hunger strike. Please help her.'

He shook his head resignedly. 'Yet again, Isoeult?' He sighed. He knew of Maud's arrest and had already tried to intervene. 'I've already spoken to Cosgrave. I told him she is 57 years old and won't be able to stand the stress of a hunger strike like a younger woman. There's little else I can do.'

'Will he help?' Isoeult grasped his hand.

'He made no promises, I'm afraid. He believes women should stay out of politics and help mind the sick. He told me that if they take part in political activities they should not be considered as ordinary females.' Sadness swept over him. 'Maud told me that if I do not denounce the government she will renounce me forever.' He looked despairingly at Isoeult. 'She cannot forgive me for becoming a senator.'

But his pleas as a senator were effective. Twenty days

later he stood outside the prison, out of her sight, watching sadly when Maud Gonne was released, carried out on a stretcher.

A few days later it was Maud's turn to once again ask for help, ignoring her denunciation of him when she telephoned him at his home. Isoeult had been arrested in a general security swoop by the government. Yet again Willie Yeats interceded on behalf of his adopted family, Isoeult being released that day.

In May there was another cease-fire and an uneasy truce, de Valera, with IRA agreement, calling an end to hostilities, ordering the irregulars to lay down their arms, issuing his orders with a declaration: '... other means must be sought to safeguard the nation's fight ... Your sacrifice and that of your comrades was not in vain.'

It was the end of the cruel and bitter civil war.

IT WAS late 1923 and the November damp of the previous week had been dissipated by the winter gales sweeping over the country, claiming the last of the leaves from the trees in the square. It was eleven o'clock at night when the telephone on the small table in the hall rang insistently. The caller was Bertie Smylie, the editor of *The Irish Times*, an old friend and frequent visitor to functions at Yeats' home. 'I have great news for you, Senator. And for this country.'

Yeats cut him short impatiently. He had been busy in his study balancing household accounts when the phone rang and it had been an irritating trek down from the first floor. 'What is it, Bertie?'

'The Nobel prize, Willie. It's yours. A very great honour.'

The significance did not immediately sink into the

exasperated Yeats. Finally he spoke, the accounts still very much on his mind. 'How much, Bertie, how much?'

'A lot of money, I am sure, Senator. But the glory, for you and Ireland. Think of it ...'

Yeats thanked him. His first thoughts were for George, for her to share the moment with him.

And then Maud. He felt a terrible sorrow burn inside him. Maud who had fought with him, worked with him and who was now so irretrievably against him. The same Maud he had loved so deeply and so long since those early days.

And then other thoughts took over, for Lady Gregory, who had done so much to make it possible.

He held his head in his hands, sudden tears of pride, of success mixed with sadness, swelling in his eyes. He lifted his head as the phone rang again. It was the Swedish ambassador to Ireland. Now it was official. He had been awarded the Nobel Prize for Literature. He feigned ignorance and surprise which gave way to modest delight.

He was sitting again on the stairs when George came from the bedroom, alarm on her face as she saw him. He stood up and held her to him, at first unable to speak as emotion overcame him.

'It was the Swedish Ambassador.' He held her close, whispering to her. 'They've given me the Nobel Prize.'

She pulled back, staring at him, her own tears welling up, interrupted even before she had time to congratulate him by the ringing of the doorbell. 'I am so very pleased for you, Willie. So pleased.' She whispered, brushing her eyes with her fingers as she answered the door.

It was well after midnight by the time all the journalists and congratulatory visitors had left. He closed the door and stood with his back to it, smiling at his wife. As ever, she was the practical one when he told her how much the prize money was.

'It will make a difference to us, Willie. £7,500 is a lot of money and we can pay off what is owing on the house.'

'And I can get the reference library I have always wanted ...'

In his enthusiasm he had already spent the whole award. George was more practical. She raised an eyebrow. 'We still need carpets and furniture. And your sisters need some help.'

He nodded. Lily had been diagnosed with tuberculosis and was in a nursing home, her expenses becoming increasingly difficult to meet. Now his feelings turned to an overwhelming sense of relief. It was the first time in his life he had been free of financial worries.

Over the following days there were congratulatory telegrams, from James Joyce and John Quinn among others. He sat and read, with hopeful longing, through hundreds of letters and telegrams. But there was nothing from Maud, the person whose approval mattered above all.

Several days later, George read from the evening paper. 'It says the Chairman of the Senate stood up: "We take great pride in this award on account of the courage and patriotism which decided Senator Yeats, twelve months ago, to cast in his lot with his own people under conditions then very critical."'

It was two weeks later, on 10 December, that Willie Yeats received his diploma and gave his acceptance speech to the Royal Academy of Sweden. He had met the King of Sweden at the palace, waiting in a long gallery surrounded by those wearing the chains of office of the Swedish Order of Merit, men of letters, the intellectual and cultural soul of the country.

To Willie Yeats it was a moving experience.

His lecture, to an audience made up mainly of women, was on 'The Irish Dramatic Movement' and covered the history of Ireland's literature up to the present day. George was amongst the audience, looking proud and striking in a cream silk blouse, a loose fur-lined jacket and a tight fitting turbanned hat.

His voice was full of emotion as he continued, almost reflectively, to speak about the contribution of others, magnanimous in his praise. '... When your king gave me the medal and diploma, I felt that a young man's ghost should have stood upon one side of me, a living woman sinking into the infirmity of old age on the other. I think that when Lady Gregory's name and John Synge's name are spoken by future generations, my name, if remembered, will come up in the talk, because of the years we have worked together. They would have been pleased to be here because their work, as mine, delights in history and tradition ... We felt we must have a theatre of our own but it was not until I met, in 1896, Lady Augusta Gregory, that such a theatre became possible.'

He finished his speech and thanked the audience with words from one of his poems:

And wisdom is a butterfly
And not a gloomy bird of prey.
... If little planned is little sinned
But little need the great distress
What's dying but a second wind?

Two days later the Theatre Royal in Stockholm staged *Cathleen ní Houlihan.*

31

THERE WERE sad times to balance the good. In 1924 John Quinn died of cancer in New York. These more success-ful years for Willie were spent without Maud, the woman who had been his inspiration. Politics had created a great gulf between them, from the day she had disowned his friendship, divorced from his life until, several years later, he saw her again. Old longings resurfaced. It was the first night of Sean O'Casey's, *The Plough and the Stars*, in February 1926.

It was a play about the Easter Rising. And once more there was controversy at the Abbey.

The cast and the manager had already been warned about the language used. The republicans in the audience, mostly relatives, friends and comrades of the rebels of 1916, objected to the scene where the Citizens' Army flag and Tricolour were brought into a pub frequented by prostitutes where men were drinking and wallowing in mawkish sen-timentality for Mother Ireland. Above all they objected to the ridiculing of the men of 1916 and its portrayal of Dublin tenement life as one of prostitution, drink and poverty.

O'Casey had refused to make martyrs of the rebel lead-ers, the play appearing to criticise the idealism of those who had given their lives to the cause, the anti-hero in the play, being a member of the Citizens' Army, joining the uprising out of vanity instead of idealism, and ultimately being killed.

Cumann na mBan, led by Maud, had organised a protest and there were continual disruptions until, as the prostitute came on stage the crowd began shouting to her to get off as she was a disgrace to her sex. On the fourth night, after the usual hissing and booing, violence erupted, some of the audience invading the stage and pelting the actors with rotten fruit.

Maud Gonne sat with Kathleen Clark several rows from the front, in cold silence, refusing to join in the protests by women in the audience that their men did not drink. After all, she had sued for divorce on the grounds of her husband's own drunkenness.

Another old and still true friend, Olivia Shakespeare, was with Yeats at the side of the stage. Yeats turned to her as he saw Maud, his voice betraying his bitterness. 'It's been four years, Olivia. Not a word from her. Now she comes here to cause trouble in the theatre Lady Gregory and I started.'

He shrugged, almost despairingly. 'I gave her so much help and advice. I always will when she needs it, whether she takes it or not.' He stared long and sadly at the once so-familiar face. She was wearing a veil of dark blue, long and down over her shoulders, her deep-set eyes, when she removed the veil, full of sadness. But her face, more lined, was still, even at that distance and in the artificial light, the face of a goddess.

Willie took his eyes from her as the trouble makers refused to stop, then, finally running out of patience, signalling for the curtains to be raised and storming onto the stage.

He waited until there was quiet, slowly casting his eye over the audience but refusing to look in Maud's direction, the familiar, mellow voice intense as he stood square onto the audience. 'I thought you had got tired of this behaviour, which started fifteen years ago. But you have disgraced yourselves again. I am ashamed to face you. Is this going to be a recurring celebration of Irish genius? Synge first and then O'Casey? The news of what has happened here will go from country to country. Once more Dublin has rocked the cradle of genius ... When you are dead and gone, buried and forgotten, the name of O'Casey will resound through the world to the glory of Ireland and of art where civilisation exists.'

There was an almost embarrassed hush when he had finished until some of the noisier members of the audience started heckling again. Yeats lost his patience, beckoning forward the police who had already been called. Without hesitation he pointed out those protesters he wanted removed, one young man staring challengingly at Yeats as he was led away. Tall, fair hair flat on his head, hollow cheeked, fine features with deep set eyes. It was Sean, the son to whose life Maud was now dedicated. He had escaped from prison after the Four Courts incident by jumping from a lorry when being transferred during a hunger strike from Mountjoy to Kilmainham Gaol. During his time on the run, working with IRA nationalists, he had married, with O'Higgins' personal guarantee that he would not be arrested if he came out of hiding.

Yeats sighed in terrible anguish. It was as if he was tearing his adopted family apart. He wondered if he would ever speak to Maud again or even see her?

THE IRELAND known by Willie Yeats and Maud Gonne was changing. In March of 1926, Eamon de Valera resigned as president of Sinn Féin and, together with Constance Markievicz, made Fianna Fáil into a political party. Another founding member was Sean MacBride who, after serving as IRA propagandist in Europe and as de Valera's secretary, now worked as a journalist. But some of that change in Ireland was terrible. And final.

The morning of 26 July was sweltering hot, the streets almost deserted, when Kevin O'Higgins left his home to walk to mass at his parish church in Booterstown just south of Dublin. The precautions he had taken in the years immediately after taking power had been relaxed, his bodyguard at that moment having a breakfast prepared by O'Higgins' wife who was at home looking after their four-year-old daughter Maeve and her baby sister.

O'Higgins' pace changed, wary and unsure as an approaching car slowed. Then sudden alarm, hardly time for fear as one of the men in the car leaped out, rushing toward him, a gun raised. A shot at point blank range: sudden noise, sudden pain as O'Higgins staggered back in confusion, puzzlement, then sudden terrible realisation as he turned and tried to run, the gunman following, joined now by two others. O'Higgins stopped, refusing to go easily. To run was pointless. He raised his hand questioningly to his murderers, his eyes turning to each in turn as the bullets ripped into him, his strength abruptly going. His legs buckled and he collapsed to the ground.

More shots were fired as he lay bleeding, before the murderers climbed back into their car and drove quickly away. They had waited a long time to settle old scores.

O'Higgins felt nothing, except that the warmth of the

sun had gone and that it was now terribly cold. There were voices, as, apprehensively, people came from their homes to help. Then the fear came, acknowledgement of his fate as, through dimming eyes he could see the priest who held his hand, an unfocused mind trying to remember prayers of contrition as they waited for the ambulance.

Kevin O'Higgins died at five o'clock that afternoon, his last words his acceptance of Ireland's suffering as he forgave his murderers.

Yeats was on the way to the Gresham Hotel for a dinner that evening when he heard, the news saddening him. He left his wife and friends and walked the streets for hours in grief over the death of a good friend. And remembering O'Higgins' words at the time of the executions after the civil war: 'Nobody can expect to live who has done what I have done.' And one evening at Yeats' house when discussing the hard line taken against prisoners, which he had resisted as much as possible, O'Higgins commented wryly, 'Soon I'll be sitting on a damp cloud with Mick!'

As he walked Yeats could only think that perhaps his friend was doing just that, staring down with Collins at the sad bitter land which Ireland still was.

The police had an immediate suspect, a member of Fianna Fáil. Sean MacBride had been identified by a gardener who had witnessed the murder and he was quickly arrested.

There was only one man his mother could turn to for help.

They had been years apart, and yet, when she needed help, he was still there for her.

Willie was angry with Maud when she came to his home. Angry with her and with Sean for his continuing involvement with the IRA. 'You come to me quite unashamedly for help and more, Maud, even though you encouraged him. Just to satisfy your own mad political ideals.' He shook his head vehemently. 'He's Director of Intelligence for the IRA, for God's sake! Why shouldn't the government hold him?'

Maud said nothing, her head held high, refusing to be humiliated by the man she had rejected so many times, still confident of the power she had over him.

'It was such a heinous crime ...' She went to interrupt but he silenced her with a wave of his hand. 'O'Higgins was the one strong intellect in Irish public life ...'

She placed her hand on his arm but he turned from her. She pleaded with him. 'He had nothing to do with O'Higgins' murder, Willie. I swear it.'

Still Yeats rebuffed her. 'He's been identified by witnesses, Maud. There's a strong case against him.'

'But he's done little against the Free State. He's just a republican, like me. He just believes, as I have since before we first met, that Ireland has a right to be independent.' She stared accusingly. 'As you once did.'

He nodded. 'I did and, like you, would have been happy with Home Rule. But you changed. I have no time for the awful hatred which still exists.'

He stared at her in silence, conflicting emotions coursing through him. He wanted her to suffer, to glimpse the hate she bottled inside her. But he felt helpless. It mattered little what she asked or what she had done to him.

He knew he would always come when she called, do as she wanted. He breathed deeply, walking to the window and staring out over the square, speaking without facing her. Even now he had to reassure her. 'You have no need to worry, Maud. The government won't harm the son of a hero and John MacBride was a hero to many of them.' He wanted, cruelly, to prolong her anguish but was unable to. 'I did try to get his release but they said he had to go to trial ...' He stopped, suddenly relenting as he saw her terrible pain for her only son. 'But the charge will be dropped. A witness claims to have seen him on the ferry from England at the time of the murder. He will have to remain in Mountjoy for the present under the new Public Safety Act.'

She held her hands to her breast, tears of relief spilling over but making no comment, no words of thanks, concerned only about her son. He sighed wearily but his voice softened as he spoke. 'You don't help, Maud. Your work for the prisoners, raising money for their families and for the republicans. It all causes resentment. And then your meetings every week, stirring up unrest. It all turns the authorities against you. And against Sean.'

The meetings in O'Connell Street had now become a feature of Dublin life, as Maud walked with slow, theatrical steps to the meeting place, dressed in clothes of flowing black, always carrying a bouquet of flowers, uniformed and plain clothes police always nearby. As she took the platform there was a burst of cheering, her voice instantly recognisable, once heard never to be forgotten, the voice of Cathleen ní Houlihan, when she pleaded the case for the political prisoners.

She looked at Yeats defiantly. 'I cause no harm to the government. I just want justice. Why don't you come and hear me?'

Yeats smiled wryly. 'You've held the meetings for years now, but to no effect. They're a part of times past. There's no point in me going because we will never change the other's politics. It's time now to let it all go, Maud.'

He held his hands wide, deep sadness on his face. 'It's over. All the speeches and martyrdom. The new republican dead will never share the glory of the earlier dead, never be remembered in the same way, their names not spoken today except at your meetings in O'Connell Street or at some prison gate.' He shook his head sadly, his voice soft. 'You are almost the sole surviving friend of my early manhood, still protesting in your sybiline old age, as once you did in youth and beauty, against what seems to you to be tyranny.'

Despite his gentle criticism, there was concern in his voice. 'I'm going away to Spain for a short rest. I can do no more for you here. While I'm away, please take care of yourself.'

There was sudden concern in her expression. 'Take care of yourself also, Willie. Perhaps we could start writing to each other again?' The old, beautiful, teasing smile returned, her voice still that of the defiant Maud of old. 'But I won't change what I believe in.'

'You know what I think of your beliefs. And I, and others like me, hate the dislike of the more ignorant sort of Catholic for our beliefs.'

She bridled at him, anger in her expression. 'You hate the Catholic church, Willie. But the Public Safety Act of yours by which anyone may be arrested and charged with the most appalling crimes, imprisoned or deported, surely that is an act of hate?' Her voice quivered with emotion. 'Go away into the sun and reflect on it, write poetry and pray to God to send men who understand what love of Ireland and their fellows means to undo these hateful things. Because you are a great poet you will be forgiven for your part in it. But sin no more, Willie.'

He looked at her wearily and sadly. 'We can only put our faith in human nature, Maud. To stop people's liberties in the name of an uninformed Catholic clergy will create embittered people. Legislation upon religious grounds opens the way for every kind of intolerance and every kind of religious persecution.'

She waved her hand at him, dismissing his criticism. There was no more to be said, their differences still irreconcilable.

They were together once more that summer as, only days later, he lost yet another good, dear friend from his youth. Eva Gore-Booth had died the previous year. Now her sister, Constance Markievicz, an opponent of O'Higgins in the civil war, had entered hospital for a routine appendectomy but complications set in. She died on 15 July, only five days after the murder of Kevin O'Higgins. The country had lost another true patriot.

Both sisters were among the dear memories of his youth. He remembered the grandeur and tranquillity of the sisters' home at Lissadell as he took time from everything else he was involved in to write a poem to commemorate them both.

The light of evening, Lissadell
Great windows open to the south
Two girls in silk kimonos, both
Beautiful, one a gazelle.

'In memory of Eva Gore-Booth and Constance Markievicz', was a requiem for lost beauty and lost youth.

Yeats stood with Maud at Constance's funeral as Eamon de Valera gave the eulogy: 'Ease and station she put aside ...

sacrifice, misunderstanding and scorn lay on the road she accepted, but she trod it unflinchingly.'

It was moving praise from de Valera, the anti-feminist who had even refused to have women serve under him at the Flour Mills during the uprising, a man sometimes accused of forgiving his enemies yet forgetting his friends.

Willie Yeats had been right. It was all over, the rousing, patriotic speeches, the martyrdom. The politics of Ireland were changing, the IRA breaking away from de Valera who decided not to work against the situation, but with it, as Michael Collins had done ten years earlier. Political stability was nearing when the new Fianna Fáil party did well in the elections of June 1927, claiming 44 seats while Sinn Féin retained only five, every candidate now agreeing to take the Oath of Allegiance.

And just as life in Ireland was changing, so also was life for Willie Yeats. It was a time for taking stock of what had been achieved, for reflection and planning for an easier future. Then, in October of 1927, his health began to fail. A heavy cold, increased by his heavy smoking, turned to congestion of the lungs, his condition worsening, with a high temperature and delirium. When he had recovered sufficiently, George decided it was time to move to a warmer climate.

Later that month, with Anne and Michael at boarding school at Villars-sur-Bex in Switzerland, Willie and George went first to Algericas, then onto Seville for more sunshine and warmth and finally, after ten days, for better medical attention, to the Hotel Château St George in Cannes, staying there for a three-month convalescence. It gave them time to search for a more permanent winter home, finally deciding on Rapallo on the Italian Riviera, moving there in February of 1928.

It was a place where they no longer felt like visitors but part of an established artistic community, friends such as Ezra and Dorothy Pound already living nearby.

Their home was an apartment in the Villa Americhe, perched high on the the fourth floor, overlooking a long, gracefully curving promenade flanked by tall palm trees, the blue Mediterranean below. It was bright and airy, his study with doors opening onto a balcony which looked out on olive trees, laurel, camellia and bougainvillaea, their perfume, lingering in the humid air, flooding the gardens.

The climate was to his liking, and time was spent lying in the sun and swimming, and enjoying the children's holidays. He often visited the street cafés of Rapallo, in long debates with Ezra Pound and friends, now dressed more flamboyantly, bright shirts, coloured ties, his face turned brown from the sun. The pale, lanky, insecure young poet was now a distant memory.

32

IN 1928, WHEN Maud returned to Dublin after completing the sale of Les Mouettes in order to give Isoeult a home at Laragh Castle in Glendalough, she called to see Willie Yeats at the house in Merrion Square. They had been a long time apart, two years since they had last met, and there was a long pause, staring into each other's eyes before she moved towards him and he kissed her gently before holding her at arm's length. He shook his head and smiled sadly. 'It's been so long and we are both growing old, Maud. Perhaps now we won't have to quarrel any more.'

There was a long, contemplative silence before she smiled, that wonderful smile which still lit up the room. 'I suppose so, Willie. Old age is terrible. I can see no redeeming features in it. I hate it, as you do, but I am more a rebel against man than you and rebel less against nature. But, you know ...' She paused reflectively. 'I think I accept the inevitable more than you and will be happy to go gently into the unknown.'

They stood facing each other, holding hands at their sides like young lovers before he spoke. 'I wrote a poem for you once. You made no comment then. Listen to it now.' He spoke slowly as he remembered it, without reading.

There is grey in your hair,
Young men no longer suddenly catch their breath
When you are passing
But maybe some old gaffer mutters a blessing
Because it was your prayer
Recovered him upon the bed of death.

She took over from him and spoke the final lines slowly:

Vague memories, nothing but memories.

He looked at her and smiled, suddenly emotional as he
saw the tears which had sprung to her eyes. 'You did
remember.' He shook his head. 'And I thought you had
ignored it all these years.'

'It is one of your most beautiful poems, Willie. But then
I was younger and not ready to face old age.'

'Everything changes, Maud.' He stood up and walked
over to the window to stare at the trees in the square. 'We
are selling this house. George is quite broken hearted at giving up such a lovely place but it is too big for us. We are
buying a flat in Fitzwilliam Square. Then we will go to
Rapallo, where I can put Ireland's past behind me and write
as I wish.'

Maud smiled. 'I'm pleased for you, Willie.' Her voice
changed, tinged with affection. 'How is Augusta? I haven't
seen her for some time. I heard she isn't too well.'

'I spend a lot of time with her. And she's been staying
with us for a month.' His expression was sad. 'She is an
infirm old lady now after the operations for breast cancer.'

'And your castle, Willie. You loved that so much. Do
you still go there?'

He lowered his head in a sudden wave of sadness. 'We're selling it. It's too remote and the dampness makes my rheumatism worse. Another part of my life going.'

A YEAR later Yeats made another of his visits to Coole Park. By now his dearest friend was very frail, walking slowly and painfully as they took their usual late evening walk beside the lake, he a large noble figure, his face masked by thin-framed round glasses which gave him the intellectual appearance he had sought so desperately in his younger years. He placed Lady Gregory's arm through his, talking quietly, shared memories revisited.

They were nearing the end of a life together, a battle against odds yet so wonderfully successful. He spoke after a long, comfortable silence, shafts of cold moonlight penetrating the trees as they watched the swans floating sleepily, a myriad of stars reflected in the still water.

'We were a wonderful team, Augusta. We achieved so much; the renaissance of literature in Ireland and the theatre, our theatre, is doing well. It has survived all the nationalist anger, even staying independent of all political, social, nationalist and religious opinion. We should be proud that its drama was not just for Ireland but for the whole world.' There was no false modesty in his voice as he continued. 'I think ours has been the greatest literary partnership of this century.'

She smiled gently as she remembered their successes. Then she had a request. He looked at her inquiringly. 'Write a poem for me about this place. As it was. As it will never be again.'

He smiled gently at his old friend. 'Of course, dear Augusta. I have wanted to do that for some time.'

She squeezed his arm in gratitude.

Several years later, in the winter of 1931, Willie Yeats became almost a permanent resident at Coole Park, though recovering from ill health himself, as Augusta Gregory's health declined further. She was increasingly frail, unable to sleep, wracked with arthritis and in great pain. It was clear the end was near and Willie was there with her, for her.

Soon after returning to Dublin, at Easter, there was a letter for him, from a noble lady to her dearest friend. It was her last letter to him, filling him with a terrible sadness as he read it aloud to his wife.

I don't feel too well, Willie. It may be time for me to slip away ... I don't want to be a burden and give trouble ... I have had a good life and except for the grief of parting with those who are gone, a happy one. I do think I have been of use to this country and for that, in great part, I thank you.

I thank you for these last months you have spent with me. Your presence here has made them pass quickly and happily ... as your friendship has made my last years ... all blessings to you in years to come.

He wept openly when he had finished reading as his wife consoled him, his head in her arms.

IN THAT same year, the IRA moved towards the left, causing the government, through fear of communism, to make them a banned organisation, together with the Women's Prisoners' Defence League and Cumann na mBan. Many of the IRA leaders were arrested, whilst others went on the run.

In February, a complacent William Cosgrave called an election which he expected to win with a comfortable majority. But Maud canvassed incessantly with the Women's Prisoners' Defence League, holding rival meetings to stop the Cosgrave government, her speeches, as always, inflammatory. '... We do this for the honour of Ireland, even though some of us, old and feeble, are roughly handled, our clothes torn, we will save Ireland the sight of murderers and traitors flaunting their crimes in public.'

Her efforts, and those of her supporters, were successful, de Valera's Fianna Fáil party, with the support of the Labour Party and the IRA, narrowly defeating Cosgrave's government. Willie Yeats cast his own vote against de Valera, whose first action when in power was to abolish the Oath of Allegiance and claim sovereignty over all 32 counties, yet acknowledging the King as the Head of the Commonwealth.

At last de Valera had become the country's leader, his supporters convinced he was the man sent to lead the country from the wilderness and away from the bitterness of the past, the greatest Irishman who ever lived. Others, the diehard republicans, regarded his entry to the Dáil as a betrayal, their militant wing, the IRA, condemning him as the greatest twister and traitor in Irish history.

After the election the Women's Prisoners' Defence League made presentations to all who had helped in their successful campaign, Maud Gonne the only one who refused to accept any honour.

But at the ceremonies Willie Yeats stood with tears of pride in his eyes as she gracefully accepted the best accolade of all when acclaimed by the leaders of the Women's Prisoners' Defence League as 'the greatest Irish woman who ever lived'.

Soon, however, his pride was to be replaced by a terrible sadness for another woman he loved.

Willie had been expecting the call for weeks, every day his thoughts turning to Augusta. The sudden ringing of the telephone on 23 May, in 1932, seemed particularly ominous. He had just come through the front door as George took the call. She glanced up and he knew immediately.

'It's Augusta's solicitor, Willie ...' She looked at him with great sadness. 'He's been trying to get in touch with you ...' Her voice was hushed. '... he says she is dying.' She went to him and held both his hands in hers. 'I'm so sorry, Willie.'

The earliest possible train the following morning was not soon enough. Lady Gregory's granddaughter, Catherine, met him at the station. But he was too late, she had died during the night, the young girl consoling him as he broke down in tears, his grief almost inconsolable.

Augusta Gregory had first said goodbye to her great house. The servants had helped her downstairs to walk slowly through all the rooms, staring for long moments at the paintings and portraits, the sculptures and bound books. Remembering. She had gazed from each of the windows at the lake and woods in its early summer colours. It was her last farewell to Coole before she was taken back to her room. Minutes later she passed peacefully away.

Yeats sat beside her bed for hours in silent homage as he too remembered. When he returned to Dublin George was waiting at the door as he climbed from the cab. He gazed sadly at his wife, shaking his head. 'She's dead and I will miss her so much. A great light in my life has gone.'

She took his arm, leading him inside. 'We will all miss her, Willie.'

He sat down wearily at the table, his hands folded in front of him. 'So much of my life was spent working with her. Her beautiful house became my home and gave me so much peace.' There was a catch in his voice as he looked at his wife, a deep sadness in his eyes. 'I think we were the last of the romantics. She was a part of an aristocratic Ireland, a place we will never see again in our lifetime. An Ireland before all the hate and troubles, before de Valera and the church and its rule over people.'

He had brought with him the picture by Augustus John which Lady Gregory had wanted him to have. It showed him in the open air, a broad-brimmed hat on his lap, his white hair blowing in the wind, the cloths of heaven in the sky behind him.

'I even finished the poem she asked for but she never heard it. I will call it "Coole Park, 1929", in her memory.' There was a deep sadness in his voice as he recited a few lines.

Here traveller, scholar, poet, take your stand
When all these rooms and passages are gone,
When nettles wave upon a shapeless mound
And saplings root among the broken stone,
And dedicate – eyes bent upon the ground,
... A moments memory to that laurelled head.

As always in time of sorrow, his thoughts turned again to Maud. As if reading his thoughts George spoke for both of them. 'Will Maud know?'

He shrugged, bitterness in his voice. 'Would she care? She is old now.' His shoulders slumped and his face saddened again. 'But she is the only one alive from my youth.'

His eyes clouded over. 'It was a grand youth, George, such inspirations. Such dreams.' And then, woefully. 'And such obsessions.'

There was no one to hear him, his wife had left him alone with his memories as he spoke aloud, as if addressing one of his audiences. 'It was such a special, close friendship. Almost a marriage.'

COOLE PARK, the great rooms, the deep, cool woods and magical lake had gone forever. And Ballylee was now another memory.

And the grandeur of Merrion Square and Fitzwillian Square were also behind him. But there was to be another romantic home for the Irish poet. It was shortly after his sixty-seventh birthday, in July of 1932, that Riversdale took the place of Coole and Thor Ballylee in his heart.

Riversdale was in Rathfarnham, south of Dublin, at the foot of the Dublin mountains, in one of the wealthiest suburbs. It was an eighteenth-century farmhouse, its walls covered with creepers and reached by a bridge over a stream. There were stables, a conservatory and a lush garden which he could step into from his study, from which he could gaze at the views of the Wicklow mountains to the south.

And there were other things to delight in – a lily pond and rose garden, wide lawns laid out for croquet or bowls, and a small orchard of apple and cherry trees, gooseberry bushes and beyond that a tennis court.

But once more a new home needed money, as did his children's private education and his taste for good wines and high living, developed over the successful years. And there were also other causes which needed support, the Abbey Theatre still one of them.

The generosity and support of Irish Americans would again be the means, and in October he left on his last lecture tour to America, to a country and people he had come to love.

It was a lengthy, exhausting and sad visit, his father's great bearded, noble face no longer there to greet him, old friends dead, his journey from New York, through Detroit and Canada, not without its problems. The majority of people gave him a generous welcome, acclaiming him both as a poet and a patriot, but again his pride in the Abbey was hurt when a Fianna Fáil group, most of whom had never seen the Abbey plays, tried to stop him raising money for the theatre. They complained that the Irish-American taxpayer should not be subsidising a theatre which advocated drunkenness, murder and prostitution, and which held the Irish character up to ridicule.

Even on his return in January 1933, the complaints of the Fianna Fáil group followed him. De Valera, a hero to Irish Americans, ever opportunistic and aware of American opinion, took up their case, warning Yeats that if the Abbey did not make their repertoire more acceptable then the £1,000 a year grant from the Irish government would be stopped. The grant had helped save the Irish National Theatre, the first state theatre in the English-speaking world.

But Willie Yeats would not to be bullied and withdraw plays by Synge and O'Casey. He refused de Valera's request to submit a list of plays the Abbey intended to perform on its next American tour. Eventually, at a meeting in March, Yeats pointed out the political cost of risking the theatre's future, and the President backed down, the theatre retaining its freedom.

Their differences, however, were not yet over. Yeats was foremost in preventing the government's repressive policies. In the Senate he made one of his strongest attacks on de Valera's Ireland: 'If you show that this country, Catholic Ireland, is going to be governed by Catholic ideas and by Catholic ideas alone, you will never get the north. You will put a wedge in the midst of the nation.'

It was a vision of the future from one of the greatest Irish minds.

33

WILLIE YEATS was moving towards old age, his health failing and even inspiration for his poetry had faded. Age brought to him an awareness of opportunities lost, the wasted nights of his youth. His life with George was unfulfilling, the auto-writing which had inspired him had long stopped and there was a distance between them. He still loved her and idolised his children but his interest in other women, beautiful, poetic women, invariably much younger than himself, had increased. Now began a frenzied zest for life, his writing spurred on by thoughts of what had been, what could have been and what still might be as he sought other loves, seeking images of Maud in them but never finding them. Or her.

George also was making a life of her own, escorted frequently now by Lennox Robinson, a platonic and loyal friend, her drinking increasing to help fill the emptiness in her life. Her husband was spending more time away from their home and their life together in Ireland.

The women Yeats now sought were sensual and romantic, without the fierce political passions which infected Maud. They were voyeuristic liaisons, seldom consummated, but which excited him to a frenzy of writing – poetry for them but still poetry for Maud.

In October 1934 he met Margaret Ruddock, an attractive 27-year-old actress. Margaret had written asking to meet him. She was proud of her naked body in front of him, a body which she felt should give people happiness.

But sexually he was unable to enjoy her. And then the pleasure she gave him turned to grief as she often became drunk and depressive, demanding that he make her a recognised poet. It was a short-lived affair.

There were others to take her place, the first, a few months later, another liberated woman. Ethel Mannin was a 34-year-old journalist and writer of romantic novels, an attractive blond with smooth, drawn back hair. Although she had other lovers, her liberated views excited him, the relationship intense and tender, even sensual.

He was living life as full as was possible, writing more than ever, but with an awful void which no one else could fill. Meetings with Maud had been infrequent, for lunch or visits to the theatre, and always at his request. Never easy, their time together was edged with nostalgia, always charged with emotional tension. Now, with age creeping up and time running out, he wanted to impress.

At a lunch, however, at the Kildare Street Club, a long-established bastion of the Anglo-Irish aristocracy, she had failed to be impressed. His membership had been another milestone for him in his recognition as an Irish statesman. But she had been a visitor there years ago, in her debutante days, when women were not officially allowed. He was lost for words when she told him, shaking his head and smiling. She had bettered him yet again.

He was excited when inviting her to lunch at Jammett's in Nassau Street, the most expensive French restaurant in Dublin, and entertain her in the best surroundings, this time dressed in a beautifully cut, corn-coloured suit chosen by George, a bright blue silk shirt and a matching silk hand-kerchief in his top pocket. Maud stared affectionately at him. He looked as handsome as ever and a sudden sadness swept over her.

When they were seated he looked at her over the table, so much love for her in his gaze, tinged with sadness for what might have been. 'I thought it time we met again, Maud. At our age there seems to be so little time left.'

'But why here, Willie?' She smiled at him. 'You have no need to impress me.' She reached over and took his hand. 'You were always a god among men to me.'

He shook his head slightly. 'And yet you refused mar-riage to one of your gods?'

She ignored the longing, the slight trace of bitterness in his voice. 'Let's not argue from now on in. As you say, there is so little time left and we have meant so much to one another.'

The love he had always had for her could not be hidden as he took both her hands in his. 'We've been apart for many years, Maud, yet you are still my dearest friend. And you still protest in your old age against what seem to you to be wrongs. Since we first met we have been having the same argument.' He turned her hand in his, gazing down at it before continuing. 'There are still things we can do togeth-er, Maud.' He sighed. 'Sometimes I get so depressed that I have outlasted so many.'

She reached across the table, gently pushing back a straying lock of white hair from his face. 'Where will you go next, now that Ballylee and Coole Park have gone?'

He shrugged. 'To the sun, Maud. We have given up the flat in Rapallo and next month George and I are going to the south of France. There are people there that I know.'

'I am going to Belfast ...'

He broke in, his tone resigned, sad. 'Your next step in revolutionary politics, Maud?'

She made no reply and he continued, shaking his head. 'I can never understand the strength of your convictions. But as for Ulster ...' He waved his hand dismissively. 'The people there are so disagreeable that I hope they never unite with the rest of Ireland ...' He ran out of words, his fingers tapping the table nervously, not wanting to argue with her again. Two men approached their table, the older holding a menu card and asking politely for their signatures. Yeats shook his head irritably, Maud rebuking him. 'Are you above that, now, Willie Yeats?'

He stared at her, his embarrassment showing. He signed the menu, adding a few apologetic words from one of his poems:

Like a long-legged fly upon the stream, his mind moves in silence.

He passed the paper to Maud before handing it to the man, muttering a brief apology.

When Willie turned back to her she smiled at him as he took a sip from his glass of white wine. She was still bringing him down to earth. 'You forget yourself. Drinking fine wines which Augusta gave you a taste for! You've done well, Willie.' She raised an eyebrow. 'And you have many lady friends now I hear ...'

'I have met many, Maud. Beautiful women, but none quite so beautiful as you.' He paused, raising an eyebrow, smiling. 'They make me feel young again.'

Maud laughed, mocking him. 'It's your work they admire.'

He shook his head, vehemently. 'No, no. They make me a passionate man again. Their beauty arouses me. As yours once did.' His voice dropped to hardly a whisper. 'And still does, dearest Maud.'

She smiled at him. 'You would have been a good Catholic, Willie. You confess so easily, so honestly.'

'It's too late for that, Maud.'

She frowned. 'How does George feel about them?'

'She is tactful. And untroubled by them. She knows I mean her no harm in the world. She has told me that when I am dead, people may talk about my love affairs but she will always be proud of me.' He played with his glass. 'George is a wife and mother to me, but she doesn't give me the artistic support the others do. With them my writing is improved and I seem to be able to work harder than ever. I suppose for that reason George thinks they are useful.'

Maud's face became sad. 'I was sorry to hear that Olivia passed away.'

He gave an almost imperceptible shake of his head, his eyes closed. Olivia's recent death had been almost unbearable to him. 'For more than 40 years she was such a part of my life in London, and during that time we never had a quarrel. Sadness sometimes but never difference.' There were tears in his eyes as he continued. 'And what beauty. It all seems so long ago.' He sighed. 'One looks back to one's youth as to a cup that a mad man dying of thirst left half-tasted.'

L IFE WAS too full and work too demanding, his writing almost continuous and interspersed with liaisons with various new loves, sensual experiences, too much for a man in his poor health. In January 1935, the year he would be 70, he developed severe breathing problems when in London and collapsed. He returned immediately to Ireland where George arranged a holiday for them both, sailing from Liverpool to Majorca to convalesce. They remained there for three months, before returning to Ireland for his birthday celebrations in June.

That year another woman entered his life. Dorothy Wellesley was an immensely rich aristocrat who was to become the Duchess of Wellington. A striking woman, with beautiful blue eyes, pale skin and heavy sensuous lips, she always dressed in elegant and expensive modern clothes, calf-length skirts, often with a blouse and cardigan over. Her home, Penn-on-the-Rock, was another magnificent house for him to enjoy and admire. He had read her poems and they intrigued him, as did her bisexuality, her marriage having already broken up through her relationship with Vita Sackville West and Virginia Woolf. She was now the lover of Hilda Matheson who lived nearby, yet another woman who admired and befriended him.

His new relationships gave him a fresh lease of life, the years from January 1936 his most productive, most of his time spent in the Mediterranean. His sexual curiosity and his poetic output were continuing with renewed force. In America, an Irish-American testimonial committee had been formed with the aim of ensuring he would be free from financial worries for the rest of his life, two members of the committee coming to present him with a cheque for £600.

The following spring he met another paramour. Edith Shackleton Head was a successful literary journalist, a plain woman with a wide mouth and intelligent eyes, favouring long skirts and flowered blouses, often with a tight, tur-banned hat on her head. She was 53, petite and unmarried and Yeats soon became a frequent dinner companion at her home, the 'Chantry House'.

Like his other new women friends she was bisexual. Yet again he was entranced and fascinated, her exhibitionism satisfying his love of women's bodies as she sat unashamedly naked for him in her garden, inspiring him as he wrote frenetically.

IN POLITICS things continued to change for both Maud Gonne and Willie Yeats. The IRA had become outdated, no longer relevant to the independent Free State and was again declared illegal. But Maud's activities continued with speeches against the persecution of Catholics in the north, the plight of the prisoners in Belfast gaols and the lack of civil liberties under the Special Powers Act.

Much to her relief, in April 1938 when the IRA approved a bombing campaign on mainland Britain, her son's politi-cal ideals changed, Sean resigning his position of Chief of Staff and resuming his law studies.

34

THE LETTER was brief. It was dated 22 August 1938 and she carried it with her for the rest of her life:

My dear Maud. I want you to come here to tea on Friday. A motor will call for you at four. I have wanted to see you for a long time but ... Yours, W.B. Yeats.

She stared at it for long moments, sudden foreboding sweeping through her. It was as if he had a premonition that the end was near.

There was no need for the car, Isoeult driving her to Riversdale. George greeted them, walking with Maud in the garden while Isoeult went first to his study at the rear of the house to see the man who had been a father to her, who could have been a husband. Near his chair and next to his desk, her portrait stood on an easel. Her marriage had by now failed and she still corresponded regularly with her former suitor. She stayed briefly, her eyes brimming with tears as she brushed past her mother on her way out.

Maud was in a long black dress, a coat over it, her hair below her shoulders, a veil covering her face. She pulled it back as she approached him. He stared at her sadly. Time, life, had passed so quickly and she was now 72, her face wrinkled but still with a beauty she would never lose.

She stood looking at her closest friend, the man she should have married. He had dressed carefully for the meeting, wearing a biscuit-coloured dressing gown which set off his light Mediterranean tan, a blue shirt and hand-kerchief in his top pocket, a monocle lying against his jack-et. He was still strikingly handsome.

She waited as he forced himself with great effort from his armchair, waving aside her help. There were tears in her eyes as she went to him and he held her to him, her hands in his as she rested her head against his great frame.

There was a terrible poignancy in the bitter sweet reunion. Nostalgia, memories, love and regret – two aging heroes of Ireland clinging to each other.

She held his face in her hands, tears flowing uncontrol-lably down her cheeks.

'Oh my poor Willie.'

He found it hard to speak, emotions overcoming him. 'Together again, Maud. You will always be my Cathleen ní Houlihan.'

'And you the greatest poet ever born, in this or any country.'

He looked at her, deep, unremitting sadness in his eyes. 'Darling Maud, we should have gone to our castle of heroes.' He reached for her hand. 'We might still do it.'

She was unable to speak, looking at him in surprise that he remembered his offer of long ago, lost in sudden reverie, his poems, meant for her but so often ignored by her, cours-ing through her mind.

He stared at her, a poet at a loss for words, drinking in every feature of the woman he had loved for so long. There was still a great haughtiness about her, her hair glossy and as fine as silk in plaits on her head. Her cheeks were deeply creased when she smiled, her nose wrinkling up, but her eyes and face were still that of the young girl he had known, her smile that which had captivated him long years before when she first entered his life.

Willie smiled. 'Even at your age, Maud, you are still the spiritual force of Ireland. With John O'Leary and Augusta Gregory you are among the greatest of Ireland's noble people. And the most beautiful of those.' He paused, tears brimming. 'You were always and forever my inspiration.' He shook his head in awe. 'You know, no artist could ever truly capture your beauty and just now you look magnificent.'

He sank back into his chair and they stared at each other without speaking, a slight smile on his lips, both wondering what might have been.

'We are both old now, Willie. But I remember much. You have been so good to me. Perhaps I shall be remembered by your poems. Do you remember one you wrote for me? Such a long time ago. I remember it so well.'

She whispered the lines to him, sinking to her knees beside him.

When you are old and grey and full of sleep,
And nodding by the fire, take down this book,
And slowly read, and dream of the soft look
Your eyes had once, and of their shadows deep.

He took over from her:

How many loved your moments of sad grace,
And loved your beauty with love false and true,
But one man loved the pilgrim soul in you,

And loved the sorrows of your changing face;

Their emotions were now too much for either of them to finish, tears pouring down both their cheeks as she rested her head on his knees. There were a few moments of silence, his hand stroking her hair, sighing deeply before taking a cigarette box from the table next to his chair, offering her one and lighting them both.

'We've come so far since that first meeting in Bedford Park. Do you remember, Maud?'

'I will never forget, Willie. You were such a beautiful youth. And so enamoured with me ... I was flattered and confused. But politics separated us for so long and we rowed. Especially when you became a senator!'

He laughed suddenly, staring at her again in awe. She had such violence in her and yet such tenderness. And still at her age an almost unearthly physical beauty. He shook his head in wonderment, throwing his arms wide. 'What a woman you are, Maud. What vitality. What energy!' His tone changed. 'And yet always such a tender and gentle woman. And caring to those in need.' His voice was soft, full of love and admiration. 'You went among people who were starved and depressed and treated unjustly. You really believed that only by freeing Ireland from England's rule could people's lot be improved. You were the first one to ask for social justice with a national identity.' His mood changed. 'I often wonder what our role really was. Did we create a new, happier Ireland? Did that play of mine inspire men who the English shot? Did your Cathleen ní Houlihan become Ireland?' He paused, reflecting, before he continued. 'I wrote a poem for it, "The man and the echo"':

All that I have said and done,
Now that I am old and ill,
Turns into a question till
I lie awake night after night
And never get the answer right.
Did that play of mine send out
Certain men the English shot?
Did words of mine put too great strain
On that woman's reeling brain?

'It's beautiful, Willie, but my favourite was always "Red Hanrahan".' She stood, tears again dimming her eyes as again he quoted softly:

... we have hidden in our hearts the flame out of the eyes,
Of Cathleen, the daughter of Houlihan...
... Angers that are like noisy clouds have set our hearts a beat;
But we have all bent low and low and kissed the quiet feet
Of Cathleen, the daughter of Houlihan.

She smiled sadly. 'That was Ireland, but everything is changing. Sean has done all he can. He's 34 now, he's finished his law studies and will practise at the bar. He says he will always have time to defend those gaoled by the de Valera government.'

Yeats nodded, relieved for her and her son. 'I'm going back to the Abbey in August. We are putting on a new play for the opening of the Irish Dramatic Movement. I would like you to be there.'

'I would love to. I would like that very much.'

He stared at her, searching her face as if to carve it into his memory. Then he sighed, taking her hand and holding

her to him again before clambering to his feet, George joining them for tea in the conservatory. Afterwards he leant
heavily on Maud as she walked with him in the garden,
past the lily pond and across the manicured lawns. There
was no need for words. They were together, souls of
Ireland, at peace on a warm midsummer afternoon in the
evening of their lives.

They stopped frequently and, before returning to the
house, he asked her to sit with him on a small bench by the
rose garden. 'When I go, Maud, in Sligo there is a churchyard where my great-grandfather was rector a century ago.
I want to be buried there. I have written my epitaph.
Perhaps you and George, the true friends I have left, will do
this for me?' He took several pages from his pocket. They
had been folded and re-folded many times. 'It is yet to be
finished. Will you read with me?'

She sat close to him, her voice faltering at the beauty of
the lines, and then continuing in her low, melodious voice:

Many times man lives and dies,
Between his two eternities,
That of race and that of soul,
And ancient Ireland knew it all.
Whether man die in his bed
Or the rifle knock him dead.

His voice joined her as they continued together:

Irish poets, learn your trade,
Sing whatever is well made,
Scorn the sort now growing up
All out of shape from toe to top.

And then he alone finished it, his tone measured as he read his powerful epitaph:

Under bare Ben Bulben's head
In Drumcliffe churchyard Yeats is laid.
An ancestor was rector there
Long years ago, a church stands near,
By the road an ancient cross.
Cast a cold eye
On life, on death.
Horseman, pass by!

Tears were again pouring down her cheeks as he folded the paper and they sat quiet for long minutes, his arm around her, two elderly lovers at last finding peace. George had watched, tears dimming her own eyes as the two friends walked and talked together. Now she came to them, his breathing heavy as they helped him to his feet, a prolonged bout of coughing racking his body.

He was tiring fast and Maud knew it was time to leave. She took his hands in hers and he went with her to the door.

They stood, facing each other, holding hands like young lovers, staring deep into each other's eyes for the memories locked there, until tears blinded her eyes and she could no longer see him.

As Isoeult drove them away down the drive she turned and saw him through her tears for the last time. His head was erect and challenging, still a beautiful man, the radiance of the sunlight behind him making his white hair a halo around his head.

Maud feared she might never again meet her hero in this life. But perhaps after that.

35

IT WAS as if he had known the end was near and he had wanted to see his Cathleen ní Houlihan for the last time. But the emotion of that meeting had taken its toll, his health failing and, for the winter of 1938, he and George returned to France, staying at a quiet hotel in Cap Martin, with rooms facing the sea. Nearby were a number of friends, Dorothy Wellesley and Hilda Matheson, who were staying at a villa at Bealieu, near Nice. When his health recovered sufficiently he and George frequently joined them for dinner.

It was to be a good Christmas. The family were together until, in January, the children returned to school in Switzerland.

Soon after they left, his kidneys began to fail and he was given morphia for the bouts of intense pain. He was breathing with difficulty and,due to the sedation, was hardly able to speak. He beckoned George close to him and whispered that he knew for certain his time would not be long. She held his hand as he smiled gently at her. 'But I am happy.'

Two days later, on 28 January, 1939, Willie Yeats died.

It was a peaceful and dignified death, Canon Carey from Monaco repeating quiet prayers beside the bed, George and friends taking turns to maintain a vigil, his features more noble and beautiful in death than they had ever known them.

The following morning he was taken on the stony uphill path to the chapel at the small cemetery of Roquebron, overlooking Cap Martin and Monaco, George following the coffin with Dorothy Wellesley, Edith Shackleton Head and other friends who lived nearby.

The body of Ireland's greatest poet lay in state until three in the afternoon when there was a simple graveside Anglican burial service, George trying to smile through her tears as she repeated his last wishes. 'He said we could dig him up later and take him back to Sligo.'

When they returned to the house, telegrams of condolence and wreaths from all around the world had been delivered. James Joyce had remembered him, as had Sean O'Casey whose tribute was brief: 'His greatness is such that the Ireland which tormented him will be forced to remember him forever.'

Among other tributes was a telegram of condolence from the Irish government and the hope that his body would be brought back to Ireland for burial, the French Government having offered a destroyer to carry the coffin back to the land of his birth.

And there was a letter from Isoeult. George read it aloud. 'She feels we have both suffered a terrible loss in his growing old and dying. The whole of Ireland, the world, has.' She read again, slowly. 'Maud is distraught and sends her sorrows. She says that he must be returned home for burial. She is writing to the President to arrange it and that there will be a memorial service at St Patrick's Cathedral in Dublin. We must all be there.'

But another war was to prevent his immediate return to his homeland.

MAUD GONNE remembered his wishes. For years after the Second World War she had approached the government and de Valera, asking for the re-internment of her dearest friend in Ireland but it was not until ten years after his death that his wishes were granted. And she was able to keep the promise made at their last meeting.

Sean MacBride was now the Minister of External affairs. In 1948 he had helped to end the government of de Valera whose Fianna Fáil party was defeated after sixteen year's continuous rule, Sean by now disliking de Valera so much that he joined in government with former bitter enemies. It was the year in which Ireland broke all Commonwealth ties with England and declared the 26 counties an independent Republic. Now that Irish Republic, which Willie Yeats had helped create, worked for the return of his body and a great ceremonial funeral, Sean MacBride arranging for the government to send an Irish corvette, the Macha, to bring his body home.

It was to be the homecoming of a hero.

On 25 August 1948, a guard of honour from the French Alpine Infantry escorted the coffin from Roquebrone cemetery to the square of the town for a lying in state. It was then taken to Nice, the coffin draped in the tricolour which Maud had designed, and brought aboard the Macha. A poem, in French, was read and dedicated to Yeats, many of those present in tears as the French and Irish national anthems were played before the Macha set sail for Galway where George, his son and daughter, Michael and Anne, and his brother Jack, went aboard before the coffin was piped ashore.

It was a homecoming which would have delighted Willie Yeats, the great romanticist. Journalists and photographers from around the world were present as the cortège started its slow journey through Galway and Mayo, the hearse preceded by pipes and muffled drums, through once-familiar streets and lanes, people working in the fields stopping, kneeling to pray as the coffin passed, until it reached Sligo, where there was a military guard of honour as it again lay briefly in state before Sligo town hall.

Slowly the cortège continued its solemn way, in misty wet weather, to Drumcliffe churchyard, there to be met by Sean MacBride, representing the government of Ireland, and by other government ministers and dignitaries who stood at the graveside, among them the leader of the opposition, Eamon de Valera.

But there was one face missing from that sad, damp churchyard. Maud Gonne was unable to face the loss of her beloved Willie.

A Church of Ireland service was held before William Butler Yeats was laid to rest near his family's ancestral home, as soft grey rain swept in from the sea and over the tiny graveyard, a veil of mist hanging over Ben Bulben.

On the grave stone of William Butler Yeats his simple epitaph was carved.

Cast a cold eye
On life, on death,
Horseman, pass by.

It was a year after her hero was laid to rest that a frail but determined Maud Gonne attended the religious ceremonies connected with the creation of the Irish Republic.

She still smoked incessantly, her body as slim as ever. Her eyes still had the sparkle they had as a young girl and her voice was still that of a rebellious young girl as she addressed the celebrations on another Easter Monday.

Maud remembered the man who had loved her beyond all and immortalised her in the beauty of his poetry. Her thoughts were with him.

'How lucky Willie was to escape into the freer life of the spirit, beyond the limitations of time and space. I think that Ireland is not doing too badly when I compare it with the Ireland of my girlhood, with the periodic famine and the wholesale destruction, by the battering rams, during the evictions. I think that Ireland is going to be a leader of the peace thought in this world of confused thinking.'

On 27 April, 1953, when she was 86, after receiving the last sacraments, Maud Gonne went gently into the unknown, tributes to her received from throughout the world.

Buried with her were a pair of babies booties she had always carried in her handbag. They had belonged to her first born, Georges. Also in that hand bag, and buried with her, was an envelope, in it the letter which Willie Yeats had written inviting her to their last meeting. On her finger was the ring he had given her some 40 years before.

At her funeral, women from Inghinidhe na hÉireann, Cumann na mBan and the IRA marched behind the hearse. The O'Rahilly, son of Michael O'Rahilly, gave the oration at the service of dedication when she was buried in the republican plot in Glasnevin cemetery. It moved those present to tears.

'It is over 60 years since she, with the minimum of association with Ireland, found herself amongst a people depressed, starved and treated with injustice. And injustice was one of the things which she could not tolerate. She realised that only by freeing Ireland from English rule could the lot of the people be improved and she devoted the remainder of her life to the Irish people.'

Now they were both gone. Willie and Maud had given all to Ireland, their wars had been for a good life for their people in her four beautiful green fields. Now the old lady had thrown off her cloak, Ireland was reborn and his Cathleen ní Houlihan was with him again.